A DUKE'S KEEPER

The Dark Dukes
Book 2

J.M. Diedrich

Dragonblade Publishing, Inc. is an imprint of Kathryn Le Veque Novels, Inc.
P.O. Box 23
Moreno Valley, CA 92556
ceo@dragonbladepublishing.com

Produced in the United States of America

First Edition April 2024
Trade Paperback Edition

ARE YOU SIGNED UP FOR DRAGONBLADE'S BLOG?

You'll get the latest news and information on exclusive giveaways, exclusive excerpts, coming releases, sales, free books, cover reveals and more.

Check out our complete list of authors, too!

No spam, no junk. That's a promise!

Sign Up Here

www.dragonbladepublishing.com

Dearest Reader;

Thank you for your support of a small press. At Dragonblade Publishing, we strive to bring you the highest quality Historical Romance from some of the best authors in the business. Without your support, there is no 'us', so we sincerely hope you adore these stories and find some new favorite authors along the way.

Happy Reading!

CEO, Dragonblade Publishing

Additional Dragonblade books by Author J.M. Diedrich

The Dark Dukes Series
A Lady's Duke (Book 1)
A Duke's Keeper (Book 2)

CHAPTER ONE

London: 1891

CAMILLE RAN.

Fear was a quick fuel in her veins, but the night air in her lungs squeezed too tightly.

She couldn't stop. If she stopped, they'd catch her, and if they caught her . . . She tore around the corner and slipped on loose rocks scattered along the cobblestones. Her shoulder slammed into the alley wall. For a moment, she saw stars.

The three men behind her taunted and jeered, their words muffled, but their hungry intent clear.

Camille's fingers closed around one of the rocks. She pulled herself up and away, cradling her wounded arm to her chest, the rock secure in her other hand. The pain shot across the joint like sparks of lightning.

She wouldn't feel the pain after that, neither in her shoulder nor her aching feet, as her weathered boots beat the cobblestones. Darkened doorways rushed past, places where no one inside would offer Camille aid. Not here in Rotten Row, where the name remained more considering than the people.

If she could make it to the docks, the Cock 'n Hen tavern would house her, and, if not the establishment itself, Scarlet would.

The steps haunting her own closed in.

Camille listened over the ragged beating of her heart.

Step, step.

Step, pause, step.

Only two of the three followed behind now. They had split up.

Camille tore around another corner, and another, and another. The maze of alleys was disorienting in the dark, but she didn't need light to see. The map of Dockside appeared vivid in her mind, like a permanent picture etched behind her eyelids.

If she took the alley to her right, she'd find a dead end. The alley to her left and she'd circle around and most definitely come face to face with the last of the three. Which left the alley straight ahead.

She could now make out their words with sick clarity.

"No use running, chicken."

"We only want a good 'pluck.'"

She shuddered and pushed through a bisecting intersection, catching sight of a shadow darting past the end of the other alley, mirroring her movements.

The map in her head shifted. Mind racing, calculating, *praying* for a path of escape, all routes led to one conclusion: She wouldn't make it to the tavern, not before the third man cut her off.

She had one last option.

Dockside's main square lay ahead. Twenty feet . . . ten . . . one.

She burst into the open space. The last standing lamppost gave off dim light, revealing the shadow emerging from the other alley.

She was out of time and out of breath.

Whirling with her back to the third, empty alley, she planted her feet.

Seeing their prey caught, the men slowed and smiled to one another, their teeth flashing in the moonlight.

Peter Hawkins, Anthony Grey, Manny Flank. Their names

and faces from Madam Clarice's files rushed to the forefront of Camille's mind, along with the unpleasant detail that Hawkins was a fighter for the 'Underground.'

Reeling, her mind flashed through every page of *A Woman's Best Offense Is Defense*. She spread her feet apart for balance, her heart hammering against her chest.

She wouldn't give in to her fear. Pain was pain. She'd felt it before.

Until the bastards ran the knife across her throat, she'd fight.

She shifted her stance a second time to accommodate her hurt arm, the movement familiar but alien, as with every detail her mind remembered when her body held no memory.

"Come now, chicken." Hawkins offered a hand in a bastardized mimic of a gentleman's escort, his black, moleskin coat and trousers lessening the intimidating height and muscles underneath and drawing immediate attention to the man's uncapped head of ginger hair. "No need to be afraid." Greasy strands of orange hair fell forward into too-bright eyes. "You gave us a merry chase."

Another of the men, Grey, laughed. With his dark hair and light coat, he was Hawkins's opposite. "Look at her face. She ain't done."

Hawkins's smile was reptilian. He licked his lips. "I like a chicken with some fight."

Camille steeled her nerves and gripped the small rock in her hand.

Rolling the rock over, she faced the worst of the edges outwards.

She would survive. She'd been born in a gutter, raised in a gutter; she refused to die in one, not without doing enough damage to scar.

Her mind knew the maneuvers. Her body, even battered and tired, was lean and strong. The lapse in speed between her mind and her body's reaction was immense and frustrating, as she knew from experience, but the basics were easy: Stay balanced and go for the squashy bits.

Her breath came in shallow pants of fear and anticipation.

Camille tucked her good arm behind her back. She'd have one opportunity for a surprise knock to the head. Coming up on her toes, she angled her body towards Hawkins, knowing exactly which head she'd bash first.

They closed in.

She held her breath.

"What do we have here?"

The low voice rumbled in her chest like thunder.

Camille whirled to see a man half-covered in the shadow emerging from the third alley, impeccably dressed in a black suit, and closing in with unhurried steps. Her stomach dropped.

A fourth man.

Her mind went into a frenzy of calculated risk and reality. How had he gotten so close without her noticing? There wasn't a chance he hadn't seen her crude weapon hidden behind her back, not with the lone lamp shining down on her like a damn spotlight.

She'd shown her hand without making a single play. Her shoulders hunched in defeat, but the immediate, blinding pain pulled her back on task. Sidestepping, she divided her attention between the two parties, still resolved to make the first move.

"Hey, now." Hawkins jabbed his chin towards the harbor. "There's a tavern along the water, friend. Go find your own fun. This chicken is ours."

He wasn't one of Hawkins's men? Camille's body flushed with premature hope.

"The Cock 'n Hen, yes. I just came from there." The man came into the light of the lamp.

He was young, tall. His hair was a rare shade of blond, like spindled gold or sun-kissed wheat. He turned, and a shocking pair of desert-colored eyes fixed on her face.

Camille gulped, unsure if the rush of heat to her belly was from fear, or from something far more dangerous.

"Chicken, you say?" The man took in her injured arm—and what must have been a mushed knot of auburn hair around her pale face—and shook his head. "She doesn't appear amused by your game of fight and fowl, sir. Hawkins, wasn't it?"

Hawkins smiled, an unfriendly twist of the mouth. "You a fan?"

"I've seen you fight on occasion."

"Then you know I don't leave my opponents standing." Hawkins took a threatening step in the newcomer's direction. "I said to move along." He cracked his knuckles. "You'll find more trouble than you can handle otherwise."

Camille had an uncharacteristic pang of concern for the stranger's well-being. She had enough on her conscience without adding the death of a young man. Well-intentioned, or looking for a bit of sport himself, he had intervened and offered an opportunity for a distraction.

Like some damn knight sent to save her.

Pride got the better of her. "I don't need your help."

The man's eyes widened. His gaze bounced from man to man to man and back to her, his brow arched sardonically. "Yes, I see now. You have them exactly where you wanted them."

She ignored his mockery, and the fluttering of her stomach at his piercing gaze. Hawkins and the others had halved the distance, so close now, she felt their wretched gazes clawing at her skirts.

"Stay out of this," she said, though she directed her words towards the fourth man.

A flash of unknown emotion crossed his face before his mouth settled into a smirk. He leaned against the lamppost and crossed his arms.

He was honestly going to stand and watch? She tracked his movements with narrowed eyes. "You won't step in?"

He raised his hands. "I won't lift a finger."

She didn't trust him for an instant, but she had other problems, literally, at her back.

Heatedly aware of those desert eyes on her, Camille didn't hesitate. Rock secure, she swung with a right hook, catching Hawkins in the cheek and sending him careening into Grey.

They fell in a heap, leaving Flank inside her guard on her bad side.

His punch flew wide.

Her mind drew up the proper counter, but as she skirted back, her shoulder gave a bark of pain. The stalling had cost her.

His next swing clipped her in the temple.

She caught the cobblestones on her hand. Something cracked. Grimacing, she pushed up on her good arm and fell when her wrist wouldn't hold her weight. Flank was there, towering over her, his grin wide and revealing rotted, gapped teeth. "Not so smart now, bitch." He reeled back.

Camille braced for a boot to the gut.

There was a sharp crack, and Flank fell forward.

Camille rolled and gasped at the pain.

Flank landed, face first, on the ground beside her with Desert Eyes digging his knee into Flank's back, his expression severe.

Flank flailed.

Desert Eyes chopped Flank in the back of the neck, and the latter's struggles subsided in unconsciousness.

The stranger gave Camille a small smile. "Well, that wasn't nearly as fun as promised."

She first eyed him and then the still bodies of Hawkins and Grey where they lay off to the side. Knowing one hit wouldn't have been enough to take the vazey ratbags down, she scowled. "You helped."

"I did." He stooped and clenched something in his hand.

"You said you wouldn't lift a finger."

He shrugged. "I couldn't resist."

"You lied!"

"This is a point of contention for you, I take it?" He raised his hand to his chest. "My deepest apologies, miss. I am, normally, a man of my word to a degree of disregard for self-preservation."

His gaze flicked to Flank, still under-knee, and his smiling eyes went hard. "But even my word of honor breaks when a man raises a hand to a woman. Please." He offered his hand. "Let me make it up to you by getting medical attention for that arm."

His words were too pretty.

Close up, Camille saw the man's suit was of fine wool and expertly tailored. The smell of expensive Ballantine hung on his breath.

She ignored his hand and sneered. "You're a gentleman."

He blinked, seeming taken aback by the force of her distaste. "One of my least offensive titles, trust me."

"I *don't* trust you."

"Obviously." He stood.

She thought it was to intimidate her into accepting his help, but she grudgingly noticed he'd backed away, as if giving her room to think or get away.

Her shoulder screamed. Her wrist smarted. Left to her own devices, she'd make it home, *eventually*. If her luck held out and no more demons solidified from the shadows.

Camille gritted her teeth. "Fine," she said, awkwardly getting to her feet on her own. She'd always had shit for luck.

She'd lost her rock when she'd fallen, not that the measly pebble would be any use with her throbbing wrist. Sprained at best, at worst, she was down two arms and at the mercy of a man more skilled than first calculated, and with no idea of his motives.

"Here," he said.

She stared at the rock he offered on his open palm.

His gaze was direct, his expression knowing, as if he suspected she didn't like being defenseless.

She didn't take it. She'd never accept anything from a gentleman. Ever. Again.

Shaking his head, amused or exasperated—it was hard to tell in the dim light—he pocketed the rock and inclined his head in the direction of the docks. "There's a doctor who lives by the water who can look at that arm of yours." He ran a hand through his hair. "I can't vouch for his bedside manner, but he's got miracles in his fingertips."

Camille watched his gestures with a critical eye. He didn't give off the aura of a man setting a trap, not that appearances and gut instinct added up to anything.

At her silence, he shrugged. "Well, I could use another drink after that bout. I'm going to walk in that direction at a leisurely pace." He tapped his chin as if it weren't glaringly obvious what he was doing. "I may even whistle, in case someone loses sight of me."

He turned and walked—*strolled*—at a most suspicious slow pace.

The man was planning to escort her all the way back to the harbor?

Camille gingerly touched her head where Flank's punch had glanced over her temple. Was it a head injury? Had her brain conjured up this scene to overcome Hawkins and his men's violence?

A charge of fire shot through her wrist. She dropped her arm and grimaced. The pain was certainly real. If she'd had a mind to overwrite the pain of being assaulted, she'd have taken the rest of the pain as well.

Which meant the man was real . . . and his tall frame was disappearing down the alley. Camille bit her lip. Home was in the opposite direction, but no one in residence would know how to set her arm. And knowing the procedure herself didn't change the fact that she didn't have the strength to set a dislocated bone. Plus, if she showed up battered and broken, the sight may set her mother's already fragile mind into another episode; she'd barely recovered since the last one.

Decided, Camille followed, finding comfort in the fact that, if the man truly meant to go back to the Cock 'n Hen, she had friends there who wouldn't hesitate to bleed anyone who meant her harm, even if he owned a title and a handsome face.

Camille scowled. The man was certainly not handsome. Trim

and clean, with an odd shade of eye and hair, didn't change the ugly fact that the man was gentry born and used to the privilege of things going his way.

She wasn't attracted to him. She was grateful, that was all. And the man hadn't proven her gratitude warranted or not. She caught up, though she made sure to keep him squarely in front of her.

"Decided to come along then, chicken?" he asked.

With two useless wings, she felt the flightless fowl, but she couldn't let his condescending tone go unchallenged. "My name isn't chicken."

"You can't possibly be a sparrow." The teasing tone in his voice was unmistakable. "And if you're a pheasant, that makes me a plumed peacock, and my fragile ego can't take that ridiculous comparison."

Her lips twitched in a fleeting moment of insanity. It had been a long night. First the incessant rush of patrons at the Prodding Pony, where the wandering eyes of Hawkins and his ape-like friends had left her jumpy all night. Then the lovely, and all-too-memorable, evening 'stroll' through the alleys of Dockside. It was no wonder she found this strange man amusing—she was too exhausted for her normal contempt. That was the only possible reason she offered, "My name is Camille Forthright."

Seeming as surprised as she, he glanced over his shoulder and gave her a grin she saw even in the dark.

A strange fluttering filled her stomach.

"A pleasure, Miss Forthright. Please," he said, his eyes brightening, "call me 'Renard.'"

She sneered. "I'd hardly call a man I just met by his given name."

"You could always address me as *Your Grace* or *the esteemed Duke of Lux.*"

The man was insufferable. "I'd rather eat my boot."

Renard chuckled.

CHAPTER TWO

"I 'VE NEVER BEEN in a brawl with a woman at my side," Renard said. He spoke of brawls with the tone of a gentleman remarking on the weather.

Camille eyed his back. The moonlight must have been kind, for the lines of muscle across his shoulders looked lean and tight. "I notice you say, 'Never *with*' a woman and not 'Never *over*' one."

"Ah, yes. Well . . ." His boyish grin resurfaced. "Sainthood never appealed to me."

That made two of them.

"You agree?" he asked.

Camille didn't agree or deny. It took too much effort to keep up with his long strides. The ground underfoot was uneven and slippery from the rain earlier in the evening. Focusing on keeping on her feet around missing chunks of mortar, Camille skirted around the sunken patches of the alley where unidentifiable liquids pooled.

The cramped quarters of hovels stacked one on top of another grew scarcer, giving way to the industrial warehouses and factories—and the filth and stench they poured into the streets and water—that ran the length of the Thames. It was a place unfitting for dogs, let alone a finely dressed gentleman.

"Do you often walk alone in the middle of the night in dangerous neighborhoods, sir?" she asked, more to distract herself from the growing pain than from curiosity.

"Please, call me 'Renard,'" he said. "After a good drink, I enjoy a stroll. One never knows when one will have an adventure with a beautiful woman in a dark alley."

"*Adventure.*"

Camille's belly filled with fire. Yes, for a moment, she'd forgotten. For her, the night's 'adventure' would have had her beaten and 'plucked,' if not dead, in the gutter. What else would a bit of violence be to a young, rich man? Strong enough to defend himself from the lowbrow and entitled enough to command respect from on high.

"If looks could cut, I do believe I'd be fit to stand as a display in Mr. White's ribbon shop," he said.

She hated his wit. Her discrimination against the *ton*, and men, may have been unfounded, but then again, experience made for excellent fodder. "It isn't personal."

"Your glare says otherwise. Is it my gentlemanly status that offends?"

"For starters."

She remembered the name now. Lord Renard Louis, Duke of Lux. He'd inherited the title after his mother and father had tragically died in a fire at their country home. The story had been in the August paper eight years ago. She plucked the article from her mind, reading it behind her eyelids like a lightless poster:

Tragedy in the country!

A stable fire caught the Duke and Duchess of Lux unawares, leaving behind their only son, Renard Leopold Louis, to inherit the dukedom at the pivotal age of fourteen. With the new title comes the responsibility of his younger sister, Lady Charlotte Ann Louis, age ten.

Fourteen. Camille remembered the age. An ugly, helpless time in her life when she'd been too old to ignore the exploitation of another, older duke, and too young to do anything except obey. She put thoughts of her past away and let a wave of pain through to keep it at bay.

Eight years ago. That put Renard's current age at two and twenty, a match to her own.

He turned and cocked his head to one side. "May I ask what other sin I've committed?"

"You're charming."

He huffed a laugh. "A capital offense, indeed."

"And handsome."

The moonlight played over his good-humored grin. "You can't possibly hold that against me. I'll be old and bald eventually."

Camille didn't believe for a second he wouldn't grow more handsome and distinguished with age.

"You, yourself, are no dying duck in a thunderstorm," he said. "Quite the opposite."

"*Like a doll.*"

The words from her childhood settled like a stone in her gut. Her hair pulled savagely at her scalp in an unflattering knot. The dresses she wore were shapeless and of poor quality, nothing flashy, nothing to draw attention to herself. But she could do nothing about her face; the fair skin and naturally rose-tinted cheeks. She sneered. "I can't help that."

His look all but said, "*I know.*"

The man had a point, damn him. Aside from his general 'maleness,' she couldn't admonish his manners or character after he'd gone out of his way to stop Hawkins and his cronies.

"Very well." She sighed. "You may remain handsome."

"Then I'm forgiven?"

"On this matter."

He winked. "I'll take it."

They continued in silence. Feeling relatively certain the man wouldn't accost her should her attention waver, Camille glanced at their surroundings, catching a glimpse of the moon through a rare break in the smog, before prodding her wrist and determining the bone wasn't broken. She sighed.

"Plotting something?" he asked.

She tucked her arm back to her side and gave him her best haunting stare. "Your demise."

He grinned. "A blow to the head?"

"Strangulation by corset lace."

He smiled.

She watched his eyes crinkle in the corners, and her own smile came unbidden. "You don't seem concerned."

"I have a younger sister."

"A sister." The admission made him seem more human. She didn't like it.

She had a brother. A different domineering duke, Lord Hamish Hurstfield, the Duke of Camine, a man who didn't know when to quit sticking his good intentions in her business. After a brief but infuriating conversation, the man had taken it upon himself to play Lord and Savior for his poor, unfortunate, *bastard* sister. If he'd set his sights on anyone else, she may have admired his persistence. But he hadn't chosen someone else, and she continued to wish he'd fall into a deep hole and not come out. Imagining Renard's sister as a spoiled and starched lady of the *ton*, she asked, "What's your sister like?"

"Trouble." His grin turned into a real smile.

Camille's head spun—probably dehydration.

"She's commanding, not that she realizes," he said. "Her mind is sharp, her words sharper. She loves nothing more than digging in the dirt or hunting for bugs. I've found more than one beetle in my breakfast after angering her. Hence, my concern." His smile faded. "She stays in the country, where it's quiet."

Camille saw something dark lurking behind his expression.

She couldn't fathom the feeling in his voice: warmth, worry. She had no experience with the softer emotions, but, coming from him, they didn't sound so awful.

Camille would give a month's pay to meet a lady with dirt under her fingernails. What a waste to keep her locked away.

They passed over Bethnal Green Road and into one of the isolated rookeries, where few 'bobbies' ventured after Scotland Yard had moved from Whitehall place to Victoria Embankment a year ago, the London rookeries now beyond help or, more likely, above notice.

As if sensing the danger, Renard lengthened his strides, leaving Camille to hobble along behind him, her breath coming in sharp gasps.

She was dizzy. The pain she refused to feel had become the pain she couldn't ignore.

The alley walls blurred. Listening to his steps, she matched the rhythm, relying on her mental map to turn when needed. She knew they'd reached the textile mills by the smell alone.

Camille's eyes stung, but she had no handkerchief to cover her nose, and she refused to ask the man beside her when he didn't so much as flinch at the stench. The smell was acidic, a mixture of chemical, piss, and cheap soap used by the immigrants brave, or desperate, enough to maintain the streets for a coin.

They worked along the narrow walls and followed the growing sound of the Thames River. A few blocks more and they'd come out on the south Dockland, where the ever-increasing traffic on the Thames would be uncommonly quiet after the recent storm from the North Sea; there'd be no one around aside from bored sailors looking to make their next port—or fill their beds with cheap company.

If *Renard* meant her harm, she was little better than a babe. She could run again, but any number of thugs or *men* lurked in the dark, and there was a distinct possibility Hawkins wouldn't stay down for long.

Camille gritted her teeth and kept pace, leaving her well-being up to fate, and a blasted duke.

RENARD'S RELATIONSHIP WITH fate was a fickle one. Like most nights, he'd spent a good few hours drinking, followed by a chaser of the most dangerous activity at hand.

Normally, the activities were drunken carriage races through the London streets. Tonight, he'd elected a merry jaunt through the back alleys of the slums, expecting to find a fist in his face, or better, a knife to his throat.

The fists he'd gotten right, but finding a lovely woman facing off with three thugs hadn't been part of the deal.

He welcomed the violence with open arms and bruised fists, but the woman complicated matters. He made a point to never dabble with the flighty creatures. The idea of being at the receiving end of some grateful, cloying wench was enough to keep most of his treacherous activities to male sport.

And yet he'd gone and saved her like some damned knight of old.

But if he'd expected the damsel to inflate his ego with lamentations of gratitude, he'd need to go back to the Cock 'n Hen to find a bar wench impressed with manners and coin, because Miss Camille Forthright seemed more likely to chop off an arm than accept his help.

Renard didn't delude himself for a second that the lady had succumbed to his charms. If the thought weren't ridiculous, he'd say the woman was impervious. She'd as much as sneered when he'd called her lovely.

She shuffled behind him, her one arm tucked to her chest, the other hanging limply at her side.

The woman was exceptional. Aside from her looks, which were on par with renderings of Venus with her flaming hair, flawless face, and eyes the color of autumn in the country, she'd bashed that ginger bastard hard enough the boxer hadn't recovered to avoid Renard's uppercut. And he had no doubt she'd have taken that skinny fiend to pasture if it hadn't been for her other injuries.

All without a whimper of complaint. Forget exceptional; she

wasn't human.

Though the way her gazes, and words, flayed his ego open, he'd yet to determine if he was in the presence of an avenging angel—or a delicious devil.

"You're staring," she accused.

"Hmm. Tell me, Miss Forthright, are you religious?"

Those lovely, brown eyes flashed in the spotty moonlight. "I've seen too much of the world to believe there's someone looking out for my well-being."

"You're a cynic?"

"I'm a realist." Her nose wrinkled. "I suppose you are a believer?"

"Heavens, no." He smiled at his joke. She didn't. He cleared his throat. "Not in the conventional sense of church and prayer, anyway. But God . . ." The blackness long buried in his mind clawed its way towards the surface. Renard pushed it down and away and answered simply, "Yes."

There was a God. Renard knew with absolute certainty. He should know; he'd been stupid enough to anger Him.

The sounds of water, and profanity, filtered down the alley with the warm light of the Cock 'n Hen tavern.

Renard felt an odd sense of reluctance to part ways. Stranger still, his increasingly sober state didn't elicit the usual panic he experienced most mornings before his drink—since not even a self-proclaimed lush of a worthless gentleman thought it right to grab a bottle before ten in the morning.

He turned down a bisecting alley, heading for the warehouse on the far side of the harbor. "The tavern is the other way," she said.

He didn't stop. "Your deduction skills are profound."

He was surprised to hear her follow. Glancing over his shoulder, he saw her jaw was locked and her wrist had turned an unhealthy shade of plum. And those lovely eyes . . . were blank; she'd near lost consciousness on her feet.

"Damn it." He scooped her into his arms, minding her injuries.

She protested—loudly.

"The man I mentioned lives up ahead," he said in hopes of quelling her struggling.

Life came back to her eyes when her suspicious glare surfaced. "There aren't any dwellings on this side of the docks."

Even half-conscious, the woman's mind was sharper than an officer's sword.

"He lives in his workshop," he said.

Gregori never stopped working. When Renard's oldest friend, the Duke of Camine, had brought the crackpot back to London after one of his tours of Europe, Renard had watched the young man work on a pair of spectacles, his first ever, for four days straight—longer, since Renard had blacked out at some point after finishing a fine barrel of German beer.

He grinned at the memory. "I'm not sure the man sleeps."

"Why would a doctor need a workshop?" Her face paled under the moonlight. "You're bringing me to a coroner?"

His brows rose at that. "Squeamish, are you?"

The woman was willing to make a trio of corpses not twenty minutes ago. He said as much.

"I was defending myself," she spat, then bit her lip and muttered, "Most people find dead bodies unsettling."

If he knew her better, he'd think her pouting over the fact that he'd found a weakness. Any true gentleman would've stopped and apologized.

He didn't apologize.

He'd been known to poke a beehive upon discovery, loving the excitement and terror of the potentiality of being stung.

"That grey skin," he said, then he grimaced. "And that awful, musky smell—"

"Stop!"

How lovely her brown eyes sparkled against her sour-colored skin. "You're looking a bit green around the gills, miss."

"Must be the pain." Her expression was dead. "My arm hurts

like a bitch."

Renard nearly stumbled at the profane language.

She glanced at him. "You all right there, Dandy?"

He adopted his best 'insulted' expression, hard to do when he was smirking. He threw her earlier words back at her. "My name isn't 'Dandy.'"

"No, it's Reynolds or something."

"You can do better than that."

"Reginald?"

"You're not even trying!"

Her mouth twitched. What a difference humor brought to her features. Features too soft and feminine for such a severe frown. Dear God, if she actually smiled, he may be rendered speechless.

"You're staring again," she said.

He noticed her accusing tone was absent this time around. He had been staring, and he found he didn't wish to stop.

He dragged his gaze away and nodded towards the warehouse at the end of the street. "We're nearly there."

She eyed the dark building and then turned a dragon-glare on him. "If you're luring me into a trap, *Renard*, I will make you bleed."

He laughed, a real one. "I may be a sorry excuse for a gentleman, but I'm not an imbecile. The way you busted Hawkins's face, I believe you, *Miss Forthright*."

She huffed and turned away.

Renard swore she did it to hide a smirk.

He kicked at the warehouse door, the resounding echo of boot on metal loud enough to rouse the sleeping sailors aboard the nearest ship.

He winced.

"Could you be more conspicuous?" she hissed.

"I could," he said, knowing the superior tone would irk her. "But my arms appear full at the moment."

"Then put me down! No one asked you to carry me."

His arms tightened around her and the fullness of her backside against his forearm felt delicious. "As you were about to collapse in a dark alley, injured and helpless, a simple 'Thank you' wouldn't be remiss."

"That was my problem, not yours."

For some reason, her words tripped his own, usually contained, anger. "Seeing as how I'd just saved you, leaving you undefended would have defeated the point."

"I never *asked* to be saved!"

His gaze narrowed. "And here we come to it. How it must needle you to know a man—no, a *gentleman*—saved you. I've known you less than an hour, Miss Forthright, but I can say with certainty, pride like that will get you killed."

To think this woman, this damn, fearless dragon was out in the world, strong and sharp and all kinds of wrong—in so many ways—and if he'd decided on another tavern, another drink, one single blasted alley over, she would most likely have died alone, in the dark. The idea was deplorable, unforgivable.

"Despicable."

Seeming to think his mumbling was directed at her, she struggled in his arms.

He caught her to him and heard her gasp in pain. His gut dropped. If she kept up this incessant flailing, her arm may fracture beyond repair.

She pushed at his chest, her wrist giving a grating *pop*.

"Stop." He pressed a kiss to her temple.

She froze.

Her skin was sweet and smelled of sweat and flowery soap, an agreeable scent in comparison to the acid-tainted smell of the streets. A low heat filled his belly, like the slow burn of good brandy down his throat. When he pulled back, he found her cold eyes filled with shock.

"Now," he said, his voice unsteady, "if you would desist, we may both avoid further injury."

She blinked, and some logical thought seemed to grab hold.

She leaned back in his arms and said with venom, "I won't thank you for acting like some reckless hero. I never will."

A stab of regret cut the muscle in his chest before he patched it up with dark acceptance. Even if he wanted to reenact some boyish fantasy of good and evil, which he did not, he knew his role wouldn't resemble anything close to heroism.

Hearing the lumbering steps of Gregori on the other side of the door, he turned to her and made himself perfectly clear. "That's where you're mistaken, Miss Forthright." He faced the door and let his expression, and heart, turn to stone before his own words cut him too deep to repair. "I'm no one's hero."

CHAPTER THREE

T HE WAREHOUSE DOOR opened, flooding the dark street with warm and bright light and revealing a young man in a wrinkled shirt and dark hair sticking heavenward around the strange contraption attached to his head.

The man squinted at the sky, then focused on Renard and, finally, her. "It's night," he said.

Camille frowned. *This* was the doctor; a young man with an oil-stained shirt, his sleeves rolled up around his elbows, and a week's worth of stubble on his chin? Her luck continued to be poor. She shook her head. "I'll take my chances with the tavern."

Renard grinned. "Good evening, Gregori."

"What do you want?"

"The lady here needs a bone set."

Gregori's indifferent gaze fixed on her awkwardly held arm. He turned back inside, leaving the door wide open and revealing a large space with tables running the length of the room.

She looked at Renard, who shrugged and brought her across the threshold and into a cluttered but well-maintained workshop.

Camille's mind switched on, taking in the room's dimensions, window count, and secondary door at the back of the space before cataloging the contents on the tables: hammers, microscopes, wiring, precision knives. There were pieces she didn't recognize as well. If those tools weren't going to be potentially used on her, she'd have been intrigued. It didn't take a genius to realize the man was a skilled man of science, but she *was* a genius.

She pinched Renard in the arm, her wrist aching.

"Ow!" he said. "What was that for?"

"He's an engineer," she said.

"He's a doctor."

"Not a *medical* doctor."

"So?"

She blew hair out of her face. "The specialties are not the same." Really, were all gentlemen idiots?

His smirk was all teeth. "They're essentially the same. One works with the mechanics of the body. The other with inanimate objects."

"They're completely different."

"No, they're not."

"He's not touching me!"

They turned at the same time, finding Gregori studying them.

"Well?" Renard said.

Gregori nodded to Camille. "She is right."

"You can't set a dislocated bone?"

"I can," Gregori said.

"But you said she was right."

"She is."

"What the hell?"

The younger man didn't use four words when two would do.

He was an engineer. Up close, she saw the mechanism on his head was a handless monocle with a collection of lenses on a rotating gear, the lenses each a different strength and magnification by the thickness of the glass. He worked with fine and intricate designs, something to do with eyepieces, judging by the stock of specialty wire and soldering.

But the man claimed he could set a bone, and more than one of the tools laid out were identical to those found on a surgeon's table.

"You studied anatomy and medicine," she said. His confidence said he'd studied under a bonesetter as well.

He glanced her way, his brown eyes alert despite the dark circles underneath. "I did."

"I can't vouch for his bedside manner."

Renard's earlier words clicked into place. The man didn't make time for petty emotions or desire to explain his thoughts when others couldn't keep up.

Given her own circumstances, she understood completely.

"I see." She pointed to the one table that wasn't covered in bric-a-brac by a far wall. "Set me there and find me a strip of leather."

"That's it?" Renard asked, his mouth bent down in a frown. "Two words and you've changed your mind?"

"Yes."

His nose scrunched as his feeble mind worked hard to catch up. His expression turned comical. "Dear Lord!" He shook his head. "You're just like the crackpot, aren't you?"

RENARD LEANED AGAINST a table, his arms crossed over his chest.

She was more than clever. He knew that look, the one a person of superior intellect used while waiting patiently for the rest of the world to understand. He'd mistaken Miss Forthright's actions and words as blustered pride. Pride she surely had, but with a mind to back it up, and none of the patience. He never thought he'd see the day when Gregori's two-word explanations were the preference.

Gregori bent close and examined her jutting shoulder before moving to the plum-colored mess of her wrist.

"How did the bone dislocate?" he asked.

"I ran into a wall," she said. At his quirked brow, she added, "I was being chased."

"Ah." His typical neutral expression covered his stupid face.

Renard sucked a tooth, his mood souring.

He'd forgotten how young Gregori was, with long hair and a

whisker-dusted jaw that never failed to turn the ladies' heads on the rare occasions he left his lair. The man didn't even have the decency to look ragged after being up all night, no doubt tinkering with some new experiment.

Renard rubbed the back of his neck. Why the hell was he thinking about the crackpot's hair or how the ladies liked him? Not that the man's looks mattered when he had the personality akin to one of his soulless machines.

Miss Forthright watched him with hawk-like precision, looking ready to shred him if he got too close. "What is your opinion on Dr. Hood's book regarding bone-setting?" she asked.

Gregori took one of the tools from a nearby table, inserted it into the side of the odd-looking contraption on his head, and gave it a twist. A *click-clack* sound later, and a round eyepiece fell over his left eye, with no need to hold it in place.

He continued to examine her wrist, prodding the joint. "I prefer Steele's more recent article."

Her brow arched. "And your opinion on Steele?"

Gregori looked up and smirked. "The man enjoys the word 'quack.'"

She smiled. "And 'qualified.'"

Renard stared, dumbstruck. The smile was captivating, tempting. His insides felt like they'd liquified into warm honey. Her smile was perfection, and it was directed at another man.

Renard bit the inside of his cheek. So they talked in riddles. So she'd smiled at the stupid crackpot. He merely felt protective. He had saved her, after all, and gone through the trouble of carrying her here. She could smile at whatever stupid, mechanical crackpot she wanted.

Except that crackpot's characteristic neutral expression just lit up in a completely uncharacteristic fashion.

"What's your take on adding bone-setting to the medical curricula?" Gregori asked.

Was that interest in the other man's voice? Couldn't be. Miss Forthright didn't have gears or any kind of wire sticking out of her body. Renard would know—her dress was threadbare and left little to the imagination when in his arms. His blood heated thinking about how her curves had fit perfectly against his chest.

Miss Forthright gave Gregori a sniff. "I think doing away with the ease and affordability of generational bone-setting families so some educated snipper-snapper's feelings don't get hurt is a waste of talent and much needed services for people who work for a living."

It was Gregori's turn to smile, a brilliant grin straight and full of white teeth that Renard suddenly wished were crooked and bloody.

"Something to add?" Gregori asked him.

Renard shot Gregori his finest glare. "Can you set the lady's shoulder or not?"

Gregori's mouth twitched.

Renard didn't have time to ask the stupid, mechanical, *stupid* man what was so damn funny because Gregori stood and beckoned him forward.

"It's a partial dislocation. The pain will increase until the muscles swell, possibly tearing in the event of further assault. The upper arm bone needs to be placed back in the socket immediately."

Renard blinked. That was the most words he'd ever heard the man string together, but why the hell was he telling him?

"I'm right here," Miss Forthright said, gaze narrowed. "Eyes and ears, and perfectly able *legs*."

Renard internally smiled at her subtle threat. Gregori was too cold a creature for a woman like her, all fire and steel. Mood restored, he gave the other man his back and asked her, "What do you want to do?"

She jolted, seeming surprised he'd asked. "*Now* I get a say?'

"All of this has been your decision." He stopped her with an upraised hand before she could skewer him with another well-aimed insult. "Aside from refusing to let you fall unconscious in a dark alley."

Her expression closed as she went through her thoughts. He hadn't forced her to follow him towards the harbor, nor to the warehouse. He'd made sure to keep her apprised of the direction he was heading and to not-so-subtly imply that he'd wait for her, but she'd walked on her own two feet, for most of the way, right up until this moment.

She shifted on the table and took in a lungful of air through gritted teeth. Part of her dress fell to the side, revealing a nasty bruise and unnatural jutting joint at her shoulder, almost as violently colored as her wrist.

Renard's fists clenched. Her body, her decision. His own guardianship over his sister, troublesome and sweet Charlotte, had taught him the fear of how women were treated outside the protective embrace of a male relative. As such, he believed a woman had the right to choose when, where, and who would touch them . . . but if Miss Forthright didn't do something in the next ten seconds, he'd have to leave the warehouse or else he may very well turn into a smog-breathing dragon and force the woman into letting the crackpot fix her. Renard would gladly take the beating from her as long as she stopped grimacing in pain.

A change of tactics, then; she was sensical and, therefore, could be reasoned with. "Miss Forthright—"

"Let me attend you or get out," Gregori said in that uncomfortable, bored tone he used. "I have work to get back to."

Renard could've strangled him.

"All right," she said. "Do it."

Renard blinked. "Really?"

She arched a severely slanted brow at him. "Did you expect hysterics? Tears?"

"I expected you to say 'no.'"

She lifted her chin, a new light of challenge sparking in her eyes. "I rarely do what's expected of me."

Women were already unpredictable creatures, confusing and, indeed, hysterical. Renard couldn't fathom why when Miss Forthright said as much, with those wide and intelligent eyes fixed on him, it in no way made him wish to dash for the hills.

CHAPTER FOUR

T HE HARD WOOD of the tabletop left Renard's tailbone aching, but the ache in his groin was more pressing. As he held Miss Forthright against his chest per Gregori's instruction, he hoped the woman mistook the hardness between them as one of the dozens of tools strewn about the warehouse and not the jutting erection straining against his button fly.

She was lean and soft against him, her back curve molding to his torso and chest indecently, perfectly. The light from the buzzing bulbs overhead bathed her profile in warm light, playing with the golden hues woven through her auburn hair. She had a beauty mark on her neck, perfectly hidden under the line of her jaw. No one would know it was there unless permitted intimately close. He liked knowing. And that smell of flowers, no perfumes or imitations, unlike anything he'd smelled on a woman's skin. It was enough for a man to appreciate the vendors selling lilies and romance on the side of the street.

Gregori offered her a strip of leather to place between her teeth.

She reached for it and gasped.

Damn it! He should've stopped at the tavern for a whiskey . . . for her. He scowled at the other man. "Don't you have something for the pain?"

Gregori shrugged.

If he hadn't been holding Miss Forthright, he'd have punched the crackpot in the jaw.

"I'm fine," she said around the makeshift mouth guard, her statement ruined when she grimaced again.

"Do something—now!"

Gregori shook his head. "I work with metal, not people."

"So?"

"Metal doesn't complain."

Renard stared at him. "You don't have anything? Scotch? Whiskey? Sherry?"

"I don't drink."

Renard eyed him, appalled.

"The pain will subside when the bone is set." Gregori watched her, that rage-inducing gleam of appreciation back in his gaze. "She should be unconscious by now. I've seen veteran boxers reduced to whimpering after such an injury." He smiled at her as if she were a machine that had learned to crave tea and biscuits. "Truly remarkable. Do you have a dulled pain receptor?"

"Compartmenlistin.'" Her response was garbled.

Gregori's face lit up. "Fascinating."

Renard growled. "What's so bloody fascinating?"

The younger man turned to him, his patience ever intact. "There's a rough theory that if one's mental fortitude is apt, a person can essentially close off parts of their body from experiencing specific emotions." His gaze went back to Miss Forthright, awe in his tone. "I'd never considered it possible to block pain."

Renard could only stare at the back of her head, her hair mussed and knotted. Block pain? A person would need to be a genius, a walking miracle, to pull that off. "Amazing."

Gregori nodded. "Indeed."

Miss Forthright spit the leather from her mouth, her tone dry. "If you two idiots are done treating me like some machine to dissect, I can't block pain entirely and my shoulder does, in fact, hurt."

Spoken like a woman who'd pricked her finger on an embroidery needle and not dislodged a bone from its socket.

Truly incredible. Renard shook his head. The woman was a dragon herself, rare and far too perfect to keep locked away. He'd figure out what that meant later.

He nodded to Gregori. "You heard the lady."

Gregori reached up and placed a hand on her upper arm, the other on the subtle curve of her shoulder. "Turn your head," he told her.

She turned away, bringing her nose a scant inch from Renard's.

He felt her intake of breath as their gazes locked. Her eyes burned golden in the light, and the loveliest shade of pink stained her cheeks.

Renard swallowed.

Her gaze fell to his lips.

His body went taut, hot, and rod straight. He'd never met a woman so beautiful. Flawless skin, words that cut a man in two, and nerves stronger than iron.

He leaned forward, breathing that flowery scent deep into his soul. "Perfect."

Her lips parted.

A nasty *pop* sound filled the warehouse.

Miss Forthright jerked away with a quick cry.

Renard removed himself from around her, giving her space to rest on her good side on the table.

He ran a hand through his hair, his body hot and shaking. He looked down at his hands. What the hell was he doing? Was he going to kiss her? A woman locked in his arms and in pain?

He glanced her way.

On her side, loose hair fell into her face. Her pants steadied into a relieved sigh before she nodded to Gregori with a quiet, "Thank you."

Gregori held up a wad of cloth. "I'll wrap your wrist now."

She offered her hand, not bothering to sit up.

She must have been in more pain than she let on, but still, to not make more than a shout . . .

Not for the first time, Renard wondered about her life, her family. The scenario in the alley earlier said something about her status, along with her ragged clothes and hairstyle. But she was educated. Her speech was impeccable, her posture board-straight, and her face . . . There wasn't a chance others hadn't taken note of her beauty.

She'd looked conflicted when he'd offered her assistance, looking in the direction of one of the other rookeries. Her home? Someone waiting for her?

The idea of a husband sent scalding acid churning in his stomach. He ignored the thought, pushed it down. She couldn't be married. No self-respecting man would be stupid enough to win a woman as fine as her and not keep her safe and off these streets. The man would have been an idiot, and Miss Forthright didn't strike him as a woman who suffered fools.

Gregori set the extra cloth on a side table after a quick snip of his shears. "Done."

He left her resting on her side and stopped beside Renard. "There's a canister of water under the table," the eccentric man said.

Renard watched Miss Forthright's lashes flutter, exhaustion winning over.

"I'm not thirsty," he said.

"I didn't mean for you."

Renard glanced at Gregori's direct glaze and quirked mouth. His brain caught up. The crackpot had been right there and could have offered her a drink easily.

Instead, Gregori had offered the chance to him.

His brain flew ahead, suspecting the crass statements and delayed ministrations had been for his benefit as well.

Renard clapped him on the back and took back almost every violent thought he'd had for the other man over the past hour. "You're a good man."

Gregori snorted. "I pay attention."

"Meaning?"

"She doesn't like you," he said.

Renard felt the words like a hammer to the gut. "Obviously."

"But she's attracted to you."

Renard eyed him. Had he not seen the death glare she'd been giving him all night? "When was the last time you spoke to a woman?" He glanced around at the scattered tools and trays of pub food, delivered by one of Hamish's other associates, no doubt. "When was the last time you opened a bloody window?"

Gregori snorted. "I study things for a living, Your Grace. I don't need to *experience* an emotion to identify it." He glanced at where Miss Forthright fought sleep and offered him a rare chuckle. "You're an idiot, even for a duke."

"Thanks."

Gregori walked to the back of the warehouse, where a small cot was tucked away in the corner.

Renard had a sneaking suspicion the callous words had been the crackpot's strange version of inducement.

TURNED OUT THE encouragement wasn't necessary. Seconds later, after offering Miss Forthright the canister of water, it became evidently clear the woman more than *disliked* him.

"I don't want anything from you," she spat.

Even half-asleep and lying down, the woman was ready to spar.

How he'd found anything about her warm or endearing must have been a credit to the excellent Ballantine at the start of the evening. He dropped the water can down on the table beside her, surreptitiously pleased when some sloshed out the top and splashed across her face.

She sat up and sputtered, "You did that on purpose."

He smiled. "Happy accident."

She picked up the can, her expression promising violence.

"Gregori told me to give it to you," he said in hopes the other man's name would forestall her from tossing the tin at his head. "Drink it or not. It makes no difference to me."

She sniffed the top, her gaze suspicious.

"For the love of—" He snatched the can from her and took a swig before handing it back. "Why would I go through the trouble of bringing you here if I'd planned on poisoning you all along?"

"You're an idiot. How would I know?"

The echo of Gregori's words voicing the separation between him and them, him and *her*, was enough to send his temper over the edge.

"Fine! You're right. I should've left you to those monsters. Should've left you at the mercy of the slums in the middle of the night. I give up. I'm an idiot because I don't understand." He threw his hands in the air and walked away. Women. He'd been right all along. Never get involved. Never form an attachment. He knew better—

Something slammed into his head.

He rubbed the cradle of his skull and stared at the worn tread of a woman's boot at his feet. His gaze shot to hers.

Her cheeks were red, her breathing labored. Those mesmerizing eyes were glazed, from residual pain or anger, Renard couldn't guess.

And she was lovely. The bun at the back of her head had finally given way and dark hair cascaded around her face and shoulders; she looked like a goddess inflamed.

His own hot anger shifted to a different heat, imagining a different flame in her eyes.

He picked up the boot. How small it was. Dainty feet. The idea of this woman sporting anything dainty was a laugh and a revelation.

Renard startled.

Since when were women lovely or intriguing? Revelation? The stale warehouse air must have addled his brain.

She'd thrown her footwear—showing a scary bit of strength and skill hitting him squarely in the head—like a child in the throes of a tantrum. Highly inappropriate, unsuitable.

"Unexpected."

"Will you return my boot, or must you continue to stare at it all night?" she said.

Renard's body warmed anew at the dry tone. He leaned against a nearby table and tucked the boot under his arm. "Seeing as it was thrown at *my* head, perhaps I'll keep it, as a remembrance of our time together. You won't mind, will you?"

"My foot is cold," she said.

Her ruffled feathers did wonders for his aching head. He hid his grin behind a mask of mock seriousness. "Perhaps I'll enshrine it, have little flowers stitched into the leather."

Her mouth curled at the corner. The lady wasn't completely devoid of humor, it seemed.

"I don't like cold feet," she said.

"I'm not so fond of being bludgeoned by ladies' footwear myself."

She held out her hand. "Will you return it?"

He shrugged.

"What?" she demanded.

"I am waiting for a better incentive."

Her grinding teeth sounded like gravel underfoot. "I have a second boot, sir, and you, a very large head."

"Then you'll have two cold feet." He walked over and dropped the boot in her lap, grinning down at her. "But that will do."

She huffed—what might have been a laugh—and replaced the offending boot on her foot. "You're an idiot."

"So you've said."

She huffed again, seeming to be mercifully at a loss for insults.

He found he liked her off-balance. He found he liked *her* despite every instinct screaming at him to run far and wide. From moment to moment, he couldn't decide if he wanted to throttle her or kiss her.

A whirlwind of conflicting emotions, an unpredictable woman in every sense, but the contrast wasn't altogether unpleasant. Aside from the lump at the back of his head, Renard would go so far as to call this evening overall thrilling. And it had nothing to do with the three cretins he'd pummeled in the square.

"You're staring again," she said.

He laughed. "Add it to my growing list of flaws, right next to handsome and being in possession of a dukedom."

Mention of his title soured her expression. "Just when I was starting to tolerate you."

A man's heart shouldn't leap at such a cold term as 'tolerate.'

"Should I regale you with my many flaws? I'm told they are vastly amusing."

She crossed her arms over her chest, the action not seeming to bother her shoulder. "This should be good."

"I drink profusely, am honest to a fault, and have lain with women without marriage."

The last on his list left a wonderful blush on her cheeks, but she didn't look away.

"Honesty is a flaw?" she asked.

"People are rarely interested in the truth."

"If it's your opinion, then it isn't truth."

God, but he couldn't relax a second if he hoped to land any hits in their verbal match. "Shall we say *my* truth, then?"

She was smiling now.

Renard's chest swelled. "And my penmanship is abhorrent."

"Really?"

"Doctor's scratch is legible in comparison."

She laughed.

He was flying.

"What else?" she asked.

That lingering look she had in the alley came to mind, and Renard's joy dimmed. "Am I not keeping you from your husband?"

He'd never heard a woman cackle, which Miss Forthright did now, loudly.

Renard wouldn't decipher his relief. "Not a fan of the institution?"

"Not a fan of the *man* part."

He blinked. "You prefer women?"

"Don't know," she said. "I've never thought about it. Have you?"

"You with another woman? Can't say I can think of anything else at the moment."

She laughed again, and the sound was musical, hypnotic.

He could spend the rest of his short, black life listening to the sound.

"You *are* honest," she said once she'd caught her breath.

He winked. "To a fault."

She pursed her lips, but her amusement was evident, as well as the lowered guard in her easy body language.

A timepiece croaked the hour, like a frog with sand in its throat, the tone muffled under the crackpot's trinkets, where it had no doubt been forgotten.

Like a lifted spell, Miss Forthright's smile vanished, and that frown returned. "I should go."

Renard would give his right arm for her to stay, which meant he'd let his own guard drop.

She was too lovely, too lively. Too long in her presence and a monster like him could forget about his debt and his past. Neither would be acceptable.

But still, he hesitated.

"Did I also mention I'm an excellent deterrent for drunkards and pickpockets?" he said.

"Because they steer clear of their own kind?"

"My muscles aren't just for show." He puffed out his chest. "I can be intimidating." It could also be the Remington 95 tucked in the back of his waistband, double barreled.

She sighed. "There's no way you won't follow me home, is

there?" She didn't wait for his response. "All right, you may come on one condition."

Anything.

"Yes?"

She smirked. "Show me your doctor's scratch."

CHAPTER FIVE

C AMILLE HELD UP the paper scrap in the moonlight, the shadows of the alley walls unable to hide the worst penmanship she'd ever seen. "Are these numbers or letters?"

Renard winced next to her.

He walked at her side, the heat from his body warding off the night's chill.

Everything about him was warm—his laughter, his smile, his eyes, all directed at her—and she was horrified to learn she wasn't immune.

When he'd held her to his chest in the warehouse, she was sure her heart had pounded hard enough to crack a rib. And when she'd turned her head at the engineer's instruction, she'd been sure he'd been about to kiss her. For one brief lapse in reason, and sanity, she'd wanted him to.

She should have insisted on leaving alone. He would have followed her, she knew, but there'd be no question of the drawn line. She'd had every intention of doing just that when his boyish smile had resurfaced. Huffed resignation aside, she'd as well as *invited* him to escort her home.

Madness and confusion, that was the trouble with charming men. They used pretty speeches and shallow desires to earn a lady's trust for their own gain and then threw them to the wolves when they were no longer convenient. She'd known a charming duke once, had let him control her life and her body as a doll on strings, and then he'd cut those strings when she'd lost her usefulness.

She let the space between their bodies grow, embracing the cold, and stuffed the paper with his illegible scratch in her pocket—kindling for the fire.

She led them into another part of town. Here, the walls were cramped, the living quarters more so. It was a nicer part of St. Giles, if nice were possible in the poorest and dirtiest part of the rookery. But the rent was reasonable and her landlord, an older man who'd been eager for company after his wife had died in childbirth along with their newborn son, more so for the kind. Tucked away in the upper rooms of a first-floor walkup, Camille and her mother kept to themselves and remained relatively safe with the older man downstairs.

"You're quiet," Renard said.

"Many men consider silence a woman's virtue."

"Only idiots."

She glanced his way.

He waved off the question in her eyes. "I've a sister, remember? When things go quiet, I lock up the rifles and liquor, just in case."

She wouldn't be moved by the tender note in his voice. "Is she really so much trouble?"

"She once set an army of ants on her governess because the woman had said a proper lady shouldn't question a man. 'The man' being me and 'me' having foolishly expected my little sister to follow my order to stay away from the stables without complaint."

"How old was she?"

"Twelve."

"She was only a child."

Renard shook his head, but she could tell his frown was for show.

"She *also* put a jar of worms in her chaperone's bed for insisting a man doesn't like his wife to read so much."

The lady sounded marvelous! "When was that?"

He smirked. "Last month."

She'd like to meet a woman who used insects to fight off injustice towards a woman's independence. "Is she coming for the summer?"

The Prodding Pony had been fully booked since Midsummer. Less than a fortnight and the balls and soirees of the elite would double up events and pull the wealthy and titled clients away, meaning she may finally get a night off.

Renard's expression darkened. "She stays in the country."

"While you're here?"

"It's safer *there*," he said.

Camille didn't understand his emphasis on 'there.' The city was dangerous, true enough. She'd been chased down by demons not three hours ago, but a well-bred lady—in a stone mansion with butlers and maids and an army of other pompous and starched servants—surely had little to worry over. The lady sounded like she'd take the *ton* by storm, or better, drop beetles in the punchbowl when the head-in-the-clouds debutante darlings needed their feet dragged back to the ground.

"You should bring her," she said. "If not for society, then for the sights."

If one ignored the lung-retching smog and urine-soaked streets, London was a wealth of grand entertainment and local beauty. Camille hadn't been to Bond Street since she'd been a girl, but even with her cynical and tainted views of the elite, she had exclaimed at the elaborate shop windows and smells of fresh pastries sold at the bakeries.

The hard look was still present on his face, but his tone was thoughtful when he said, "Charlotte does like to paint, and the bookshops have the latest edition of Dickens."

Camille imagined the buttery and flakey texture of croissant on her tongue. "And pastries."

His brows rose. "You liken bread with literature?"

"I'd take a lemon tart over Shakespeare any day."

His frown vanished and his grin reemerged. "Many claim Shakespeare's plays are the best food for one's soul."

"Then they're never had a tart."

"I confess I've never had one," he said.

She snorted. "No wonder you read plays."

He shook his head, all traces of that darkness in his expression replaced with amused light. "They're that good? Better than *Romeo and Juliet?*"

She stared him dead in the eyes, perfectly serious. "Better than *Hamlet.*"

"Now I know you're mad. *Hamlet* cannot come second to a pastry. Do you also prefer sticks to flowers?"

"Of course. Though the stick burns better in the fire."

"Madness!" He was smiling. "To win your heart, a man mustn't use flowers or poetry, but a tart?"

She enjoyed his teasing. The lack of scolding in his tone was full of sincere attention. Since it was unlikely she'd ever see him after tonight, she didn't see the harm in indulging in a bit of amusement at his expense.

"Don't think me so easily caught, *sir*. It would take at least ten."

"Ten tarts." His smile was all teeth. "Is that all?"

She was glad when the moon drifted behind a passing cloud, else the man would witness her grinning like a fool. "Perhaps a pair of satin slippers. I do have an inclination for footwear."

He laughed. "To use as weapons, I've no doubt."

He was too easy to talk to. She hadn't meant to offer so much, but he'd looked sad talking about missing his sister. Truthfully, she struggled conversing with most people. The way her brain worked, having to explain herself was tedious. But the duke had more than kept pace.

He spoke genuinely, honestly. She believed him when he'd said he wasn't a hero. Most men would bluster and lash out at her lack of gratitude, whereas Renard had laughed it off.

What a strange man. Tall and fair-haired, the man would put

the great statues to shame. A gentleman, no less, and yet, he walked the streets at night, as if hunting for a fight.

"Admiring my good looks?" he asked.

"Yes."

He stumbled and righted himself, muttering something that sounded like, "Unexpected."

She grinned . . . then frowned. They were deep in the rookery now, a stone's throw from the flat she shared with her mother.

The modest dwellings gave way to mostly standing four-walled shacks. Camille felt a module of shame—and then let it go.

She wasn't interested in pity or charity. Though the pay at the Prodding Pony was generous, there were still years' worth of debt to repay; the duke's inattention harmed them even in death. Until the collectors' threats were gone, they'd make do. She had plans for whatever was left over, and she'd make it count.

A light shone in the upstairs living space where her mother must have left one of their precious candles to waste. She should go inside and save what wick was left, but she found herself hesitating to leave the night air. Maybe not just the air. Tonight, she hadn't been the girl who'd ruined her mother's life, or Madam Clarice's errand girl.

They stopped at the corner, and Renard nodded to the light. "This is home?" No disgust, no pity.

She could have kissed him for that. The fingernail she pressed into her shoulder was sharp, a reminder. No good would come of letting herself like him. Certainly no good would come of kissing.

"You're frowning," he said.

The moon had yet to make its reappearance.

She huffed. "There's no light. How could you tell?"

"You went quiet."

"And silence equates to frowning?"

"You frown when you're thinking."

She snorted. "I'm always thinking."

"As I said."

Her frown deepened. Charming, handsome, *and* observant;

she was at great risk of *not* hating him.

He moved closer, his body heat chasing away her cold thoughts.

She swallowed away the sudden dryness in her throat and forced her brows to smooth. "You're mistaken," she said.

"Am I?"

He stood so close, his words brushed her cheek, low and rumbled.

She shivered.

Camille held her breath as the tip of his finger traced her chin and trailed up her cheek and to her brow. Their earlier heat from the warehouse rose up, alien and wonderful and terrifying.

He whispered against her temple, "You shouldn't frown."

Her body was on fire, her brain a cold machine—mostly. "I'll do what I like."

Those burning lips followed his finger's path across her forehead. "And what *do* you like?"

Her brain's focus narrowed. There were only his lips at her cheekbone, his fingers tilting up her chin. And the ache in her belly, growing and charting a wanton path to her core.

Her brain informed her of the word 'heat.' An animal husbandry term to describe the sexual awareness of a female. An apt name when the spot between her legs felt like liquid sun.

His lips skimmed the sensitive skin below her ear. "What do you like?"

"You," she said breathlessly.

His teeth nipped at her lobe. "I like you too."

She gripped his shoulders to keep upright. "You shouldn't." She gasped.

"Neither should you."

"Then we're in agreement?"

"Yes."

His tongue ran the seam of her lips, tempting, taunting.

She flicked his tongue with her own.

He growled low in his throat, but he kept his distance.

Her body trembled, her breath coming in pants. She needed something, something she suspected he withheld. She leaned forward, but he pulled back.

The disappointment felt cold in her chest. "Won't you kiss me?"

He stiffened. His voice, when he spoke, was low and hungry. "Is that an invitation?"

Lord forgive her. "Yes."

His smile was dazzling, even in the dark. His fingers worked through the rushed knot at the nape of her neck, loosening the curls until they tumbled around her shoulders. He cupped the back of her head and leaned down to whisper against her lips, "Good." His lips sealed over hers.

Camille's body flushed, the heat unbearable. Needing him closer, she gripped the front of his overcoat with one hand and pulled the lapels together until she felt his hard body everywhere.

Every flick of tongue, every brush of skin, was madness. She understood now how some of the women at the Pony said they enjoyed their work. The excuses of kissing she'd suffered in the past had been the artless fumblings of boys. Renard was all man.

Her hips ground against his, seeking pressure, the friction lovely. Back and forth, back and forth. This feeling, this frenzy, was exquisite.

He broke the kiss and pressed his forehead to hers, his voice unsteady. "Slow down."

"Like hell." She pulled his face back to hers and ran her tongue along his lips as he'd done to her.

His grip tightened on her hips, his hands like fire through her thin dress.

She wanted those hands everywhere. She guided his hand to her chest, where her breasts felt heavy and aching.

He pinched her nipple through her dress. "Camille," he moaned.

Her name on his lips set her ablaze, and she went up in smoke.

CHAPTER SIX

H E WAS GOING to combust any second. She was like a raging fire, and he'd been dry for months. They were on the streets, standing on a dilapidated corner of cobblestone more dirt than stone. It was dangerous and dirty, and he couldn't have cared less.

This had to stop; his hands on her hips were too tight, his touch too rough.

Buxom widows, ladies bored of their old, infirm husbands—he had his choice of lovers—yet he'd never struggled with restraint in the bedroom before. Then why the hell was he going mad keeping himself from pushing her against the nearest wall and jamming himself to the hilt between her legs? She was a force of nature, a deadly combination of ice and fire a man could willingly lose himself in.

Her hand reached down to guide his to her breast.

He gritted his teeth, his restraint threadbare. "Camille." Her name came out like a prayer. He rolled her nipple through the fabric.

"Renard."

A primal roar of triumph rose from the pit of his existence, lost in passion. He wanted his name on her lips, wanted her to know she was his.

Except she wasn't.

From that same deep place, he found the will to pull away.

Moonlight broke through the cloud cover, revealing her lust-filled gaze and swollen lips.

The soft look on her face did something odd to his chest. He wasn't a pious man, but Renard found himself wishing, *praying*, he'd be forgiven this one moment to deserve this woman.

Past darkness coiled in his chest, choking the warm and bright seed that had sprouted.

He'd let himself forget. For the first night in eight years, he hadn't seen the haunting faces and felt the burn of his future in the fiery pit. There'd only been *her* and that stubborn resolve and unforgiving nature, challenging him to be more, *expecting* him to be more.

He set her away from him and watched her soft expression harden. He welcomed her anger and disdain, another gentleman who used an opening to take advantage. It was better that way. He'd never deserve the woman in front of him. No amount of scrubbing would wash away the blood on his hands.

"I'm sorry," he said, knowing she'd misinterpret his words.

For all his speech about not being a hero, he'd deluded himself into believing saving her, giving something of himself, would mean he wasn't an irredeemable monster. He'd laughed and flirted, all part of his mask—the 'rogue' duke—a gentleman who was always charming and not to be taken seriously.

But somewhere over the course of the evening, amidst alley brawling and sparring in verbal matches he'd had no chance of winning, that laughter had rung sincere.

All because of her.

"It wasn't a mistake," she said.

He wouldn't hurt her and deny it. Better she did not know how close she'd come to a real monster.

Her jaw set for a fight. "Don't tell me it was."

Even now she surprised him, delighted him, made him want more. He shook his head, knowing he'd never allow himself what he wanted.

"I won't," he said. Kissing her *had* been a mistake, but not one he'd regret. Her kiss would be one bright memory in a sea of ugly shadow.

CAMILLE WATCHED THE darkness of memory steal the light from his eyes. She knew how the past latched on to one's mind and refused to let go. It poisoned joy, haunted hope.

He was waiting for her anger at being rejected; she saw it in his shifting gaze.

He *had* rejected her, and she *was* angry, but not at him.

She'd let herself be swept away in the moment, knowing better. Emotion was too flimsy and changeable to rely on.

That flimsy sensation reared its ridiculous head now, determined to undermine her and prove her wrong. She wanted to continue her exploration of lips and skin and brush off the weight of responsibility on her shoulders. The resounding quiet in her brain as he'd touched her had been a relief from the constant thoughts and images, the constant regret. It was an epiphany so overwhelming, she would have willingly stayed in his arms forever and let her body take over.

But she couldn't rest. There was too much relying on her skills and brain. Always on, always making up for what she'd been born lacking.

"I'm sorry," he said again.

The two words grated against her freshly secured mental armor. She looked up into his handsome face, wishing she could hate him. He represented everything she loathed, the young embodiment of the man she'd despise long after she was dead and in the ground.

All she saw was *this* duke's straightforward nature and self-deprecating smiles. Honesty may have been a flaw to the conniving matrons and debutantes of the *ton*, but she respected the guts it took to state one's mind at the risk of rejection. And, unlike that self-serving narcissist of a duke from her past, Renard had morals.

Guilt. Even as charming and kind as he was, he knew how inappropriate a connection between them would be. He was a member of the gentry, and she was . . . unsuitable. If he'd spouted poetic nonsense about love and passion, she'd have spat in his face.

At least, in this regard, she could assuage his conscience without betraying herself.

His lips parted, a third apology inevitable, when she held up a hand to stop him.

With her emotions back in check, she looked him in the eye, not feeling anything. "Do not concern yourself, Your Grace. You've hurt no feelings as there are none to harm. I asked you to kiss me and you did." She stuck out her hand. "Let us call it a mutual exchange and leave it at that."

His laugh was a huffed puff of white air between them. "Kissing is an exchange?"

"Isn't it?"

He laughed again, some of his former humor returning. He took her hand, his eyes dancing.

The fingers curling around hers were warm. Camille still felt their heat on her chin, her lips. She dropped his hand and gave a terse nod. "Good evening, Your Grace."

His smile didn't reach his eyes. "Goodbye, Miss Forthright."

She pivoted on her heel and crossed the street. At her doorway, she removed the key from the string around her neck, and opened the door, refusing to glance back at the man bathed in moonlight.

Tonight would be a night of adventure and memory, an unlikely dream she would take out and examine when the desire for whimsy struck, but nothing more. For this evening was but a fantasy.

Renard Louis, Duke of Lux, lived in a foreign world, full of manners and obligations, whereas her world was defined by rough freedom. Rich and poor, etiquette and slums, low and high—they were perfect opposites. Their meeting had been chance, an event not meant to be repeated. She'd close off her memories just as she closed and locked the door behind her. They would never see each other again.

It was simpler that way.

TALL, DARK HAIRED, and with a smattering of faint freckles across her cheeks, Scarlet had decided to attend the bar as herself today instead of donning one of her half a dozen disguises she wore aiding the Merry Men gang. She slid a shot across the bar, her mouth set in an amused line. "Did you walk into a wall?"

Camille arched a brow at the offered whiskey. "It's ten in the morning."

Scarlet shrugged, her swept-back hair looking ready to escape out its knot atop her head. "You looked like you could use it. That bump on your head looks awful."

Camille touched her temple and winced. She'd been so pre-occupied with her shoulder and wrist last night, she'd forgotten Flank's lucky punch. And she'd been so concerned her mother would see her sorry state this morning that she'd left the flat early and come straight to the Cock 'n Hen.

Luckily, no one other than Scarlet and Manny, the owner, would be here this time of day. With its gleaming, mahogany countertops and oversized window overlooking the bustling harbor, the tavern was a world set apart and a haven for a woman who needed to avoid men with a score to settle.

"So what *did* happen?" Scarlet asked.

"I ran into a wall."

"Why?"

Camille picked up the shot of amber liquid before setting it back on the bar without drinking. "I was running. It was slippery.

Hence, wall."

Scarlet leaned forward on her elbows, her look hard, and waited.

Camille sighed, knowing this wasn't a battle she'd win. "Hawkins and his friends wanted an extra session away from the Pony."

Scarlet grabbed the whiskey, threw it back in one shot, and set it on the bar with a loud *clank*. "Shit."

Enough said.

Scarlet knew about the unwanted attentions of men. Before her father had returned from America, she'd worked at the Prodding Pony, where *fantasies came alive* . . . at the drop of a coin.

It was where Camille had found her in the alley out back— that same awful night months ago when her own life had shattered—her lip and dress torn and silent understanding passing between them of what had happened. After half-carrying, half-dragging Scarlet to a free, but secret, clinic run by the Underground, Camille had marched back to the Pony and informed the Madam she was a shitty excuse of a woman and that if she was going to let her 'girls' be assaulted not two feet from her door for free, then she was an even sadder excuse of a businesswoman.

Expecting the silk-wrapped woman to have her thrown out of her 'establishment,' Camille, without two pence to rub together, had been dumbstruck when the older woman had apologized to her, by name—infamous as the first of the scandal sheets had circulated in the rookeries' deadly playhouses before being sent to entertain the *ton*—and offered her a job on the spot.

Luckily, Scarlet had found her own employment at the tavern less than a week later. The patrons still got handsy when deep in their cups, but the shotgun behind the bar remained enough incentive to keep the petting to a minimum.

"Those bastards." Scarlet's fists white-knuckled around the glass. She didn't bother asking the outcome of Camille's night. A lone woman against three assailants were impossible odds and all too commonplace in this part of the city.

There was also no pity, not between two sisters-in-arms.

They both knew what had happened, or would have, if a certain golden-haired gentleman hadn't intervened. Determined not to think of the duke, Camille focused on her friend, who was cursing Hawkins and his cohort in colorful detail.

"Careful, Scar," she said, "your accent is showing."

Scarlet nodded to the room. "There's no use pretending for empty stools." She shook her head. "Leave the Pony, Cam. You can work here. Manny is certainly smitten and would hire you, no questions asked. Flutter your lashes at him and he'd be on one knee in seconds."

If only wishful thinking paid. She'd never pay off their debt working for sixpence at the tavern. And marrying a tavern owner, no matter how kind the man was, would never happen. She had plans for the money when the collectors' greedy appetites no longer dragged them to her door, plans too important to worry over things as trivial as comfort and safety.

"I can't," she said.

"If it's about the money, I can ask Pops—"

"No." Camille didn't doubt Scarlet's Pops, the leader of Dockside's 'Merry Men,' had a stash of blunt big enough to pay off her debts and those of every other sorry case in the rookeries, but those funds were what kept the underground clinic and the shelter for injured officers running and out of the grasping hands of the elite, who'd describe the additional attention and funds as 'unnecessary.'

Her cause was as important, and urgent, but she wouldn't rob the baker to pay the grocer.

"I'll make do," she said.

Scarlet sighed. "I knew you'd say that. At least let one of the Merry walk you back and forth to the Pony until someone informs Lucien his prize dog is up to his old tricks."

Camille rolled her eyes. "Because Hawkins won't take being fired personally."

"He knew the rules," Scarlet said. "Maybe Lu will do us all a favor and put him down."

"Wishful thinking again."

"What?"

Camille waved her off. Having one of the Merry follow her around would secure her comings and goings, but they'd also scare off business at the Pony, something Madam Clarice would take more than personally. The men may have been skilled and nimbler than the feral cats patrolling the waterways for the ever-infested rats, but they were also big, loud, and carried the air of death around them like winter-worn cloaks.

All except one.

"Any chance Pops will let me borrow Syd for a few days?" Camille asked.

Scarlet shoved a finger in her face, the nail worn and chipped from helping in the back kitchen peeling potatoes day after day. "Don't go encouraging her. She's too wild as it is. Why Pops lets her run with the men is beyond me."

Camille smiled at the sisterly affection. "Syd will be leader of the gang in the next year."

"She's sixteen!"

She shrugged. Camille had a rare soft spot for Scarlet's little sister. Upon her father's return to London, Syd had made it her mission to learn everything she could about self-defense. Fourteen at the time, the 'Merry Men' expanding into protecting local businesses had been her idea. Two years later, everyone looked to Markus Laundry for leadership, but anyone close to the family knew Syd called the day to day. The mind of a business-woman, and the heart of a bruiser who didn't yet weigh eight stones.

"Escorting me has to be safer than what Pops has her running," she said.

Scarlet gave her, and her wrapped wrist, a dubious look.

Camille pushed. "We both know Syd could take Hawkins."

"Easily," Scarlet said with no small amount of pride, her hard expression softening as her gaze slipped back to Camille's injuries.

"Fine. I'll ask."

"Thank you." Camille checked the clock. It was early for her shift, but it wouldn't hurt to get to the club before the morning rush. She had stacks of files to work through and convert to memory, and a proposition to finish.

She stood. "I'll see you tomorrow, Scar."

Her friend waved her off, then shouted when Camille was at the door. "Hey, Cam, I forgot. There was a bloke in here earlier asking after you."

Camille's heart leapt before she strapped it down. "Fair-haired? Light eyes?"

Recognition lit Scarlet's eyes. "Something you need to tell me, Cam?"

Damn. "No." Camille offered a pasted-on smile. "The man?"

Scarlet smiled knowingly but mercifully dropped her inquiry. "Dark hair. Blue eyes."

Camille frowned, unfathomably disappointed. Who had she expected?

"A sailor?" She'd kept a close relationship with the captains who frequented the harbor, a natural carry over from her time rubbing elbows with the merchants as a child.

"Nah. He wasn't dressed for the sea," Scarlet said. "But he was a gentleman, I've no doubt."

Description and opinion aligned, and Camille gritted her teeth. Only one man would come looking for her here. "Hamish."

The damn duke didn't know when to quit. First the Prodding Pony and now the Cock 'n Hen. Apparently, a shoe to the head wasn't enough to get through his thick skull. It was only a matter of time before her half-brother found the flat where she and her mother lived. If he showed up while she was away—looking so much like their father with the same dark hair and piercing eyes—and her mother answered the door . . . Camille made a mental note to send *another* scathing letter, telling the man to keep his nose out of her business, or lose it. Like she didn't have enough to worry about.

She turned on her heel and went to the door, calling over her shoulder to Scarlet, "If he shows up again, do me a favor and shoot him."

CHAPTER SEVEN

"**Y**OU'RE EARLY," MADAM Clarice said.

Camille shut the door to her boss's office and slid the bolt over before moving to the hidden panel in the wall, the entrance to the *real* office where every ledger and client file was stored.

"Camille."

She didn't turn around. She suddenly became interested in the elaborate moulding of vines and leaves carved into the walls' center lines. "Yes, Madam?"

Papers rustled, then, "Where did you get those?"

Camille shut her eyes. She wouldn't insult the other woman by playing dumb. She'd forgone the cloth sling the engineer had given her for her shoulder, but her bound wrist and bruised temple weren't as easily hidden.

"I ran into some trouble on my way home last night."

"Who were you running from?"

Camille turned and crossed her arms over her chest, her shoulder muscles protesting.

Powdered coif and cheek faded on one side, Madam Clarice busied herself with the papers on her desk, a desk identical to the one in the secret room at Camille's back. But whereas Camille's desk was full of files and papers in neat piles, Madam worked with her documents fanned out in front of her like a parchment barricade between herself and her clients.

"You shouldn't sleep at your desk," Camille said. "The position isn't good for your neck."

Madam didn't look up, didn't need to. With a single word, her iron will and refusal to change the subject was clear. "*Who?*"

"Flank and Grey."

A pause. "Anyone else?"

Camille looked away. "Hawkins."

Still reviewing the documents in front of her, Madam lifted a small bell from her desk and rang it once, twice.

Trapped inside the office until whatever attendant arrived, Camille leaned against the panel to her office and picked at her fraying sleeve. She'd need to take a morning to peruse the ready-made shops for another serviceable dress before month's end. The burden on her income would set back her plans, but while the sacrifice wasn't necessary, it was practical.

Even working as she did in the secret office with only Madam's company—and fleeting visits as the Ponies came and went from their shifts—Madam enforced a modest dress code of taste and acceptable wear, not letting the smallest tear go unnoticed.

The thread at her wrist came free, more grey than blue in color after a year of repeated laundering. A new dress would be in order anyway if she was to have anyone take her seriously in the career she aimed to have one day.

The secondary door behind the desk opened—the door leading from the depths of the club—and Sensa, Madam's second-in-command, walked inside.

Brunette hair pulled back in a severe bun, Sensa looked and played her role as governess for her clients with precision, and no small amount of strict delight. "Yes, Madam?"

Madam flipped one of the pages over, dripped wax at the bottom, and pressed the seal of the Prodding Pony into the paper. She repeated the actions with two other papers before handing them to Sensa, all without looking up. The papers had been sitting there before Camille had walked in.

"These patrons' memberships are revoked. See they're handled accordingly."

Sensa noted the names. "Grey is in the club presently. Shall I remove him?"

Madam raised her head at that, and the smile she wore was the same coy tilt of the lips that had won her the hearts of the gentry two decades ago. And the one she wore even as she dominated her clients with whips and chains hard enough to break skin.

"I've a better idea." Madam trailed a finger up Sensa's arm. "Be a dear and bring him to me. No need to ruin the surprise with the papers."

Sensa brought Madam's fingers to her mouth and kissed the tips. "Yes, Madam."

When the door closed, Madam held out the club's seal. "Put this away, would you?"

Camille palmed the metal stamp and shook her head. "Why did you ask their identities if you already knew?"

Madam leaned back in her chair, the full weight of her blue-eyed gaze unsettling. "I wanted to see if you'd tell me the truth."

Instead of experiencing outrage, Camille laughed. "You enjoy your tests."

Madam inclined her head. "You've never failed one."

"How did you find out?"

"I have my sources."

Camille didn't doubt the alley walls themselves had confessed. The woman had a knack for learning secrets.

"Hawkins won't take your decision graciously," she said.

Madam stood and went to a secondary hidden panel and pushed the latch in the moulding. The door swung open, revealing a shallow cubby lined with six riding crops in a descending order of lengths and thicknesses, all blood red—to hide the stains.

She chose a mid-length crop with finger-width tassels on the end and shut the panel. "Hawkins will be fortunate to fuck his hand after Lucien breaks him."

Camille dropped her arms, her shoulder giving a dull ache. "You told him?"

Madam arched a brow. "Why the surprise? Hawkins knew the rules."

It was the second time she'd heard that line that morning, and Camille shuddered at the implication. She knew how 'rules' worked to intimidate and bully those outside of power to behave. She knew this intimately.

Madam twirled the crop in her hand before catching the tassels against her palm with a swift *crack!* "Hawkins is lucky Lucien gets to administer his punishment. He'll only have his arms and legs broken. I would have removed his fingers and toes with a butter knife."

Camille shuddered again. There was a reason Madam Clarice remained the sole and undisputed owner of the Prodding Pony despite heavy competition from local clubs and the grumblings of the clubs' owners, all brutal and all men: She was ruthless.

Between Madam's harsh punishments, Markus's far and skilled reach through the Merry Men gang, and Lucien's unforgiving nature, it was a wonder idiots like Hawkins continued to so much as take a piss on the streets in Dockside without wiping it up on hands and knees. Pleasure, business, entertainment—the three Underground leaders represented the three faces of the rookeries like a bastardized collage of Catholic saints.

Madam offered her the crop handle. "First strike is yours."

Camille swallowed the acid in her throat. She wasn't naive enough to ask for leniency. Dockside justice was swift and brutal. It had to be, else monsters like Hawkins wouldn't stop. Grey and the rest deserved what they got, but . . . the sound of those tassels slapping Madam's skin sounded just like a different hit, one she wore across her back as a permanent reminder of what happened when rules were broken.

She shook her head.

Madam dropped the riding crop to her side and frowned. "You're too soft, Angel."

Camille ignored the pet name, used in disdain and disappointment. All clients knew Madam didn't tolerate violence towards her girls. Even before the new regulations had been drafted into the current client contracts, courtesy of Camille, the script above every sign outside and in the club spelled it out in bold script: *Upon consent.*

"I thought you'd take a personal interest in punishment," Madam said, the memory of that day Camille had stormed into her office and demanded retribution clearly present in her mind too, six months later.

Camille ignored her disapproval. "I've no interest being the one doling out punishment." She'd been raised on it. "There's no pleasure in it."

Madam gave the younger woman's body a heated onceover before she clicked her tongue. "A pity." She nodded to the panel. "Shall I close the screen?"

Camille looked to the mirror at the far end of the room, an ingenious one-way glass that allowed an occupant in the hidden office to see and hear what transpired in the current room without detection. As far as she knew, only one other club used the mirrors, the Sally Draw, Lucien's personal clubhouse.

A knock came from the inner door along with Grey's grating voice. "Asked for me personally, eh? The other chickens been boasting?"

Camille ground her teeth at the derogatory term and turned to the panel before Sensa entered. She pushed the latch and told Madam to leave the screen open.

She wasn't a real angel, after all.

AFTER THE FIRST scream, Camille shut the screen and went back to the files on the desk.

There was no need for a fire since the outer walls' heat kept the small space regularly sweltering, but today, the secret office was cozy. Nothing as lavish as the main office with its low firelight and plush fabrics meant to seduce wealthy clients into parting with their purses. Here, ingenious electric bulbs provided by a nameless benefactor granted the windowless room the brightness of the day with the privacy of the night. The polished, oak desk gleamed in the flickering, white light and Camille's backside sank into the worn, leather chair comfortably. Bookshelves lined the walls on either side of the screen, reminiscent of a gentleman's study. All in all, it was her favorite room, so much like the neglected study in the townhouse she'd grown up in. The one room her mother had never entered, thus giving Camille a haven of written word accompanied by the smell of parchment.

The smell of ink and papers were of little pleasure now. Camille flipped through the files, counting as she went. There were two dozen today, a slow morning.

All the Ponies—an unimaginative descriptor for the women contracted to the club—kept detailed reports of their sessions. Camille read through her third report, noting red flags for potential problems. Clients ranged from low-level fighters with heavy purses to the titled gentlemen, and a sparse few women, of the *ton*. Most understood and appreciated the fantasies the Prodding Pony provided, but some liked to blur the lines between fantasy and reality.

Camille closed the file and pinched the bridge of her nose. When the tedious and disgustingly specific accounts of male depravity were done, she had membership requests and potential clients to vet. Backgrounds, finances, vices: Madam was known to trade secrets and favors for time with the Ponies, though the more damning information, the older woman kept to herself in a ledger hidden somewhere in the club. Which served Camille fine.

Her mind was permanently filled with the names and innermost desires of hundreds of clients, filed away in her mind with more precision than any solicitor's cabinet.

She eyed the stack of requests and sneered. Sixty-three more men vying for entry.

Camille pushed the stack of sessions away, needing time to

mentally scrub Mr. Pendor's fantasies of being nursed like an infant from her mind.

She picked up the top file on the secondary stack—a blue file indicating a prospective client scouted by one of the Ponies—and flipped the envelope open.

Her hissed inhale was loud in the quiet room as she read the man's name.

Renard Leopold Louis, Duke of Lux
Age: Two and twenty
Height: 183 centimeters
Weight: Fourteen stones
Features: Blond hair, brown eyes
Vices: Scotch, whiskey
Mistress: None noted
Past: Parents perished in fire. The duke was fourteen at the time.
    (Approach fire-play with discretion.)
Family: Sister, Charlotte Louis, age eighteen

Camille read the information twice, even when there was no need. The nine lines were burned into her mind like a cattle brand at a glance. She flipped the page over. Empty.

That was all the information Madam's scouts had gathered?

One of the Ponies had approached him, probably at one of the taverns. Had it been Sensa? Victoria?

All the Ponies were beautiful and skilled, roles ranging from fair and docile to dominating and exotic; whatever a client's preference, the Pony would provide. Though none of the remaining Ponies were half as successful as Scarlet had been. Madam still grumbled about losing her 'prized mare.'

For new clients, the Ponies offered a free session. Had Sensa offered her governess fantasy to the duke?

Camille couldn't grasp why her gut twisted at the thought.

"Brown eyes."

Vague information as well as minimal. Brown eyes, as if the

duke's sand-swept gaze was so easily categorized.

"No mistress noted."

The twisting in her gut loosened. Not that she cared if the man slept his way through every ballroom, pleasure house, and brothel in England. She'd met him once for but a few hours; he was a stranger. What did she care for Renard Louis?

"The Duke of Lux," someone said.

Camille's head snapped up. Madam stood in the office doorway, her face flushed and blood staining her skirts. Grey must have looked a fright.

"The duke?" Had she spoken out loud?

Madam indicated the stack of blue folders. "Have you been through the duke's file?"

"I have it here."

Crossing the room, her heeled shoes clicking against the wood, Madam lifted the sheet—all nine pathetic lines on it—and asked, "Any concerns?"

Camille hesitated—and then hesitated a moment longer for hesitating. Why wouldn't she want him as a member? He was rumored to be as rich as a king and the girls would enjoy a handsome rider . . .

"There isn't much information," she said.

Madam glanced her way.

Camille's jaw clenched. She was being ridiculous. They both knew she'd vetted men with less. She picked up the next file from the stack and turned her thoughts to work. "He's fine."

Madam replaced the paper and snapped the file closed. "That uncomplicates things."

Camille frowned as Madam placed the duke's file in the accepted bin at the edge of the table. "What things?"

"The duke," Madam said. "I'd have hated to turn him away."

Camille watched Madam head for the main office, her brain working uncommonly slow. "Turn him away? From where?"

"He's in the club." Madam stopped and smiled, the bank notes practically dancing in her eyes. "And he's requesting a ride."

CHAPTER EIGHT

C AMILLE'S BRAIN RACED ahead as her stomach dropped. "He's here?"

"I sent Victoria to break him in," Madam said.

Camille couldn't respond. The electric bulbs were too bright, the room's heat leaving sweat running down her back. The duke was in the club. Any minute Victoria would show him to her chamber, a particularly decorated bedroom meant to give the impression of a fantasy in the clouds, all white cotton and teasing feathers.

With her light hair and gentle nature, Victoria was the most sought-after of the Ponies by the more refined clients. She played the innocent, the untouched, a common fantasy of the experienced.

Madam tapped the desktop.

Camille looked up. "What?"

"Grey has been removed from the grounds." The older woman studied her with a cryptic smirk. "In case you wished to stretch your legs."

Camille nodded, not fully processing. The twisting in her gut was back, along with a wave of profound anger. She and the duke may have been strangers, but that hadn't stopped him from kissing her senseless not eight hours ago.

And it had been good.

Now he was here, looking for fictional fantasy when he'd had perfectly decent reality.

Camille shot to her feet and stalked to the door where Madam had exited. The cad! She'd tell Madam the duke was unsuitable—on the grounds of his sheer stupidity—and to send him on his way. Checking the screen, she opened the hidden panel to discover Madam wasn't in the main office.

She must have been making her rounds.

Camille crossed to the inner door and locked it behind her. Through the screens, she saw the cursory rooms—the chambers for clients to wait in, either for a Pony to finish a previous session or to increase the anticipation of a current one—were empty.

She entered the deeper rooms in the club, where black silk gave way to unadorned brick. Preparing to drag the duke from Victoria's arms if necessary, Camille turned down the Pony's wing, surprised when Victoria herself appeared, her character's mask in her hand.

"Oh, Camille, thank goodness," she said. "Lord Reiner is here and has requested me."

Lord Reiner? What was a personal friend of Madam and the main investor for the Pony doing here at this hour?

"What of the duke?" Camille asked.

"He's in the Nest, waiting." Victoria's blue eyes darted to the hall behind them, where the luxury chambers lay for Madam's most distinguished patrons. "I need to change before I go to Reiner." She shoved a clipboard into Camille's hands. "Can you do the duke's interview for me?"

"Interview?"

Victoria's impatience rolled off her in twitched waves. "It's easy. The questions are on the paper."

"I can't." She wasn't a Pony.

"You don't have to screw him." Victoria's face softened. "Sorry, I didn't mean it like that. All us girls know you don't think less of us because of what we do." She grabbed Camille's other hand and placed her mask in her palm. "Please help. I need to go. I can't leave Madam or Reiner waiting."

Victoria was a widow and mother. She needed this job just like the rest of the girls. Just like so many others waiting for someone to step up and do the right thing.

Guilt sinking in, Camille merely nodded.

"Don't fret," Victoria said. "Just pretend to be me."

Camille stared after her as she vanished into the next wing. This was madness. *She* was to conduct an interview with the duke?

Her stomach bottomed out this time. Her brain scrambled. One of the other Ponies must have been available.

But she knew the schedule; she wrote it.

Anything before ten at night was minimal staff during the season, when ladies stayed out at balls until the wee hours, and the men could slip away for a quick ride before returning to escort their women home.

With Victoria called away, only Sensa and Madam remained. Sensa's clients were notorious for midday rides, meaning the Pony's second-in-command need always be available for her regulars. Madam had her monthly meetings scheduled the rest of the day, meetings she couldn't avoid else the kitchens and laundry would not be stocked for the next few weeks.

Which left . . . her.

Like the rest, Camille needed this job, or she would have walked out. Of all the perverted, narcissistic, vazey ratbags of the *ton*, it had to be *him*.

Her misfortune continued.

She dragged her feet to the door and stopped. The look on his face when he recognized her . . . Would he think she deserved Hawkins's attentions? Would he regret helping her last night? Most people believed working in a pleasure house meant a lady had no right to say 'no.'

She shouldn't have cared what he thought. He was here, after all; he must not have found the practice of paid pleasure too reprehensible.

Her gaze settled on the basket of props and costumes by the

door, Victoria's cape and elbow-length gloves a perfect match to the white mask in her hand.

Her brain leapt to the perfect solution.

The gloves whispered across her skin, covering her bound wrist. The cape, cropped short and made of the softest silk, fluttered around her shoulders. She weighed the mask in her hand, knowing it would hide the bruise on her temple.

The knot of hair at the nape of her neck gave easily, freeing her curls along her shoulders to better hide her homespun dress. Looking down at herself, Camille felt the freedom of the disguise and the beginnings of appreciation for the fantasy.

Maybe *she* wouldn't need to face the duke at all.

RENARD EYED THE white silk and feather-embroidered cushions against the white, linen bedsheets—too reminiscent of Biblical descriptions of the Lord's skyward house—and regretted his decision all over again.

He'd no idea what had possessed him to come here, where men paid to bed 'Ponies' in the manner and setting of their choosing. There was no shortage of bored misses and willing widows begging to share his bed. The Prodding Pony dealt in fantasy and fixation; he had no business dabbling in either.

Somewhere between last night and this morning, old lovers and stolen moments had lost their appeal. In truth, he'd come here to clear his system with a faceless partner and a detached tumble, the opposite of the woman plaguing him.

He couldn't escape her. Every redheaded woman from Dockside to his city home had caught his attention, whipping his head back and forth until his neck pinched. It was a matter of emergency that he'd come here after he'd passed a Brittany Spaniel and had nearly been run over by a carriage in his distraction. He drew the line at dogs.

It had been the excitement of an eventful evening. Emotions high, of course he'd found Miss Forthright fetching. In the light of the day, she'd lose her appeal. No woman could be that lovely.

One meaningless tumble with some buxom blonde and he'd forget all about the less-than-lovely Miss Forthright. Except he was in no mood to bed some random woman. The idea soured his stomach. He sighed and stood to leave, now seeing this errand as a terrible idea.

The door opened, parting the clouds that had been painted across the room and the door.

Renard cursed himself for a fool. He'd specifically told the Mistress of the house what he wanted, and this Pony wasn't it.

Auburn hair, like a low, burning fire, skin finer than china. Her gaze found his, her brown eyes flashing with intelligence.

His body electrified with awareness.

He couldn't see her face fully with the mask, but he knew. It was *her*.

Somehow, she was here, standing before him as if his very fantasies had taken flesh.

The mask she wore was white laced and covered most of her face, but he knew those eyes, recognized the challenge in them like a calling to his soul.

She crossed the room and sat on the bed across from his seat on the chaise, her short cape draping around her chest in tantalizing reminiscence of bird wings. Reclining against the pillows, her legs tucked beside her, she gave off every impression of a submissive lover.

Fate was cruel. He'd come here looking to wipe the slate clean but instead had found the very object of his desire. The hard-won woman who'd taken on three monsters had a secret life. This coy and decorated dove was nothing like the sharp-tongued falcon from last night.

"Unexpected." She was everything she'd declared and more.

She was spectacular.

"Your Grace?" she asked. "Is something the matter?"

Even her voice was too quiet, too sweet, marked by a slight tremble, as if she were nervous.

He'd give Madam Clarice credit; her Ponies' acting abilities could rival the theatre's most popular debut actress, Miss Crim.

Why was she here?

Client confidentiality or merely not to ruin the fantasy, she would pretend not to know him, he knew.

A game, then.

Suddenly, his need to rid himself of her shifted to delighted anticipation.

"Nothing is wrong." Renard sat back in his seat and shook his head. Her working here changed everything. "Please, ask me anything you wish."

She blinked in surprise. "Anything?"

"Anything."

Nothing was off limits, not when he had every intention of winning this match, and all the others to come. After all, who was he to say 'no' to fate?

⇶⇷

CAMILLE COULDN'T HEAR over the relentless pounding in her chest.

She'd been sure the duke had recognized her. She had no mastery of fluttering lashes or coy smiles. Her imitation of Victoria's staged character was laughable but apparently good enough to fool the attentions of an indifferent gentleman.

He sat back on the chaise, arrogance and entitlement like a second coat across his shoulders, though the hunter-green coat he wore made him look infuriatingly like a mythical satyr that could lure women into the dark woods with a smile and a rub of his bristly chin.

Must the man be blessed with such handsomeness?

He only saw a faceless bedmate.

Camille swallowed silent fury. All men were the same. She'd been a blind fool to expect more.

She lifted the board, inkwell, and parchment from the bed and placed it on her lap. As she ran the feathered end of the quill under her chin—embracing the flighty and innocent persona with ease—her gaze lingered on his face, when all she wanted was to smack the stupid grin from his mouth.

"Name?" she asked.

He smirked. "You don't know? Didn't you address me as 'Your Grace'?"

The glint in his eye made her stomach uneasy. She forced a laugh and indicated the paper. "For the record."

"Renard Leopold Louis."

"Income?"

His brows rose, but he answered, "Fifteen thousand."

"Annually?"

"Yes."

"Connections to the Pony?"

"Excuse me?"

"Any acquaintances who frequent this establishment?"

"Is that relevant?"

"It may be," she said. "We pride ourselves on client anonymity, but gentlemen talk." Boasts and retelling of conquests, really, as if they didn't finish early and leave their partner unsatisfied. Camille smiled. "We wish to avoid hard feelings should a question of property arise."

"An issue of sharing, then?" He scoffed. "Women aren't property. Any man believing he can dictate whom a woman decides to take to their bed is a selfish prig." He cleared his throat and color crept up his neck. "Apologies, miss."

Camille's façade cracked in an astonished smile at the fierceness of his claim, and the boyish contrition of his apology. "That's . . . quite all right, Your Grace." God, were his eyes always so bright? She'd been certain she'd find a spoiled, titled man waiting, the roguish flirt from last night a fluke of an adventure-rich night, but Camille needed to reconsider her approach. Renard Louis was not what she'd expected. At the risk of shattering her solidly erected distaste for all things elite, she may have rushed to an improper conclusion about the man.

She looked up to find his gaze on her, his mouth twitching at the corners.

"You're frowning, miss." His voice had gone low. "Are all the questions so *personal?*"

The way he'd said 'personal' . . . He was trying to seduce her.

Which was preposterous. Seduction was *her* job. Well, her fake job.

Ignoring the thrill up her spine, she latched on to the charade. "We've yet to touch your *personals,*" she teased, knowing the mask hid her burning cheeks.

His answering grin set her belly burning.

He leaned forward, his eyes dancing. "You have my attention."

A giggle burst from her lips, a most outrageous and humiliating sound. She scrambled for control and read the next question on the parchment, nearly dropping the quill at the words.

"Is there a problem?" he asked.

Her jaw tightened. She was going to kill Victoria! Smile pasted on, she ground out, "Of course not, Your Grace."

That's right, he was *His Grace.* Teasing and flirtation aside, he was nothing but a potential client for her employer. This was a game, a farce. If he knew who she was, he'd never say such delicious things.

'Delicious'? Heaven above, what was wrong with her?

"Do you need a moment?" he asked.

"No!" She cleared her throat. "How many partners have you had?"

What kind of question was that? As if a gentleman would state so blithely—

"Two hundred, perhaps," he said.

She choked. "Two hundred?"

"More?" he shrugged. "I stopped counting after I hit triple digits."

Forget cad. The man was a walking curse on all womankind. What a disgusting . . . Her thoughts trailed off at the mischievous glint in his eyes.

She huffed. "You're teasing me."

"You make it rather easy."

She tapped the paper. "You were informed of the paperwork."

"But not the content of the questions."

"You said to ask you anything."

He grinned. "How many partners have *you* had?"

Camille threw out the first number that came to mind, a *two-digit* number that seemed respectable for a woman in her supposed profession.

The duke's grin vanished, and an enjoyable paling of his smug face told her she'd regained the upper hand.

"Any preferences or fantasies you wish to enlist in sessions?" she asked sweetly.

He sat back and crossed an ankle over his knee, his gaze narrowing. "I've a fondness for rescuing damsels. A recent experience turned me on to the merits of a grateful woman."

She managed a casual, "Oh? Recent experience, you say?"

Was he here to relive what had happened last night?

"Very recent," he said. "The woman was in shock, you see. Poor thing could barely walk. Naturally, I carried her to safety."

Her teeth ground together. "How valiant you are, sir. And you wish to act out such"—*falsehoods*—"heroics here?"

At the mention of 'heroics,' he flinched. "How could I not? Especially as the lady had the same hair color as yours."

Camille forced herself not to play with the curls at her chest. "Hair like mine? What a coincidence."

He stood. "And the same fair skin." He moved closer, his gaze no longer distant.

Camille stood so fast, she knocked the board and parchment

to the floor in her haste to reach the door. Ink spattered the floor. "This is a great start, Your Grace. An excellent place to begin." She turned the handle and smiled over her shoulder. "I'll file your answers and we will place you on the schedule for next week—"

"Why wait?"

He was right behind her, his arm placed beside her head, his hand on the door, making escape impossible.

Camille felt the heat of him through her cape and knew if she turned around, she'd expire on the spot.

She swallowed. "There are rules, sir, a process. You must be checked . . . for illness." That sounded plausible. "The health of the Ponies is Madam's priority."

His arm was removed. "All right."

She turned around. A mistake.

He hadn't retreated. He stood a scant foot from her, his honeyed gaze hot on her face. Untying his cravat, he slipped it through his collar and dropped it to the floor. His coat followed. When his hands went to work the buttons on his shirt, she panicked.

"What are you doing?"

"Undressing." His gaze didn't leave hers. "I wouldn't want you to ruin your process."

"Process?" What the hell was he talking about? Her brain stuttered, starting and stopping with every exposed inch of tanned skin.

His shirttails pulled free of his trousers, leaving his chest and waist visible.

Her mouth went dry.

"Miss?"

She looked up. "Did you say something?"

His slow smile left her head spinning. She leaned back against the door.

He sloughed off his shirt, where it joined his coat and cravat at their feet. "I asked your name."

Name. All the Ponies had stage names. Scrambling, she said,

"Angel."

His smile curled sardonically. "I see."

He did? What did he see?

The place between her legs ached as his finger played with the waistband of his trousers. Dark-blond hair led down his abdomen and trailed where she couldn't see. He was beautiful, muscled but lean. Now that he'd removed his arm from the door, she should flee, but his finger . . . the way it slid back and forth had her core clenching.

All thoughts of running stilled. She'd never seen a naked man before; this may be her only chance. If one was to observe a specimen, surely, he was a choice subject.

His gaze darkened, and his voice was unsteady. "Would you like me to continue?"

Her teeth tugged on her bottom lip, but she nodded.

His fingers went to the button-fly and worked the trousers open with maddening slowness. The way his thumb pushed through the holes had liquid heat collecting between her legs.

She rubbed her legs together to keep the wetness inside, but the friction sent a spasm of sensation through her. She gasped and closed her eyes.

She couldn't do this. A good girl didn't ask a man to undress, and she certainly wouldn't be aroused watching. Shame, hot, ugly shame, pulled her thoughts from the heat of pleasure and brought her mother's words into sharp focus.

"You filthy, worthless wretch. Good girls listen. Good girls do as they are told. Good girls—"

A featherlight touch turned her head to the side.

"You're frowning again," he said. "There are so many nicer things we can do with your mouth."

His words, whispered in her ear, had her toes curling. The fantasy he wove with words and touch did more than the room and disguise. With her eyes closed, she could be anywhere, be anyone else.

Maybe the mask was a blessing. Here, now, with this man

who wanted the most basic of desires from her, the damning label forced on her as a child had no place. With him, her mother's words faded into the recesses of thought and memory, as if it were possible for her to forget.

She'd spend the rest of her life alone, chaste and quiet, making up for a mistake that had cost her family everything.

This once, she wanted more.

Willing her brain quiet, she put herself into this moment—and nowhere else. She turned her head, feeling the rough scrape of a day's whiskers against her cheek.

"Please," she said. *Make the thoughts stop. Make me feel something other than shame.* She rose up on her toes and whispered against his lips, "Please."

CHAPTER NINE

T HAT WORD, WHISPERED between them, brought their match to a freezing halt.

No. A match required both parties' participation. Renard had deliberately kept his knowledge from her like a lie. She had lied too, but her circumstances dictated anonymity. The club may very well have strict rules on a Pony revealing her name and face.

He cursed inwardly. *He'd* been playing games. A game she unknowingly had taken the upper hand in.

Stripping himself, cornering her, he was like some damn hound on the scent. He'd apologize for his abhorrent behavior. She deserved that at least.

He pulled back from the door to give her space. "Forgive me—"

Her lips snatched his apology, along with his sense of balance.

He caught himself on the door, resting his forearm above her head and pinning her against his instant hardness.

She smelled like parchment and tasted like spring, sour and sweet, the perfect blend of lemon and honey she must've added to her morning tea.

The detail pleased him. She was a woman of opposites, of constant surprise. If he weren't careful, he'd lose himself to the excitement that was *her*.

If he hadn't already.

She licked his bottom lip and he let his body take over, his hands running up her arms and displacing her cape to expose that same woolen dress she'd worn last night, the hem frayed and scratchy against his fingers.

Silent outrage had his fingers bunching into the fabric. She should have been in silks, wrapped, draped, every floor lined underfoot as she walked.

His fingers dipped below her neckline, teasing the valley of smooth skin.

He captured her moan in his mouth, its sweet, alto tone in perfect harmony with his growling base.

Music. She was like a clashing symphony of notes he couldn't take in all at once or he'd rend apart from the rich sound.

Her white cape's tie loosened with a long pull and slid from her shoulders to join his clothes at their feet. He put to task unfastening the fine hooks of her dress until that too slipped down around her shoulders and caught on the womanly flare of her hips.

She shivered, her body cold no doubt with the exposure of skin to the fireless room. She pressed closer, and Renard was all too willing to share his heat.

"Put your arms around my neck," he said against her lips.

He flicked his tongue against hers when she complied, earning another unfettered moan from her throat.

Without breaking their kiss, he grasped her skirt, one-layered and too damn thin, and pushed them up . . . up until they revealed those luscious hips. She didn't wear stockings or knickers and the bare skin of her shapely thighs was like a dinner bell.

His mouth watered. Fingers digging in, he lifted her and pushed himself between her legs.

She clung to him, her fingers snaking into his hair. Her pants were erotic, animalistic, driving his own passion wild.

His body was pushing forward at an alarming rate, the sounds and feel of her ripping away at his composure. A quick shift and his throbbing cock sprang loose, finding the apex of her legs and nudging her open.

Nails dug into his scalp, clawing him closer.

One second more not being inside her and he'd go mad.

He drove upward, impaling her on him. The heat was scalding. "My God!"

He nearly came then—the folds of her so tight, he couldn't breathe, else he find his release—but her sharp gasp held more than pleasure. He drew back and stared into her eyes, dark and lovely, half-glazed in her passion. The other half . . .

His gaze caught on the door they leaned against, the white, painted clouds swirling into a nauseating baby blue of heaven's sky. His stomach plummeted.

He'd pushed her against a door without a thought. And that sound of pain . . . "Are you all right? I'm . . . I didn't mean to be so rough." *I didn't mean to be a rutting monster.*

She shook her head, her expression scrunched. "It's just so much." She wiggled against him, lifting her bottom up and then down, pulling him in and out.

Her wince left him cold.

She'd been a fucking virgin!

Withdrawing to her folds' edges, her legs tightened around his hips and drew him back inside with a seductive sound of slapping skin.

"Oh!" She ground down on him and threw back her head, his name on her lips.

He gritted his teeth, knowing the harm was done. Taking control, he set a smooth pace, that edge to heavenly bliss so close, his toes skimmed the clouds. Pushing that pleasure away, he focused on her.

He tasted the top swell of her breasts and rubbed circles in her curls above where their bodies connected.

She arched, her fingers tangled in his hair pulling. "More," she demanded.

He grinned and moved, inside and out . . . out, then slammed back in. Out . . . out, in. He moved faster, the little thrusts of his hips making her mewl and writhe.

She was so tight, so hot.

He barreled to that edge and fell off the side as she found her own climax with a scream.

Their chests rose and fell and slowed together. Renard slid her to her feet, keeping an arm around her waist should her legs give out. Winded, spent, he felt wholly satisfied for the first time in his life. He held her to him, feeling the weight of her against him, feeling the perfection of how their bodies fit.

This was the moment, he realized. That same swelling of feeling he'd had as a boy watching his father and mother rose to the surface now, twice as consuming, ten times, a hundred.

Love.

He was not like his fellow peers, believing love a lie and affection a waste. He didn't balk at the revelation or hide. His flaws and darkness were no mystery to him. Nor was he mindless or unaware. Just as God was real, that fickle emotion too had turned its attention to him, unworthy though he was.

He leaned his forehead down to hers and didn't bother tempering the awe in his voice. "Amazing."

That smile, so rare and mesmerizing, surfaced. "We aim to please."

He didn't take the bait. She was a warrior. He should've suspected the second after a soul-shattering coupling, her impenetrable mask would fall back into place, the real one nothing so delicate and inviting as the white feathers currently adorning her face.

He traced her cheek with his finger, and something tensed in his chest when she closed her eyes and bit her lip. Even now, she responded to him.

He couldn't let her go. Fate, that miserable and miraculous mistress, had offered a sliver of mercy for him to find her again.

She eased out of his arms, righting her skirt, and pulling her sleeves up over her shoulders. "If you approve of our services, Madam will contact you when your paperwork is filed." Her gaze didn't meet his. "I'll make a note you are clear of . . . disease."

He wouldn't tolerate the shame in her voice. "You have a filthy mouth, Miss Forthright, and a terrible poker face."

She froze, her gaze darting back and forth as if she could catch a lie in the corners of her eyes. "You've mistaken me for someone else." Her hand shook as it grasped for the door handle behind her. "I've other clients to service, sir, so if you wouldn't mind—"

"I was your first." He didn't make a habit of deflowering virgins. He'd picked none in his decade of debauchery, but he wasn't a fool. Her gasp of pain had said enough without the blood that stained her thighs and his flagging arousal.

The knowledge of being her first, her only, eased the ragged edges of jealousy he'd experienced upon discovering her here. But that demanded the question yet again: Why *was* she here?

Her eyes widened. "You can tell?"

"A demirep doesn't call out a man's name in the heat of the moment. Risk of using the wrong one and all."

Her expression hardened, the coy dove driven away by the hawk. "Now that that unpleasant encounter is over, I suppose the others will be more enjoyable."

It was a lie. However she'd found her way of employment to the Prodding Pony, she was no painted lady. Still . . . "Others."

He gripped her arms and held her against the wood as his mouth sought out hers. He teased and nipped until they were once again gasping. Dragging a hand down her backside, when her lips opened in a moan, he said against her lips, "What did I say about that mouth?"

She bit her lower lip again, but the heat in her eyes cooled, assessed, knowing he'd see through another lie. "You knew the whole time?"

"I stayed *because* I knew."

Her gaze shot to his. "Why?"

He lifted her chin with his knuckles and let his honesty bring his feelings into the open. "I came here, of all places, to forget you. After last night, I swore I wouldn't seek you out. I'd let you live your life." He grinned. "But then you walked through the door, and I knew I couldn't walk away this time."

He swore her breathing hitched, but then her eyes narrowed. "You expect me to believe that?"

The doubt in her gaze, the challenge in her voice . . . He wouldn't back down. As a lad, he'd always pushed himself to the point of torn knickers and broken bones if it would keep his ego from a similar break. The need to win rose to the surface now, past sins and future damnation consequences for another day. He'd promised to never play the hero, never sully his good father's name, but there was no fear of pretending with her.

Miss Forthright saw him for who and what he was and was not impressed. But she'd responded like a siren caught in her own trap: passionate, and angry, and perfect.

He grabbed her chin and watched those brown eyes flicker with a spark of fire.

"I'll make you a deal, my dear." He licked at her lips until her mouth parted. When he pulled back, her hot gaze was on him, for him. He smirked. "You stop pretending this isn't fate, and I'll see you tomorrow."

HIS WORDS HAD been a promise. Even after they'd dressed and Camille had escorted him, blindfolded, to the Pony's exit, those words, that look of predatory delight, kept flashing in her mind.

She'd been so distracted, she'd left the Pony late that night, long after the usual patrons had gone home to their marble mansions and unsuspecting—or uncaring—wives. Long after Madam had slunk off home to whatever conniving rock she lived under. Long after the lighters had ignited the row of lamps, the only row in Dockside, meant to draw the illusion of safety and warmth in a gutter known for its cold and merciless embrace.

Picking her way through the dark alleys, she noted the uncommon quiet. The usual riffraff was absent; no demireps loitering around the club in hopes of winning a coin as a bargain deal, no senseless drunks sleeping off the liquor in the alcoves. Not even the sailors were out, on their way back seaside after a night of drinking and gambling. Camille's hand wrapped around the letter opener in her pocket. The one she'd taken from Madam's office.

A shadow picked its way out of the darkness ahead of her, the wraith-like figure familiar, and the only reason Camille didn't scream.

"Your father agreed to let you off the leash?" Camille asked. No wonder the streets were clear. "I hope you left the bodies intact? The coroner's work is hard enough as it is."

Syd, Scarlet's younger sister and the unofficial leader of the 'Merry Men,' smiled and tucked her hands in the pockets of her long trench coat.

"I asked the sirs to move along is all. I was rather civil, I thought," she said.

Camille shook her head, feeling insanely grateful the 'wolf' of Dockside was on her side and not at her throat. "It's not civility when you threaten to stick a knife in their backs."

Syd pressed a hand to her chest, looking anything but innocent. The hood of her coat swept back, and her dark hair—straight as a rifle barrel—fell down her back, instantly changing the 'wolf' persona into a big-eyed, sixteen-year-old girl. She jutted out her chin to indicate where Camille's hand had disappeared in her skirt. "You know how to use that blade?"

Camille let go of the letter opener, leaving it concealed in her pocket. "Pointy end out?"

Syd smirked. She picked at a nail and admired its jagged crescent. "I could've sworn Anthony Grey's sorry ass was dragged out of the Pony this morning. Hard to tell with his face all bloody." She glanced Camille's way. "Your *pointy end* know anything about that?"

Camille gazed into the dark alley ahead, keeping alert, and

avoided Syd's feral grin. "You know how Madam enforces her rules."

Syd snorted. "The only rule worth that enormous purse she charges is keeping her girls safe." Syd froze, her cocky grin slipping. "*You* were the chicken Hawkins went after last night?" Her predator nature vanished entirely. "I'm sorry, Cam. The Merrys were sent to break up a brawl at the Sally Saloon last night. I was stuck on a nearby rooftop till dawn thanks to Pops's paranoia."

Camille waved away the apology. Even with their six men— and one woman—crew, the 'Merry Men' couldn't be everywhere at once. She said as much.

Syd wouldn't accept anything easy, regardless of logic. "Zans is on patrol until we get our 'fresh blood' trained. Till then, I'll be your faithful shadow."

The mention of 'fresh-blood' made Camille roll her eyes. Any new recruits the Merrys got would be four years Syd's senior and two stones heavier and still never measure up.

There was a time when Syd had gone by the name Sydney Laundry, the daughter of a respectable officer in Her Majesty's army, and in love with everything lacy.

Then the Battle of Tell El Kebir had happened, their father was dishonorably discharged for refusing to slaughter innocents, and the little Laundry girls had left childhood and pretty things behind, like many girls in the slums, finding employment any way they could so their bellies didn't go empty.

Camille swallowed the guilt, letting it settle back in her stomach, where it would fuel her resolve. Miss Forthright's House for Female Companions would be a reality. A place where girls wouldn't have to give up their innocence to make ends meet when their fathers went off to war. A place where a woman could be her own hero, raising herself up to respectability by her mental acuity and will. A place to learn and make connections, a community of women supporting each other's betterment, without the interference of men . . . or ambitious mothers.

Realizing she'd stopped in the alley—a death wish, considering her surroundings—she returned from her thoughts.

Syd leaned against the parallel wall, waiting. At Camille's focused gaze, she said, "Want to talk about it?"

Camille wouldn't condescend. Sixteen was more than old enough to see the ugliness of the gutter, but she shook her head. "Would you?"

That amused grin was back. "Not for a tray of freshly baked scones."

Camille laughed, remembering a time when she and Syd had shared an entire service of scones and clotted cream to the indignant rage of Scarlet, who'd spent the entire morning in the kitchens. Aproned and flour in her hair, she'd come into the main room with a tray of heavenly lemon tarts so good, the girls had barely heard her epic lecture about patience and manners over their chewing.

The memory of tarts brought another, more recent, memory front and center, along with a boyish grin of a most definite man. Camille shook herself and gave Syd a smirk.

"You won't share, even for a lemon tart?" she asked.

Syd's grin grew into a real smile, telling Camille she remembered as well.

"Maybe ten," she said.

Camille laughed again, the action chasing away the anxiety and excitement of what and *who* tomorrow would bring.

CHAPTER TEN

"THERE'S NO USE sneaking out."

Camille winced at her mother's voice coming from the bedroom—a luxury in this part of the rookery when most families had to share a single room or floor with sisters, brothers, fleas, and worse. Knowing she'd look guilty with her boots underarm, Camille laid the worn, leather footwear in front of the door and threw back her shoulders before walking to the opening, where a door should have stood.

Her mother, rail thin and looking more and more like one of the hangers that used to suspend her shimmering costumes than the actress who'd once worn them, sat up against the pillows already dressed in her signature scowl and every meager blanket they owned.

Camille went to the open window to cut off the harrowing chill.

"Leave it," her mother said, a wisp of stringy, graying hair escaping her nightcap. "I won't be poisoned by our air."

Camille left the window ajar but pulled the torn and holed curtain over to block more of the morning breeze. There wasn't much movement between the buildings at least. Idiots like Doctor Arnott, spouting that a window must be left open or else the air turn sour, were responsible for countless cases of frostbite and pneumonia. Even if their claims of air quality held true, she'd take labored breathing over the dampness any morning, especially as they had no coin to spare for fuel or rug by the fire. Leaving windows open overnight was ludicrous. It may have been June, but London held a perpetual draft when the sun went down throughout the year.

"I didn't mean to wake you," Camille said.

Her mother sniffed. "I'm thirsty."

Camille crossed to the nightstand. After pouring a half-glass of previously boiled water from the pitcher, she handed it into her mother's waiting hands.

When she'd finished, she held the glass out without looking, expecting Camille to put it back despite the nightstand being less than a foot away.

Camille took and replaced the glass without comment.

"Punishment." Madam Clarice's fascination with and pleasure from asserting control over another person was unsettling. Camille wondered, not for the first time, if her clients felt as helpless and worthless as she did.

"Would you care to wash?" She nodded to the near-full pitcher. "I can fetch the flannel."

Mother clutched the blanket tighter and shook her head.

"Are you hungry?" she asked.

"I want meat pie."

Camille nodded. "I'll pick up some on my way home."

They both knew she wouldn't eat anything until she was well too drunk to taste the cheap meal.

Her mother lifted her chin towards the empty bottles in the corner. "And more brandy."

Camille nodded again, deciding to forgo this morning's outburst by reminding her mother she wouldn't be paid for two more days.

The clock in the main room sounded the hour. Camille waited until the eleventh chime concluded before saying, "I have to go to work."

Her mother stared at the corner and her collection of bottles in answer.

Camille didn't offer a kiss or farewell, not wishing to feel her mother pull away. She made it to the door before glancing back at her mother's gaunt face and dead gaze, and her guilt pressed down on her like an overturned carriage.

⟫⟫⟪⟪

"I HAD A most interesting talk with Victoria yesterday," Madam said from the panel door between offices. "Seems the Duke of Lux never signed his membership contract."

Camille didn't flinch, didn't pause. She read the file before her, jotting notes in the journal to her right. "Unfortunate."

"It is," Madam said. "Seeing as how you were asked to step in and interview him."

"Victoria should never have asked me to do her job, and you should never have lied and told her Lord Reiner was here. Victoria told me she waited, but he never showed."

"Are you accusing me of meddling?"

"I'll accuse you of worse things."

"But not to my face. Turned into a coward since yesterday, Angel?"

Camille's quill scratched the last of her thoughts down before she laid it on top of the desk. She closed the file and offered it to Madam. "The Marquess of Slasbury's petition for membership is riddled with inconsistencies. Sensa needs to take a second look. Or is that my job now as well?"

Madam didn't take the file. "Why didn't you finish the interview?"

Camille threw the file down. "You know why!" She met the other woman's gaze, the rage in her chest holding her humiliation at bay. "You saw the whole thing."

Madam didn't balk at her anger. She shrugged. "It's my job to check on my girls."

"I'm not one of your girls!"

"That's not what it looked like from my angle."

Camille's lip curled. That damn screen! If she'd have been thinking clearly, she'd have locked it. But she hadn't been in any mind. She'd kissed the duke willingly and more, all while the screen had been up.

It didn't matter that Victoria's wing should have been empty, or that Madam had had appointments scheduled until dawn. As soon as Camille had gone to retrieve the interview sheets from the room after Renard had left, she'd seen the side room door open, when it had most definitely been firmly shut when she'd left the room two minutes earlier. And she'd known Madam hadn't made her meeting.

Camille didn't lower her gaze or temper the steel in her voice. It was her body; she'd made her own decision, one she wouldn't regret. "I hope you got your money's worth, Clarice? The Pony charges extra for a voyeur fantasy."

Madam shook her head, her mouth set in an approving smile. "I've always liked you. From the moment you stormed into my office, that anger in your eyes was like cold fire. Nerve and pride earned by sheer grit and intelligence."

"I don't want flattery," Camille said.

"What *do* you want? Apologies are empty words, as any woman knows. If you want the duke banned from the premises, I'll sign the removal now."

Madam cared for her girls, but the world, their unfair and skewed one especially, ran on favor and money. As the duke was in possession of both in criminal quantities, the offer was more than suspect.

"You don't have the conscience to turn away a fat purse," she accused, daring the woman to lie to her and say she did.

Madam grinned. "Business is business." She quoted her favorite line, her eyes flashing. "But a man in love is bad for my business."

Camille crossed her arms over her chest, her shoulder still sore, to hold in the fluttering spasm underneath. Indigestion, no doubt. "He's not in love with me." The very idea was madness.

With a mocking arch of her brow, Madam said, "I take back my comment about your intelligence."

"He came here for a *ride*."

"He came here for *you*." Madam held up her hand, her fingers stretched wide. "His stipulations when he arrived were that his Pony could not be above average height, strong-willed, or pale-skinned, and that she could not possess red hair of any shade." Madam curled down a finger for each item and looked at her pointedly.

"He didn't even know I worked here. If anything, he asked for anyone but me."

Madam smirked. "A man does not pay a fortune for a woman that specifically unless he is either married to her likeness or wishes to be. I'm a woman who delivers for her clients. I gave him exactly what he wanted."

That fluttering in Camille's chest felt like silken feathers. Stubbornness clung to her words as she grumbled, "My height isn't above average."

Madam rubbed her temple. "He is to return tonight?"

Camille glared. "You heard what he said."

"Shall I turn him away at the door?"

Try as she might, putting her thoughts of Renard, *the duke*, aside had proved useless. Stabbing pain in her shoulder and wrist, she could ignore, but one brief 'exchange' and she forgot every resolve.

Madam watched her, seeming to garner her answer without words. "I'll bar the doors, then."

Camille inclined her head in gratitude. She didn't need distractions. Whatever nonsensical feelings she had mistakenly allowed for the duke would pass. She hadn't lain with him for any hope of a future. The best someone like her could hope for was a flat in a nice section of the city and a line of credit to the local modiste. But she had no intention of being any man's mistress. Men like him expected obedience and access for security, but she hadn't asked for his protection or attentions. Madam's assessment of the duke's affections was too deep. He liked her, he'd admitted it himself. Two encounters were not enough for anything beyond attraction.

"As soon as he realizes I don't wish to see him, he won't make any more trouble," Camille said.

Madam laughed. "You know nothing, Angel, if you think denying a man what he desires will *deter* his intentions."

"That's nonsense."

"Rule six," Madam said. "Leave a man wanting more."

Camille cringed at the mention of rules, remembering a different set that had run her life, until that awful night. "Not even children follow rules," she said quietly.

Madam scooped the marquess's file off the desk and tapped the edge on her open palm. "Mark my words: The man will be at the door before sundown."

Those flutters turned the air in her lungs breathless. "Why?"

Madam's gaze turned pitying. "He won't be able to resist."

RENARD DIDN'T RESIST.

Whether the Amazonians clad in silk togas were women of strong nature, or a rumored branch of special Ponies Madam kept for clients of *particular* male tastes, the outcome remained the same.

Coattails bunched and his arse bruised on the cold cobblestones in the narrow back alley, Renard considered his issued demand to Camille may not have been as charming as first thought.

"I'll see you tomorrow."

Apparently, the woman disagreed.

"You should have tipped better," came a voice above him.

Renard glanced up at a person looking over the edge of the building, their face obscured by a dark hood.

Yes, an amused audience was precisely what this situation needed.

He scowled and got to his feet, making a grand show of straightening his torn coat. "What would a street urchin know about money?"

The hooded figure chuckled. "There's never enough."

Renard grinned at that and noticed the thin creature was leaning over the building like they'd sprout wings instead of falling the hundred feet and bleeding out slowly from the head.

"Boy, you shouldn't loiter on roofs. Come down where it's safe and there's a copper in it for you."

That chuckle again. "My, you're arrogant for such a hand-some man." A pause. "Then again, most handsome ones are."

Hearing the distinct *feminine* lilt in the hood's voice, Renard glanced up to find the figure—and her unwelcome while most dreadfully apt observations—had vanished.

He ran a hand through his hair, not entirely sure he'd imag-ined the person or not. A day of sobriety after years of steadfast abuse did things to a man's mental health. His bruised bum was a solid reminder the throwing of his person into the dirty streets had *not* been in his head.

A strong drink awaited in his library for his return. If the woman didn't want him, he was in no mood to freeze his toes off in the streets. But if he left now, he'd fail whatever game they played. A sneaking suspicion told him if he left now, he'd miss a prize far beyond a bottle of fine scotch.

Taking in the metal, reinforced door to the club, Renard threw his hands in the air. "Now what do I do?"

On the sour and salty breeze coming from the direction of the harbor, he swore he heard faint woman's laughter and the sage advice, "Wait for her."

With his strained relationship with the good Lord, Renard had no choice. Be the strange, possibly fictitious, creature heaven sent or hell's messenger, his own stubborn nature agreed. He crossed himself and prayed the rats here were friendly. Whoever had said love was a beautiful thing had never had to huddle in a piss-drenched London gutter. He hunkered down, flipping his collar up to block the damp from seeping to his bones.

He waited and waited.

CHAPTER ELEVEN

"H E STILL OUT there?" Madam asked from her desk.
Camille didn't turn from the view from the tinted window—a rounded peephole that anyone outside would mistake for an ill-placed exhaust vent—and nodded.

The duke huddled in the street, his coat collar up around his ears, his top hat pulled low to shield his face from the light drizzle that had started a quarter of an hour past. He'd been there for hours; if he didn't find himself a warm drink and a hot bath soon, the great rumored charms of the 'rogue' duke may very well hereafter be known as the 'rogue' duke sans a handful of digits.

"Must be soaked through by now," Madam said, a note of reprimand sounding.

Camille bit her tongue and watched the stupid man rub his hands together to return feeling to what must have been numb fingers through ridiculous gentlemen gloves. "It's his own fault if he's cold. No one is holding him here."

Madam snorted.

Hands going to her hips, Camille whirled on the older woman. "What?"

Madam leaned back in her leather chair and fixed Camille with an amused look. "We both know who is keeping him here. If you were hoping for a declaration of affection"—she nodded at the window—"there's your answer."

"In what sane mind is catching a chill romantic?"

"Men are idiots, Angel."

Camille sneered, her gaze cutting to the man on the street outside. "He wants another tumble is all. Since working here, I've seen clients, grown men, for heaven's sake, ambush Victoria with rites of love." Mr. Richmund's poetry was so painful, they'd all sworn off sonnet fantasy for the foreseeable future. "Men spout flowery nonsense until they get what they want."

Madam stood and crossed the room to share Camille's view. "I've always believed the louder a man shouts his feelings, the shallower the depth." Her gaze turned to the duke, wrapped up like a sausage in a pastry crust. "Funny, he didn't say a word after he'd been escorted out."

'Escorted' was a fine term after the guards known as the Stallions had thrown him out on his ass.

Camille frowned. "Spit out whatever you have to say."

Madam rolled her eyes. "I'm saying, *Angel*, no one is *that* good a tumble to gracefully and *silently* suffer one's toes rotting off for." She tapped her nose and pointed to the alley. "And if you have any interest in seeing that handsome face in your bed again, or *anywhere else*, a cup of hot Earl Grey wouldn't be out of the question."

CAMILLE FOUND TEA too civil a drink for what must be done. The man could not stay in the streets, where the dampness was known to take even the healthiest of men. But he would not be permitted to stay, either.

When she stepped into the streets, steaming cup in hand, his gaze shot to her, though he made no effort to stand or speak. Camille's body tingled at the intense stare. With only his eyes visible between his hat and collar, the pale-brown color glowed.

She extended the cup to him, careful to stay under the overhang and out of the rain. "Here. It is hot water and lemon."

At the idea of hot anything, he stirred from his heap of coat and limbs and accepted the cup with a "Thank you," though he remained seated. He took a sip, his gaze fixed on her face, as if she would disappear the moment his eyes left her.

Camille had never realized the power of someone's stare. The man did nothing but sip down hot water, but the silence between them was alive. His gloved knuckles wrapping around the cup conjured images of leather whips and embraces against her breasts and shoulders, while his lips on the cup suggested other, more scandalous, embraces someplace lower.

Her growing arousal felt like a weak betrayal of her body. This was not acceptable behavior, from either of them. She'd accepted their intimacy yesterday as a gift, one she was not permitted to enjoy again. Once was forgivable, a continued liaison was not; selfishness would only lead to ruin. "You're an idiot."

He didn't answer until he'd drained the cup and set it gently on the cobblestones. When he looked up at her, some color had returned to his pale face. "Yes, well, I make up for it with stubbornness and excellent hair."

She wouldn't smile. "Why are you here?"

"I told you I would come."

She scoffed. "And you're a man of your word."

"I told you I was."

"Men say things all the time. Rarely are they true."

"You are a cynic."

His easy assessment pricked her temper. "Two interactions and you make great leaps to claim knowing my character, sir. You overstep yourself."

"Ah, yes." He leaned back against the alley wall, somehow managing to look distinguished with his knees pressed to his chest. "There's that pride again. I admit our acquaintance has not been long, but I can claim to know you better than most, a fact you cannot deny."

Mention of their intimacy and her lack of experience shifted the power in the conversation, and Camille could find no way to take it back.

"And the point is mine," he said, though there was no smugness in his expression.

"This is not a game."

He gave her a pointed look. "Yes, it is. You've played since we first met and are now sore because I have landed a blow you cannot reciprocate. Don't worry, my dear, you are still well ahead."

How aptly he understood. Forcing indifference into her words, she said, "I am not *your dear*. We are nothing to each other." She hated how her heart rebelled at the words.

"I'd like to change that."

Hated more how her heart fluttered at *his* words. "We mustn't."

He stood then, his tall frame not nearly as concerning as his growing smile. "I hear you said 'mustn't' and not *cannot*. Which means you wish for it as much as I."

Another point. *Blast!* "A simple slip of the tongue."

He drew close, his eyes darker than normal. "I find your tongue exceptionally skilled. Hard to believe it would fail at anything."

He was flattering her even as he seduced her. Camille was not naive, not as much as before. The tone of his voice had shifted like his eyes, lower and silkier. And as before, she was not immune.

Backing away, she pointed to the cup on the ground, thankful for something besides his eyes to draw her attention. "I'll need that back."

He smiled again as if he knew her new game and retrieved the cup. He did not hand it back.

"The cup?" she said.

"The china is still warm and my hands so very cold. You'll permit me if I wish to keep holding on to it for a bit longer."

"The cup or the conversation?"

"See?" he said. "Back on top score already."

She huffed. For a blundering idiot, he was eloquent in his own right, knowing just how to appease her wounded pride. She leaned against the club door, her fear of falling victim to his expert skills dimming with the familiarity of his company. He was charming and amusing. Two traits lacking in most men in equal quantities. For all his reputation, the 'rogue' duke *was* easy to talk to.

"I see you're warming up to me again," he said.

He saw too much. "If you state your business, then you may leave and we may both be warm."

"I'd much rather be cold here with you." He put up a hand to stop her. "Yes, I know; I'm an idiot."

She closed her mouth and fought a smile. "Well, then, out with it."

"I want you to come home with me."

The smile came regardless of her efforts. "That's bold of you to ask."

"Another flaw, you think?"

"Not quite." She waved him on. "Go on, sweep me off my feet with your reasoning."

"Is such a thing possible?"

"Doubtful." She'd needle him into professing some such nonsense of love, as Madam had said. "But I permit you to try your hardest."

"You are magnificent."

"Noted. Anything else?"

He licked his lips, his gaze no longer self-assured. "And brilliant."

"I've been told that before."

His gaze narrowed. "You refuse to make this easy."

"You are correct."

He sighed and removed his hat, his hair springing about in an attractive dishevelment of light waves around his ears. Efforts clearly not working, he dropped the charm. "Come to the country with me. Meet my sister," he said. "Let me wrap you in silks and satin, as you deserve."

His speech was artless, but his words hit their mark. Camille was glad for the wall behind her, for her legs would surely have given out without the support. Meet his sister . . . Such things were not done. Ever. His sister was a lady, and Camille . . . was not. She'd expected him to offer her an insulting but well-paid position as his mistress. She might have even considered it. For a moment, at least. What he was offering now . . . She had no idea.

"One does not pluck a low creature from the gutter and bring her home like a pet to be groomed. Not even a duke."

"Is that how it sounded?" He muttered something about being an ass. "I meant what I said before. My sister is a terror but perfect company. I've no doubt you'd be thick as thieves before the first course at dinner, and, while your loveliness would raise a mere sack to heavenly standards, that dress you're wearing is impractical for London streets."

"And silks and satins are?" Is that all she had to say? He'd as good as offered her a position as his sister's companion, which would only be acceptable with Camille's background if he first made her his ward. Even so, that simply was not done. Her own father hadn't even considered . . . Renard made no sense. Did he mean to take her to bed or not? He'd clearly not thought of the repercussions of introducing her to his sister.

Her heart froze against such pretty fantasies. She was surrounded by them, after all; she knew when things were too good to be true. "What is it you want from me, Your Grace?"

"You," he said simply. "I want you."

Her patience evaporated. "I don't even know you!" What a cad to come here and weave this beautiful future for her when they both knew it was impossible.

"Then get to know me," he said.

He was there in front of her in an instant, his gaze serious, calm. No desire or delusional heat evident to cloud his judgement.

"And if you can stomach my awful personality and dreadful handwriting," he said, "then allow me the privilege to know *you*."

The ice in her heart was thawing at an alarming rate. "It's not that easy."

"Of course it is. I want you. I like you. Plain. Simple."

"Ha!" she shouted in triumph, ignoring her disappointment. "I knew this was all a game to you."

"Huh?"

"You're speaking of feelings; you must not mean them. Didn't scratch the itch the first time? There won't be a repeat of yesterday, *Your Grace*, so you might as well leave."

"Excuse me." He shook his head as if removing water from his ears. "The water must have flooded my brain, because nothing you say makes any sense."

"You said you like me." Madam's experience aside . . . "Your actions are the ones that don't make sense."

His eyes went wide. His hands shook at his sides from emotion, though the trembling could have been attributed to the cold.

"You are the most maddening, wonderful, infuriating, charming, lovely, *maddening* woman I've ever met."

Emotion, then.

"I tell you I want you and you shout how it proves me a what—cad? Sexual male? Yes, I'd like to have sex with you again, preferably with you naked this time. No, that isn't what I'm talking about. I'm—" He shook his head. "Damn it, I don't know what I'm saying. My life was simple before you arrived. I was content to spend my days as a worthless gentleman, and then you showed up, proud and right, and made me want something more for myself." He paced as he spoke. "If I were a smarter man, I'd have left hours ago, after it became abundantly clear you want nothing to do with me." Back and forth, he walked, his hands gesturing in big sweeps, the cup still in his one hand. "But I am an idiot, as you've mentioned numerous times." He stopped in front of her, nothing but sincerity in his gaze. "But I do want you— your mind as well as your body—and I'll be damned if my idiocy and your madness keep me from getting that through your lovely, stubborn head!"

Camille stared. Her heart pounded wildly, the useless muscle flying with unfathomable emotion and warming her cold limbs.

He *cared* for her or believed he did. She'd be the idiot to deny what was plainly written on his face.

She cleared her throat and lifted his collar that had fallen during his impassioned speech. Keeping her gaze down, she said, "As far as proposals go . . ."

He seemed to stop breathing. "Yes?"

"It wasn't bad."

She bit her lip and looked up into those fathomless eyes, seeing her insecurities reflected in their sandy depths, as well as relief.

He saw it too. "We'll take it slow."

He was real, and flawed, and haunted, and everything she wanted.

Wanting anything was a dangerous thing. The world wasn't gentle or loving to her kind. She'd fought what had been plain in front of her since that night in the warehouse. Deep down, she'd known all along he was different. *She* was different when she was with him; she was someone she didn't hate.

"I've no experience with . . ." She refused to say something as ridiculous as *affection.* "Relationships."

"Good," he said. "Me, neither. I'd hate to be on uneven footing with you."

She grinned. "You wish to continue our rivalry?"

"Heavens, no! I'm tired of losing." He brushed a stray hair from her cheek, his eyes going soft. "But I wouldn't be averse to stumbling through it together."

"*Together.*"

Camille had never felt the warmth of that word until this moment. Trust, support—there were facets of affection she'd never touched, never hoped to find, and now that she'd found them, she was terrified.

What if she wasn't good at them?

"You're frowning." His smile was dazzling; his touch on her brow was feather soft. "I'll have to do something about that, my Milly."

Camille's heart swelled at the sweetened form of her name. He knew. Somehow, he saw her fears and knew what she needed.

"*Together.*"

She wouldn't be alone. Equal rivals could become equals on an altogether more treacherous battlefield. That was what those eyes said. What her heart told her.

And faith. Caring was a leap her brain couldn't calculate, not when everything in her past told her such feelings weren't enough.

"What do you say, Milly?"

That vulnerability returned to his gaze, the only thing that could reach past her doubts.

She smiled up at him, feeling exposed and cherished. "Very well," she said, her voice husky from emotion. "*Slow.*"

Perhaps, this once, *affection* would be enough.

CHAPTER TWELVE

S YD DROPPED DOWN beside Camille in the alley outside the club, taking two years off her life.

"Stop doing that!" Camille said.

Syd etched a low bow. "Apologies, miss."

Camille rolled her eyes and fell into an easy stride. After her afternoon with Renard, she was looking forward to crawling into her cot on the floor at home to relive his touches and his words over and over until she convinced herself she'd imagined it all, but her mother's request came first. "I have an errand to run on the way home."

"A detour?" Syd's eyes flashed with amusement. "To a gentleman's house, perhaps?"

"When did you become a meddler?"

"When I was forced to sit and wait up on the roof all day and night."

Camille's irritation ebbed. "Have I thanked you for that?"

"Not yet. Buy me a whiskey and we'll call it even."

Linking arms with Syd like when they'd been children, Camille smiled. "What a coincidence. My destination happens to be the least offensive tavern on the river."

Knowing instantly where she meant, Syd sighed. "Any chance there's a bossy older sister working there?"

"How *did* you know?"

Syd gave her a look. "Don't tell her about your man. You

think *I'm* a meddler . . . Tell me you're not going for advice? She won't approve. Her ideas of men are akin to puppet masters wishing to play women for fools." She shook her head. "Scarlet is insufferable when she gets that 'I-know-better-than-you' tone."

That, Camille knew too well. "Fear not, friend. We go for pie."

Syd's mood shifted with the prospect of warm food. She bowed again and offered her arm once more with enthusiasm. "Then by all means, milady, let's be off."

〉〉〉✷〈〈〈

AS LUCK HAD it, the Cock 'n Hen had been so busy, Scarlet had little more than minutes to say hello, though still plenty of time to tell Syd to wash up before she got sick eating with filth on her hands.

Deciding to forgo the shadow on her way home, after procuring two meat pies, Camille ducked out of the tavern and walked the rest of the way to her flat in alert silence.

When she returned home, it was to find her mother in bed and deep in her cups.

Camille picked up a half empty bottle of gin. "Where did you get this? Did you leave the flat?"

"Me, go out into the dirty streets?" She scoffed. "Mr. Rockford stopped by, the melancholy little man." She saluted with a limp wrist. "But the man is a Christian. Wouldn't hear of me going without fortification for my pain."

"You lied to our landlord for free liquor?"

Her mother's drunken sneer was ugly. "My pain is internal. At least *someone* cares what I've been through."

Camille didn't comment further. She'd take Mr. Rockford aside later and explain her mother's 'pain' and offer another penny for his trouble. The man hardly asked for anything for rent and losing his good will would be a financial disaster they weren't yet able to face.

A small sound from the outside alley stirred her from her planning: one of the knocker-uppers tapping the glass of a nearby neighbor as he made his early morning rounds for the factory workers.

She set the crockery from the tavern on her mother's nightstand. "Meat pie, like you asked."

Her mother sniffed, snatched the bottle from Camille's hands, and took a long drag of gin instead.

That sound came again.

Camille looked towards the window, where little, tan stones sprinkled the sill and floor below. She strolled over and picked up the nearest one to examine what looked like finely ground gravel. There must have been two dozen of them scattered across the floor.

"Mother, where did these come from?"

Her mother's glance was unfocused and blurry eyed. "Hmm? Oh, some urchin has been tossing them at the window for the past hour. I yelled for the riffraff to move along, but the filth must be deaf."

Urchin? The space between the back of the flat and the next cramped building was suffocating for even a small dog.

She poked her head out the window, nearly hitting her face on the opposite building's wall, and looked down the thirty feet to the narrow alley at a fair head of hair in the dim moonlight.

Her gasp had the figure's head shifting and a face looking up. Camille nearly fell out the window at Renard's boyish grin.

Heart leaping, she silently motioned to meet at the end of the row before turning back to her mother. "I'm going for a spot of air. I'll be back shortly."

Mother waved her on, taking another swig from her bottle.

Camille raced out the door and down the back stairs, careful to keep her tread light so as not to wake Mr. Rockford. When she got to the back door, she unbolted the lock with shaking hands.

He was here. She'd seen him that afternoon, but she'd convinced herself he hadn't been real. The wonderful warmth in her chest and fluttering in her belly had been the work of girlish fantasy.

Settling herself, she flung open the door and there he was, strapping in a dark, wool-lined coat, trousers, and a flat cap in his hand full of tan stones.

When he saw her, his smile was dazzling.

"Hello," he said.

Managing to catch her breath, she smiled back and said, "Hello, yourself."

"Were you sleeping?"

She shook her head. The breeze on this side of the building was strong with the alley tunneling the wind between buildings. She shivered through her thin dress, having forgotten her shawl on the hook next to the door.

Renard sloughed off his coat and wrapped it around her shoulders along with the smell of his bergamot and lemon cologne.

She pushed her arms through the sleeves, his body heat lingering in the fabric. "Now you'll be cold," she said.

"What cold?" he asked, his teeth chattering.

She bit her lip and did her best not to smile. "I hate when you're charming, remember?"

"Ah, yes, I'd forgotten." His brows pushed together in a more charming-than-grumpy furrow. "I do say, chivalry dictates a man share his coat with a freezing damsel, but it's damn uncomfortable." His face smoothed. "How was that? Gruff enough? Should I have used more profanity?"

Her smile came full force. "I can't believe you fit in the alley."

"It was a bit tight," he said. "I find I have more sympathy for a woman's hat box now. Speaking of boxes." He nodded to his coat pocket. "There may be a small something in there I couldn't wait until tomorrow to give you."

She startled. A present? She reached into the outer pocket and pulled out a lovely, velvet box. Opening the lid, she found a slim, glass vial in the box's plush lining, delicately decorated in white swirls that reminded her of the waves crashing the shore where the Thames met the North Sea. Tears pricked her eyes.

"You don't like perfume!" He shut the lid and took the box from her hands and hid it away in his trouser pocket, his expression fallen. "I should have known. I'm sorry. I'll find something more suitable next time. My first instinct was a box of coal, but black cinders hardly seemed like an appropriate offering to a woman—"

Camille pressed a finger to his lips. "I've never had anything so fine."

His shoulders relaxed. Taking the box back out of his pocket, he offered it on his open palm. "You like it, then?"

She placed a firm kiss on his lips. "Does that answer your question?"

"It makes me feel less like an idiot," he said. "Not to worry. I'm sure I'll say or do something to prove myself an ass and all will be right with the world again."

She frowned at his words, not the first time he'd said something self-derogatory. Hardly acquiring the skills, or historical desire, to set a man at ease, she drew him closer and whispered in his ear, "Not to worry, Your Grace. I like a man part fool."

He chuckled low and grazed a searing kiss along her jaw. "Good to know, Miss Forthright. Then I shall state with pride I am your fool and no one else's."

Her mind coiled around his words as her hips naturally pressed against his body in her growing desire. "I like that."

His hands fell to her hips to press her more squarely against his hard erection. "What else would you like, my lady?"

He ground against her core in a melting friction of heat and steel.

She gasped and clutched him tighter. "You. Now." She had no idea where the wanton words had come from. His masculine smell enveloped her, addling her thoughts until they narrowed down to the single ache between her legs.

He growled and pushed her into the dark alley with her back against the wall. His hands were already under her skirts and parting her petticoats. His thumb ran around her intimate lips once, twice, infinitely in a tortuous circle that had her shredding her nails on the stone at her sides.

The knowledge of what they were doing, out here in the street where anyone could stumble upon them, was scandalous, provocative, further pushing her towards that sweet oblivion. It felt as if a tight string pulled, tighter and tighter, until she'd snap.

"Renard! I need you."

He fell to his knees then and lifted her skirts to the bitter night air.

She had the mind to grab his head for support before his mouth clamped down on her.

Her nails dug into his scalp. She clung to him, urging him to suck harder. He was unparalleled in his skill. Camille needed no other experience to know he was unmatched. He threw her leg over his shoulder for better access. The way his teeth nipped at her sensitive skin, or how his hands kneaded her hips to keep them wide, she moved and opened with the slightest of direction.

He was there as her legs folded, supporting her, easing her open.

Her other leg thrown over his shoulder, her back pushed against the cold alley wall. He lapped at her, sending her hurtling towards another climax.

She arched, pressing her palms against the wall above her head. "Renard!"

So close.

When his tongue slid inside her, that thread inside her broke and she willingly fell into her puppet master's waiting arms, her strings no longer able to hold her up.

CHAPTER THIRTEEN

RENARD NEVER KNEW such obsession. He'd taken her here, in the alley, without a second thought. He'd known only his desire and a need to touch her, and then when her passion had ignited, his very essence had become about her needs and pleasure, unrelenting until she'd come on his tongue with his name falling from her lips like scripture.

My, but she was a miracle.

Imagining a long night of shared bliss, he pulled down her skirts to keep out the damp of the alley and kissed her gently on the lips. "May I come in?"

Her body, so wonderfully weighted and soft, stiffened. "It's late. I must rise early for work."

The idea of her working any labor was repugnant.

It was a test of his will allowing her to return to this filthy place. He'd have snatched her from the Prodding Pony and set her up in a golden palace if she'd be receptive. But her pride and independence were easy to decipher, and he refused to step beyond her wishes. If she continued to stay in this dangerous rookery, he might have to find his own hole to lay his head in, if only to keep his fears for her safety at bay.

He kissed her again, working his charms until she was once again soft in his arms. "If I promise not to keep you up too late, may I stay?"

She shook her head, a delicate wrinkle forming between her

brows. "I can't let you come up."

That tone was disarming. "If it's a matter of the state of the home, I have no objections to your life, Milly."

"It's not that. There's—"

"Camille! Where'd you go?"

A woman's shout came from the open window down the lane, shrill and slurred.

Camille winced and pulled out of his arms. "Coming," she replied to the faceless voice. To him, she said, "I must go. My mother is indisposed. She doesn't suffer company well."

Her mother? Ah, the faceless voice that had screamed at him earlier. He'd thought it had been a nosy landlady. He'd assessed his Milly hadn't a husband or children, but he'd never considered she may have had siblings or parents to watch over.

Fool as he was, he'd never asked.

"What of your father?" he asked.

"He's dead."

He didn't imagine the temperature dropping around them from the ice in her words. There was history there, an ugly one, by the sound of it. He knew that feeling too well.

"I didn't mean to pry," he said.

Her frown softened. Fingers lacing behind his neck, she kissed his lips with a featherlight touch. "Will I see you tomorrow?"

Renard savored the taste of her before his spirit dimmed. "I must leave for the country tomorrow." Truth was, he'd put off his trip after that first night. "Charlotte's latest chaperone keeps sending me letters." He adopted a shrill voice to mimic the older woman. "'The lady is out of control. I'm at my wits' end.'" He ran a hand through his hair. There'd been another letter this morning, this one from his housekeeper, insisting he make for Lux estate with all haste.

Camille smirked, no doubt rooting for the recalcitrant lady. "Your sister will be happy to see you."

He loved how certain she sounded. He tucked a curl behind her ear that had fallen from the bun at the back of her neck. "I've decided to bring her to London next summer, as you suggested."

"Why not this summer? There's plenty of time left."

He sighed. "*I* need at least a year to prepare for the antics to ensue."

She chuckled. "I'm sure she'll enjoy the experience."

"I think she'd appreciate the city more if there was someone she could talk to about dresses, and fashion, and . . . womanly things." He gritted his teeth. This shouldn't have been so hard to ask. He was a grown man for goodness's sake. "I was hoping you might accompany me?" He rubbed the back of his neck. "Who knows? If I bring home a companion of a sort, maybe Charlotte won't run off every chaperone within fifty miles."

Her gaze widened. "To the country? Tomorrow?" Her eyes brightened. "I would love to meet your sister!" Expression falling, that horrible frown surfaced, the one that spoke of troubled thoughts. "I'm hardly appropriate as a companion. I never received the proper education and my pedigree would bring embarrassment to your family should my parentage come to light. Besides, I am needed here. My mother, the club. I have obligations."

He didn't give a fig about her connections, familial or other-wise, but she didn't seem likely to respond favorably to him snubbing society. "We can take your mother with," he said instead. The sooner he got her away from that club, the better. It was a matter of time before one of the patrons saw her and made assumptions, like Hawkins. Anger boiled to the surface thinking of those three men. He'd have to do something about them soon. "Fresh air is said to cure most illnesses," he pushed. "Or at least ease the suffering."

"It's not that kind of—" She cut herself off and started again. "Thank you, but I must remain. When will you return?"

The prospect of not seeing her every day was enough to make him want to write back to his housekeeper that Charlotte may decorate the very walls with spiders if it meant he could stay in London. But that wouldn't do. He owed his sister a visit. He owed her far more.

He raised Camille's hand to his lips and pressed a kiss to the inside of her wrist. "I won't be gone long if I can help it."

Not when you are here.

He knew she'd heard the words he'd left unspoken when that brilliant smile of hers chased her frown away.

"Come now, Your Grace. A few nights' reminder of the peace of the country and you'll be pained to part from it."

"I much prefer the diversions of a particular young woman." Her teasing didn't help his plummeting spirits. Going more than a day without a fresh insult from those luscious lips may prove harder to bear than sobriety. "I will write, if that is acceptable?"

She nodded, but her voice held a hesitant note. "When you're there, you should consider what you truly want, Renard."

"What do you mean?"

"I will not be your mistress."

He blinked at her sudden fierce expression. "The thought never crossed my mind." And it hadn't. Mistress, what a waste to keep a woman like her a secret. Was that what she thought his actions implied? Damn it all!

He frowned. What *did* his actions admit? He cared for her, would protect her if given the chance. Setting her up as a companion to his sister would be a faux pas society wouldn't take quietly. Anything more than that . . . If society railed against an improper companion, they'd never approve of making such a woman a duchess.

Society could eat bricks. His parents and grandparents were gone. Aside from that insidious Mrs. Norris and her increasingly nosy letters pertaining to her would-be son heir, who'd do their utmost to interfere, he was a duke! The damn title should come with some perks.

Not that he was considering marriage. He was courting, that was all. And there were no laws against that.

"Milly." He took her face in his hands and pressed a long kiss to her forehead. "Aside from some rather erotic positions I'm keen to interest you in, not many thoughts have crowded my brain. I've thought only of you and the pleasure you bring me. Talking, arguing, sex . . . It's more than physical." He shrugged. "I know you would never agree to being a kept woman and I respect your choice."

"Then what is this?"

"This?" He hated that generic word to describe what was between them. His thumb ran across her mouth while he imagined something else pressing between her lips. "*This*," he said, "is an ambiguity in fate's design that I have no interest in questioning. I want you desperately, you want me marginally. Allow me the title of friend, lover, confidante. I will take all I can get, but don't throw away what could be." He kissed her once, twice, in quick succession. "I will do as you ask and think over our relationship, if you will promise the same? But know this, Camille Forthright." He kissed her a third time for good measure, knowing with certainty his next words were spoken by fate herself.

"Until you look me in the eyes and tell me, resolutely, to leave, you will never be rid of me."

HE LEFT HER at her door, stunned and wanting. His words burned through her, leaving even the drafty stairwell feeling steamy. She made it back to the second story and locked the door behind her before falling into the stained cot in the corner.

He was mad. To invite a commoner to meet his sister, one who worked in a pleasure house for that matter, was improper. Neither of them would be spared the shame or mockery of the gossip papers. The 'rogue' duke fallen, and she . . . She would never put herself in a position to be used as gossip fodder for the *ton*. Never again.

How her heart had pounded at his invitation. To ride to the

country, to meet his family. For a moment, she'd forgotten their stations and her responsibilities and let herself dream.

She'd wear her best dress and her only surviving ribbon from her childhood. She'd walk up to a beautiful fair-haired lady, easily identified as the duke's sister, and introduce herself as Miss Forthright with a perfect curtsey.

"A good girl curtsies low to her betters."

Lady Charlotte would have invited her to sit in the garden—a perfectly trimmed and primed space befitting the grounds of a duke—and they'd take tea and biscuits while talking of easy topics.

"A good girl never brings up weighty topics." "A good girl is always agreeable and pleasant."

Her mother's rules slowly seeped poison into her dream, tainting the beautiful image she'd concocted. Camille screamed, letting her limp pillow muffle the sound. How many nights had she lain awake as a child, fantasizing about her father's home at Camine Manor and a lovely garden in which she would take afternoon tea?

Renard's offer had been tempting, if only for a real image of a duke's home to occupy her mind.

She couldn't understand him. He'd bought her an expensive gift, lured her into fictitious dreams of a future, but he hadn't once implied her workplace was unsuitable or that he would set her up in a flat in town.

If he acted like any other gentleman and encouraged a mutual physical relationship, she'd understand his expectations. But he'd made no demands, set no expectations. He'd as much as said he'd taken no time to consider the matter. But he *had* offered himself and that which held value to him, almost as if he was asking for more without realizing.

No. She turned on her side and stared at the wall, letting the cracks and watermarks ground her back in reality, and willed her trail of thought to end. That way lay danger. Anything beyond their next rendezvous was satirical nonsense. He may glance over the logistics of what a real future between them looked like presently, but for how long?

She'd said he should take some time to think over their relationship, but the advice went both ways. Their time so far had been a whirlwind of passionate arguments and more passionate couplings. Despite the reprieve from her less-than-ideal circumstances, a wealthy and handsome duke didn't fit into her future, no matter how her mind wandered into the realm of romance.

Marriage was out of the question, and she refused to be a kept woman like her mother, relying too much on a relationship that left her dependent and vulnerable without the freedom to walk around in society.

She curled into a ball and listened to her mother softly snoring in the other room, on a mattress of rags and torn curtains taken from the last of their possessions from the flat off Burkley Street, the house the duke had kept for his 'dolls' to stay in.

Camille bit the inside of her cheek to keep her next scream inside. How far they'd fallen; a year ago, they'd been living in a small but tidy home in a respectable neighborhood. Now they were lucky to share a two-room flat with the rest of the freezing vermin in St. Giles.

She watched a roach crawl across the floor and disappear through the gap under the door and shuddered. This was her life, a life mirrored by hundreds more in the surrounding buildings. People who had no way of dragging themselves from their hellish circumstances, not alone.

She was needed here.

The country, attachments, affections: they'd all have to wait. She had work to do.

CHAPTER FOURTEEN

C AMILLE EYED SYD'S shifting gaze. "What's the matter?"
The girl jolted from her search of the dark streets as if
she'd forgotten Camille was there. "What? Nothing." She shook
her head and gave a reassuring grin, but a second later, her gaze
slipped back to the alley shadows, her expression indecipherable
with the sliver of moon overhead.

Camille stopped. She knew better than to ignore the nose of
the 'wolf.' And she'd pay her week's wages to distract herself with
someone else's drama. "Want to talk about it?"

Hearing her words repeated from the other night, Syd
glanced her way, her grin flashing. "The streets feel off is all."

Taking a moment to make her own assessment of their surroundings, Camille did have an odd sense of shifted intention in
the air, a sense she should have noticed at once. Gone for less
than three days and Renard's absence was an unforgivable
distraction. "What is it?"

"Don't know." Syd shook her head. "Probably a fight gone
bad at the Sally Saloon. Anytime Lucien crawls out of his
underground lair, the night walkers get jumpy and the rest make
themselves scarce."

"We should ask Lucien to venture into the streets more often. The Merrys could use a night off."

"That'd be nice," Syd said.

"But you don't think that's the reason for the quiet?"

"Probably nothing." Syd stopped her fidgeting and shrugged. "Pops says I got a sense for trouble, but that sense rarely leads to anything."

"Are the Merry Men still running thin?"

"With the fat purses in town, there've been pickpockets pinching the pockets of gentlemen when they visit one of the clubs by the harbor. Nothing unusual. Then there're the white collars."

Nothing like priests spouting about the pits of hell to make the sinners run for the steeples. "Think one in particular is causing a fuss?"

"Hard to tell. Some bloke's been sniffing around, asking questions. Discreet, I'll give him, but stuffed monkeys talk."

Camille smiled at the pastry reference. The Jewish immigrants made a fruity dessert on par with English tarts.

There wasn't a stone you could throw anywhere in the Houndsditch or Whitechapel rookeries without hitting at least two Jewish families who'd fled to London from East Europe, clumped together in unreasonable conditions just to make ends meet. Which also meant there was always someone watching.

No wonder Madam stayed so well informed.

"Any idea what he wants?" Camille asked. The rookeries had seen a rise in missionaries and priests along with the rush of inhabitants, young men fresh from the seminary who came with bright intentions and pure speeches of love and compassion, only to leave with haunted expressions, their belief in a higher power disillusioned by the ugliness of the real world. "Another representative of the church, maybe?"

Syd shrugged, the subject only as interesting as the possibility of intrigue and violence. "He'll leave soon enough. They all do."

Camille didn't mistake the envy in the girl's voice. "But not us?" Syd was young, bright, skilled, and beautiful. As a child, she'd shown a proficiency for music that had bordered on prodigy. If any of them could make something of themselves, Syd could.

"The day I accepted the streets as my home, I became vermin

to this world. You know better than anyone, Cam," she said, her smile dark. "None of us can escape our birth or past, no matter how much we may wish to."

The pessimistic and altogether truth of her statement tore at Camille's heart. It was women—still a girl, really—like Syd who would benefit from a home for girls and women. But for others. For Syd, Camille's dream was three years too late.

"There's still time." The words were for them both. "Someday, someone will come along and make a difference for the better."

Syd's grin held nothing of the carefree life of a young woman. "You're too smart to believe that, genius."

"Even geniuses can dream."

"Hmm. Do those dreams include a certain gentleman?"

Most decidedly *not* wishing to discuss Renard, Camille gritted her teeth. "No."

"No? You looked rather chummy last night when I came to check on you."

Camille stopped and gave her friend a hard look. "You're spying on me?"

Syd continued on, and Camille was forced to follow.

"Don't look so irate. I've taken over that section for patrol so I can keep an eye on you, as promised."

Camille's anger burnt itself out, the emotion replaced with something strange and disconcerting. "You overheard us?"

"Only the last bit when he asked you to come away with him." Syd huffed. "I hope you realize how hard it was for me to hold my tongue when you turned him down."

"So . . . you think I should have gone with him?"

Syd glanced at her from the corner of her eye. "You're asking my opinion instead of rejecting the idea outright? My, you must be in love."

Camille tripped in surprise and caught herself before she fell on her face. "What? That's ridiculous!"

"No," Syd said. "What's ridiculous is you pretending like you haven't completely changed since you met him, for the better, I might add. Questioning, moody—you might be human, after all."

Emotions piled one on top of another until Camille couldn't decipher anything she was feeling. "If this is what it's like to be human, I'll pass."

Syd laughed.

Their discussion waned as they turned from Church Street to Church Lane, silently agreeing to avoid proximity to High Street and beyond in case the constables had decided to patrol the main roads for prostitutes. The repeal of the Contagious Diseases Act years ago had led to less and less detention of women under the guise of checking for disease, but some of the older officers kept to the practice with personal satisfaction. Even with her modest neckline and combination of shawl and bonnet to identify her as a woman of the working class, at this late hour, no one would believe she was innocently walking home.

The tension in the air shifted again, and the welcoming warmth of easy banter was replaced with cold silence that matched the night air.

Camille's steps slowed. Her hand slipped into the pocket of her skirt to grip the letter opener.

Syd drew her hood up and disappeared and reappeared as she wove in and out of the shadows provided by the sunken doors of the homes and shops along the alley.

The short stroll from Phoenix Street to Plumbtree was endless, the growing sense of danger thick enough to cut. Crossing over a deserted Broad Street, Camille breathed a sigh of relief when her home came into view with the usual washing and bric-a-brac left in the door by her neighbors. She'd retracted her hand from her skirts when Syd shot in front of her.

"Don't look," she said.

Camille angled a glance over Syd's shoulder and stilled.

Not washing piled in the gutter.

"Stay here," Syd said.

Syd crouched next to a body, her subtle touching at the

turned-over wrist telling Camille she looked for a pulse.

Camille moved closer, noting a familiar profile in the dim moonlight. Upon seeing the man's crooked nose and splotchy complexion, she pressed a hand to her throat.

Flank's body was tossed into one of her neighbors' doorways like garbage, his limbs thrown about at puppet-like angles too contorted for anyone breathing.

"Grinning at the daisy roots," Syd confirmed.

Camille swallowed hard. She'd seen corpses before. London winters were hard, especially in the rookeries where fuel was scarce, fires and heat more so. When the temperatures plummeted to dangerous digits at night, coroners would come with wagons to take the frozen bodies from the streets the morning after before warmer weather caused the unfortunates to thaw.

But the stiffness in Flank's body had nothing to do with the cold. He'd been here for hours, overlooked by others rushing on their way home from working the factories or the docks.

"Think he was visiting one of the local girls?" Camille asked.

Most of the prostitutes took up residence in St. Giles, as the rent was the cheapest in the city.

"Wouldn't be the first time a lover's quarrel got ugly." Syd poked at Flank's pockets and sleeves, finally drawing back the collar at his neck. Ugly slashes crisscrossed the skin in a sloppy pattern. She cursed. "Not a quarrel."

Camille didn't hope to believe it was a robbery gone bad. Not when a clean slice to the throat was quicker and valuables were visible from his pockets.

"Has his timepiece," Syd said, agreeing with her. She stood and backed away, leaving no evidence of her search. "A sick way to exact punishment."

"Lucien?" The Underground leader was known for his brutal measures.

"Flank's not his business," Syd said. "But someone thought he was theirs. Those cuts are shallow, meant to inflict pain."

Torture.

Camille turned into a nearby alcove and dry-heaved, thankful she'd been uninterested in eating anything all day. When she'd finished, Syd handed her a handkerchief.

She pressed the linen to her mouth. "I'm sorry."

"For what?" Syd tsked. "*One* of us should have a conscience." Her assessing gaze darted up the lane and back. "Let's get you inside. I'll make a courtesy call to Mr. Bowler on my way back to the Den."

Knowing the sooner the coroner was called, the better, Camille nodded. "Will you be all right walking back?" The Merry Men's headquarters was a good ten-minute walk, more than enough time for a killer to find his next victim. "You can stay here tonight."

"Nah. Coroner's office is on the way." She stuck out her chin in the direction of Camille's flat. "Go on. I'll wait until you're inside. Give me a signal through the window so I know you got in safe."

"All right." Camille hesitated. "You sure you don't want to stay? Mr. Bowler can wait until the morning."

Syd shocked her with a quick embrace. "Thanks, Cam. No worries. I'll be here before you leave for the club tomorrow. Don't step foot out your flat until you hear . . ." A hushed, whistling sound rushed between her teeth, like a birdcall. Her gaze followed in the direction of the Prodding Pony. She shook her head. "What a lark."

"What is?"

Syd's grin was too tight to be with humor. "There is one escape we all make in the end."

Camille patted the girl on the head, which Syd allowed. "Make me a promise neither of us will meet that end anytime soon."

Syd pushed her hand away, not unkindly. "All's the same. Personally, I plan to meet the Devil with both arms open."

"Then you'll be safe," Camille said, forcing lightness into her tone. "No Devil wants to take on a ragamuffin like you."

Syd laughed before slipping into the shadows.

Camille crossed the street and locked herself inside her flat, praying the Devil didn't come for any of them before the night was through. Not when Camille couldn't shake the feeling Flank's body had been left out in the open as an invitation to her specifically from Death himself.

CHAPTER FIFTEEN

C AMILLE DIDN'T DEVIATE from the path to the club and back for several days at Syd's behest. There'd been grumblings over Hawkins's dismissal and lack of suitable replacements from the patrons at the club, leaving the streets tense and rife with boredom, a combination even the least talented nose could sniff out.

Flank's lifeless body didn't help matters. Boredom gave way to conjecture and rumors of a new wave of garroting infesting the rookeries. The Merry Men soothed the growing discord with a firm presence on the streets, but Syd's hope for new, able recruits was proving too optimistic, and a six-crew gang was no enforcement for dozens of alleyways across the city.

At Syd's fourth plea for her to 'bar the windows,' Camille locked herself inside Madam's secret office at the club after an easy promise from the landlord he'd check on her mother every so often should she need anything *non-alcoholic*.

It was in that very space, amidst stacks of ink-scrawled parchment and an incessant hum from the electric lights Madam had installed, that the woman herself found Camille.

"A letter arrived," Madam said.

Camille waved towards the bin with the rest of the merchant bills for the club. "I'll get to it later."

"It's from your duke."

Camille shot out of her chair and took the letter from the

other woman's hands. She'd waited, most impatiently, for word from Renard. A week without any correspondence could only mean he was taking her request seriously and considering their future.

Heart pounding, she broke the seal to find another duke's hand, a most legible and unwanted one.

Dear Miss Forthright,

I admire your affront to any attempt at outreach, but your efforts are in vain. Should you wish to go through another party as to avoid interaction with me, I will of course make the arrangements. Since all previous grocers, servants, and errand boys have been turned away with a most unbefitting character, I shall endeavor to break down your resistance with more flattering persons. A renowned modiste shop assistant will arrive at your location in two hours' time . . . one, by the time this letter receives you. I ask you to put aside your normal stubborn behavior and be reasonably tempered, as it is not the woman's normal house call, and it is essentially not her doing.

As always,
Hamish Hurstfield, Duke of Camine

Unbelievable! Camille tore the paper in two and regretted not having a fire burning so she could singe the domineering popinjay's words to ash.

The man didn't know when to quit!

"Good news, it seems," Madam said.

Camille went around the desk and threw the torn letter into the cold hearth. "Be prepared to turn away a seamstress in the coming hour," she spat.

"A seamstress?" Madam glanced at the parchment at Camille's feet. "Ah. The other duke. My mistake."

There was no way the Madam hadn't been explicitly aware of the sender of the letter.

The other woman tapped a perfectly crested nail on the desk's edge while she surveyed the neat stacks of files. "You haven't left this room in three days."

Camille placed the current file she'd been working on in its designated pile. "The Pony has never run so smoothly."

"You've barely touched your plates."

The trays of food offered by the club's cook lay by the door, untouched.

"I'm not hungry," Camille said. More like everything she put in her mouth brought on a wave of nausea that eventually led to undignified gagging. Images of a dead body tended to ruin one's appetite.

"That is concerning," Madam said. "And telling."

"What do you want, Clarice?" Camille leashed her temper with effort. She hadn't left this sweltering hole in *four* days, eating, sleeping, and more, all in an eight-by-eight-foot box, not that she'd offer up the information as more fuel for Madam's nagging. She'd worked that entire time, switching off parts of her mind when exhaustion took her, allowing herself to continue processing the words and files. Eating, sleeping, Camille only knew the passing hours from the clock on the mantel and the ache of muscles from her backside.

Madam didn't flinch at her outburst, ever in control. "Did you tell him how you felt? Is that why he left?"

Temper flaring again, Camille knew exactly which 'him' she meant. "The duke *left* because he has a duty to perform, and so do I, which you are now interrupting."

"Careful, Angel. Wouldn't want to expose the truth and ruin all that self-denial."

Camille stood and went to the panel door, wrapping her shawl around her shoulders with jerky movements thanks to stiff muscles. Her words were cold when she said, "Don't expect me for a few days."

And she left.

SYD DROPPED DOWN from a nearby eave and offered Camille a grin. "You lasted longer than I anticipated."

Unaccustomed to the brightness of midday after months of nocturnal life, Camille shielded her eyes and aimed for the tavern.

"Scarlet won the bet?" she asked.

"Pops, actually."

Camille smiled despite her agitated mood. The Laundry family's gambling would rival any official gentleman's book; opposition had become an art form. Anything from how many rocks in a horse's shoe to how many bodies would turn up on the bank of the Thames.

"Any progress on who did in Flank?" Camille asked.

"Nah. Nobody saw anything, and Lucien is 'not receiving visitors at this time.' But Zans won't stop asking until someone remembers." Syd rubbed her fingers together to indicate the exchange of coins and rolled her eyes. "Our white-collared friend is gone, though. A bonus."

"Too saintly for you?"

"Too many lectures on the church steps about propriety and the damnation of greed, or was it sloth? One of those sins."

"Good thing poor listening didn't make the commandments."

Syd shrugged. "We're in hell already. Why worry over minor flaws?"

They made the turn at the end of the alley. Both stopped cold at a body lying in the street.

It was Grey.

Syd's intake of breath sounded like a knife freeing from a sheath. "Fucking quims." She approached the body, taking precautions to keep her slippered feet out of the growing pool of blood. The kill was fresh. Syd's hawk-like gaze darted from roof to alley to roof and back again. "I didn't hear anything from up top." She pulled back Grey's collar, revealing small cuts across his throat identical to Flank's.

Camille's voice came out quiet. "It must be Lucien, right?" Who else was bold enough to work in broad daylight despite the risk of washerwomen and children stumbling upon the scene at any moment?

"Hmm." Syd didn't discount the fighter's involvement outright this time.

Lucien's reputation wasn't one of kindness or compassion. Anyone claiming otherwise was likely to lose more than a mouthful of teeth.

"I haven't seen the Devil work before," Syd said. "Flashy, though, leaving Grey out here like this."

Camille nodded. That was right; Pops didn't let Syd anywhere near the Ring in case a fight broke out and her gender was revealed.

She latched on to the information, anything to keep her mind, and stomach, from the body at her feet. The oath she'd sworn to Markus after Scarlet had been hurt: his girls would be safe, untouchable. Only a select trusted few knew the connection between the three Laundry family members and Syd's secret. Markus had set out specific rules, rules Camille didn't balk at, their purpose making perfect sense when so many others in her life had not.

"A good girl never visits on a rainy day." "A good girl does not warm herself by the fire without invitation." "A good girl never uses two hands to raise her skirts when crossing the street."

"A good girl should never let a smell get to her."

"What?"

Camille startled from her trance, realizing she'd said the last rule out loud. She shook her head at Syd's questioning expression. "Never mind."

The choice of victims had to be more than a coincidence. If the Ring's master was exacting justice on her behalf, she'd need to set the record straight before more bodies littered the streets. She'd go tonight, after Syd left her watch and before the revelry of the Underground grew too dangerous.

It had to be Lucien. The alternative was too ugly to bear: a killer hunting the streets for unsuspecting men. Thank heavens

Renard remained in the country, where it was safe.

THE STREETS SMELLED of fear.

Mr. Bowler had made quick work carting Grey's body away, but hours later, the lingering presence of death clung to the slums like permanent fog, coating every stone in a wet and vicious rot.

Camille hastened towards the Sally Saloon, the anxious energy dogging her steps. A dim lantern sent a yellowish glow upon a black door and silent streets. Worried the evening's fight would be cancelled after a second body was found, she tracked through the near-deserted pub and into the back room, where rickety stairs led down into the Underground, just as rumors from the club claimed.

As she neared the bottom, the sounds of jeers and shouts grew deafening, telling her the fight would not only go on as scheduled, but she'd missed her chance to talk to Lucien without hundreds of ears around.

A liquor-soaked floor stuck to the bottoms of her boots, boots she tripped over when the Ring and its spectators came into view.

Bodies pressed together in a violent riot of bets and sport around a roped ring in center stage. Dozens of lit lanterns hung from beams in the ceiling, looking old and rusted enough to have been from the original tunnels when Parliament had forced excavation for sanitation's sake.

Tunnels bisecting beneath the city for miles where no 'bobbie' would think to find illegal gambling, a fact that had served Lucien well in becoming the greatest bit of bloody show in town.

Camille tucked her shapeless coat around her and pulled her cap low. Her skirts were an unfortunate addition to her disguise that couldn't be helped. Anyone looking her way would know she was a woman, but the rest of her worn and stained ensemble should deter all those but the most amorous or drunk.

She skirted around the edge of the crowd, aiming for the hidden stairs carved into the wall, which led up to a chamber she only knew was there because the same one-way mirror Madam used in the club ran along the upper edge of the cavern with a perfect view of the Ring. Whatever nameless patron supplied the Prodding Pony must have been in the pockets of all the Dockside leaders.

A collective gasp and cheer went up as one of the fighters made a particularly good strike to his opponent's face. Curiosity turned her fully towards the Ring when a steely voice had her ripping her gaze back to the hidden crook in the wall.

"This staircase is off limits."

The easily recognizable man sitting above her—glaring down with hard eyes and a harder jaw—had defined muscles that would have no problem silencing weak men like Grey and Flank. His hulking overcoat could neither hide nor deny his carriage-width frame, or the violent energy he wore like a second skin. He was also young, younger than any man who held the power of the Devil in his hands should have been.

Camille swallowed and removed her cap. "Mr. Greymore."

The Devil's brow rose, momentarily ruining his icy expression. "What's this? A Pony in hell?" His mouth curved into a dangerous smile Camille didn't believe for an instant was from amusement. "Did Madam send you, or did you arrive at my doorstep of your own volition?"

"I came on my own . . . for other reasons," she clarified.

That seemed to amuse him. "Since when do messengers have such angelic faces?"

"I'm not a messenger, either." Camille edged farther onto the staircase and out of the view of any curious crowd members who happened to glance their way. "My name is Camille Forthright. I am—"

"I know who you are," Lucien Greymore said, eyeing her in a completely different and calculating manner. "Madam's prized foal. Genius, she says, and off limits." His tongue raked across his front teeth as his gaze raked down her body. "It's not wise of you to enter a demon's lair, no matter what threats the old woman throws around."

Camille squared her shoulders at his thinly veiled threat. She was not here to be bullied or terrorized. If the man in front of her was indeed the demon hunting on the streets, then it was her duty to stop him for good.

"I came to ask if you had anything to do with Flank's and Grey's deaths."

Those dark eyes blinked in seeming surprise, and a sound of real amusement crawled out of his throat. He leaned back on the stairs, that predatory gleam in his eyes replaced with utter indifference. "You are a bold one, I'll give you that. Does Madam know you're here? Does anyone?"

"I came alone . . . and for an answer, which you have yet to give me."

He leaned forward, his gaze growing intense again at her challenging tone. "And if I say I killed them both, say I left their worthless corpses in the streets to send a message, what would you do?"

Camille blew out her breath, seeing exactly what she needed in his gaze—amusement but no triumph or gloating—though her relief was short-lived. "I'd say you weren't responsible." Which meant someone else was.

His smile was terrifying. "Seems Madam wasn't exaggerating about you."

"Do you know anyone else with a grudge against them?" Maybe it'd been a coincidence. Maybe there'd been a different connection between the two men. Lucien would know.

"Besides you?" he asked. "I'd say a woman scorned was a dangerous enemy indeed."

Madam's warnings about Lucien's quick mind hadn't been exaggerated, either.

"If I wanted them dead," she said, "I'd have left them on Hawkins's doorstep, not my own."

He barked a laugh that had the closest spectators flinching and glancing around. "If you ever tire of the old church bell, you are welcome here. I've use for someone with your skills . . . and boldness."

The crowd's swell of screams didn't drown out the unspoken innuendo in his offer.

The Devil was handsome in a dangerous way. Aside from the constant aura of a man itching for a fight around his person, his smile was straight, his nose and hair likewise. A few weeks ago, she may have been tempted by such an offer for adventure. But that was before she'd met the Devil's fairer and gentler reflection.

"Thank you." She donned her cap and tucked her curls beneath its brim. Having learned what she needed, lingering here would be unwise. "But we'd both find I am not suitable for your usual clientele."

Hearing her polite refusal, he shook his head. "A pity. You're wrong, of course. All kinds find sport here." He jerked his chin in the direction of the Ring. "Even the most refined have the blood of the Devil in them."

Camille followed his gaze, taking note of a new pair of fighters in the Ring. The one with his back to them laid into his opponent with brutal fists.

The crowd's shouts of approval seemed to drive the fighter wild. His fist connected with his opponent's cheek, once, twice, until blood rained on the unfortunate individuals who viewed closest to the mat.

It was a savage display, one that Camille struggled to turn away from, especially when a nagging feeling kept her focus on the man attacking.

Blood dripping down his face, the man turned and Camille recognized familiar light eyes bright with fervor and a parish pickaxe identical to the nose on the face of her nightmares.

She gasped and lurched towards the stage at where Hamish, the Duke of Camine—her half-brother—continued to strike his opponent over and over, even though the other man had lost consciousness.

Gut wrenching, she watched in horror and elation at seeing his twisted face. That anger, that blind rage was like nothing she'd seen. No, she'd seen its match once, on that horrible night.

Two men strained to pull Hamish back from the man on the floor until a third came and hauled him from the Ring.

Was that truly Hamish?

"Magnificent," Lucien said behind her, having stood and descended the steps without a sound.

She jumped at his towering form, blotting out the entire staircase behind and her view of the one-way mirror overhead; a carriage was an apt description. "You think a man beating another near to death is something to praise?" Men really were idiots.

He noted her disdain with a grin. "Violence has always plagued a man's spirit. Here at least, men can settle their differences in an honorable bout of strength and not with pride-filled boasts or unreliable guns. Though…" He glanced at where Hamish had been dragged out of the Ring and into the fighter's quarters out of view. "That one there has hate in his veins."

"Hate?" Was that what she'd seen on his face? Her heart pounded raggedly against her chest. There'd been blood all over him. She hadn't a mind to verify if it all belonged to his opponent.

"Like a rabid dog." Lucien sighed, as if disappointed. "Won't be able to bring him back for a while. Crowds love the spectacle of a bloody gentleman, but death matches are murder on long-standing schedules."

Camille didn't acknowledge his joke. There was nothing funny about the rage or violence she'd seen. Madam's exacting punishments were cold, passionless. Judging by the constant rumors around the Underground, Lucien himself was an indifferent fighter, never engaging in fights over petty arguments and never needing more than a single blow to win one. Even Markus, the most hotheaded of the three leaders, left his personal vendettas to Syd or one of the other Merry Men, to keep punishments clean and fair.

What would drive a man to such merciless lengths? Would Hamish have stopped of his own volition before he'd killed the other man?

"You should go before the crowd gets restless for another bout." Lucien rolled his shoulders as if he were in fact the restless one. He nodded towards a break in the crowd and offered a brief word of concern, and there was a Scottish tilt to his words she hadn't noticed before.

"Careful on your way home, foal. Madness be spreading the streets."

"Madness." The word haunted her as she retraced her steps up into the pub and out into the night. The heaviness in the air now had a name and a purpose.

"Madness."

Perhaps the man at Hamish's mercy had given a personal affront. No one could harbor such ugliness for someone they barely knew. But an insult wasn't an excuse for such behavior.

Had that really been the man who'd come to the Pony months ago to offer her a life of comfort? The same man who relentlessly shoved grocers and physicians her way to assuage a misplaced sense of guilt and responsibility? Why would he come to the Underground, a vile place of brutal and beast-like sport?

Before, she'd never questioned the extent a man's rage could take. Men of all stations fell from grace with secret vices of drink and violence. But she knew not all men were bad. One gentleman proved there was goodness despite her best efforts to assign flaws to his actions.

Camille drew her coat around her and prayed for a familial relation she'd never wanted, a peculiar protective nature taking hold.

"Madness."

It must have been catching, for Camille doubted that which her own eyes had seen and that which her brain would never forget.

No matter how many times she saw her brother's face, twisted in a sneer of ugly emotion so much like their father's, it was not Hamish.

It couldn't have been.

CHAPTER SIXTEEN

S YD WAS WAITING on Camille's steps when she arrived back at home. Her friend's gaping mouth as she'd approached from the wrong direction would have been comical if the ensuing lecture hadn't laden her with such heavy guilt.

"You went to the Ring? *The Ring!* Are you insane?!"

Camille took the lecture quietly, her mind and body in tumultuous battle. Hamish in the Underground. Bodies in the street.

Her stomach gave a twist that had her retching in the alley.

"Camille, what's wrong?" Syd was instantly there, her anger postponed to offer comforting pats on the back.

Camille stared down at the stones at her feet, at the pool of sick she rarely succumbed to, even as a child. The chaos of her thoughts cleared for a single devastating understanding to wash through her, along with the ever-present teachings of her childhood.

"A good girl does not complain of illness." "A good girl does not eat more than what's proper." "A good girl does not encourage affection without the promise of marriage."

Syd fluttered behind her. "Do you need a physician?"

Camille glanced unseeing at the young woman beside her, recognizing the panic in her friend's voice but unable to quell the feelings when her own gripped so tightly. She should soothe Syd's fears, no doubt as she whirled through a list of fatal diseases more tragic than the next. Cholera, typhus . . . The rookeries were a breeding ground of internal battle.

Camille would take a quick death over the long-suffering future to follow. She managed a simple "Yes" to Syd's question before she took off in the direction of the free clinic, and an answer to a question she feared she already knew.

CAMILLE RETURNED TO the Pony before dawn, with a quiet Syd in tow.

Humming to herself, she left her friend to scale the building and perch on the roof. Camille worked vivaciously on the file before her, a new urgency driving her to perfect her proposal to Madam. The violence in the streets and the Underground had proven one thing for certain: the Merry Men's presence wasn't enough to keep violence off the streets.

The Den, as Syd had so affectionately coined their base, was a refuge for men looking for righteous justice and honorable means to put food on the table. The free clinic too was a means of safe and clean rest and reinvigoration for those who knew of its existence, usually factory fathers and brothers whose families relied on their contributions when an untended injury could spell infection and starvation.

Working-class women and girls had one of two options for honorable employment, and none at all if the dangerous conditions resided *in* the home and not at work. Attempts had been made by the government for compulsory schools for the children, but boys' education took precedence no matter the station. Changes had been made the farther out in the country one went, the agricultural and rural areas attempting to teach not only intellectual skills, but practical ones as well.

Here, the need for child labor abounded, and the feminine mind and body, forever inferior in the eyes of society to that of their male counterparts, got the mangle.

A knock on the inner door into the club gave Camille pause. Having elected to work in the main office with its cozy fire and cheerier colors, she'd forgotten she'd be at the mercy of the other Ponies' company.

Sliding her proposal into a bottom drawer of Madam's desk, she turned in her chair and said, "Come in."

Sensa opened the door, her cheeks flushed and eyes bright from her last appointment. "Oh, hello, Angel. Where's Madam?"

Camille didn't have the energy to rebuke the pet name, nor did she have the interest in using Sensa's rather misleading stage name, Mistress. "Up in her apartments, I suspect. She has yet to come down. Did you need something?"

Sensa handed her a session file. "Lord Trager wishes to increase his visits from two times a week to three. I need to confer with my schedule before I give him an answer."

Already calculating the days in her mind, Camille nodded, pleased to have something else to occupy her thoughts. "There's an hour block of time on Thursday afternoons you can designate, between one and two."

"It's astounding how you can do that." Sensa smiled at her, a pretty expression it was a shame her 'character' wasn't allowed. "I'll let him know." She turned to leave but hesitated at the door.

"Yes?" Camille asked.

"Maybe you could help Victoria too. Mr. Richmund is here and going over his time."

Camille groaned. "Sonnets as awful as we remember?"

"Worse. He was likening her beauty to the purity and majesty of minx hide when I passed by," Sensa said. "I'd get Madam, but I have two clients waiting in the cursory room."

"And Victoria has Mr. White waiting." Camille stood, making a note to add more padding to the Ponies' schedules in the event of overtime play. "I'll encourage the gentleman to move along."

"Thank you." Sensa winked. "You're an angel, Angel."

Camille shooed her away and left for Victoria's wing.

Upon entering the Nest's viewing room, Camille had the

unfortunate opportunity to not only hear Mr. Richmund's inclinations towards Victoria's 'nurturing bosom of innocence,' but also the misfortune to see the man on his knees in nothing but his underclothes and top hat.

She tapped the glass three times in quick succession, Madam's normal call to reinforce house rules. Camille didn't miss Victoria's sigh of relief.

"Mr. Richmund, my mistress is calling me," Victoria said. "I do so hate to part ways, but I am needed."

Victoria's acting ability was astounding.

In her full bird garb, Victoria assisted the man with his shirt, coat, and standard blindfold and walked him from the room with a quick 'Thank you' mouthed in Camille's direction.

Camille sighed. "Men."

"I see what you mean about poetry."

She whirled to find Renard in the open doorway, his eyes on her.

It was another, less composed, woman whose unladylike squeal sounded. The same woman who bounded across the narrow room and flung her arms around his neck. And the same still, when she pressed a kiss to his lips with a smile wide enough to show all her teeth.

"You're here!"

His dazed expression cleared to one of amusement. "If I'd have known I'd be received so well, I'd have come sooner."

She glanced behind him at Victoria's smiling face as she passed with her blindfolded man.

Camille's eyes widened looking back at Renard's non-blindfolded face. "How did you get back here without an escort?"

Renard shrugged. "Madam has taken a liking to me, it seems."

"It would take a bag of gold and an invitation to St. James to ease her rein on the rules."

He smiled. "Did I mention I'm filthy rich and am in good standing with Her Majesty?"

She returned his smile. Maybe 'charming' wasn't so bad after all.

"You are pleased I'm here, then?" he asked.

Camille laughed. "Did my embarrassing loss of composure not give you a great enough clue as to my pleasure?"

"A man should not assume."

"You *are* learning." Her heart was flying. Ten days apart had torn her hopes and certainty to shreds. But a moment together and those doubts had vanished . . . for her. Joy dimming, Camille at last reined in her emotions and asked seriously, "Did you discover anything while in the country, Your Grace?"

"I never left London."

Camille's gaze locked on his contrite expression.

"I had every intention of going," he said. "But what you said, about thinking over our future, I couldn't *stop* thinking it over. I was so distraught that next morning I mounted my horse backwards."

He flushed at his confession. "Not wishing to risk running into a lake by mistake when I couldn't focus on the road, I stayed. I've contemplated every possible reason we can't be together. Status, family, fortune, disagreements over Shakespeare." He gazed down at her as if his epiphany had manifested between them. "All my doubts and concerns concluded in one simple answer."

Camille couldn't breathe. "Yes?"

His passionate expression slipped into that grin she loved so dearly. He offered her a brown parcel bag. "Here."

Startled, she took the bag without question, a familiar smell from her childhood bringing to mind a sunny day and a walk in the city. "A present?"

"No need to look suspicious. Open it."

She peeled open the bag and squealed, "You brought tarts!"

Not caring she had yet to eat luncheon with the girls, she bit into flaky crust and moaned as the tangy lemon curd sparked the nerves on her back teeth.

Renard chuckled. "Good?"

She took a second bite, not waiting to finish chewing before replying, "Better than any play ever written."

"They taste all right?"

Camille popped the last piece of crust into her mouth and frowned at his expectant expression. "Did they fall on the ground before you got here?"

"No!" His conviction was honest, but he shifted from foot to foot, quite a display for a composed gentleman.

Camille's eyes widened. "Did *you* bake that?"

His ears turned pink. "Not entirely. My cook instructed me on everything."

Camille didn't think the fluttering in her chest was normal. "You baked me tarts." She could kiss him for his thoughtfulness.

So she did.

He responded with enthusiasm, neatly plucking the bag from her hands and threading their now-empty fingers together as his tongue mimicked the action inside her mouth.

He pulled back after a thorough taste and said, "I should have brought more. Nine others, was it?"

His light teasing chased away the shadows and apprehension of last night. "Good sir, are you attempting to seduce me?"

"Is it working?"

She twined her arms around his neck. "The baking was exceptionally done."

He laughed. "Famished, are you? There's no way my cooking could reach exceptional. Tolerable at best. But I will do better next time."

"*Next time.*"

Camille's heart soared. There was no reason to fear. He'd all but said he'd stay with her. There'd been no promise of marriage or comfort, but she didn't need those. She had everything she truly needed here, in this precise moment. She wouldn't repeat her own history because things were different. *He* was different. And things had changed.

She smiled up at him and gave up all pretenses to place a hand on her belly. "Cravings are normal, the physician said."

The lighthearted and easy camaraderie between them vanished at his sudden intake of air.

When he did respond, it was not the warm joy she'd expected.

"You're with child?"

She nodded, waiting for his shock to pass. "It's early still, but the signs are present. The physician confirmed this morning." Syd had stayed outside on the roof, but a knowing look had crossed her young face before they'd parted ways outside the club.

Renard's expression grew darker. He ran a hand through his hair and began pacing with growing agitation. His hand snaked into his coat pocket as if reminding himself of something.

"Renard—"

"Not now."

The tone he used was sharp. Her hand fell away from her belly and a sinking feeling started from her chest to her abdomen.

He muttered to himself something that sounded dreadfully like, "Conniving, manipulative wench."

Camille's insides turned to lead. "You think I did this on purpose?"

He whirled on her. "What else do you expect me to think? You work in a pleasure house, for God's sake! Did you not think to take anything after to prevent unwanted surprises?"

"*Unwanted.*" The word ricocheted inside her chest like a bullet, its lead ball ripping her apart. Her words, when they came, were from a year ago, when a different duke had used the same word to describe her. "I expected you to believe I would never reveal anything that would compromise you or your family. What would I possibly have to gain?"

"Who knows? Women are always scheming to keep a man entangled."

"Entangled?" Camille saw the true panic on his face. He didn't trust her. He thought she'd intentionally become pregnant to keep him close. The knowledge struck her deep.

She stood from the table and kept her voice low so as to not disturb Victoria next door with Mr. White. "I have never asked anything of you. Not once. I made no demands and held no expectations because I knew reality is not as kind as the fantasies of dreamers." Her rage turned to frigid stone, as did her words. "But I suppose an assuming, arrogant dandy too self-important to take a shit without a valet's admiration of his skill could never understand that a woman could simply care with no more incentive than the warmth in her heart." She strode for the door, her final words following her even as the door clicked shut behind her. "Good day, Your Grace. I find I'm no longer interested in tarts—of any kind."

RENARD STARED AT the closed door.

What the hell had happened? He'd been set to profess himself like a besotted fool. How had this ended in a row? A row that felt damning to more than his idiotic manners.

He was angry. How could she let him go on about tarts when she should have told him about the baby first thing? The smile when she'd put her hand on her stomach . . .

He couldn't believe Camille would intentionally withhold something so important.

Truth was, he didn't believe it. Despite his idiocy, he knew women didn't know these things instantaneously. Hadn't she said the physician told her this morning? She hadn't withheld anything.

He cursed.

He'd accused her of attempting entanglement, but *he* had pursued her. She'd been an innocent when he'd taken advantage. Despite working for a notorious pleasure house, she may not have known what medicines to take to keep her womb infertile.

Who knew how much she interacted with the other girls? *He* was the one who'd camped out in the streets until she'd shown up, no doubt from a guilty conscience, to keep him from growing ill. And it was indeed he who'd bought the exorbitantly priced three-stone emerald necklace from the jeweler's on Bond Street on his way here, thinking the green coloring would flatter her complexion as the perfect betrothal piece. He patted his coat pocket again to make sure it was still there.

With child.

If he were honest with himself, he was overjoyed. His shoulders hunched with some invisible weight hearing he was to be a father, but there was lightness too, far more radiating through his body than any sense of responsibility could drag him down.

And he'd been seconds from dropping to his knees and begging her to marry him.

The new Duchess of Lux, heirs, and a little laughter were a future he wanted. He'd never allowed himself to hope for any of it. Even if he could extract the foot from his mouth and convince Camille to marry him, Mrs. Norris and her son could make a case of illegitimacy and say his child wasn't well-bred enough to inherit the title and estate.

"Simply care with nothing more than the warmth of her heart."

Renard shot out the door after her, his temper redirecting its fiery scolding inwards.

Hang the title!

The woman he loved was pregnant with his child. More miraculous, she wanted him back. Instead of professing his affections, he'd driven her away. The timing was sooner than he'd expected, but surprise over her announcement was no reason to lose his head.

Not when all he'd wanted to do was to confess he'd gone and thoroughly lost his heart. She had a head start and a firm knowledge of the area, which left him at a clear disadvantage. His Milly could be anywhere by now.

God damn, he was a fool.

CHAPTER SEVENTEEN

C AMILLE WAS NOWHERE to be found. After scouring the club, before he was kindly reminded his access was a privilege and not a right by a large woman in a toga, he'd raced to Camille's flat in St. Giles, only to be turned away by a balding man by the name of Mr. Rockford, who said Miss Forthright had yet to return home.

Less than a quarter hour later, Renard was back in the main office of the Prodding Pony, his mind and purpose clear after the vigor of his hunt.

"Whatever her debt, I'll pay it," Renard said.

Madam watched him from the other side of her desk, her gaze on a document written in a delicate hand. "There's no debt."

"What do you mean? You must have something over her for her to stay here." He doubted Camille would take kindly to him interfering, but she need not know his involvement. If she were to choose him, he wanted it to be her own decision, without any financial need to force her hand.

"This is not a prison, Your Grace," Madam said. "While the circumstances that bring my girls here may be demanding, indeed, I am not their jailor. They may leave when they please."

Renard hadn't expected the woman's harsh tone. The woman meant it; she didn't keep her girls like so many of the pleasure houses who demanded unreasonable control over women in already poor conditions.

Then why did Camille stay here? Surely, a woman as bright and educated as her could pass for a schoolteacher or a nurse in the lower income areas of town.

Which meant there was more than security on the line.

Renard frowned. Debt of another kind. Collectors, family—she needed money and fast to keep someone at bay. He'd be damned if he let his son or daughter be at the mercy of the slums and the lowlives who took advantage of those already disadvantaged.

"Do you know the names of the creditors she owes?" he asked.

Madam's eyes widened, then crinkled with an amused smile spreading her mouth. "I know of some, the more persistent ones who have called on the house when they believed, wrongly, that payment was due."

He heard venom in her voice. "You turned them away?"

"This is a house of pleasure away from reality. I informed the creditors they were not welcome unless it was them who offered a sum." Madam's smile remained, but it looked anything but friendly. "Then I asked them to leave."

"Like I was asked to leave?" Renard still couldn't sit on his backside for any length of period after being tossed into the streets.

"Just so."

Good, he thought. His bruised bum aside, any fears he had over Camille's involvement in the club were assuaged by Madam's candidness. She was a fierce and exacting woman, if the stories he'd heard at White's were any indication, but that fierceness extended to loyalty to her girls.

Meaning, the older woman had more than cold calculation beating in her chest.

He set a stack of notes on the desk between them. "Compensation for the names, then," he said. "And a promise to not interfere if the lady wishes to leave your employment after her debts are settled."

Madam leaned back in her chair, her brow cocked. "I do not speak for the lady. Her business means her names to give."

"You will not bargain with me?"

"I never said that." That calculating look was back. "I do not dither in simple coin, Your Grace."

"What do you want?"

"I trade in secrets."

His gaze narrowed. "You mean leverage?"

She smiled as if to repeat, "Just so." Her hand waved towards the door and the streets outside. "I am a businesswoman in a world of men. Money is parted with and exchanged like water between fish. My currency keeps the most powerful men in England indebted to me and this club."

Security. Renard's gut twisted. The woman had a point, and a devil's instinct. Her associates had no doubt returned with little in the way of blackmail material to use against him in case of his membership. A woman like Madam wouldn't be satisfied with a paltry confession that the Duke of Lux liked to leave the house with his stockings un-ironed. He was a man of his word, and he lived by the philosophy of truth above all, except in one instance.

Darkness, pitch black and all consuming, rose from his very soul, a whisper of ruin that begged to be set free after years of suffering in silence.

He did not hesitate. "Very well." Renard swallowed down acid in his throat. For Camille, he would do this. For his son or daughter, he'd find Camille and marry her immediately. That idiot cousin, Norris, could make his life difficult regarding the title, but Renard *would* protect his family. Somehow. If he had to beg his friend, the Duke of Camine, for a place as a tenant on his estate, he'd learn how to milk a cow or till a field.

He would admit to his sins and suffer the risk of ridicule and possible imprisonment. He would need to set out immediately to find prospects for his sister, Charlotte, before his guilt was made public when there'd be no chance of settlement. He'd find her a husband, someone who'd weather the scandal and give her the family and status she deserved.

He raised his chin and looked at Madam directly. "May I ask a boon?"

Madam merely blinked.

"I need two weeks before you use this information to your advantage." He licked suddenly dry lips. "So I may put affairs in order."

Madam leaned forward in her chair, clearly more interested than her blank expression implied. "The Pony does not release information on a whim, Your Grace. If your currency is as damning as you suggest, you have my word. I will not reveal it without just cause."

"Thank you." Renard released his breath, but relief did not come. There'd never been anything but twisted self-loathing and responsibility since that afternoon, and a hope he could one day let the past rest in peace. But for Camille, he'd bleed the darkness from his soul, inflicted when flame and despair had eaten the very sunshine from the sky.

"The fire at Lux estate when I was a boy was set deliberately," he said.

He turned his heart to stone and offered up himself as a sacrifice to hell, knowing heaven would never take him.

"*I* killed my parents."

"I'M SENDING YOU on an errand." Madam handed Camille an embossed envelope from behind her desk, her focus remaining on the stack of files in front of her. "You leave tomorrow."

Camille opened the sleeve and pulled out an invitation, her name sweeping across the gold cardstock in black calligraphy. How official and proper her name looked. She could almost imagine it was an invitation to some grand ball, some debutante's debut. A duke's sister, perhaps. The invitation shook in her hand as an ache pulsed in her chest, knowing her name would never be proper. *She* would never be proper. Clenching her jaw, she noted the location of the party and looked up, brows drawn. "This is to an estate in the country."

"Lord and Lady Quickner are patrons of the Pony, silent benefactors. I need you to retrieve this year's contribution."

"You want me to attend a garden party?" Camille glanced down at the details. "It starts tomorrow! Why not wait until the couple arrives in town?"

Madam's normally direct gaze cast wide, seeming unable to meet Camille's. "The viscount and viscountess enjoy their . . . *privacy* away from town. They are unlikely to return anytime soon, and the club doesn't run on credit."

'Privacy' meant one thing: They enjoyed scandalous bed sport like the rest of the Pony's patrons. Camille wouldn't think of what kind they enjoyed if they needed to stay out of society to keep it quiet. "Wouldn't it be less risky for me to wait until after their guests have departed?" Her brain lighted on the most likely scenario. "The guests are part of the cover." She knew exactly what kind of bed sport the Quickners partook in.

"Very good, Angel." Madam waved her off. "These are important clients; I expect civility and a respectful innocence on your part."

"I'm not one of your Ponies. I've no intention of acting like anything I'm not."

"You should learn." Madam's lecturing tone made its hourly appearance. "There are all kinds of ways to gain status and connections. Stubbornness and admirable scruples are one." She inclined her head in acknowledgment of Camille's character, but her expression was facetious. "'Course, you'll find a module of flattery clears the field more readily than sharp observations."

Camille shook her head. "This should wait until Victoria can go."

"Why are you making excuses? This is a simple task, one you've done before." Madam's tone hardened. "Or is three days too much time away from a certain gentleman?"

Camille fought against another pang wrenching through her chest. She wouldn't think of Renard. He'd turned out to be everything she thought he'd be.

Camille's gaze narrowed. Her mind combined the other woman's shifting gaze and impatient tone. "You're separating us on purpose. *You* were the one who encouraged a liaison."

"I did."

Camille didn't miss how Madam's right hand stalled on flipping the new file open, only for her left hand to take over.

She must have known about their fight. Victoria needed only mention the Duke of Lux had left alone after their too-brief visit and the older woman would have connected the pieces together like a spider weaving her web. But that didn't change the unlikely timing of this 'errand.' Suspicion laced her next words. "Something has happened."

"You are paranoid." Madam fanned out her fingers on one hand to admire her nails.

"And you're a terrible liar."

Madam grinned at that, finally looking Camille in the eye. "You are the only one who sees it."

"You have a tell." Camille nodded to the woman's hand. "You fiddle with your left hand when you lie, never your right."

Madam looked down at her offending hand on the surface of the desk and curled the fingers into a fist. She relaxed her fist and hid both hands in her skirts. "You are extraordinary, Angel."

Camille didn't take the compliment. "What has happened?" Her stomach soured. "Another body?"

"No, no. Nothing like that. Sit down," Madam said. "You look pale as death."

Camille was relieved to hear of no more bodies in the streets, but she sat anyway, her feet swollen and her energy waning of late as her body refused anything except water for the baby growing in her womb. *Another* topic she loathed to discuss with the woman sitting across from her.

In due time, she told herself. While her baggy and shapeless dresses could hide her condition, she'd continue as if nothing had changed. She'd work for what needed doing up until the moment of birth. Gaining donations, renting suitable apartments, calling in favors . . . If she worked hard and was uncharacteristically lucky, Camille would be the first to person to benefit from the generosity of Miss Forthright's House for Female Companions. If she had to use Madam's alleged ledger of secrets to blackmail every sick bastard who darkened the Pony's door, she'd do it. For her baby, she'd do anything.

And to do that, she needed to keep Madam happy.

Camille placed the invitation in her skirt pocket. "I'll leave tomorrow morning."

Madam nodded. "Good. Come here, to the club, before you go. I'll arrange transportation and proper attire."

The mention of attire made Camille wince at her current worn ensemble. She'd never gotten a chance to peruse the ready-made shop. Not that a mass-produced dress wouldn't stick out like a weed in the rosebush.

Camille cringed. At the mercy of proper ladies. Even in the less formal setting of the country, she'd never fit in. Three days would be an eternity without a single woman to talk to who'd understand her circumstances.

Camille brightened. "I have a favor to ask."

Madam startled. "A favor?" She recovered with a knowing smile. "An official one?"

Camille rolled her eyes. "You may subtract one of the favors you owe me if you can arrange the letter arrives to its destination today."

Madam couldn't hide her interest. "A letter? To whom?"

Camille hesitated. No matter what would happen between her and Renard, she had no real right to interfere with his life or family. But the desire, the need to reach out, wouldn't abate, and it hadn't since the first time Renard had mentioned his sister.

Camille reasoned, it wasn't really *she* who would reach out anyway. *Diana* was a warrior's name, a strong name of a woman who didn't back down, and Camille needed all the strength she could muster to spit in etiquette's face and force an introduction.

She pressed a fresh sheet of parchment to the desktop. "I need you to send a letter to a lady."

Dipping the quill in the ink blot, she marked the return address care of the bakery off Fleet Street, though the place had been out of business for some time. Boarded up except for a neat trap door only a handful knew about, the storefront was one of the Merry Men's safehouses and any mail addressed to Camille would go straight to the Cock 'n Hen tavern.

She penned the intended recipient's name, a sense of rightness settling over her.

To The Lady Charlotte Louis:

Camille tried out the name before she wrote. "My name is Diana . . ."

She bit her lip and wracked her brain for a surname. Smith? Wilkenson? Every name sounded like a governess with a hooked nose, and Camille knew how much the lady loved those.

Camille glanced around the room, her gaze falling on the chair by the fire, a pillow embroidered with a fat, striped bee across the front. She smiled at the harmless image and wrote her opening greeting.

My name is Diana Yamsbee, and I hear you are a woman in great need of an adventure . . .

CHAPTER EIGHTEEN

C AMILLE HAD RIDDEN in a proper carriage twice in her life. The first at the age of ten, on a day of many firsts and with uncommon joy. The second had not been so joyous, nor as long in duration. Despite her impeccable memory, the devastation of that night had been over in an instant, the carriage ride being the highlight of the evening.

She settled into her third and, hopefully, second-to-last ride upon her exit from London. Madam's personal victoria was too fashionable and ridiculous to take the entire twelve miles into the country. But a representative of the Pony must arrive in style, and Madam's usual closed carriage was needed in case of emergency, and discretion.

The passing of industrial buildings into dust-covered road and green grass was disconcerting. She'd spent her entire life surrounded by the grey smog and cold stone of the city. The open horizon with its blue skies and untouched beading of morning dew over the road left her exposed in a manner she rarely allowed. No wonder highwaymen were so successful. Without the continuous oppressive presence of smoke and people, one could quite easily fall into peaceful complacency.

At least the incessant bumps from the cobblestone streets had lessened to an occasional terror of a dip in the road. Camille was grateful for the driver's calm demeanor and seeming expert hand, but at this slow trot, they'd make the Quickners' country seat well after dinner. If Camille were a more suspicious person, she'd say Madam had deliberately slowed her pace to keep her away.

But she *was* suspicious, and the older woman had been hiding something.

One of the wheels bounced over a divot in the road, which Camille felt from tailbone to jaw. *Stupid, worthless,* clean *roads.* Too much more jostling and she may be sick.

"You all right back there, miss?" the driver asked.

Camille smoothed her skirts, the ridiculously starched monstrosity Madam had forced her into, and called up her affirmation.

"With the fine weather, we'll be there in no time," he said. "Not to worry."

Camille wouldn't pout. Even if the driver's good-natured optimism grated. Especially as her only view of the man revealed fair curls escaping his hat. Not interested in any reminders of Renard and how they'd parted ways, she forced her attention back to the picturesque scenery and went over Madam's instructions for her meeting with Lord and Lady Quickner.

"Upon arrival, you will introduce yourself as an ambassador of the club. No word or discussion of business will be allowed until the following evening. You are to take your meals in your room until that time. When Lord Quickner invites you to discuss business, you will decline. When he invites you to the nightly festivities, you will decline. Wait until Lady Quickner approaches you. You will exchange one envelope for another and make your departure." At which time, Madam had handed Camille a crisp envelope.

Camille had scoffed at the ridiculousness of it all, making the mistake of asking why she couldn't go to the lady of the house first thing and offer the letter so she wouldn't need to suffer the festivities at all.

Whip in hand for its monthly oiling—an orchestrated ploy used for intimidation—Madam had smacked her palm with a nasty *crack* before replacing the leather rod to its rightful place, successfully ending the discussion.

"Are you going to ignore me the entire way?"

Camille eyed her allotted and wildly inappropriate 'chaperone' and the startling transformation from gang leader to young woman. "You told me not to look at you."

Syd picked at her finery, having protested more emphatically than Camille when Madam had demanded they change into presentable outfits. Nevertheless, the younger woman wore the mauve, satin dress with an innate grace Camille could never duplicate.

"I didn't appreciate the staring, considering you look far sillier than I and won't stop fidgeting," Syd said.

Noting how she absently played with the lace at her collar, Camille dropped her hand. The rules she'd inherited since birth had never come easily. While she never forgot a single ridicule of her manner, her body had always worked independently from her mind when stressed.

"You gonna tell me why we were sent out on this embarrassing errand, anyway?" Syd asked.

"You didn't have to tag along."

"Sha-dow," Syd stressed. "Hawkins is still unaccounted for; I'll see this job through till the end."

Neither of them voiced the thought that Hawkins would show up soon, probably face-down in the Thames.

Camille pasted on a smile and backtracked. "Most women would call the opportunity to dress well and mingle with the peerage a novelty."

Syd snorted. "Most women have boring lives. Any chance they'll turn me away, seeing as I am without invitation?"

"As I am an unmarried woman, Lord and Lady Quickner will assume I have a chaperone." She smirked at Syd's disappointment. "I'll introduce you as my married cousin to make your younger age more acceptable."

"*A good girl introduces mutual acquaintances with care: a commoner to a lord, a woman to a man, inferior to superior.*"

Camille never imagined she'd be grateful for the years of

etiquette drilled into her by her mother.

"A refugee from Ireland sharing the same table as the elite?" Syd said. "Talk about novelty. What excuse did you give your lover for leaving?"

The horses veered suddenly—most likely from another insufferable pothole—and Camille locked up her response behind clenched teeth until the victoria had settled back into a smooth pace.

She glanced at the driver's stiff shoulders and whispered at Syd, "Keep your voice down."

Syd rolled her eyes but lowered her voice. "Like our driver cares. He was probably hired by Madam just like everyone else."

"Not everyone need know my business with Renard."

"'Renard,' is it?"

"Don't look at me like that, *Sydney Laundry*. Where does Scarlet think you are right now?"

Syd shrugged. "I told Pops the game. That's good enough. And don't change the subject. What did *Renard* say when you told him you were leaving?"

"I didn't."

Her smug expression pinched.

"For the love of—we are not wed. I may come and go as I wish."

Syd shook her head. "After all the rain he suffered through to get your attention."

"Whose side are you on?"

"Yours." Syd didn't hesitate. "Which is why I'm telling you the man is perfect for you."

"Ridiculous. He's a gentleman, a duke, a complete and utter idiot, and I'm . . . me."

"He did seem to notice that last part."

"You've suffered too many blows to the head if you believe such blindness is acceptable to the *ton*."

"I never thought I'd see you run from a fight."

"I'm not running."

Syd looked back out at the scenery. "If you say so."

Syd's words drew up images of Renard and the severity of their last argument. He hadn't said a word about the baby. Racking her brain, she had no idea why he'd gotten so angry. Gentlemen were notorious for siring illegitimate children with mistresses. Was he afraid she'd keep him from a proper marriage?

Rutting arse! The debutantes could have at him. She'd told him because a child changed their relationship, if only linking them in a way previously absent. Most bastards were carted off to orphanages so as not to impede a dalliance with a rich man. But Camille's ambitions had never strayed towards that life. She'd thought Renard would see a child differently. The way he'd spoken of his sister, she'd seen his compassion and familial ties. She hadn't gone and foolishly fallen for an unattainable man. Good thing too. Accusing her of trapping him! Idiot man. She wouldn't have him if he begged on his knees. Her heart was intact, her thoughts clear. The painful tearing in her chest was from her condition and nothing more.

AFTER BEING TURNED away from Camille's home once again by the fine-whiskered Mr. Rockford, then hearing from the Madam that Camille had left London for a few days—and refused to tell him exactly where she'd gone—Renard knew sitting idle would do no one any good. He left a letter with the Amazonian at the Pony for Camille, explaining his departure from London and the necessity to check in on his sister in the country. He wished he could have offered the information in person, along with a heartfelt apology.

His knuckles tightened around his horse's reins. He wanted their child. He wanted everything! If the strength of language in his missive—likening himself to the worst and smelliest parts of a particular barn animal—didn't express his disdain for his actions properly, he'd make his feelings clear when he returned.

Somehow, he'd convince Camille to marry him. If he had to offer up what black cinders remained of his soul, she had but to ask. He'd confess everything, his past, his impending fall from society. There was hardly more he could do to claim his child's legitimacy when he'd be stripped of far more than his title. If Camille never wished to see him again, it would all be worth her disgust if she but agreed to be cared for somewhere safe and comfortable in the country. He'd find a suitable house with a secluded wing to house her mother, keeping that shrill and haunting voice from interfering until Camille's condition was over.

Renard spurred his horse faster, the Lux estate coming into view over the ridge. He placed his plans for Camille and the baby aside. First, he'd sit down with Charlotte and covertly gain insight into her desires for a husband. He'd find her someone suitable and have a marriage contract secured by the end of the week. His sister's only chance of happiness with a respectable man of title had to be before the news broke.

He congratulated himself on his stupid luck for finding the most impossible women to dedicate his short life to. Maybe the two women would strike up a friendship while commiserating over the Louis name's stain.

He shook himself to task: find Charlotte a husband, marry Camille, secure both their futures before the noose. Let that horrid Mrs. Norris and her son claim the title. There were more important things than status or wealth.

Two weeks, he told himself. He'd make it all happen in two weeks come hell or incarceration.

"WHAT DO YOU mean?" Renard asked.

His housekeeper's pinched expression was one of disapproval

he knew too well, usually from a lady he knew better.

"Lady Charlotte has gone to attend the Quickners' garden party, Your Grace."

"Where's Mrs. Chiselhurst?" He'd paid the chaperone a small fortune.

"Quit last week. My letter did mention your visit was a matter of urgency."

"Of all the—" Renard brandished the party's invitation between them, ready to storm Lord and Lady Quickner's estate and drag his sister home by the bustle. "The party is a two-day affair. Does she plan to spend the evening there?"

"I do believe that was her intention. She packed a small trunk and reticule."

Renard did indeed go for his horse then, fully prepared to make an utter fool of himself to save his sister's reputation. Of all the times for his sister to take an interest in mingling and forgo the rules of society when he needed to secure a match based on her pristine reputation—fate wasn't done interfering yet, it seemed.

Lord Quickner's property was another six miles west of Lux estate, the only other neighboring property aside from Camine Manor. He glanced at the fading sun in the direction he must travel. If he rode like the Devil, he'd be there before nightfall.

"Your Grace." His housekeeper stopped him before he could mount his stallion. "If you wish to smooth the ripples of Lady Charlotte's actions, might I suggest a fresh shirt and coat?"

Renard looked down at his dust-coated ensemble, filthy from his haste to make it to the estate before dinner. Panic and anger made way for practicality.

He offered his horse's reins to a stableboy with an order to brush and feed the poor animal in the twenty minutes it would take for him to wash and dress for a party. At least he and Charlotte would have the proper family carriage for the journey home.

Making for the house, Renard kept his gaze from wandering

to the stables themselves.

Renard avoided the country for good reason. Upon setting foot back on his family's ancestral grounds, the memories and guilt pressed down on him tenfold, until the simple act of standing became unbearable.

But he'd stand, ride, *run* wherever he damned well needed to find and return his sister where it was proper and safe. He'd expected his usual soft-spoken sister to be working quietly in the drawing room with a new species of insect.

His pleasure at her showing an interest in more than her entomological machinations for her chaperones and their staff was subdued by cautionary feelings over whatever had prompted her to leave the estate, unchaperoned of all things.

Women! They were maddening and completely . . . Renard smiled to himself, his thoughts trailing off on the word that should have infuriated him. But he'd learned *unexpected* pleasures came from unexpected places.

Entering his chambers, Renard stripped off his soiled clothing and washed the dust from his body the best he could with the pitcher of water one of his footmen brought in.

What a pair of women he had in his life: one fiery and passionate, the other kind and troublesome. Despite the impending flurry of action he must take to settle both Camille's and Charlotte's futures, Renard appreciated a moment of contentment. There was no doubt the women would get along. With a baby, whatever unpleasantries that followed his downfall would be lessened by the joy of laughter, a sound severely lacking in this family these past eight years.

He'd accepted his penance would be to never hear his child's voice or see to it there were siblings with which to play.

A knock on the door preceded the footman's voice. "As your valet has yet to arrive, Your Grace, if I may be of service, I can help you dress?"

Renard scrubbed the dust from his face, reaffirmed in his resolve. "Come in. I'm ready."

CHAPTER NINETEEN

"W HERE ARE YOU going?" Syd asked from the four-poster bed they were to share for the duration of their stay.

The bed that was as big as Camille's two-bedroom flat.

Controlling her jaw to keep it from dropping at every gilded surface and brushed oil on the wall, Camille secured her—Madam's—dressing gown around herself, forgoing the chaos of attempting to put back on that monstrous dress with its buttons and lacing that had taken Lady Quickner's maid fifteen minutes to navigate.

"I'm hungry," Camille said, door handle in hand. "Want anything?"

"Why not ring the bell? Madam said to keep to our rooms when the sun went down."

"Madam didn't take into account my *chaperone* would eat my entire supper before I had finished undressing." Truth was, Camille needed to stretch her legs after sitting in that carriage.

Syd winced. "The jellied yams were too good to stop."

"Shall I bring back the vat, then?"

"You know me well."

Camille rolled her eyes and slipped from the room. The sun had gone down, and Madam's warnings whispered through her head as she traversed deserted hall after hall and down a back staircase she assumed led to the kitchens.

When she hit an invisible wall of warm air, she knew she'd

chosen correctly.

The Quickners' kitchens were as opulent as the rest of the house, as the viscount and viscountess themselves. Stepping from the victoria—well past the courtesy of arriving the appropriate fifteen minutes before dinner—she'd been welcomed by an older couple in matching lavender robes, the golden threads swirling around the floral, printed fabric looking like the threads of fate. It had been a shock to realize the couple was actually the viscount and viscountess and not the expected low-level servants.

The kitchens too were wallpapered and pristine, all in matching floral print. A single lamp had been lit, highlighting a large tray of cold meats and fruit on the cook's block, as if waiting for late-night visitors.

Camille glanced around. Finding herself alone, she picked herself a fine array of meat and grapes and divided it between two plates.

"Seems I'm not the only late-night eater."

Camille whirled around to find Lord Quickner watching her from a chair in the dark corner, his robed body near indiscernible from the surrounding wallpaper. He uncrossed his legs and stood. His robe gaped in front, revealing naked skin of a surprisingly muscled chest.

Blood racing, she subtly turned to face him, consciously placing the table between them, Madam's *other* warning making her uncomfortably aware of the deserted halls.

"*When Lord Quickner invites you to the festivities, you will decline.*"

Camille edged around the table in the direction of the stairs. "Apologies, Lord Quickner. I'm aware I should have used the bell instead of giving in to restlessness. I am not interested in your advances, so"—she picked up the plate—"if you'll excuse me. I will return to my room."

He leaned into the light, his eyes dancing. "No need for concern, my dear. I am not lying in wait to ravish some unsuspecting party." He smiled. "Unless they ask me to."

Camille had heard enough lies in her life to recognize the truth when spoken. She set down the plates, thoroughly chastised. "Forgive me, my lord. That was unfair of me just now. I hope you didn't take offense?"

"Not at all, Miss Forthright. I appreciate a woman who is so delightfully . . . *forthright*."

Camille smirked at the man's joke, feeling an odd sense of comfort in the older man's company, like what she suspected a grandfather might be like.

"And for being such a good sport and laughing at an old man's bad jest, I'll share my guilty pleasure with you." Lord Quickner beckoned her towards a small pot on the range, his eyes brightening with mischief. He lifted the lid, and the sweetest smell cut through the lingering smoky air that plagued all kitchens.

"Is that cocoa?"

"Do you fancy a cup?"

"I've never had it before. Is it better than tarts?"

Lord Quickner laughed. "Nothing is better than tarts, but this comes close." He ladled a spoonful into a cup and handed it to her. "Careful it doesn't burn your tongue."

Camille took a sip and came dangerously close to moaning. "That's sinful."

Lord Quickner plucked the cup from her hand and ladled two more spoonfuls, earning her eternal love.

"Thank you."

"You're welcome, my dear. Now, if you're interested in a more daring venture, there's a lovely game—"

"I'm not interested in any poking or prodding."

He *tsked* at her, his smile warm. "I was inviting you to a bit of archery for tomorrow's lawn game. What a perverted mind you have, Miss Forthright." He sounded delighted. "I promise, the only prodding will be with the proper equipment at intended targets."

"Nothing you said makes it sound any less filthy."

Lord Quickner hooted. "What a gem you are. Clarice called you an angel. I'm so very pleased to disagree."

"You know Madam well?"

"Going on near . . . thirty years! What a most unpleasant realization. I do believe that makes me properly old."

Thoughts of Renard baking tarts came unbidden. She pushed the thought away and said honestly, "I'll take a distinguished man who knows the worth of cocoa over some puppy any day."

A feline smile took those thirty years off a still-handsome fifty-year-old face. "Now you've done it, Miss Forthright. I do believe you have renewed this old body's youthful vigor. I insist you join me for archery tomorrow."

Camille hesitated. Conversing with a houseful of aristocratic party guests sounded like a good way to *become* the target. If any of the partygoers connected her name with the article from six months ago . . .

That mischievous glint in Lord Quickner's eye was back. "I'll have Cook set aside a tray of tarts just for you."

Knowing Syd would kill her if she refused, Camille laughed. "Done."

➤➤➤◄◄◄

CAMILLE DECIDED TO take a more direct route through the main house, her plundered plates in hand, when she came to the main staircase and felt an invisible tug that had her turning towards the foyer.

She glanced over her shoulder to see a young man arriving, his relinquished hat revealing fair hair.

The man waved away the butler's attempts to escort him through the house and took long strides towards the hall that led to the library. He stopped suddenly, and that invisible bond seemed to claim him as well. He turned.

Their eyes met, and Camille felt her body jolt with awareness.

Renard's eyes widened. "Camille?"

He crossed the foyer, moving around the massive center table, two chairs, and three busts of Lord Quickner's ancestors as if she'd vanish before his eyes. Stopping before her, his wide eyes looked like he refused to blink for the same reason.

"What are you doing here?" he asked. "You're supposed to be in London."

Camille's body shuddered at his nearness. It took more will than she cared to admit not to toss the plate of food and throw her arms around him like she had the last time they'd spoken. Reminder of their argument had her squaring her shoulders and a harder edge sounding in her voice. "I'm working. *You* were supposed to be in London."

"Working? Good God, Lord and Lady Quickner are patrons?" He ran a hand through his hair, strands damp from a recent bath. "I have to find Charlotte immediately."

Camille startled and glanced around as if the lady would materialize any second. "Lady Charlotte is *here*? Why?" Though she had a suspicion a particular letter had something to do with it.

"I'd like an answer to that myself. To think of my sister in any social gathering is unprecedented. To think she'd come here with these kind of people is downright suspicious timing." He took her by the arm and pulled her towards an alcove half-hidden behind a bust of what had to be Lord Quickner's ancestor with a marbled chest.

"More importantly," Renard said, "you shouldn't be anywhere near these people, either. Go pack your bags, and I will escort you back to Lux Manor."

Camille pulled her arm free, his demanding tone making her dig her heels in. "I am here on business. I can't just leave."

"Certainly you can. Whatever matters Madam Clarice needs resolved, I shall do in your stead. I daresay, I can handle a gentleman's agreement far better than a woman."

Camille stared. Of all the arrogant, chauvinistic . . . "No."

"No?"

"That's what I said."

His brows furrowed. "You can't tell me 'no.'"

Camille laughed, a better reaction than throwing one of Lord Quickner's ancestral busts at his person. They did look expensive. Throwing the plate in her hand was more out of the question. Syd really would kill her for wasting food.

Camille threw daggers with her gaze instead. "Did you go and hit your head on the ride here, Your Grace? You *must* have suffered a head injury to believe I would let you dictate to me anything about where I go and what I do."

Expression hardening, his voice turned to steel. "It is more than your safety that needs worrying about."

Worry. Camille stilled, hope kindling. "I thought you didn't want this baby?"

"Damn it, Milly. That's not what I said."

Something in her chest loosened, only to tighten with renewed anger. "No, you said I was trying to trap you!"

"I know! I'm an idiot, what else can I say? I handled the news about the baby badly." At her glare, he amended, "I took it like an ass! A rutting, stupid ass. I'd never considered you'd be with child. I was so blissfully ignorant, I expected everything to fall in line at the right time like the pompous ass I am. When you told me, I was shocked, angry. I actually thought, 'How could the world not obey my wishes?' But I was never unhappy about the news." He took her free hand in his. "I would love any child I had with you." He pressed his forehead to hers, and she let him. "I'm sorry."

Camille's heart soared even as she pulled back. "You hurt me." She clung to her anger like a shield. "This relationship is impossible as it is. If there's no trust, then there's nothing left between us."

He reached for her, his expression pained, only for his hand to drop away, as if he knew his touch wasn't what she wanted right now. "Please," he said. "Please give me another chance. I won't fail you again. I won't fail *any* of us again."

Mention of their child had the last of her anger melting away. That didn't change the fact that her memory was long.

"Words don't mean anything without actions to back them up," she said. She wouldn't forgive him. Not yet.

"I know."

The grandfather clock chimed the late hour from the hall.

Renard glanced at the time. "I must find my sister and make sure she is safe." His attention returned and he took her hand once again. "I want to make this work, Milly. Please, tell me, we can start again?"

Camille didn't fight the hope rising in her this time, but she didn't accept his apology outright. "Take care of your sister. We'll talk tomorrow."

He nodded, his expression fallen though his voice was determined. "Tomorrow." He looked towards the stairs, seeming at a loss.

Camille took pity on him. Confusion over their relationship was no reason to put a lady at risk. "Check with a housemaid," she said. "They will know which room is hers and if she's supped." She hoped someone had informed his sister to steer clear of the back gardens until dawn.

Renard's gaze went to the balcony doors, where a beckoning light in the distance revealed the night's festivities had already begun. "I can't imagine what Lord and Lady Quickner are thinking, inviting innocents while they gallivant like witches in the dark? Anyone could stumble upon them."

Camille's tone was dry. "I do believe the risk of being caught is part of their pleasure. And innocence . . . that is willingly given."

"You mean proper ladies join in when they find out? But the idea that any of them would find pleasure is more than unlikely."

Camille had shared his horror the first time she'd heard such a thing. To think of individuals enjoying what was supposed to be sacred between a man and a woman in a group where any number of pairs and trios may go off together. But then again, no one invited was underage and only consenting adults were encouraged to join, or watch. And Lord Quickner had seemed more than a decent man, for a viscount.

"Is it so surprising the sheltered succumb to temptation when they have been given no education? Ladies are shamed into thinking they are to know nothing of their own bodies until a husband comes along, and then it becomes *his*."

Renard turned to her, his color high. "I never said I agreed with the idiocy of society, but *my sister* has lived more than a simple 'sheltered life.' I'm not sure she's spoken to another peer since we were children. She may not understand the innuendo of an invitation to such . . . such . . ."

"Indecency? Fun? I must say, the red in your face brings out the green flecks in your vest."

"This is serious, Milly."

The comfort of their usual banter had her blurting out, "I've missed you." His eyes widened as he mirrored her own surprise at the confession. Taking her words as encouragement, he said, "Meet me in the garden tomorrow morning. Please." He smirked. "Preferably when the 'festivities' are well over."

"Squeamish, Your Grace? All those legs and mouths and hands—"

"You tease, my dear." His boyish grin made her heart flutter. "I am no prude, but I found I like living under a code of pleasure: one woman. It was what my parents had, and what I want."

"One woman at a time only?" She'd heard plenty of stories of young men gallivanting through London and testing the limits of brothels with multiple partners at once, the 'rogue' Duke of Lux being one of them. "Now who's talking unlikeliness?"

"Not *at a time*." He leaned down and whispered in her ear, "I meant, one woman for life." His gaze flicked towards the second level and back.

To stay and fight to win her affection or go save the sister he'd always looked after; she saw the indecision in his eyes. No one had ever fought *for* her.

"Go," she said.

Camille stood there for a long time after he'd gone in search of a housemaid, his absence up the stairs like a string growing taut between them.

A string that Camille suspected, if she looked inward, would be knotted to the heart in her chest.

THERE'D BEEN NO time that next morning to meet in the garden. After confirming his sister was indeed in her room and safe—though not from an epic lecture from her older brother—and seemingly ignorant of the party's actual purpose, Renard had laid his head on the pillow but a moment before a crashing sound echoed through the manor.

For prurient nobles who prowled the nighttime for group fun, they were surprisingly lively for ten in the morning—and their servants were quite adept with a larger-than-necessary dinner gong.

Renard stood in Lord Quickner's side lawn with the rest of the party. With the dozens of guests milling about in their striped dresses and coats, his neck and eyes strained for a glimpse of fiery hair in the unending sea of lines.

She'd been like a phantom last night, standing at the bottom of the stairs, looking domestic and lovely in a silk dressing gown with a tray of snacks in her hand. How he'd wanted to wrap her in his arms and take her on those stairs, her hair spilling down around her shoulders, and eat those snacks off her naked body.

Of all places for Madam to send her, it was fate once again, he decided. The emerald necklace was packed away in the small trunk at the foot of the bed for guest use. With a bit more of fate's hand, he'd give it to her and then secure both her and Charlotte's futures today.

"Looking for someone, Your Grace?"

Renard bowed his head to the lady of the house. "Admiring

the grounds, Lady Quickner. They are well maintained."

"Lord Quickner will be glad to hear it." The lady snapped her fan closed and tapped him playfully on the shoulder. Blue eyes flashing, the color matched perfectly with her silk kimono and the look of mischief on her aged but fair face. "But you were looking for something else, or some*one*. No use denying it! A woman knows."

Renard eyed the lady with growing apprehension. Women were terrifying creatures. A man may do serious harm to himself and his reputation by underestimating their powers of perception.

He turned on the charm and gave the woman a conspiratorial grin. "Don't tell anyone my secret."

Her fan clicked open in her burst of triumph. "A budding romance. I knew it!" She nodded approvingly. "It's good of you to confide in me. None of these other young men will tell me anything. Think I'm a meddler or something equally hurtful." She pouted. "As if a grown woman of five—" she cleared her throat. "Four and six would be at all interested in their shallow liaisons."

Renard smiled at that. He supposed his sex wasn't entirely hopeless. A flash of red hair over the lady's shoulder had his heart skipping. He scowled at the crowd between him and Camille. Getting her alone now would take near divine intervention . . . or an experienced woman used to slipping away. He was awfully glad Lady Quickner had decided to meddle.

He walked a few paces, pressing lightly on Lady Quickner's elbow for her to follow, and all the while keeping that red hair in sight.

"You know, my lady, it is terribly crowded on the lawn, a credit to Lord Quickner's and your renowned hospitality."

The lady bobbed her head in silent appreciation for the compliment, her eyes sharp. She whipped open her fan and made a good show of fanning herself in irritation. "Crowded is right." She raised her voice for the closest couples to hear. "So hard to have any kind of civil conversation with an amiable young lady with all this noise." She glanced towards the lake in the distance. "But you know, no one would be walking the path this early in the day.

And seeing as how it is so visible and public, no one would utter a word about impropriety. Wouldn't you agree, Your Grace?"

Renard smiled, finding he enjoyed a bit of meddling. The lady's reaction verified one thing: More than Charlotte must be unaware of the nighttime activities. "I think I may do as you suggest. It is a fine day, after all, and your grounds *are* so well maintained."

Lady Quickner folded her fan and tapped his shoulder once again, her smile wide. "To be young again. Go on, then." Her attention went to the crowd, but her next words were for his ears only. "I'll have Lord Quickner start the archery tournament early. That should give you plenty of 'quiet' time to walk."

Renard bowed over the lady's gloved hand and gave her a wink. "Any of these puppies utters so much as a grumble in your direction, and I will set them straight."

The lady's dazzling smile was that of a younger woman. "I will watch over Lady Charlotte while you are away." Her gaze went to where his sister stood off to one side, shifting her weight from one foot to another. Lady Quickner's expression softened. "A sweet girl. And wonderfully curious, though of a different variety than I expected. Asked me about the local insect population not two seconds after arriving." Her attention returned to him. "Have no fear, Your Grace. She is in good hands and far too innocent to be the subject of prey for anyone here."

Renard's shoulders relaxed as he bowed again. His words were wholly sincere when he said, "Thank you, my lady."

"Make sure to write her a note, begging for her to slip away to meet you," Lady Quickner said with a sigh. "It's more romantic."

Renard thought of his poor penmanship and winced. Then he remembered how Camille had teased him for his bad handwriting the night they'd met. Deciding her humor at his expense was well worth another round of his humiliation if it put him one step closer to her forgiveness, he made his way towards the house in search of writing supplies.

CHAPTER TWENTY

C AMILLE LOOKED DOWN at the note the servant had handed her a moment ago, the words so mangled and such an eyesore, the sender had to be Renard. She glanced at the partygoers around her in their ridiculous, cheery patterns and top hats and searched for one particular man with fair hair and desert eyes.

Syd's scrunched face appeared over her shoulder, telling Camille her friend had had no luck reading Renard's message, either.

"Did a child write that? Is it code?" she asked.

"Code for what, exactly?"

"Another lawn game, or a clue to a scavenger hunt . . . or perhaps directions to a secret rendezvous from a handsome duke? No use feigning shock." Syd put a hand on her hip. "You should realize by now I know everything that goes on with you. I knew Mr. Lover was here the minute you returned last night and didn't balk when I ate the rest of the food on your plate. Did he follow you here?"

"It is a coincidence." Though it felt anything but.

"It's fate!" Syd's younger age made an annoying appearance as she clutched her chest in a dramatic gesture of adolescence. "It's a love letter? What does it say?"

Camille bit her lip and shook her head. "I have no idea." Really, this message was more illegible than the last he'd written for her to read.

"Never mind." Syd nodded towards the treeline. "I caught a glimpse of fair hair heading in the direction of the lake a minute ago. Go. I'll cover for you."

Camille glanced around at the dozens of elegantly dressed ladies in their wide-brimmed hats, and then at herself and Syd, hatless and in simple day dresses.

"You sure you'll be all right 'rubbing elbows with the elite'?"

"No need to worry, friend." Syd's grin was not comforting. "I've always wanted to shoot a bow and arrow at a crowd of peacocks."

Camille groaned. "Be civil, please."

"I'm always civil when threatening fowl."

Camille headed off in the direction of the lake, fearing a very real conversation with Pops on why his daughter had been detained by the local magistrate for misuse of sports equipment.

Following a well-trekked path in the lawn, Camille came to the lake in no time and used the shade of a large willow to survey the lakeside for Renard. Short cattails framed the lake's edge, and she leaned against the tree's trunk and breathed in the country air. He must have taken a less direct route.

The breeze was slight, leaving the lake's surface glassy as it reflected a sky of cloudless blue. A pair of iridescent green-and-blue-headed mallards splashed in the shallows, ducking their heads under the water and sticking white feathered rear ends in the air.

Camille watched in wonder, the brilliance of color like nothing she'd seen in the city—aside from some rather ostentatious gowns and vests worn in the newest fashions.

"Enjoying the view?"

Camille pushed off the tree, expecting to find Renard. But when she turned, it was to find a different gentleman, the golden curls on his head wild when he tipped his hat.

"Excuse the intrusion. I did not mean to startle you," he said.

The man's intense gaze reminded Camille of a hawk and had

her feeling the unmistakable disadvantage of being the mouse. She glanced back at the party, easily in view and close enough to call attention from if she raised her voice. Remembering her manners, she dipped a shallow curtsey. "It is I you must excuse. I was expecting someone else."

A single, blond brow rose at that. "A friend? Your companion, perchance? I do believe she's making a good show of beating every woman here at firing arrows and earning a horde of male admirers."

Camille shook her head, her stomach knotting. Syd's porcelain face and forward manner would earn far more than admiration. She'd be sure to resist teasing Scarlet next time she complained about the headache of subduing the antics of her little sister.

"Would you care to take a turn about the lake?" the man asked, his smile charming.

His charm did nothing for her. "A woman does not permit an escort she's not been properly introduced to, sir."

He paused, whether from shock or amusement at her cutting tone, his reaction was hard to discern. "Then let us rectify that at once." He bowed. "I am Gunther Flarborn, Marquess of Slasbury. And you are?"

The name brought Madam's files to mind, a file she'd flagged due to inconsistencies in his application. The fact alone raised caution, but she had no reason to deny societal pleasantries, and she had no wish to shame her host by being taciturn.

"I am Camille Forthright."

"There now." He winked. "Now we are no longer strangers." He held out his elbow. "What do you say, Miss Forthright? Would you care for that walk? It is not far, and the other side does seem to have a picturesque view of the woods."

His manners were pretty. His smile was wide, like a friendly crocodile before its jaws snapped shut.

Camille had no reason to suspect anything untoward. His invitation was nothing but natural, and the lakeside path was visible from every angle, but she hesitated.

She glanced back at the party, a smattering of applause sounding after someone had gotten in a considerably proficient shot to the distant target. Angling her body in the direction of the crowd, she offered Lord Slasbury a polite smile.

"I do believe it is time to return to my friend."

The man's smile didn't slip. He continued to offer his arm as if she'd said nothing.

"Really, my lord." She backed up a step. "I thank you for the offer, but I must decline."

He stepped towards her, that same side smile like a slash of paint across his face.

Camille's stomach dropped.

"There you are!"

Camille whirled with relief to see Lord Quickner hurrying in their direction, his overcoat and pants a perfect match to his mauve cane and top hat.

He stopped a short distance away and nodded to the other man. "Good day, Lord Slasbury. I'd heard you'd arrived. I'm glad you could make it."

The marquess's smile had an edge to it, but his words were nothing but pleasant. "Of course, Lord Quickner. I wouldn't miss one of your legendary garden parties."

"I see you've met Miss Forthright?" Lord Quickner offered his arm to her. "Come now, the tournament is near half over already and I've had to fend off more than one attempt at our tray of tarts."

Camille accepted his arm gratefully. She dipped her head to the marquess. "Excuse me, Lord Slasbury. It seems I'm needed elsewhere."

His responding nod was accompanied by a quiet, "Another time, then."

"Glad that's settled." Lord Quickner steered her towards the party and a large, white-clothed table filled with light pastries and lemonade. As an afterthought, he waved back towards Lord

Slasbury. "You are welcome to join us?"

The other man followed at a distance, and Camille felt his gaze on her neck like a brand.

Lord Quickner patted her hand. "I hope I wasn't intruding?"

"Saving me, actually," she said. "Thank you."

The older man smiled. "Lord Slasbury has an intensity about him. I've heard from more than one lady that he isn't much of a conversationalist, but it seems he merely lacked a good partner."

She laughed. "You make conversing sound like one of your lawn games."

He gave her a knowing smile. "When you find the right person, everything becomes a game. It's what keeps the relationship alive."

Camille couldn't help thinking of Renard. From the moment he'd shuffled into that poorly lit alley, every word had been like a challenge, a dance.

She followed Lord Quickner's soft gaze to where his wife stood in a group of young men, each one leaning in to listen to something she said.

"Is it that way for you two?" she asked.

"I love my wife," he said without shame. "Even after thirty years of marriage, Lady Quickner surprises me, tempts me."

Camille would never understand the 'love' that people spoke of like poetry or song. "Then why the 'nightly' party? If you were truly happy together, wouldn't you wish to keep her to yourself?"

He scrunched his nose at her. "Don't be boring, Miss Forthright. It doesn't suit you. You're an intelligent woman. I'm sure you can grasp that unrequited love is no less impassioned."

Lady Quickner didn't love her husband. At least not the same way he loved her.

Camille's heart gave a painful *thump*. The viscount's admission resonated in the corner of her mind she'd blocked off. Rejection, acceptance, loneliness for a person he could never truly, at her core, touch. Marriage and marriage rights didn't guarantee the man his wife's affections.

"You do all this for her." The parties, the multiple couplings: The man was a saint, not a sinner.

His smile turned sad. He patted her hand again, the warmth in the action the same as the kindness he'd shown last night. "When you love someone, you'd do anything to make them happy. Absolutely anything."

Camille nodded, though she would never agree. The kind of affection the man spouted was fiction. No one loved enough to overlook infidelity. Jealousy, rage, and resentment tainted any innocent emotions, no matter how selfless their origin, and left every party in ruin.

She would know; the lie of love had brought her into this world, and it was her own form of love for her father that had destroyed them all. But that wasn't right.

She knew love by its real name: romanticized obsession. And obsession faded. Some people like Lord Quickner could cling to those softer edges, it seemed, but it was a fruit mixed in poison. The sadness in his voice as he spoke of his wife proved her theory. No one loved unconditionally. And doing 'absolutely anything' to make a person happy . . . well, happiness was a condition of affliction as well, along with hope and joy.

And any 'good girl' knew not to expect those.

FATE CONTINUED TO be as fickle a bitch as ever. After sending his note and retrieving the emerald necklace from his personal effects, Renard had been waylaid by every servant, gardener, and lady who knew the words *Your Grace*.

By the time he'd extricated himself from the rehearsed and expected introductions and pleasantries, the archery tournament had been long over, and the morning meal cleared away in preparation for a more formal late luncheon in the dining hall. Seeing as the party would conclude by that evening, Lord and

Lady Quickner had foregone tradition and decided on one last flamboyant display of extravagance and floral dress, because they could.

Renard searched for Camille along the lakeside and gardens before he was forced to return to the house to bathe and redress before escorting Charlotte downstairs to a packed drawing room of guests making idle chitchat.

"Having fun?" he asked.

Charlotte's expression was as grey as the dress buttoned all the way up to her chin. "Conversing is harder than I imagined." She tucked a piece of her fair hair behind her ear before pushing her spectacles up her nose. "Lady Quickner is lovely, but the rest of the guests seem so eccentric."

"You've no idea," Renard mumbled, searching the room's occupants for signs of Camille. "If only you had a chaperone to keep you company."

Charlotte scowled. "Chaperones are horrid and make everything far more boring."

Hard to argue with that. Mrs. Chislehurst had regaled him with her many exploits discovering the best shops for embroidery thread during her interview for a position in the Lux household. "Entertainment is not the point," he said. "A chaperone is meant to keep you safe. Now I'll have to find another to keep you in check . . ." A flash of red had him angling to see over the other guests' heads.

"What's the point?" Charlotte said. "There's little need for safety when I'm locked away at home."

"Hmm."

Slender fingers snapped in his direct line of vision.

He focused on his sister's furrowed expression. "What?"

"You seem distracted."

"Me? Whyever would I be distracted?" He placed her hand in the crook of his elbow and forced himself to focus on his sister. "*I* happen to have the perfect chaperone this evening."

She snorted. "Even I know an unmarried woman is an inappropriate chaperone."

He ducked his head and smiled. "That's what makes it perfect."

There was hesitation in her eyes, but she returned his smile. "I've missed you, brother."

The weight of her hand on his arm seemed to shift to the place above his heart. He swallowed hard, but, for once, didn't pull away. "I've missed you too."

That infamous gong sounded the meal's readiness.

Renard parted ways with his sister to escort the lady of the house into dinner, leaving a young but handsome marquess to bring Charlotte to her seat. Through it all, he searched for any sign of Camille. As she was not titled, he watched the last of the couples entering the dining room, but she did not show.

Was she angry he hadn't met her at the lake? Had she been unable to make out his handwriting?

He'd perfect his penmanship in the pen, he thought darkly. Nothing was going according to plan.

A flurry of activity at the entrance to the room drew all eyes to two late arrivals.

Renard's gaze bypassed a young woman with dark hair and fell on a goddess in yellow silk.

Eyes bright, Camille pressed a hand to her chest, drawing attention to her full chest and the intricate lace along her hem, the same lace that wove through her hair to make a most beautiful bouquet of rose curls at the back of her head.

The dryness in his eyes reminded him to blink.

She curtsied low to the table with so much elegance and poise, he doubted anyone attending would find fault with her tardiness.

It was the other woman beside her who spoke up, her voice clear and unashamed. "Dressing took longer than expected. Buttons!" She indicated the back of her dress with a slight turn and swish of her hand that bordered on vulgar. Her gaze went down the table. "Don't tell me I missed the soup?"

Renard bit back a smile, seeing more than one gentleman doing the same.

"Not at all, Mrs. Laundry. We were just about to serve." Lord Quickner indicated two chairs on either side of him at the head of the table. "Please, sit. Your seats are here."

Renard glanced at their hostess, imagining the woman had had a hand in the seating arrangements. Lady Quickner's grin acknowledged in the affirmative.

Whether or not Camille took note of the great honor of the seat placement, she nodded subtly, seeming to offer a silent thanks to their host. She glided to her place and looked up at the seat directly across from her.

Renard stilled at her gaze. The rest of the room faded away and only those lovely eyes, sharp and soft all at the same time, consumed his being. *Beautiful*, he mouthed the word and watched her eyes sparkle in understanding.

Having finished seating her companion, Lord Quickner held out the seat for Camille.

"Miss Forthright?"

She blinked. "Oh, thank you." She sat, her cheeks flushed. When the viscount reclaimed his own seat, she offered Renard a quiet apology.

Lord Quickner shook his head. "All of us enjoy a grand entrance. I'm ashamed to have not thought of it myself. Though I could never have pulled off that dress!"

The old man was a good sport.

A clinking glass brought the focus to the viscountess, who stood at the end of the table.

"Honored guests, Lord Quickner and I are grateful for your attendance and continued friendship. To mark the occasion, please indulge us a bit longer as we serve before-dinner champagne to toast to the good health and fortune of those friends and neighbors around us."

The viscountess clapped her hands and servant after servant entered the room and poured sparkling liquor into glasses.

"My lord." Lady Quickner nodded to her husband.

Lord Quickner smiled at his wife and rose to his feet, his glass in hand. "Seeing as how my lady wife's words are better than anything I could manage, I'll keep my remarks to a minimum." His words were met with chuckles around the room.

"My father used to say, 'Good fortune is the byproduct of a sharp mind and unfailing fastidiousness.' I say, good fortune is reflected in the kind and steadfast friends granted to a blessed man." Lord Quickner smiled at his wife and lifted his glass. "It seems I am a truly fortunate man."

"Here, here," came a voice down the table.

The viscount chuckled. "Enough of the speeches. Let's drink!"

Each guest took a sip of champagne, a sense of warmth spreading around the room with the viscount's words.

And then Lord Quickner fell atop the table, rattling the silverware and knocking plates and bowls to the floor in a shower of porcelain.

Lady Quickner was out of her seat and across the room before anyone else thought to rise. "My lord, what's wrong?!"

The viscount's face was turning the same unhealthy shade of plum as his velvet coat.

No one moved, seeming frozen in place. Except one.

"Stand him up!" Camille ordered the nearest footman. The moment the viscount was dragged to his feet, she pushed the servant away and wrapped her arms around Lord Quickner's midsection from behind and made a series of sharp thrusts in and up.

The room watched in suspended horror as the Lord gagged and a dark shape flew from his mouth.

The projectile struck the flower arrangement down the table, the unmistakable sound of metal on glass sounding.

Lord Quickner sucked in lungful after lungful of air, his color improving, all while Lady Quickner fluttered about him like a mother bird at the nest.

"My lord, are you well? Can you breathe? Sit down." She pointed to a footman, seeming on the verge of hysteria. "Fetch him a glass of wine."

Lord Quickner patted his wife's hand where it rested on his arm. "I'm quite all right now, darling." He glanced over his wife's head and gave Camille a nod. "You are an angel, after all. You have my gratitude."

Lady Quickner turned and embraced Camille like a long-lost daughter, sharing her husband's sentiments. "You are a godsend, Miss Forthright. That maneuver you did was extraordinary. Wherever did you learn such a thing?"

Sheepish, Camille ducked her head, her face red. "It was nothing. I read about airways in a medical journal and figured air pressure worked both ways. Anyone could apply the appropriate force."

"What modesty! You should be accredited for such heroics."

The viscountess took note of the reanimated room and the skittering whispers. Ordering a footman to assist her lord, she begged the room to take their seats and enjoy their meal while she excused herself and Lord Quickner. With a last, whispered word to Camille, she quit the room, trailing behind her husband.

Order restored, the conversations in the room livened as the first course was brought out, a new sense of mortality leaving even the most reserved among them with a lively word to say.

Renard caught Camille's gaze and leaned forward to keep his teasing quiet. "That was *unexpected*."

Her responding grin made his chest tighten, among other lower extremities.

"I couldn't bear to disappoint you and your ridiculous ideas of quiet propriety," she said. "Be thankful there were no baked goods involved. The evening would have taken a violent turn."

He shook his head. The woman never ceased to amaze and delight. If there weren't a roomful of witnesses, he'd have jumped the table and kissed her soundly. In that brief and aptly described moment of 'heroics,' all his doubt and worry over the social gap between them vanished. She was a warrior and a saint. Given an hour in her presence, even the harshest society crone would be charmed. He'd been an idiot to ever suspect her of manipulation. The necklace in his jacket pocket was a taunt. If only they weren't stuck in this room with dozens of witnesses, he'd get down on his knee and beg her to marry him.

"There'll be a whirlwind of invitations for you after this," he said. "To the heroine who saved a viscount's life after he made such a speech of blessings and fortune. You beat out fate herself."

She groaned. "I should have left the man to choke."

He laughed at her obvious lie.

Her expression softened. "Did you find your sister?"

"Third lady down on the left." He nodded towards Charlotte, where she sat eating the first course of pea soup, her eyes downcast.

"She looks miserable."

That's because she'd not been introduced to a single person. He scowled at his blunder. "I'll fix that tomorrow." Charlotte would need connections and friends—even eccentric viscountesses—if she were to survive the future.

Others engaged Camille while he contemplated where best to start. Lord and Lady Quickner were acquaintances already on neighborly acquaintance. The Stratfords held a sizable estate up north.

Camille's nervous laughter drew his attention at the curious questions and words of praise from more than half the table. Renard raised his glass to enjoy watching her squirm when his gaze locked on the unidentified object Lord Quickner had spat across the table.

Under the guise of replacing his glass, Renard plucked the object from beside the flower arrangement and stared down at what would have been Lord Quickner's last meal, befuddled at how a ball bearing would have found its way into a gentleman's drink.

He rolled the ball between his thumb and forefinger, the

perfect size and shape to block a man's airways. It had been an idiotic mistake. An egregious one. If Camille hadn't been here and known the exact maneuver, Lord Quickner would most definitely have suffocated.

Glancing her way, he saw Camille's lady companion doing a remarkable, but futile, job redirecting the attention of the gentleman beside her while Camille made a good show of lifting the soup to her mouth without taking a bite.

For a woman who despised the *ton*, she was well on her way to ingratiating herself to every renowned family in attendance. Lord and Lady Quickner were wealthy and well-liked, not to mention patrons of an elite pleasure house with its own tight-knit community. She may as well have saved the queen for how every partygoer fawned over her sparse but articulate words of what she called, "An educated deduction in leverage and pressure."

The woman had figured out how to clear the viscount's airways through a miraculous moment of calculation, a complicated problem he suspected would take modern physicians years to solve. Women were a marvel. He was reaffirmed that engaging special tutors all these years for Charlotte had been the right decision.

He clasped the ball in his fist and felt his skin tingle against the cold metal.

An unforgivable mistake. A life in the balance.

A feeling of fate's kiss left him shivering despite the warm and inviting atmosphere.

It seemed history was destined to repeat and reinvent itself over and over, leaving innumerable deaths in its wake. But today, history's machinations had lost to a superior mind.

An angel, Lord Quickner had called her.

How Renard prayed it was true. Fate's grip on him grew persistent, the unseen noose tightening around his neck with each minute he didn't settle his affairs.

His gaze went back to Camille and lingered, the swelling of emotion in his chest more than awe. She defied every natural and tragic event. Defied fate itself.

He'd been damned with the darkest of futures, and it would take a miracle, an angel herself, to break his curse and set him free.

He hoped, when the time came, she'd say 'yes.'

CHAPTER TWENTY-ONE

C AMILLE WAS ALL too happy to excuse herself from the suffocating praise and attentions of those at the dining table to read the missive the footman had laid discreetly beside her plate. Seeing Renard engaged in a lively debate with his table neighbor, she met Syd's hawk-like gaze and slipped out of the room.

In the quieter adjoining hall, Camille tore the envelope open and read Madam's new orders.

Angel,

Forget the donation. Return at once.

M

A flood of thoughts had her stomach twisting. Another body? Had her mother had another episode? Camille checked the back of the letter, inside the envelope, any place Madam may have left a clue to what had prompted such an urgent call home. Camille bit her lip, her gaze flicking back to the dining room.

She still needed to talk to Renard. Her gaze returned to the summons in her hand. But there were others whose needs were more important right now.

She cursed and hunted down a footman to fetch her writing supplies and to find the lord and lady of the house immediately.

After Camille left a note for Renard explaining that she was being summoned back to the Pony and that she would be happy to receive him there when he returned to town, her and Syd's sudden departure not an hour later meant a scramble to find a driver to take them back to the city, a concession Lord and Lady Quickner were more than happy to make.

The rifts in her relationship with Renard remained not entirely uncrossed, but as all the interruptions thus far had proven, now was not the time or place.

She stood in the drive outside the manor, Lord and Lady Quickner offering, again, the use of their six-horse phaeton.

"It will be far more comfortable and quite fast. You'll find no other vehicle a match in two counties," Lady Quickner said.

"That's most kind, but we will take Madam's victoria," Camille said for the fourth time.

"I do believe she means what she says, my lady," Lord Quickner said, looking the picture of health.

"You will not be dissuaded, then? But you are sure you cannot stay another night? Longer?" Lady Quickner glanced at her husband, his nod of agreement prompting her to say, "We would like to show our gratitude accordingly. How about a holiday to the coast? We've been meaning to visit Scarborough, and I could use a companion when my lord goes off to his hunting endeavors. If you have no swimwear, we can easily remedy that."

Camille felt Syd's smug smile from the victoria behind her, already seated and watching the scene from above, as per usual of the 'wolf.'

Ignoring her companion, Camille shook her head. "Madam writes I must return. Paperwork has piled up and I cannot put off my work, else the place fall to chaos." Exaggerated nonsense, but the viscount and viscountess wouldn't allow her to leave otherwise.

"Very well." Lord Quickner offered his hand in a rare breach of etiquette, which she shook humbly. He winked. "An angel's work is never done."

Lady Quickner outdid her husband's eccentricity by throwing

her arms around Camille for a brief embrace and tucking an envelope—the donation to the Prodding Pony—into Camille's reticule. "You will be received here anytime, Miss Forthright. You and your lovely friend." She exchanged a nod with Syd. "I do mean that. Call night or day and you will have a room for as long as you desire."

Camille's throat grew tight, the couple's sincerity embroiling her cool logic in a tangle of emotion. She curtsied and ascended to her seat. "You are most generous."

"Nonsense!" Lady Quickner's gloved hand curled around the victoria's leather siding, her expression serious. "Promise me, if you ever need anything, you will think of us first."

Camille nodded, feeling, not for the first time, that she'd found herself in a world to which she did not belong. How long her infallible brain had envisioned the world in definite colors of black and white. The reality of a world in varying shades of grey, as dense as the smoke that hung above London, was a test in humility.

A test she'd failed before, with a different member of the peerage.

As the viscount and viscountess watched their footmen load their guests' trunks, Camille took the opportunity to gaze at the southern-facing windows, a piece of her hoping to catch a glimpse of fair hair and a boyish grin beyond the grey-tinted glass.

"Miss Forthright!"

Camille glanced at the man coming out the house, her heart dropping when she noted it was a different fair-haired gentleman.

Lady Quickner squeezed her hand and drew her husband towards the house. "We'll leave you to say your goodbyes." She nodded to Lord Slasbury as he passed.

Hat askew, the Marquess of Slasbury stopped beside the vehicle, his expression furrowed. "You cannot be leaving? There is still the shooting to enjoy before anyone is expected to depart. And you still owe me a walk. I've not forgotten."

Camille ignored his charming smile and teasing tone, the

waiting was maddening. Two killings in Dockside wasn't uncommon as far as criminals and gang activities, but multiple murders with the same signature, it was enough for even the worst of the runners to lie low. No one who frequented the streets had yet lost the instinctual caution after the killings seven years ago. This new string had the potential to be much worse.

But if Madam's letter had nothing to do with the recent murders, something must have happened to her mother.

"You think he's next?"

Camille glanced at Syd. "What?"

"Hawkins," she said. "I thought after Lucien denied his involvement, it meant Grey and Flank were a coincidence."

Camille left useless conjectures over her mother aside and mentally backtracked. She *had* concluded Lucien had no stake in the killings. Except for some widely known gambling debts attributed to the trio, there was no other reason to connect the murders to one another. But something—that fallible gut again—told her this killer wasn't done, not with the three connected men and not in terrorizing the people of Dockside.

"I don't know," she said finally.

They came to the back entrance of the Prodding Pony, the flickering light of the lantern adding tension to their morbid discussion.

Camille wished they'd returned to London in the daylight. Her gut tightened at the unnatural quiet on the streets, a quiet that whispered of violence to come.

More disturbing, despite her gut's incessant interruptions, her mind appeared to agree.

HEARING STRAIGHT FROM Sensa that there'd been no messengers from St. Giles regarding her mother, Camille rifled through Madam's desk until she found an envelope and letter addressed to her hidden under the monthly expenses. Frowning, she read the letter Renard had left at the club for her before he'd left for the country, a letter—nearly legible—explaining his obligations to his sister and how he'd return from Lux estate after he'd fulfilled his duty. A letter that had been opened and read, most definitely minutes before the note demanding her return to the club had been sent to the Quickners.

It wouldn't take much for Madam to realize any invitations to a garden party by the Quickners would be extended to the neighboring Lux estate. What did Madam think? She'd have a run-in with Renard and dismiss her duties to the club?

Renard had made sure to inform her, *through action*, where he'd gone. Her heart squeezed. Next time she saw Madam, she'd tear out her powdered hair.

She rubbed her temple, irritated her wrath must be postponed. She should have known Madam would be abed at this hour. Standing outside the club door, she contemplated rousing the meddlesome woman at her residential address around the block, but it was late, and she should return to her flat to relieve her landlord of his duties overseeing her mother.

Her anger would keep.

"Syd?" Camille squinted up at the dark rooftops, surprised her shadow hadn't dropped to the street the instant she'd locked the club door behind her.

Maybe Syd had made a run to the Den to check in with Pops, thinking her conversation with Madam would take longer. Clever girl.

It was the knowledge of that cleverness that let Camille turn in the direction of St. Giles; Syd would know she'd gone home by the lack of smoke from the chimney.

Camille wrapped the familiar cold and shadow of the streets around her like the shawl looped over her shoulders. The country had been a nice reprieve from the constant caution and threat of danger, but complacency bred death. It would never do to get too comfortable with the elite, no matter how different and kind some seemed.

Lord Quickner's wide smirk came to mind, and that of a steaming mug of cocoa. The image warmed her against the night's chill and chipped away at the ice coating her feelings of the *ton*.

How her views of the titled had changed. Almost without realizing it, Camille found herself smiling and taking precious moments to talk idly of nothing of consequence, as if the bright memories of the elite world had somehow brightened her own.

Comfortable cocoa, warm partings, laughter: her growing circle of acquaintances had rendered more cheerful memories in the past weeks than in the whole of her childhood.

And it had all started with a handsome duke.

Camille crossed over to the next street and stopped dead.

She gasped at a figure leaning over a body in the street. Images of Grey's and Flank's bodies flashed through her mind.

Camille tore through her skirts for the letter opener, her heart hammering and her hands shaking. She ripped the steel out with a tearing of seams and advanced. "Stop!"

The figure whirled, the moonlight catching the unmistakable cut and style of a man's haircut. Camille gasped, certain the light played tricks over fair hair. The body groaned, a whining, animal cry of pain.

At the sound, the man took off down the alley and vanished into the maze of the rookery.

Camille reeled, her feet frozen beneath her. What she'd seen, it hadn't been real. She rubbed at her eyes, nicking her ear with the letter opener. The sting brought the alley, the smell of rot between the cobblestones, the body before her, all into sharp focus.

It couldn't have been Renard. He was back at the Quickner estate. Camille rushed forward, steeling herself for another broken corpse. She rolled the body—so slight and thin—until a face appeared with a smirk Camille knew well.

"Hey, Cam."

"My God, Syd!" Camille wiped at the blood on her friend's face, looking for the source of the bleeding. "What happened?"

Syd's breathing was shallow and her face pale, but her eyes were mercifully clear and focused.

"We need to get off the streets before the animals come sniffing," Syd said.

Camille pulled Syd to her feet and threw her small arm over her shoulder, the girl's weight nothing. This scenario was too much like that night with Scarlet, and Camille gasped around her own panic.

To think anyone could take on Syd . . . "Was it Hawkins out for revenge?" she asked. The moonlight *must* have played tricks with the man's features. Anyone could wear a wig. Syd nodded in the direction of the free clinic. "Later. I need to get you safe first."

"*Me?*" She'd break Hawkins with her own two hands. She pulled Syd closer, noticing a patch of red spreading up her side.

Camille swallowed that panic down, the taste like coal and smoke down her throat. Now wasn't the time to fall apart. Shoving the emotions into a box in her mind, she bolted the lock. Pressing a hand to her friend's side, Syd gasped and put her own hand over Camille's as if she could contain the hurt.

"Syd—"

"It's just pain." Syd smirked through trembling lips. "I'll survive."

Deep-seated hatred sprouted up from Camille's soul. How many times had she thought that same thing? Pain was pain, and she'd accepted it as part of life.

Life held more than pain. There was surprise, and joy, and moments too precious to label. One need only grit their teeth and ignore the demons of the past.

"Hold on." Camille hefted her friend's small frame onto her back. "This is going to hurt."

CHAPTER TWENTY-TWO

EVERYONE KNEW THE moment Markus Laundry arrived. The clinic walls, whitewashed and bare, seemed to shrink at his nameless bellow; even Mrs. Banner, the heartless creature—more bone and beratement than flesh and blood— winced.

"In here, Pops," Syd called.

Heavy footfalls sounded down the hall, into the room, and then the separator was torn away, revealing the middle-aged man, his normal stoic air replaced with lethal rage.

He took in his youngest daughter's wrapped midriff and the shaved section of her head where Mrs. Banner stitched sutures with iodized catgut.

They stayed in silence as the woman finished, pressing a bandage to Syd's stitches and securing it with adhesive.

Markus watched, his hands twitching at his sides as if he'd take the needle and remaining gut on the table and stick it somewhere personal if Mrs. Banner so much as *breathed* wrong.

Mrs. Banner finished and nodded at Markus before she quit the room, the white towel she used to wipe her hands stained red.

Still, Markus waited, an officer holding his breath after a battle of which he had yet to learn the number of casualties.

Syd smiled at her father. "I'm all right, Pops."

Expression sagging, he stalked across the room and scooped her into his burly arms.

Camille looked away. That tenderness, that rage: It was the same look he'd had when she'd first met him, when he'd barreled through the door after learning Scarlet had been hurt.

That night, that horrible night. She'd been shocked then at the love on Markus's face—a father who cared for nothing more than his child—and her heart had broken at the relationship she'd never know.

Markus pulled back, that cold-killer glint back in his eyes. "Who did this?"

Camille stepped out of the corner. "Was it Hawkins?"

Syd gave her a look, so much like her usual self, Camille felt relief ease the tightness in her chest.

"Like that piss-poor puppy could get the jump on me." Syd shook her head. "I didn't notice this man until he was right behind me. I panicked and fell."

Camille frowned. *"You* fell?" The man she'd seen could very well have seen Syd fall and gone to offer assistance. But why would someone else be on the Pony's roof?

"I was lucky Madam keeps up maintenance. The new sign at the back held long enough for me to slow my fall." Syd patted the side of her head. "This could've been a lot worse."

Worse—as in her head cracked open like an egg on the cobblestones.

"You fell off the roof!" Markus picked up the surgeon's tray, the tools and cloth crusted with his daughter's blood, and threw it across the room, where it crashed against the wall.

Camille shrank back, instinct and memory screaming for her to make herself as small a target as possible.

But Syd didn't flinch.

Markus rounded on Camille and came around the table, his eyes locked on her.

Camille dropped her head. It was her fault Syd had gotten hurt. Syd had been alone because of her; the Merrys traveled two or more, for this exact reason. God, if she'd but stayed inside the club ten minutes longer—

Strong arms wrapped around her, the embrace strange and foreign and so gentle, tears burned her eyes once the shock had passed.

"Thank you," he said. "That's twice you brought one of my girls back to me."

Camille bit her lip, not deserving his kindness. She pulled away, her shoulders stiff. "If she hadn't been watching over me—"

"Finish that sentence, Cam, and I'll slap you." Syd stood with a wince. "And I'd rather not reopen my head wound."

"But—"

A brunette blur dashed into the room. "Sydney!"

Scarlet threw her arms around her sister, her face pinched in concern and her stained apron still tied around her waist, as if she hadn't taken the time to remove it after the messenger had relayed Syd's condition to her at the Cock 'n Hen.

The small space was eaten up with Scarlet's flurry of questions. "Are you okay? How did this happen? Did that vampire woman sterilize the wounds first? Who the hell did this?"

Syd pushed her sister away. "I can't breathe. Stop fussing," she said, but her expression was pleased. "I got spooked by a shadow is all. Go back and wait on those slobbering fools at the tavern. I'm fine."

"You mean someone was stalking you?" Scarlet said, mirroring Camille's thoughts. She glanced at Pops and Camille, her gaze turning murderous. "I'm going to scoop out that bastard's intestines and force-feed them down his throat."

Camille wanted to smile at the whole family's bloodthirsty but loyal nature, but she couldn't.

"It wasn't Hawkins," Syd said.

"I know it wasn't Hawkins," Scarlet snapped. "That mutt couldn't *shit* without filling his boots."

The sisters' grins were identical. Pops crossed the room to wrap an arm around each girl.

Camille watched the threesome, each more violently tempered than the next, and something like longing twisted the heart in her chest. Family. Where hers had manipulated and schemed to use their relations for personal gain, others, like the Laundrys, would beat and threaten their way through the whole of St. Giles to keep their loved ones safe.

Was this what it would be like if she stayed with Renard? Was this what it would be like to have a child?

Her longing was replaced with a seed of joy.

She rubbed a small circle on her abdomen and let the seed grow into the tiniest sprout of hope. Hope she prayed wasn't mixed with poison.

THE RAISED VOICES coming from Madam's main office had Camille leaving the pile of files on her desk and walking to the one-way window.

Through the tinted glass, she saw Madam had visitors: Markus Laundry and Lucien Greystone, the two remaining leaders of Dockside and the collection of the rookeries peppered throughout London. The three heads coming together: An inconvenience for the coroner was forthcoming.

Taking in Lucien's oppressing frame and dead eyes, Camille shuddered, feeling death's presence for the fifth time in as many days.

Markus thumped his fist on the edge of Madam's desk. "Something must be done!"

Madam cocked a brow at the man's ire. "Your anger is under-standable." She waited until Markus took his seat. "How is Syd?"

His expression softened a fraction. "Better."

Lucien stood in the corner, his back to the only wall without doors or the glass mirror, as if refusing to open himself up for an attack, even in the presence of comrades. His gaze flicked to where she stood hidden behind the glass, as if he knew she was listening. "It's the Merry's job to keep the scum off the streets.

Your renowned captain isn't as untouchable as led to believe, it seems. Send him my way." Lucien cracked his knuckles. "I'll get him up to snuff."

Markus was out of his chair in a flash and pushing the younger man against the wall, their heights and weights a laughably uneven match. "Say that again, Lu, and I'll gut you."

Madam sighed. "Sit down, Markus. No one is questioning Syd's skills. This man would have to rival the devil himself to avoid all the Merrys despite the round-the-clock rounds. And Lucien is as guilty as you for not keeping his fighters in line." She steepled her fingers and leaned her elbows on the desk. "Are we in agreement that this is the same bastard who's been leaving bodies on our streets? At both men's nods, she continued. "I was convinced it was you, Lucien, cleaning house until the attack on the Merrys."

Lucien waited until Markus had regained his seat to respond. "I'd never be so sloppy."

Markus snorted. "No, you'd dump the bodies in the Thames and let the corpses drift out to sea." The man sounded approving.

"Could there be a new player on the streets?" Lucien asked.

Madam shook her head. "My spies haven't seen or heard anything."

"Then the bastard is trained," Markus said. "No ordinary thug could catch Syd unawares, especially not from the roofs."

"Meaning it's someone who's been seen before, but who hadn't been labeled a threat." Madam's expression looked worried. "That isn't good news."

"What about that dandy?" Markus asked. "Been coming to the tavern every other night looking for 'is sister. Word has it she works here."

Camille gasped. She'd never considered Hamish would go after Hawkins's men. If Markus thought it possible, it meant Scarlet had reservations about the duke and had told her Pops. Camille leaned closer to the mirror, watching the other two's faces for signs of agreement. Hamish may have borne a disturbing resemblance to their father, but she wouldn't suspect him of anything so violent.

But she'd seen how far his anger could push him. Dread churned her already nauseous insides. If he'd learned what Hawkins and his friends had intended to do to her that night, would Hamish have made it his mission to stop them—permanently?

How would he have found out? After Camille had asked her to, Scarlet had made it plain to any of the Jews and Irish that any gentleman poking around after her would be met with silence. No one would betray Scarlet, not one of their own.

Madam shook her head. "That particular gentleman is no threat."

"He's called here too, then," Markus guessed. "It must be him."

"The Duke of Camine is an honorable gentleman," Madam said to the stunned occupants of both rooms. "He has called here, offering nothing short of a king's ransom for his sister's well-being. Even as he's been escorted from the club, he's never once used title, insult, or force to gain the upper hand. If he had found out about the history between Hawkins's men and his sister, they'd be rotting in a cell, not dead on the streets."

Markus paled. "His sister is . . ." He cleared his throat and leaned back in his chair, most certainly guessing exactly which of Madam's employees had been attacked.

She'd have some explaining to do when she saw the old man next.

Lucien, who'd been decidedly quiet, gave Madam a hard stare. "You said 'that *particular* gentleman.'"

Madam stilled, her gaze darting to the mirror and back. "I did."

"There is another man, then, whom you suspect?"

Madam's expression smoothed into a blank mask. "Several." She indicated the piles of files on her desk with a flourish of her hand. "Dozens of men who may hold a grudge against one of my girls."

Camille didn't miss the other woman's misdirection, or her motion using her *left* hand. Madam knew something important, something she was refusing to share with her partners, a different gentleman she fostered suspicions of.

"There have been sightings, whispers of a man in black watching from the shadows," Lucien said.

Camille shivered at the mental image his description conjured, along with a nagging feeling she discarded.

That person from last night had been a phantom, a fear of her own making. Any number of people who stumbled upon a body in the streets would run. The figure she saw could just as easily have been a working man on his way to a morning shift at one of the cotton mills.

Logic interrupted her self-soothing thoughts. The mills were on the other side of the city, and any sailor or merchant would have been abed at such an hour with their days starting with the dawn. The whispers of warning in her mind grew clearer.

She ignored them.

There were plenty of other fair-haired men in London, and wigs continued to hold on to the fashion fringes despite the itchy and indecorous nonsense they provided to society. Some dandy may have stumbled upon the body after an unfortunate separation from friends while on a drunken crawl. Explanations for what she'd seen abounded. Plus, there'd been blood everywhere, enough that even her flawless mind could have been wrong.

But she wasn't. Camille prided herself on her ability to separate her emotions from her thoughts. Strip away the terror and dread from the memory of that night and the image in her mind became unbearably clear.

And Camille knew the truth.

The man hadn't been stalking Syd. He'd been stalking *her*.

Her throat constricted. She clutched her chest, but the air coming in wasn't enough. Did she truly believe Renard would kill those men?

No! Her inner voice screamed. She slid to the floor, her face in her hands. Her mind and her heart warred.

Renard wouldn't hurt anyone.

But he'd gotten into a bloody brawl the first time we met.

He was protecting me.

His angry words hurt you.

But his touch is always gentle.

Men are always gentle until they're not.

I'd know if he were a killer.

No one suspected your father of anything until it was too late.

Her heart couldn't deny the last point.

Camille screamed into her hands. It couldn't be true. The man had apologized, had said how much he wanted their family. Had that all been a lie?

There had to be a way to know for sure. Some record or witness, some piece of clothing with blood that proved Renard had secrets too unforgiveable and awful . . . Her gaze latched on to the stack of files on the desk, files filled with the darkest desires of men.

There was a way.

Her head popped up and she flew into a flurry of movement, rifling through the desk drawers, checking the undersides for hidden latches. She cursed when she found nothing. "Damn it, where is it?"

Her attention went to the only other piece of furniture in the room. Crossing to the fireplace, she ran her hands along the mantle, the shelf, behind the portrait above. Then a flaw in the tiles—one seated a breath higher than the rest—along the hearth caught her eye.

Crouching, Camille dug her fingers under the tile. It gave. Setting the tile aside, she removed a leatherbound book, no bigger than her palm, from its hiding place. The madam's ledger, where the biggest and worst secrets of the club's clients were recorded to keep powerful men from ever crossing the woman who ran it all. The real currency of the club.

Camille stilled, her hand on the cover. Did she really want to know? Whatever the Madam had on Renard, once seen, couldn't be unseen.

But she had to know.

She opened the book to the most recent page. Her heart stalled at Renard's name and title scrawled across the top. She swallowed and forced her gaze down to the only other word on the page, a word that damned her and Renard both.

Renard Louis, the Duke of Lux:

Murder.

Camille pressed a fist to her mouth, her broken sob filling the room.

No matter how many times she pinched herself, the words didn't change. It was a waking nightmare.

When the stiffness in her legs could no longer be ignored, Camille dragged herself to her feet, using the fireplace mantle to steady her balance. She glanced around the room, her eyes unseeing. Her mind a whirling mess.

She knew what she needed to do, but no matter how many times she told herself to find Markus, her feet stayed rooted to the floor. The idea of Renard being taken away, imprisoned, worse . . . Acid crawled up her throat at the thought.

She couldn't condemn him to that fate, especially with her knowledge of the remarkable Lady Charlotte and how her brother's crimes would ruin her life as well.

Revulsion spread through her mind. Not only of the things Renard had done, but her unwillingness to act against him. Because the worst truth was, despite their fights, despite her anger against what he'd accused her of, despite the killings, she loved him.

Her fingers curled into a tight fist and then relaxed. Open. Shut. Open. What Renard had done was unforgiveable, but he'd done it out of a sense of love, hadn't he? He'd been protecting her. Protected them.

"I would love any baby I had with you."

Her fingers closed once more into a determined fist. He was a good man at heart. She'd could make him stop. Somehow.

She worried her lip.

Could she keep him from hurting someone else? What if the next person who was found was Hawkins? Someone would eventually connect the murders to her and then to Renard.

She froze, and a darker thought took the last's place. Would there ever be a time when they'd be safe? There would always be threats, always be someone who opposed their relationship, some distant heir to object to their child. What if Renard hurt someone more established in society, someone with family who'd seek revenge?

Her hand rested on her abdomen. As long as they stayed together, it wasn't just *her* life she risked.

The answer hit her like a bullet to the gut. Renard *would* stop, because she wouldn't stay.

Heart wrenching, she forced her body to move, to pack up files and to yank on the boots she'd left discarded near the hidden entrance. She pulled the letter opener from the desk drawer and hid it in the slit of her skirts, preparing to take to the dark streets.

She'd rush home and use precious coin to hire a hack as soon as she could drag her mother out of the house and into a more maintained section of the city and they'd flee . . . where?

She thought of Lord and Lady Quickner's offer to house her and dismissed it just as readily. Too many witnesses had watched the older couple's graciousness as she'd left the garden party. If she disappeared, the Quickner Manor would be the first place Renard would look after scouring the city.

Crossing any kind of border without the proper payment for a coach was out of the question. Traveling across the sea was more so. She and her mother could make a good effort by keeping ears to the ground if they stayed in London, but her face was not one even the smallest urchin would forget. She needed somewhere safe where no one knew her, a place not even the church bells in the slums could gossip and speculate about. A place her baby could be born and looked after.

Camille stilled.

There was a place. A quiet place, and an infuriating gentleman who'd leap at the chance to take her from London, no questions asked. The man would be so elated, he'd probably not bat an eyelash when she demanded her mother go to the country as well.

"Tarnation!" Camille scribbled a single sentence on the back of whatever paper lay on top of the desk and sealed it with a press of the Pony's insignia. She'd grab the first decent-smelling boy she found on the street and offer him a penny to take the letter to the Duke of Camine's residence in Piccadilly and return to the Pony with her brother's answer.

Upon reflection, Camille penned another short missive, this one to Madam explaining dire circumstances had arisen and she was going away.

She signed the letter and stood back, watching the tight, black letters gleam as they dried.

Madam,

I must go for the safety of Dockside. You have my eternal gratitude.

Don't come looking for me.

Angel

Camille grabbed another piece of parchment, one last letter to pen, and the hardest to write. Swallowing the lump in her throat, she put quill to paper:

Dear Duke of Lux,

You once made me promise to think about our relationship and what I want.

Camille wiped at the tear on her cheek before it could fall and stain the paper.

I now understand that I could never be tied down by any man. Your responsibilities to your family are of the utmost importance and now, so are mine. If you have any nagging feelings of obligation or remorse, rest assured. With the savings I've acquired with my work for Madam, we have no need for charity, and with my mother to help me, this baby will be well looked after.

By the time you read this letter, my flat will be empty and I will be gone. I've told no one where I'm going, so interrogating those at the club won't do any good. And seeing as how any involvement on your part would cause us both hardships, I ask that you respect my wishes to not seek me out. As it stands, I doubt I will return to London for many years.

I wish you the greatest happiness in life, Your Grace.

Sincerely,
Miss Camille Forthright

How had it come to this? One letter and all her plans were forfeit. A life she'd planned to use to better the lives of those born like her: abused, unappreciated, manipulated. Frustration welled up with a fierce internal roar of denial. She needed to stay, needed to set right so many wrongs in this world.

But her chances had vanished the moment she'd chosen Renard over everything else.

Camille pressed a hand to her stomach, feeling the warmth of life growing there. Her child, *their* child.

Camille's hand went higher to her chest, where she willed her heart to freeze one last time, to turn to stone so she could march into the Den, confess her suspicions, and damn the man to whatever dark fate Dockside and the Merry Men administered. But the only thing her heart did was break. Lord Quickner was right; she'd do anything for the man she loved, even shield him from the attention of those others she cared and respected. Love existed, and it was darker and lonelier than anything she'd imagined.

She jammed the rest of the files into Madam's drawer for safekeeping and returned the ledger to its hiding place by the fireplace. Taking the key from around her neck, she locked the desk and tucked the club's seal back in its hiding place in the pocket on the underside of the desk. She pulled her reticule into the fold of the cloak she strapped around her neck. With one last glance, she took in the office—a lingering look at where her proposal for a space for her Home for Women lay waiting for her actions, actions she must betray for the sake of all Dockside—that had become her sanctuary.

She switched off the lamp and waited for Markus and Lucien to take their leave, knowing once she fled from Dockside and the other rookeries, the killings would stop.

Once Renard knew she'd left, he'd come for her, no matter how far she ran.

CHAPTER TWENTY-THREE

I T TOOK LESS than an hour to pack the few belongings they owned and bribe her mother into a hired hack with a fresh bottle of gin.

Heartbeat thundering in tandem with the death trap of a vehicle as it bounced haphazardly along the cramped alley streets, Camille had no breath left to catch as the boy messenger had returned with not a message, but a man.

The hack stopped with a jolt in front of the Pony club. Camille descended the stairs and offered her mother aid in making it to the street. Paying the driver, she waited until the hack left before coming forward with her mother on her arm.

The man seemed to watch them approach, the bowler hat he pulled low hiding his face, hair—any discernable features—but unable to conceal a predatory-like shuffle of silent steps as he closed the last remaining steps between them.

"Miss Forthright? Me name's Ralph. I be sent by the Duke of Camine ta retrieve ya."

Camille eyed the suspicious man, her instinct to run. She glanced at the boy, not deigning to respond to the *messenger* until she verified he was indeed the recipient of the message.

"Was he the man you handed the letter to, boy?"

The boy, maybe seven, shook his head, displacing a hat that must've belonged to an older brother. "No, miss. Was not what ya told me. I asked fur the lord o' the house, like ya said. Fella who got the note were dressed better, with scary, blue peepers."

Hamish.

She nodded and offered the boy a precious crown from her savings for his good work and told him to run along. When his frayed coat vanished down the lane, she turned back to the man.

His amused grin pulled the expertly applied facial hair on his cheek. "Quite the fortune ya gave 'im, miss. Not likely ta forget yer kindness, neither."

"What's your real name?" she asked.

The man's hesitation was but a fraction. "Ralph be me name."

Camille wouldn't acknowledge the man's accent was identical to the boy's. Why Hamish would employ a conman was not a question she needed answered at this moment. He had dealings in the rookeries; she'd seen it firsthand. That was his business. Stopping murders was hers.

"We best be off, miss," the man, *Ralph*, said.

She glanced over at her mother, who watched the exchange through glazed eyes, too far in her cups to ask where they were going.

Camille swallowed, knowing the trip would be a hard one for her mother, and the destination . . . like throwing grease on the range.

She glanced up and down the empty street. "Where is your carriage?"

"Round the corner. Did'n wan to cause a fuss out 'ere in the open."

At least the man's sense of secrecy was better than his prosthetics. "Lead the way."

The door to the Prodding Pony opened and Madam stepped out into the alley with her 'Mistress of the Dungeon' mask firmly in place.

"You will go nowhere until we've spoken." She nodded to Ralph. "You, take the woman's mother into the first room on the left and do not leave until you are summoned. And you," she said to Camille. "My office. Now."

MADAM CLOSED THE secret door behind them and threw Camille's note at her feet. "What the hell is this? I return to my office after being informed I must find a new driver, as my most recent hire just quit without notice, and find papers shoved in drawers, chairs upturned, and *that*." She sneered at the note. "With that shady character loitering outside. I'd thought you were taken hostage, the way this place was ransacked."

Camille's cheeks burned. The office *was* a mess. She hadn't considered what her hasty actions would appear like to an unsuspecting third party. "I apologize, Madam. I need to leave . . . for personal reasons." She wouldn't speak of Renard or share any of her fears. "I've decided to take my mother and get her the care she needs."

"You're a worse liar than I am, Angel. I know why you're leaving—don't say a word."

Camille closed her mouth watching Madam's gaze flicker to where the ledger was hidden.

She *knew*.

Camille dropped all pretenses. Her voice when she spoke was low, tired. "All that work to keep me away from him. Why didn't you just tell me or turn him in?"

"For your sake. I may be old and jaded, but I know love when I see it."

Camille looked away, heart in her throat. "You know what he's done, but you don't know why."

"The why hardly matters, not if you're leaving anyway," Madam said, her gaze downright anguished—a trick of the firelight; the woman cared for nothing and no one.

A philosophy Camille would need to adopt in the coming days.

"Please," Camille said, taking the letter for Renard from her reticule and handing it to the other woman. "Give him that, and he won't hurt anyone else. If I go, he will stop." She knew it in her gut. "I will run as long and as far as it takes. My brother—the Duke of Camine will help."

"You will tell him your suspicions? You are aware the Duke of Camine and the Duke of Lux are childhood friends?"

She hadn't been. "It doesn't matter. I'll be careful."

"There's no changing your mind, then?" Madam sighed and placed the letter for Renard in her reticule as she took out a different envelope, this one made a heavy stock.

"What is this?" Camille asked.

"Your response. One of the Merrys dropped it off not two minutes before you."

Camille frowned. "Response?" She stared at the name on the letter, the formal title like a lifeline thrown to her in a time of chaos; Lady Charlotte had responded. "So quickly."

Madam crossed her arms over her bosom. "My rider said the lady was overwhelmed. Said she wouldn't let him leave until she penned her response. His words were, 'Nothing like a proper lady.'"

Camille tucked the few words in a special folder in her mind as she broke the seal of the envelope.

Miss Yamsbee,

Thank you for your letter. I'm not sure what prompted you to reach out, but I will be forever grateful. After your insightful words about adventure, I made up my mind to attend a neighbor's garden party for the first time in my life. To be honest, it was quite frightening, and I had little in the way of conversation, but it was an experience.

I'm not sure why I'm telling you all this except I feel like I know you. Like you understand me. Seeing as how we've never met, that must sound ridiculous! But I've had a taste of boldness, and I find I can't stand the thought of being timid any longer. So here I go: Please, let us be friends? I don't have much in way of gossip to report being stranded as I am out in the country, but I have a wide knowledge on many subjects. I await your reply with hope.

Charlotte Louis

P.S. Please, call me "Charlotte." "Lady Charlotte" if you must. "The Lady" makes me sound like an old crone.

"A fine friend you've made," Madam said. "I hope you find many more along your way."

"A friend I'd like to keep." Camille glanced down at the envelope. "Madam."

The other woman chuckled. "I feel another *favor* coming on."

Camille smiled. "I have my mail forwarded to the tavern right now—"

"I'll have someone intercept any mail addressed with your name and sent to the duke's townhouse. What you do with it from there is up to you."

"Thank you," she said, and she meant it. There'd be no question of the woman's discretion or that of her runners. The clock tolled the hour. "I must go."

Madam nodded but stayed her with a light touch to the arm. "Leave your mother here."

"What? But the creditors—"

"The debts have been taken care of—don't say a word," she said. Camille snapped her mouth shut as Madam continued. "My apartments are well furnished and my staff more than capable of tending to a woman in her condition. She'll be nothing but a burden for you wherever you end up. Here she will want for nothing, except a stiff drink."

That stone heart Camille had vowed to keep was in great danger of cracking. "Why would you do that? Why take on more when it is not your concern? No, my mother is my responsibility." *My punishment.*

"Do you really not understand?" Madam shook her head. "The Pony will never betray you."

Camille was dangerously close to tears. Whatever emotional gate had opened to let through her new sense of loyalty and camaraderie had also let out obnoxious blubbering. "That's not how business works. Don't coddle me. Not now." Not when her entire life had fallen apart.

"This has never been about business." Madam's tone sharpened. "This building is but wood and nails stuck together. The girls' safety and desires are what make this business a success. The moment you marched into this office and demanded recompense for Scarlet, you became one of us."

"I did nothing for you. I convinced your leading lady to leave the Pony."

Madam embraced her with unexpected force, her voice shaky when she said, "You little fool. You made all the difference. Your mother will remain here, and I won't hear another word about it."

Camille's own voice was unsteady when the hug ended. "Why are you doing this?"

Madam gave her a conspirator's smile. "I'll tell you one day." She glanced at the door as if she could see Ralph pacing outside. "Now make haste. Your window is closing."

Camille nodded, the consequences of any further delay overcoming her curiosity. "Thank you," she said again. Now that her mother was taken care of, she had no need to flee to the country right away. She could stay in her brother's London townhouse and know everything that happened in the city almost instantly from the staff until she started showing.

Five minutes later, she left with the shady Ralph into a world she had never been meant to touch, holding her past to her until they became like distant memories with each passing mile out of the rookeries and into the unknown.

CORRESPONDENCE BETWEEN THE Lady Charlotte Louis and Miss Camille Forthright (Diana Yamsbee): Two days since Camille's disappearance.

Dear Charlotte,

I consider you a friend already.

I'm glad you decided to join a party. They can be quite amusing as long as you avoid the more snake-like marquesses. As for lack of conversation, there are plenty of other diversions well spent, even in the country. I hear the insects found outside the city, for example, are beyond diverting.

Sincerely,
Miss Diana Yamsbee

Correspondence between The Lady Charlotte Louis and Miss Diana Yamsbee: One week after Camille ran.

Dear Diana,

I can't tell you how overjoyed I am to hear about your interest in entomology! It is truly a fascinating area of study. Just the other day, I caught a vanessa atalanta *in the ivy (I suppose most people call it the "red admiral." Which only prompts me to envision a formidable-looking naval man in a bright-red suit). Let me know if you have interest in a drawing of the species—the butterfly, not an admiral—and I would be happy to include one in my next letter.*

Your friend,
Charlotte

P.S. What are your thoughts on the onthophagus joannae? *(More commonly referred to as a dung beetle.)*

Correspondence between The Lady Charlotte Louis and Miss Diana Yamsbee: Two months after Camille ran.

Dear Diana,

I hope this letter finds you well. It has been several weeks since your last correspondence and I've tried (and failed) to dismiss the idea that I've in some way earned your disapproval over my excitement over a beetle. They truly are intrinsic creatures when it comes to keeping an environment thriving and free of disease, but I have come to see now how such a topic may be less than ideal for proper discussion.

Please know I meant no offense, and I look forward to your next letter no matter what chastisements over my choice of subject may be included therein.

Your true and contrite friend,
Charlotte

Correspondence between The Duke of Lux and an anonymous sender: Two months, one week after she ran.

Dear Renard,

I lost him.

Correspondence between The Lady Charlotte Louis and Miss Diana Yamsbee: Two months, two weeks after she ran.

Dear Charlotte,

Please know, my lack of correspondence has nothing to do with your interests or choice of subjects. Even if I cannot fully appreciate the value of such a beetle, I can revel in your passion for life at its most basic.

The truth is, I've felt little in the way of wishing to reach out to anyone.

I've lost something precious to me . . . More than precious.

The real truth is, I'm broken. Angry and broken with no way of knowing if I'll ever mend. I had such joy, such hope, and now it's been snatched from me right when I'd finally thought I'd found a reason to start over.

I'm so sorry. I know I'm not making any sense.

Nothing makes sense to me right now.

Diana

Correspondence between The Lady Charlotte Louis and Miss Diana Yamsbee: Two months, three weeks after she ran.

Dear Diana,

You never need apologize for your grief. I will not pry and ask for specifics but know when I lost both my parents tragically when I was ten, it took months for me to speak. I was so distraught and ill. Even after I'd regained my strength and started talking, I thought I'd never smile again. There was so much sadness in me, so much confusion.

That said, you have every right to suffer in silence if that is your wish, but you are not alone. Grief makes lonely souls of us all, but know you have but to ask and I will fetch the carriage and ride to you straight away. No questions asked.

Please be kind to yourself, dear friend.

Here and waiting,
Charlotte

Letter unsent by Renard Louis, the Duke of Lux.

My Milly,

Every day, I search for you in the crowds across London, and every night, I stumble my way through the rookeries wishing for a glimpse of your red hair or the scent of flowers on your skin. I'm living a half existence without you.

I will find you.
I have nothing else.

Yours always,
Renard

Correspondence between The Lady Charlotte Louis and Miss Diana Yamsbee: Many months and letters later.

Dear Charlotte,

I couldn't believe your last letter. You are at last coming to London! It's hard to imagine that overprotective brother you

*mentioned allowing you anywhere near the city. Beware, my
friend. I suspect wedding bells are ringing in a particular duke's
ear.*

*If your brother has come to the idea of matrimony on your
behalf, make sure to have some fun first. You're always talking
about finding an adventure and I would be remiss in my duties
as a terrible influence if I didn't inform you that I have lists of
eligible bachelors who are known around town as the worst
kind of rakes and very discreet. The Duke of Hurstfield's name
being at the top.*

*Your friend and conspirator,
Diana Yamsbee*

Correspondence between The Lady Charlotte Louis and Miss
Diana Yamsbee: Thirteen months since she ran.

Dear Diana,

*The duke and I have been married for less than two months and
have finally settled into life at Camine Manor. After so many
years of loneliness stuck at Lux estate, I thought the quiet would
weigh on me returning to the country, but there was no need for
concern. Between my darling husband and his delightfully
combative sister, Miss Forthright, I feel like one big, ridiculously
happy family. My dearest sister-in-law made a quip the other
day about how a man's brain lay in his pants and not under his
top hat. I nearly lost my tea through my nose when I heard.*

*You and Miss Forthright would be fast friends should the
occasion ever arrive for us all to meet, I am sure. Your humor is
much alike.*

*Hoping, at last, we may finally meet face to face,
Charlotte*

Camille smiled down at Charlotte's letter from where she
read by the light from Camine Manor's front window. The letter
had traveled in a merry back and forth game from country to
London, through multiple establishments in the rookeries, to her

brother's city townhouse and back, arriving not ten minutes ago by postman. Even after all these months, Madam had kept her word to intercept Camille's letters from her friend.

Folding the letter, Camille looked out at her brother's well-maintained lawn, watching the moonlight cast the flowering bushes planted along the drive in stark shadows.

The past year had brought many changes in her life, including the recent marriage between Charlotte and Camille's brother, Hamish, the Duke of Hurstfield. The two women had grown close as sisters since they'd all started living together, but even now, Camille couldn't bring herself to reveal her alias as the fictitious Miss Diana Yamsbee.

The past month had also brought a less desirable imposter into their midst, a man Camille had detested the moment they'd met.

Lord Slasbury had wormed his way into a verbal marriage contract with Renard for Charlotte's hand, only for everyone to find the lord had been assuming the real marquess's name and title in order to extort a considerable amount of money through White's betting ledger. In the end, the man had proven a raving madman, going so far as to blame not only Charlotte for her part in the botched scheme, but also Hamish for some imagined slight over "borrowing" supplies on the docks.

No wonder the man had been annoyingly persistent at the Quickners' garden party. Any criminal worth his salt would have researched the scandal sheets for lords and ladies down on their luck. He must have read the notice about her connection to the previous Duke of Camine and thought he'd found an easy way to make her brother's acquaintance.

Luckily, the horrible conman had been caught and locked up just the night previous, permitting the past weeks of chaos running through the household to finally settle down. Her family was at last safe.

Her hand went to her stomach on reflex, any thought of family coming with a mix of joy and sorrow.

She was happy for her brother—even if he remained an un-compromising ass—and her friend, but Camille ached inside. With Charlotte's connection with Renard, it wouldn't be long before his visits became irregular and hard to predict. She'd been fortunate so far to anticipate him and avoid a meeting, but her luck wouldn't last. Soon, she'd have to leave again, this time, away from England.

She pressed a hand to the windowpane and gazed off in the direction of Lux estate, where a certain duke was known to reside. That ache worked its way up to the muscle in her chest.

"Renard," she whispered.

"Milly."

Camille froze.

That voice. Her heart swelled.

She turned, the action slow so as not to dislodge the image of the man standing in the open doorway, his hat and gloves seemingly forgotten in his hands. Desert eyes ensnared her. The breath caught in her throat. Her eyes drank him in, her mind ravenous for the smallest detail.

He'd grown thin under his coat. Dark circles hung under his eyes and the hair on top of his head lay long and unruly around his face, but he was as handsome as he'd always been.

His gaping mouth closed and spread into a smile. He repeated her name, the one word filled with the purest joy. "Milly." Hat and gloves dropped to the ground. He walked to her with long strides. He stopped less than a step away and gazed down at her, those eyes burning. "I found you."

She swayed forward, compulsively needing to feel his warmth against her skin, before she returned to her senses and locked herself in place.

Her body rebelled at the distance, but her mind had wrested control. As had cold determination that she now wrapped around herself like a shield.

"What do you want, Your Grace?"

He stepped back, as if her words had come with a physical

blow. His brow furrowed. "I want you." Said like it was the most obvious thing.

Three little words that snuck under her shield like water through a sieve. Camille swallowed down a wave of emotion. "I made myself clear, Your Grace. I do not wish to continue a liaison with you."

"I don't understand." Renard shook his head. "I thought we'd agreed to work through things." He glanced around. "What are you doing *here*?" His eyes lit up. "Did you come to the wrong estate by accident? Lux estate is the next plot over."

The hope in his voice hurt. Camille forced herself to hold his gaze, forced herself to lie. "I never had any intention of seeking you out. There is nothing left between us."

His expression fell. "You don't mean that, Milly." His eyes were pleading. "I know I made mistakes." He ran a hand through his hair.

The familiar action sent a cascade of longing through her.

Camille clenched her jaw until pain pushed the feeling away. "The mistake was mine." She crossed her arms over her chest and forced her face into a mask resembling granite. "Even after being rejected, you can't let go. I told you I don't want you. You had no reason to come looking for me."

"No reason?" Anger chased away the hope on his face. "You'd vanished. Of course I came looking!"

Charlotte rushed in from another room, her cheeks flushed, with her husband quick on her heels. "What's the matter, brother?"

"Matter? *Matter!*" Renard whirled on Hamish. "Is this what all those letters were about? The summons to visit so late? You wrote of a threat to Charlotte, but I should have known that was just a ruse to get me to come . . . You should've told me sooner that you'd found her!"

"Exactly whom was I keeping from you?" Hamish sounded infinitely patient.

Renard's hard gaze turned. *"Her."*

Camille flinched. There was no hiding anymore.

"I didn't realize you'd met Miss Forthright before," Hamish said. "My sister."

Renard blinked, anger momentarily forgotten. "Sister?" He pointed to Camille. "No, *her*."

There were more words exchanged between the men. Then Hamish said something to Camille that had her responding unconsciously. For once, her brain wasn't working, couldn't handle the overwhelming flood of reactions from all parties.

Until Renard's next shout dragged her attention back to her surroundings.

"What do you mean, she's living with you?"

"Forgive me, Ren. Allow me to make the formal introductions," Hamish said. "Renard Louis, Duke of Lux, this is Camille Forthright, my sister."

"No." Renard stared at her, that one word filled with anguish and betrayal.

"It's true." Camille swallowed the next wave of emotion and buried it in the pit of her stomach. "I'm the bastard daughter of the former Duke of Camine."

"Don't say that word!"

His passion-laced remark drew her up short, and then she remembered why she'd run from her life in Dockside. Why she'd run from *him*.

After that day at the Pony, she'd never told another soul about what he had done. Neither had Madam, out of loyalty for her or with the same understanding Camille had when she'd fled that the killings would stop with her absence. But now that he'd found her, now that Markus and Hamish had grown close as business partners, Renard wouldn't be safe.

Protectiveness gripped her. Camille threw back her shoulders and stared Renard down. "You should leave."

"Like hell I will!"

Charlotte stepped forward, her hands raised, and her bespectacled face drawn into a concerned expression. "Ren, please.

There's no need to shout."

Hamish rubbed the back of his neck and inclined his head towards the library. "How about a drink? The good kind."

When no one responded, Hamish shrugged and headed for the door.

Charlotte, clearly indecisive about following her husband or staying to mediate, worried her bottom lip and looked to the open library door and back.

Renard growled. "Go!"

Camille watched her best friend come to attention, Renard's outburst having the opposite effect of cowing her. Her friend had truly come into her own these past months.

"Not until you regain your senses," Charlotte said. "I won't have you lashing out in your tantrum."

If words had edges, Camille was sure, Renard would have a slice across his chest.

"I would never strike a woman." His voice was quiet but firm. "Not ever."

Satisfied, Charlotte nodded and went in search of her husband, leaving Camille to face the Duke of Lux alone.

Silence descended between them, a silence wrought with anger and longing and so painful, Camille dug her nails into her palms to keep from pressing them to her heart. "You should leave," she repeated.

"Are you sure you wouldn't prefer to go?" His eyes went hard. "You are infinitely better at running away than I."

She refused to flinch. Her armor, her cool indifference and easy sarcasm, wouldn't crack.

"This is my home. The duke and duchess are my family." It surprised her how the words matched her feelings. She'd lost so much over the past months, been broken and bleeding inside, but the two people in the next room over had patched her up and given her a purpose.

"Charlotte is my sister," he said.

Not even he believed that lie past the most basic claim. Charlotte may have been his sister, but he didn't act like a brother.

She had no idea how he'd become so irresponsible and cold with Charlotte. A year ago, his bright and wonderful little sister had been all he'd talked about, and how much he'd wanted her to be happy. In the thirteen months since she'd run, something had happened. No, it had happened before that, when he'd been so consumed with someone he'd turned into a monster. Her. *She* was what had happened.

He'd arranged a marriage against his sister's will.

Camille let her love for her friend bolster her resolve. "You mistreated her. Used her. It is what *you're* better at."

His flinch was violent.

Camille bit her tongue to keep from snatching the words back. Words were important, forever. Once spoken, they weren't allowed back. She should have been better than anyone at choosing the right ones to use, but those horrible memories, unacceptable *feelings* pounded at her armor from the inside.

Her legs readied to flee, unable to contain the overwhelming need to move when cornered. Too much more of her heart pounding and her ribs would be little better than powder under her linen dress.

Renard stepped close, seeming to battle over touching her or not. "You can't run from me. Not anymore."

The words were a challenge and truth. She couldn't run from him, from what he'd done and what she'd lost. She'd deluded herself into thinking he wouldn't find her. Not when he was her shadow, her dream. The connection that had forged between them was fate bound; escape had never been an option.

She pressed the emotion down, down. "Go home. You don't belong here."

He reached for her then. "We belong together. I've done nothing but search for you. I went mad with worry when I returned from the country and read your letter."

She tore away, the cracks fissuring into yawning chasms. "I asked you to leave, resolutely, as you once said I ought to if I wanted you to stay away."

"No, you wrote me a letter and *ran* without a word. But wait, there was one more letter." His gaze was so cold, it burned. "Three fucking words to tell me our son had died."

Camille flinched at the accusation. She'd promised herself after she'd run that she'd never contact him, never give him any hope that any connection between them remained. But that night, the night the bleeding had finally stopped, and their child had been lost, she'd been too ravaged by grief to think straight.

"I'm sorry," she said. "You shouldn't have found out that way."

He cursed softly, and all the anger seemed to go out of him. "I'm sorry too. I didn't mean that." He pinched his nose with his fingers. "I'm confused. I don't understand what happened, Milly." He gestured to the space between them. "You say you don't want me, but your body is saying something different."

Realizing she'd come within arm's reach again, she drew back. His hand raised as if to stop her.

"Don't touch me."

His expression collapsed. "Milly. What is wrong with you? God, you're looking at me like I'm a stranger." He pressed that hand to his chest. "I'm sorry I yelled, but your letter, you disappearing, it destroyed me."

Camille's heart ached. She knew what it was to be destroyed by someone you thought you knew.

But the man she'd fallen in love with had been another man, one of her mind's making. The man before her bore the same face, the same name, but he *was* a stranger.

She plugged the worst of her bleeding heart and fought for the last ounce of control as she turned away, truth and lie so seamlessly tangled, she didn't know which she spoke.

"Go home, Your Grace. I don't claim to know you at all."

"I won't leave you." He reached for her again.

"Please." The word came out a sob. She couldn't be touched, or she'd break. Not by anyone, but especially him. Not when she'd spent thirteen horrible months missing him. "*Leave*, Renard. And don't come back."

CHAPTER TWENTY-FOUR

RENARD HAD IMAGINED, rehearsed, every word he'd say when he'd found her again. Words of love, words of anger, words filled with youthful naivety and manly feeling.

But when at last he'd found her, beautiful and fine in a lady's shirtwaist and dark skirts, the only thing he could manage was her name.

Of course, the anger and scorn came swiftly after. The past weeks worrying over Charlotte's relationship to his best friend worsening his already wasting body, now more liquor than flesh and bone.

"I don't claim to know you at all."

Renard stared at the Camine Manor's drive, having no recollection of opening the door and walking out; none of it mattered if he wasn't walking towards *her*.

His scuffed boots and worn trousers looked poor, even in comparison to the sunbaked gravel underfoot. The rest of his appearance was just as ramshackle, lacking all the pride of a gentleman.

Frankly, he didn't recognize himself.

She'd been so close all along. What cruel fate. The mere door's thickness apart was unforgivable. Not that she'd suffer his touch or company.

She'd changed as well over the past year.

That strong but passionate woman was gone. The woman

he'd saved and watched over a distant memory. A statue stood with her face now, exterior so hard and cold, he'd broken his heart against the surface. But . . . the cunning and clever eyes, that ridged spine, a woman, a hardened general stood in her place.

And he loved her.

Thirteen months of torment and worry had solidified his paltry description of want and desire into a true depth of emotion.

Renard took off down the drive, needing the fresh air and laborious walk back to Lux Estate to clear the Scotch fog from his mind.

She claimed she didn't know him, but he'd change that. Was it something the Madam at the Pony had said? Had she revealed his past about his parents and the fire?

He kicked a rock in his path and watched it skid towards the future. His hand went to his pocket, where a second rock lay hidden, smaller and more precious than any gravel, owned by a duke or not. There was a chance. If he held that piece of her and their time together, their bond couldn't break.

Now that he'd found her, he'd never risk losing her again. His past transgressions and impending doom had hung over him in suspended animation these months, as if waiting to crash his life to pieces only after he'd made amends.

Temper, secrets, the drinking; he'd leave it all behind. He wouldn't tempt fate after receiving this second chance.

He wouldn't need one. He'd do it right this time. It didn't matter if Madam had told her the truth. *He* hadn't.

He'd reveal himself to her, the lies and blood on his hands, the love and wishes of his innermost desires, and his heartfelt apology for being a ruddy ass.

All before she ran away for good this time.

CAMILLE SHUT THE library door behind her and watched Hamish's and Charlotte's gazes silently search the space behind her.

"He's gone," she said.

Hamish settled into his high-backed chair, expression pensive and annoyingly patient. Charlotte, God love her, had no such control.

She flung her arms around Camille's shoulders and squeezed. "Are you all right? Gracious, of course you're not. How indecorous, my brother. Next time I see him, I'll bloody that ridiculous nose."

A bit of sun shone through the gloom hanging over Camille's head. "You have the same nose."

The Duchess of Camine sniffed and stuck out her chin. "But I wear it better." She looked over at her husband. "Don't I wear it better?"

Hamish didn't hesitate. "Yes." He cocked a brow at Camille, as if to say, *"Care to share what the hell is going on?"*

Camille eased out of Charlotte's arms and plopped down in the chair by the window. She pulled at her high collar, not giving a fig when she heard the lace rip.

She had no more energy to even pretend manners. "I know the Duke of Lux."

Hamish steepled his fingers, his tone dry. "I gathered."

She massaged her temple where a sudden ticking made her head ache. "I know the duke, *intimately.*"

Silence.

She didn't know what she'd expected. A gasp of surprise from her friend? A curse of outrage from her brother?

Like always, Charlotte showed the beautiful curiosity of an open and clever mind, and better still, the loyalty of a fierce friend.

"If it wasn't consensual," she said, "I've read of a scorpion with a venom that can fell a man. We can poison him without leaving a trail back to us."

Hamish didn't bat an eyelash. "No one would find his body in the peach grove."

Charlotte's expression lit up. "We have a peach grove?"

"We will."

A well of emotion blurred Camille's vision before she blinked it away. Family: This was what it felt like to have people who loved unconditionally, people who'd risk the hangman's noose to dispatch a duke and use him for fertilizer. Even though she knew neither of them would ever go that far.

If she hadn't given up such nonsense emotions that day at the Prodding Pony, she may have cried.

Things would change now that Renard knew she was here. It wasn't long before she'd have to make the decision to run again or confront him. Either way, her peaceful time here with her family was done.

Camille looked up to realize her brother had gone very still.

"Did he force you?" he asked.

Camille loved the violent edge to his question. The tone emboldened her, steadied her, allowed her to shed one of the secrets haunting her past so she could force out her next statement. "No. He protected me from the men who tried."

The stillness spread around the room like creeping death. Charlotte became like another bust statue against the wall.

And her brother . . . Her brother's cold expression surpassed that of even their father at his most sadistic.

The way he stared through her, Camille knew, from experience, his mind was far away, most likely imagining the most vicious way to rip genitalia from a man and force it down his throat. She loved them for not considering pity. Loved them for overlooking the shame that rose like bile to redden her cheeks and fill her chest with acid.

It was Charlotte who broke the silence at last. "The man you were running away from wasn't Renard, was it?"

"Yes." Camille smiled sadly. "And no." She shook her head. "I ran for many reasons."

Hamish jerked himself into the present. "This monster is still walking free?" He stood quickly; his chair cracked into the nearby bookcase. "He won't be for long."

Charlotte's voice was quiet compared to his. "Who was it?"

Camille shook her head. "It doesn't matter anymore. Truly nothing happened, and two of the three are gone."

Hamish looked as if he'd be sick. "Three?"

She saw his mind churning, guilt building. Thinking if he'd gotten her out of her old life sooner, things might have been different, but the truth was she'd refused to go when she'd had the chance.

"This is my fault, not yours," she said.

Charlotte blustered. "Bullocks! Neither of you is at fault."

"You said two of the three," Hamish said. "What's the third's name?"

Camille hated how she hesitated. She wasn't afraid of Hawkins. Truthfully, she'd barely given the scum a thought since she'd come to Camine Manor.

"What's his name, Camille?" Charlotte asked.

Camille looked at her friend, seeing the truth and love in the concerned expression on her face, and she realized her faith in others hadn't been lost entirely. "His name is Peter Hawkins."

Hamish crossed the room and went to his knees at her feet. He took her hand, his gaze intense. "I swear to you, sister. However long it takes, I will find that monster, and I will put him in a cell, where he will spend his days wishing he'd never met you."

For a woman set on never relying on the strength or fleeting kindness of anyone again, she was shocked to find she believed him. Guilt bit deep. She'd known better, *knew* him better. Hamish would never use violence to exact justice. He was a man of scruples. Even with his good work in Dockside, she knew he remained conflicted over working outside of the law with Markus—offering the poverty-stricken spectacles for reduced prices—asinine and unjustly enforced as the law was.

Not wishing to alarm either of them with her sudden thawing

of heart, she made sure her next words came out hollow and flippant.

"Whatever you say, Your Grace."

She couldn't stop her mind from adding a silent, *Thank you.*

HAMISH QUIT THE room, leaving Camille to drag herself from the settee before Charlotte stopped her with a soft hand.

"That's not everything, is it?" she asked.

Camille smiled at her friend's knowing tone. Hamish had to watch himself; he'd never get away with so much as sneaking a biscuit from the kitchens without his duchess figuring it out.

"It's not," Camille said.

"You don't need to tell me, but I am here if you need to talk." Her smile was kind. "There are no rules that say women must suffer alone. That's for ridiculous men to believe."

The mention of rules drew the buried scars of Camille's past from the depths of memory, the drama of the day giving way to trauma of a young girl whose existence had balanced on how well she managed the rules that dictated every moment of her life.

"It's an ugly story," Camille said.

Charlotte wrapped her arms around her, her new set of spectacles framing her kind, green eyes. "I already know some of it," she offered.

Camille smiled. That's right; Charlotte knew pieces and had never admonished her actions. "The rest is worse."

Charlotte pulled her to the settee by the fire and waited until they both sat before she said, "Tell me."

CHAPTER TWENTY-FIVE

C AMILLE WENT TO the window to look out on the garden, hearing Charlotte quietly follow. "I learned what a bastard was when I was ten." After her not-to-be-named father had bloodied her mouth when she'd made the mistake of asking why she couldn't meet her brother.

"You are a bastard! A mistake. Without that mind of yours, you'd belong nowhere. Be grateful I have use for you."

Camille's fingers curled into white-knuckled fists on the windowsill, the duke's words as fresh and ugly now as they'd been fourteen years ago. A bastard was all she'd ever be, the only title she'd ever earn. And one she'd been cursed to share alone.

Her hands slipped to her stomach, and the ache there felt like the absolute absence of hope. "I was pregnant when I ran."

Charlotte made a strangled noise behind her.

Camille knew without turning that her friend understood. Charlotte's mind was quick and made connections like no one else she'd met. If it had been a matter of an unwanted child, there were orphanages and herbs a woman could take, but there was no mistaking the anguish in her voice.

"Did you . . .?" Charlotte's whisper tapered off.

Camille's armor ripped open, spilling her heart at her feet. She choked on a sob and hit the sill with her fist.

A baby. Another bastard to a duke, a painful and ugly cycle she'd vowed she'd never repeat. Anyone else in her situation would have been relieved. But she'd wanted that child, *her* child. It wouldn't have mattered if the babe had been born with her eyes or Renard's nose. Red-blooded or blue. She'd loved that baby growing in her, with her, and she'd known her mother and not-to-be-named-father had been wrong.

When the bleeding hadn't stopped that night, not two months after she'd gone into hiding at the Camine Townhouse, she'd paid off one of Hamish's seasonal hires to take her into St. Giles and to the free clinic, a lad not likely to stick around long enough for proper gossip.

The pain had grown worse with every mile. Minutes, hours later, she'd fallen at Mrs. Banner's feet, barely conscious, and begged the woman to save her child.

When she'd woken, Mrs. Banner, stone faced, had offered her condolences with a pat on her hand and the words, "These things happen," before leaving Camille to her torn body and broken heart.

"I didn't get to say goodbye," she whispered through her tears. "She took the body away before I even got to hold him."

Through her memories, Camille heard the library door open and shut with Charlotte's departure.

Camille closed her eyes and leaned her forehead against the cool glass. She didn't fault Charlotte for making her escape. As far as society demanded, women didn't lose anything so precious. And if they did, it was never mentioned. She'd not even been allowed a proper mourning period.

She bit her tongue and tasted blood. Her mother's words, controlling and wrong—and worse, right—cut through her grief as only the woman's venom could.

"A good girl wouldn't sniffle over small things." "A good girl never shows she's in pain." "You got what you deserved. A good girl would have known better."

How many mothers were out there now, suffering alone with a grief too profound for anyone else to understand? How many were told 'these things happen,' as if having lost a bonnet or parasol to a windy day? How many bastards were left alone and ashamed, not realizing they deserved love like any God made creature?

The door opened and Camille turned to see Charlotte had returned, and not empty handed.

Charlotte offered her a half-glass of amber liquor and raised her own in silent salute. Her cheeks were tear-stained, her eyes puffy, but her voice was steady. "To those we've lost and will love always." She clinked their glasses. "And to the surgeon I'm going to find and boil alive for taking your baby away."

The tears broke free. Camille let them come, welcomed the feeling, along with a wet laugh. "A new string of crime for the *ton* to twitter over." She shook her head. "Not even a duchess could get away with murder." The sick irony of her words didn't elude her.

Charlotte smiled. "I'll have a peach grove soon, remember?" She threw back her drink, emptying the glass in one shot. Eyeing the last drops in the bottom, her gaze went to the window. "It was my brother's, wasn't it?"

"Yes."

She nodded. "Did he know?"

"Yes."

"And Hamish?"

"He knew only that I refused to leave my rooms when I first got here. Until one night, I did. I came back weak and covered in blood. He never asked what happened." It was a rare show of restraint on his part. "No one else knew."

"Your strength humbles me," Charlotte said. After a moment, she continued, her voice soft. "I wish . . . I wish I had words of comfort, but I lack my friend's gift for advice."

"Diana Yamsbee?" Camille chuckled, knowing it sounded guilty. "I'm sure she'd have no words for this. Because *I* have no words for this."

Charlotte's eyes widened. "You're Diana?"

Camille swirled her drink. "You're not mad, are you?"

Charlotte threw her arms around her friend and squeezed. "I love you." Camille sighed and returned the embrace.

Charlotte pulled back. "How did you know? How could you possibly know the perfect things to say? You'd never met me."

Camille smiled sadly.

Charlotte's expression tightened in understanding. "My brother. Why write at all?"

"Curiosity. The way Renard described you was like a work of fiction. The bug hunting and the terrorizing governesses. I'd thought, 'A woman like that wouldn't care who I was or where I came from.'"

Charlotte shook her head as if in disbelief. "Then why change your name? You could've written as yourself."

"At first, I was ashamed. I'd been the topic of scandal not long before I reached out and the details were still circulating through society. And because I had no way of knowing if a proper lady would respond to my bold introduction at all." Camille smiled, remembering. "You sure did. 'What are your thoughts on dung beetles?' I couldn't believe a well-bred lady would say anything like that to me."

"What about some of your letters?" Charlotte asked, then quoted, "'If a fearless creature can't be seen terrorizing the stuffed shirts, there's no point leaving the privy.'"

Camille grinned. "I stand by that assessment." Her humor faded. "After you married my brother, I suppose the letters had gone on too long. I couldn't find a way to tell you without it seeming as if I'd orchestrated everything. In a way, I guess I did."

Charlotte touched her hand. "I'm grateful, truly."

They lapsed into a comfortable silence, the joy of reconnecting still dampened by their earlier conversation.

Camille set her untouched drink on the windowsill, watching the action send tight ripples through the liquid. Cause and effect. Action and reaction. She saw her life in those ripples, the moment-by-moment decisions having far-reaching consequences that never seemed to stop. One effect could bring people together to become lifelong friends and sisters. Others left devastation in every life it touched.

But Camille had known this moment would come. Her past with Renard was a living shadow, never more than a step behind.

No more running. She'd sent Renard away, but away he would not stay. He was as bound by the thread fate had woven between them as she was bound. A real confrontation, away from prying eyes and ears, was thirteen months past due. A debt that had cost everything and would continue to accrue collateral interest until she faced the collector.

Her amends would start this afternoon.

And then tonight she'd go to Renard and finish the foolish game they'd started all those months ago. A game that had gone too far.

Tonight it would end. One way or another.

CAMILLE PAUSED ON the Cock 'n Hen's doorstep, the violent wind ripping at her bonnet as the drizzle of rain falling turned pounding.

As far as apologies went, this was long past due. So much had changed in the year since she'd left the rookeries—without a word to Scarlet or Syd—a lifetime in this harsh-paced, harsher-lived world beneath the *ton*'s attentions.

Syd could have died from infection from her injuries. Scarlet may have left the tavern. The whole family may have moved back to Ireland now that the waves of devastating famine had ebbed.

She hadn't so much as thought after her friends' welfare to the paper boy on the corner, never knowing which informant worked for Madam Clarice and which worked for the local gang. Madam may have agreed to Camille's request to stay away, but Scarlet and Syd would never have listened.

Camille rested a hand on the doorknob. Would Scarlet want to see her? She'd up and run away from her life here, including those she'd cherished like family. Knowing this visit would be the hardest, she'd stopped here, bypassing the Pony and the inevitable upheaval her presence would create with Madam, with Markus, with *her mother*. But now that she was here . . .

The doorknob turned before the door opened and Scarlet herself was there, leaning a hip on the frame, her mouth set in a grin, her ever-present rag flung over her shoulder.

"You gonna come in or just stand here and get soaked to the bone?" she asked.

Hearing her friend's teasing tone made her stomach twist with new guilt. "That depends. Are you more or less likely to lecture me if I'm sufficiently wet and pathetic?"

Scarlet sucked a tooth and gave her a onceover. "Odds aren't good either way."

"Then I guess I'll come in."

Scarlet stepped aside and let Camille pass into the warm room.

"So that's what happened?" Scarlet rubbed her chin with her thumb and gave a low whistle. "No wonder Madam was the only levelheaded of the monsters."

Camille set down her sipped wine on the bar, letting the sweet taste coat her dry throat. She'd given Scarlet the simple version of why she'd left—how she'd become with child, how she'd stumbled upon the killer one night on her way home from the Pony, how the killer had seen her face, even how she'd gone into hiding and come to live with her brother. And more: How she'd lost the baby and now couldn't stay away from those she loved any longer.

Scarlet accepted her last statement with a nod and a smile.

"What do you mean, *monsters?*" Camille asked.

Scarlet huffed. "A whole lot of chaos happened when you left. You'd have thought Pops and Lucien were parents searching for a child the way those two grown men prowled through the streets, upturning every gaming hell and brothel thinking you'd been taken against your will. Syd damned near burned St. Giles to the ground."

Camille winced at the mention of Syd; another apology she had to make. "Lucien too?"

Scarlet smirked. "You made an impression. Who knew Lucien was flesh and blood under all that brooding? And charming devils *is* one of your finest qualities. Pops and Syd have a side bet going on how soon after you returned Lucien would wait until he proposed."

Camille laughed at the predictable and comforting things that never changed. "What is your take?"

"I'll make a fortune when you turn the Devil down." Scarlet smiled at Camille's surprise. "Lucien has no chance, not when a duke holds your heart."

"How did you—"

"The man was beside himself when you vanished. In here every night begging for a word to anyone who'd listen. Said *his girl* was missing. Wasn't hard to put the two events together. Not when he described you down to the shade of the beauty mark under your jaw." Scarlet's brows furrowed, the woman clearly lost in thought. "When you left him as well, I too thought you'd been abducted or worse. But then, a year ago, I caught some henchmen of Madam's pilfering letters with your name on them, and I remembered you have a knack for surviving. Too smart to die." Shadows formed in her eyes. "I know better than anyone how our secrets can destroy those around us." The darkness fled and she shrugged. "I knew you had to have a good reason." Her voice steeled. "That doesn't mean you're forgiven."

Camille's heart clenched at the mention of Renard and his nightly efforts of search. No one had ever offered so much of themselves to her well-being. In a way, he had become like a dark hero, sacrificing his life and compromising his morals to rescue her from the evils of this world. Worse, she cared for him still; neither of them should be forgiven.

"I know," she said.

"And you better be prepared for an ear-bending lecture from Syd," Scarlet said. "She's gone and grown into a woman since you left, all 'checking in' and wanting to 'talk.' Damn miracle."

"That's why you aren't skinning my hide?"

"It is a nice bonus." Scarlet's smile slipped, her actor's mask falling away to show real feeling. "You worried us good, Cam. Don't go expecting an easy welcome from the rest."

"I'm to see Madam next," Camille said. "And my mother."

Scarlet nodded and slid her a shot across the bar. "Then you have my pity."

CAMILLE DIDN'T KNOCK. Slipping the chain from around her neck, she placed her key in the Prodding Pony door's lock and let herself in.

The smell greeted her first. A mixture of lavender and rose perfume the girls had taken to wearing to mask the smell of the streets outside. Then came the two stairs to the right leading up to Madam's office, the wooden boards scrubbed clean every morning to bring out the faces in the grain. Then stood the door, a simple wood that looked forbidding and authoritative despite its bright-red color.

This time, Camille *did* knock, and the sharp sound of her knuckles against the wood sounded like logs snapping in the fire.

"Enter!"

Camille steeled herself against the tone of Madam's command. She took a steadying breath and opened the door to find the woman seated at her desk as always, her mushed hair and ruined paint the same.

Madam's concentration stayed on the file before her, identical to every other in the growing *six* stacks on her desk and overflowing off the chairs.

"Leave your report on the floor or wherever you find space," she ordered.

"Looks like a storm went through here."

Madam's head shot up. Her gaze latched on Camille as if she and her voice were apparitions. But after a careful assessment of her person, the older woman leaned back in her chair with a lazy grin, the undisputed mistress of her kingdom once again. "You've returned, then? About time." She glanced around the room. "Start anywhere, throw the reports in the fire, or out the window, for all I care!"

Camille didn't smile. "Is that what it will take for you to forgive me?"

Madam straightened at that. "A spell in the good life and you've grown soft on me, Angel?"

"People don't change that much," Camille said. "But perspectives do."

The things they'd discussed before she'd gone into hiding had been just words, but Madam's offer to house the Duke and Duchess of Camine not three days ago after the marquess imposter had snuck onto Camine grounds and near drowned Charlotte had put those words into actions. Actions that might have saved both her brother's and sister-in-law's lives.

"For what you did for my brother and sister"—Camille bowed her head—"I am in your debt."

"Enough of that!" Madam stood from the desk and crossed the room. "I owe you far more and we both know it. Besides"— she tapped a nail on her bottom lip in remembrance—"what fun they were. A fine pair. That duchess has fire. Her Grace, previously the Lady Charlotte Louis, if I'm not mistaken. The lady you wrote those letters to." Madam gave her a nod of approval. "Well done."

"You're not going to scold me?"

"I'm not your mother." Madam shuddered. "Good thing too. It's a wonder you learned any compassion with that dragon blood in your veins. She'll remain here, if you don't mind? I've come too far breaking that beast for you to ruin my efforts with your coddling."

Camille winced, unable to imagine her mother beyond anything but a broken shell. She'd been putting off the subject and her visit. "How is my mama—"

"That's not what you wish to ask me." Madam interrupted, giving her a knowing look.

Camille huffed a laugh, all pretenses dropping. "No, it's not."

"Well?"

Camille bit her lip. She'd be damned to hell for what came next, but there was no option. Not when she'd given up such things as innocence and purity when she'd given her heart to a devil. Gaze unwavering, she looked Madam in the eye and said, "I want your word you will tell no one of the duke's secrets. His fate is to be left up to me and me alone. I'll cash in every one of my favors if that's what it will take to ensure your silence. I'll owe you this time."

Madam waved her plea away as if expecting it. "He found you, then?" The older woman sighed at Camille's silent nod and turned back to her desk. "Keep the favors. I like having someone not owe me anything. The days would be unbearably dull without an equal."

Camille held her breath. "And the duke?"

"His fate has always been in your hands, Angel. Damnation or salvation, you were aptly named."

Her relief was a mix with befuddlement. "I don't understand. You benefit off the secrets and predicaments of others. Your business depends on it, but you've never once held my own over my head. It defies logic."

"Logic." Madam chuckled. "My Angel, so clever and pure, still can't see the truth."

"Which is?"

"You're tenacious, opinionated, and, better, far more often than not, right."

Camille blinked. "And?"

Madam cocked her head, angling a sharp gaze at her like an owl from a tree hollow. "Did you know, adultery is a learned behavior with nobility? Sons learn from their fathers. Sons, in turn, view wives as a means to continue their lines and then discard them for more scintillating entertainment, and the cycle continues. Generation after generation, only needing a single man of merit and fidelity to break the course, but rarely does it happen. The irresponsibility of siring bastards and neglecting them, however, is as old as the aristocracy itself."

Camille's brain eased into the subject change and the connection. "Your father was a member of the gentry. That doesn't explain anything. Dozens of bastards walk the streets. Your charity doesn't extend to them."

Madam's smirk was approving. "Worse than any old titled man. He was a duke." She paused. "The Duke of Camine."

Shock sped Camille's brain into a frenzy. Not *her* father. Madam was too old to be a long-lost sister, which meant it was the previous Duke of Camine . . . her and Hamish's grandfather.

"You're my aunt."

It didn't make sense. The duke's line was notorious for scandalous dalliances, but no duke, especially not the vain and conceited line of Camines, would have left their 'kept' women unprovided for. Like her, Madam—Aunt Clarice—must have had other opportunities.

Camille indicated the club with an all-encompassing glance. "Why here?"

Madam leaned back against her desk, displacing a stack of papers in a haphazard leaning tower. "I wished to help women like me, like us. I had not your mental prowess or stubbornness. I was born with beauty and charm and a need to control that which controlled me."

She shrugged and Camille felt the overwhelming weight of years of toil and hardship in the gesture.

"When the duke died, I decided: I could follow in my mother's footsteps and find a rich benefactor until my beauty faded, or I could build an empire where those same men would bow before their pleasure at my hands, at their expense."

Camille didn't hide her admiration. "An easy decision."

Madam smiled. "I thought so."

"Is that why you offered me a job?"

"Partially." Madam didn't apologize for the deception. "If you had shown up at my door pathetic and mindless, I would have thrown you out for your own good. No woman should choose this life out of desperation, though many do. But you were proud and fierce, and I saw myself in your refusal to cower under the threat of destitution." Madam leaned over and extracted a file from her top drawer and set it in her hands. "Which is why I know you will make good use of this."

Camille frowned and opened the file. There lay her proposal for her shelter for women, along with a deed to an old, abandoned school on the outskirts of Caring Cross.

"What is this?"

Madam cocked her head. "A counter-proposal. The space is yours."

"You're giving me a building?"

"It was payment for services rendered by a man who could not afford membership. A man *you* vetted and claimed the girls would enjoy. The deed was offered up willingly, and the man has never whispered a regret about the exchange. And neither have the Ponies."

A space for her shelter. She literally had the deed in her hands. "You're giving me a building."

Madam snorted. "Don't be grateful. It doesn't suit you. Yes, the building is yours, along with the full support of the Prodding Pony."

"But the taxes? The maintenance—"

"You may thank Lord and Lady Quickner for the ease of transition." Madam rolled her eyes. "The way those two went on and on about repaying the kindness of *their* angel, it was a relief to demand the money and shut them up. Don't be surprised if they ask for their names painted on the door in gauche, golden letters."

The obstacles that had lined her path all these years were falling one after another like toy soldiers overturned. Camille's joy was laced with suspicion. It couldn't be that easy.

"What is it *you* want in return?"

Madam's smile was exacting. "When you acquire the funds to get up and running through benefactors or tuition or whatnot, I ask only one thing."

Camille's chest felt so light, she'd fetch the woman the moon. "Bastard girls will pay nothing," she said. "Any gentleman thinking to dump their *mistakes* will pay through the nose."

"Good." Madam offered her hand and her condition. "And bastard dukes pay double."

Camille grinned. "It will be a charitable institution." She took her new partner's hand firmly and shook to a like mind. "They'll pay triple."

Madam threw back her head and barked a laugh.

CHAPTER TWENTY-SIX

T HE VISIT WITH her mother had shown Camille that Madam had done more than promised. Fresh-faced and weighing a healthy two stone heavier, her mother had greeted Camille with a nod of acknowledgement and an offer to ring for tea, an embarrassing display of affection coming from the woman. Camille had been unable to do anything but blink and sit before the tilting room proved she was conjuring the stranger's image with her mother's face. The conversation that followed was stunted but cordial and by far the nicest interaction she'd had with her mother. Ever.

Feeling emotionally drained, Camille stopped by the Camine Townhouse to rest before making the twelve-mile journey back to the country, only to find the duke was in residence and waiting for her in the library.

Camille leaned in the doorway and crossed her arms. "You rang, Your Grace?"

Hamish looked up from the book in his lap and teased, "You're supposed to call me 'Hamish.'"

"So informal, Your Grace. What would the neighbors think?"

"Let them think what they like. How did your visits go?"

Her gaze narrowed. "Having that awful man of yours follow me again?"

"Hardly. You told Charlotte, Charlotte told me, and here I am."

"Why?"

He cocked a brow. "I thought your reunions may be difficult."

Camille blinked. "You came all the way to town . . . to make sure I was all right?"

"Partially. I also came to offer you unsolicited advice."

Camille smirked at the gleam in his eye. "Taking this brother thing a bit far, aren't you?" Expecting another lecture on formal greetings or a discussion on what position she'd take now that the Duchess of Camine no longer needed a companion, she plopped down in the chair opposite and crossed her ankles. "Out with it, then."

"You need to talk to Renard."

She had not been expecting *that*. "It's not that simple."

"When did love become simple?" Hamish looked around. "Do you have any idea the madness I went through with Charlotte to get her to the altar? And all that was *before* I realized she'd gone and won my heart."

Like a knight of old. For some reason, imagining Charlotte, in her starched dresses and fine coiffures playing heroine to the formidable Duke of Camine, made the image bearable.

"It's not the same. There are . . . circumstances—"

"Do you love Renard?"

Camille startled at his directness. "Love." She scoffed. "You are the exception, the *only* exception to that fairytale lie. You saw what 'love' looks like for people like us, with parents like ours. Love is a joke, a well-spun story for children to believe they weren't a line drawn on some ancient family registry. Any adult believing such notions is bound for tragedy."

"Camille." Hamish shook his head, his expression insufferable. "Family is important above all things. There is no place for treachery or disloyalty. Not in my future."

Camille snorted, wondering if that self-righteous speech would change after discovering the connection between their family and a calculating madam they both knew. "Marriage has made you an idealist."

"Perhaps," he said. "But I believe I'm the better for it."

"Not everyone gets their happy ending, Hamish. Some people were meant to be alone."

"I understand," he said. "Lord knows I lived by that philosophy for too many years, but . . ." He sat forward in his chair, his words thoughtful. "*We* are not our father. We are capable of genuine kindness and love, more than that entitled monster could ever dream up. The day I stopped believing I was anything like him was the day I took my life in my own hands and *believed* in myself. He had his hooks dug into me so deep while he was living, I refuse to let him hold me in death."

The passion in his voice hit her square in the chest. Camille felt a thread deep inside fray apart, along with the knowledge her father had taken a hold of her as well.

She was not her father. She was not her mother. Every lie they'd told, every action they'd taken to belittle her, cage her, use her—the effect those actions had had on her had been of her own making. No one had a right to her mind or body, not without her unequivocal consent. And her heart, that was hers to give as well.

The sudden absence of tension was head-spinning. She clutched the edge of her chair and sank deeper into the cushions before her body gave up entirely and slid to the floor.

All this time, her father's ghost had held her back from giving herself over to emotion. Emotions were weak and fleeting. She had to be hard and cold to keep others from using her as *he* had done.

All she'd ever done was doubt. She looked at her *brother* anew, seeing the sharp edges from when they'd first met had all but vanished by the power and smoothing grace of love. The epiphany was life-changing. And the ridiculous man had come to it first.

She scrunched her nose at him. "When did you become so insufferably wise?"

Hamish smirked. "My wife's words, not mine. I was too

thick-headed to see it too."

"Are you calling me stubborn?"

He leaned back in his chair. "Frankly, it's an improvement. You've been a cold fish since the day we met. After so many months living with you, I was beginning to think you incapable of delicate feeling. But one conversation with Renard and I see it now; *I* was the cold one." He lowered his head. "I expected you to act a certain way based on my own ignorant observations and prejudices. And then I made inaccurate assumptions. Forgive me?"

Once again, a taut thread snapped, one that had knotted around her lungs. With it gone, she breathed in an equal footing between them, a foundation to build.

"Should I thank Charlotte for this new humble side of you?" Camille asked. "Or have you done the unthinkable and realized your flaws make you as fallible as the rest of us?"

Hamish didn't take the bait. He *did* grin. "You're fallible now? Seems I'm not the only one learning self-discovery."

Camille rolled her eyes. "I've had enough emotional revelations today. Any more *discovery* and I'm likely to become violent. Unless that is your hope?"

"Depends." Hamish looked down at her booted feet. "Do you have any more shoes at disposal for throwing than the two on your feet?"

"I could use the books on the shelves."

"Too heavy to throw."

"Not when angered."

Hamish eyed the hundreds of volumes. "Wait until Renard visits to test your theory, please."

"I never said I'd talk with him."

Hamish inclined his head. "No, you didn't."

Camille smiled at his confident expression, and it felt good. The bridge forming between them did as well.

The emotional ride of the morning continued to dip and turn in directions she'd never thought possible. Discovering, mending, and now deepening relationships; who'd have thought humans capable of such growth and change? Of course the change wasn't all happy awakenings. The bruises and heart ache previous had been nothing compared to the torture to come.

One last relationship needed to change, but what kind remained shrouded in uncertainty. Seeing Renard again, being touched by him, those awakenings had been the same as before; her body demanding control from her mind. But her mind would lead the next steps going forward. A mind that grasped that emotion and logic weren't clashing enemies, but a harmonizing of thought and soul.

Hamish rose from his chair and offered her a hand up. "Shall we take the carriage back? If we leave now, we'll make it back in plenty of time for dinner."

"Eager to ride back to your wife?"

Hamish didn't hide the confirmation on his face or in his one-word reply. "Yes."

Camille took his hand. She liked his directness and shameless feeling. Another few months with Charlotte and the man may learn to be more than *tolerable* company. "Very well." She'd need to manage the gut-churning bumps and turns eventually before that evening.

When she'd need to take the carriage out for one last visit.

CHAPTER TWENTY-SEVEN

I T WAS ONLY natural for Camille to answer her brother's door that late afternoon after so many months of anxious vetting. It was instinct and memory and, since Mr. Frendstone was quite taken with his new role as the duchess's unofficial bodyguard, someone had to take over the old man's diligent post.

But when the door opened, it was not to admit a formal caller to Her Grace. It was a call of a much more intimate nature. There'd be no need to take the carriage to Lux Manor.

Renard bowed to her, tipping his hat and offering a guarded smile. "Good evening, Miss Forthright."

Camille rebelled at the formal greeting, so distant and cold. The cut of his coat still showed the loss of frame, but the fine fabric and expert press of black moleskin made him look dashing and dangerous in a way that had her core tightening.

Camille ignored her body's reaction. The conversation to come would be best without bestial desires complicating matters. "Good evening, Your Grace."

"May I come in? There are things we must discuss."

She opened the door wider and closed the door when he crossed the threshold.

He followed her silently into the library, waiting for that door to close too before he spoke again.

He removed his hat almost sheepishly, his smile warming. "I was a cad for not saying so earlier, but that dress style suits you."

Camille blinked at the sudden compliment and glanced down at her high collar and lace-lined sleeves.

"Not what you were expecting me to say?"

She turned her head, shaking off the spell of his presence and easy nature. "Charm is a weapon in and of itself I suppose. I should have prepared myself."

He frowned. "This is to be a fight then?"

"Isn't it always?"

"No," he said quietly. "It wasn't always."

Camille turned to the cold hearth, the longing in his gaze undoing all her erected mental barriers. Barriers that must remain in place. The balance between her mental fortitude and emotion was precarious at best.

"You forget yourself, Your Grace," she said. "If you wish to cross boundaries, I will call for a servant to act as a chaperone. Someone you cannot charm."

"Ah, yes." He rubbed his chin and grinned. "'Assuming, arrogant dandy too self-important to take a shit without a valet's admiration of skill.'"

Her eyes widened. "You remembered?"

He snorted. "I may not have your talent for insult or memory, but one does have a tendency to remember such a specific personal attack."

"You deserved it," she said, scales tipping towards the nonsensical. "You called me a conniving, manipulative wench."

"You ran." He crossed his arms over his chest. "*You* deserved it."

There was that feeling again. That flutter of excitement. Wit and humor, like a physical acknowledgment from one opponent to another.

As it had always been between them. A battle, a dance, a duel of minds and compatibility of bodies that would leave even the most rational mind spinning with the idea of soul mates.

But important parts remained missing after that horrible day at the Pony. Thrown out as easily as words too cruel to be forgiven: mutual respect and trust.

"I didn't hide anything from you," she said.

"I know," he said quietly.

That tone and that face speared her heart like an arrow to the target. Just as it had always done, as it would continue to do. This was the deciding moment.

She would leave. Nothing was left to say. Too much had passed between them, happened to them. Some relationships couldn't be saved. The close bond she'd felt—the connecting of fate's string—was left threadbare and gaping. They'd grown too cynical, too different in their grief and struggles. There was nothing left between them at all.

Until he said the words that would connect them forever.

"I grieve for our baby too." Unbuttoning his coat, he slid one arm free to reveal the black band.

A sob burst through her lips, too violent and sudden to stop. And then he was there, holding her in his arms, spreading slow kisses across her crown. She allowed the comfort and solace, knowing her legs and heart would buckle without the support.

"Thank you for sending that letter," he whispered. "I was beside myself not knowing what became of him."

Camille wept anew.

When her tears had finally subsided, he asked quietly, "What happened to him?"

"He was buried in Westminster, behind St Martin-in-the-Fields."

"He doesn't belong there." His arms tightened around her. "Would you let me bring him home to Lux estate?"

Camille drew back, tears turning her vision blurry. She wiped at her eyes, needing to see his expression. "You would bury him in your family's cemetery?"

"He *is* my family," Renard said with conviction. Then his mouth curled into a small smile. "Besides, I don't think my mother or father would have it any other way."

Somehow the idea of family, of her son resting in the same

place as the people who would've been his grandparents, people Camille knew had been good and kind in life, made the separation in death easier to bear.

Camille closed her eyes, envisioning a little boy with her red hair and Renard's bright eyes. "I'd like that."

He nodded. "I'll have him moved tomorrow."

"Thank you."

His hands rubbed soft circles on her back, the touch gentle, familiar. "Milly, will you come back with me?"

That name, the one he'd used in private while they lay in each other's arms, filled Camille with joy and pain. They'd known each other but a few weeks and had fallen so hard. Even now, she couldn't understand the changes over that brief time. She wished to go back to that time—before the pregnancy, before the obsession which had led Renard to harm those whom he perceived had hurt her—and assess those feelings to pinpoint exactly when they'd both lost all sense of right and wrong. But she couldn't go back, not when her memory was long and objective.

She pulled away. "No, Renard. I cannot go with you."

He buried his face in her hair, as if her rejection hurt him physically. "Why must you keep running from me?"

The emotion in his voice pulled at her own. They were both creatures of dark things, selfish wishes. But they were not the same. No, even as unforgiveable as Renard's actions against Flank and Grey were, he'd committed sins for the sake of someone else. While she had destroyed three lives, more, for her own pride.

"You know what I am," she said, hating how her position and circumstances had damned her since the cradle. "I am bastard born, a blemish on society and the good name of bad men. Our first encounter was coincidence, the ones that followed were destined to ruin."

"That's nonsense, Camille." Renard's voice was firm, even as his touch gentled. "We are all more than our parents' names and expectations. We are what we make of ourselves."

"Then I am still a monster."

Renard released her then, but not to retreat from her admission. He tipped up her chin and asked, "How could you think such rubbish? A second with you in a dark alley and I knew you'd fallen from the heavens."

She pushed him away. "That's unfair." Her chest burned, her throat ached. "I'm not some angel to place in the clouds. If you knew what I'd done"—she bit her lip—"you'd never look at me the same."

"You are a devil, you wretch. Not even hell would forgive what you've done!"

He cradled her face in his hands. "Then tell me. Make me understand."

"It was me," she whispered. "*I told the gossip sheets about the duke's affair.*"

Renard's brows pinched. When his face cleared with understanding, his voice was incredulous. "*You* threw your own life into scandal? But why? Weren't you taken care of?"

"There was a roof over our heads, and food for our bellies, if that's what you mean. But my *father*"—she couldn't say the word without snarling—"kept my mother and me like pets. She, for his own satisfaction, and me . . . I was no more than a commodity to gain power."

"What do you mean, Milly?"

Fresh tears blurred her gaze, but these were not from grief like the previous ones; these were droplets of pure rage. Rage and hurt she must share now, no matter how much it stung. Because the man before her had committed such atrocities believing she was an angel, when she'd been a vengeful spirit all along.

"I've had a good memory since I was a child," she said. "The *duke* used me to impress benefactors for his foundations, put me on display for dinner parties under the guise of me being a distant relative. I was the perfect child, you see. I had to be. My mother raised me with the knowledge that a girl who obeys is safe. A 'good girl' is allowed to eat and wash and wear pretty dresses.

"But as I grew, and my beauty as a child did not fade, the duke's interests in what I may gain for him changed." Revulsion replaced the anger. She shuddered, remembering the hands that had run over her body, assessing her 'true worth.' "The duke sent for me one night to meet a friend of his, I thought to encourage the man to invest in one of his schemes, but I was not summoned for business, but for pleasure."

Renard froze at her side, but he did not ask. Did not push. He waited for her to regain her composure.

"I would not let the man touch me." She waited for Renard to breathe again before continuing. "The duke raged and threatened me, struck me, bullied me, beat me until my skin broke, said he would have my mother throw me out into the streets if I did not obey." She could still feel the sting of the belt across her back, the memory of the pain lasting long after the skin had healed.

Remembering her father's slackened jaw when she'd spat in his face and walked from his study, head held high, the blood running down her back, brought a smile to her face . . . until she remembered the rest of that night.

She'd wandered through the rookeries, her triumph tainted knowing the duke would keep his word. She'd be left destitute, homeless, and friendless.

Then she'd found Scarlet behind the Prodding Pony, her clothes torn and her body bleeding—as Camille was torn and bloody—and they'd formed an instant sisterhood. After she'd settled Scarlet in the clinic, Camille had stomped back to the club and released her full ire at Madam Clarice, not caring what happened to her when the older woman took offense.

But Madam had done the one thing that had saved her: She'd offered Camille a job and protection. It was that boon, that brief moment of belief she'd bested her father, that had led her to make the one mistake that night.

"The next morning, I went to the papers," she said. The reporter had lapped up her story like a horse at a trough. "The story was printed that same day as a special edition. I was so caught up in justice for my father's actions, I forgot how the scandal would affect my mother."

'Affect' was too kind a word. Left without benefactor or offerings for any other bedmate, her mother had retreated into herself, not emerging for anything save drinking or screaming insults at her ungrateful daughter who'd destroyed their lives. In place of freedom, Camille had led herself into another cage, one of resentment and responsibility.

"That bastard." Renard released her to pace, his hands gesturing wildly. "Of all the insidious acts, using his flesh and blood for advancement. Good thing he's dead. Not worth the privies he pissed in."

Renard stopped and pivoted back towards her. "You are perfect, you hear me? You could have been born with a tail and horns and you'd still be worth a damned king's fortune over that idiot. Of all the asinine, evil deeds in the world, making you believe you were less than a miracle. The duke was the monster, Camille, not you."

Camille stared, not fully comprehending the pain in her chest was her torn heart stitching itself back together. Still, her head wouldn't relinquish the guilt. "I ruined our lives—"

"Whose lives? The duke's? Your mother's?" Renard huffed. "Good riddance. You did what was best for you that day, probably for the first time. The only one to blame is the duke."

Camille clutched her chest as Renard continued to spout all the ways the duke should have been punished, sure her heart couldn't take much more. She knew about the body's anatomy; she knew the heart was but a muscle, but the way the tears mended at his words defied medical marvel as the truth rendered her guilt and past to shreds.

"If I'd but known three years ago, I'd have poisoned the duke's scotch and hung for it, gladly."

Camille blinked as her brain processed Renard's continued rants, and his admission brought their conversation—and the purpose of this meeting—back into focus. "Is that why you killed

Grey and Flank? Out of a sense of familial responsibility?"

Renard stopped. "What are you talking about?"

"The bodies of Flank and Grey you left in the streets." She ran a hand over her face, too tired to play this cerebrally. "I'd forgiven you the moment I realized what you'd done, though I'd still stay away from Dockside. I know Syd falling off the roof was an accident, but Markus tends not to listen to reason where his daughters are concerned."

"Camille!"

Her head shot up at his alarmed tone. His eyes were wide, his face pale.

"Y-You think I had something to do with bodies in the streets?"

Camille wouldn't trust the hope flaring in her gut at his stunned expression. "You didn't?"

He ran a hand through his hair, his body trembling. "Wait! Is that why you ran? You thought I was killing people to keep you safe? I would gladly have beat those three ratbags to the ground for what they put you through, but I would never kill someone—" His voice cut off. He squared his shoulders and his expression darkened. "I have to tell you something."

She stilled, heartbeat erratic. "What is it?"

"I didn't touch those scumbags after that first night. I swear it on Charlotte's soul. I would never put you at risk like that. You said Flank and Grey, which means Hawkins is still out there. He probably did his men in to frame you. Though the man doesn't seem to have the brains for such schemes." He shook his head. When his gaze met hers, his eyes blazed. "If you doubt me in everything else, know I did not do this."

Truth rang in his words, but she couldn't give into relief. "Madam had a file on you. It said you admitted to murder."

Renard cursed Madam's name. He ran a hand through his hair and seemed to collect himself. "I swear to you, Milly, I had nothing to do with those deaths in Dockside. Ask that snake of a woman and she'll confirm I never confessed to anything like that."

"But . . ." Hope sprang anew. Only for confusion to take its place. "Then what about—"

"Madam was right. I *have* killed before."

Camille's insides squeezed.

"But it's not what you think." He took a deep breath, one of courage and acceptance.

"My parents. Their deaths were my doing."

Her mind stopped. She blinked as confusion flared again. She'd read about what had happened years ago. "Renard, your parents died in a fire."

"*I* started the fire."

"You . . ." She shook her head, not bothering to entertain the idea. Renard had loved his parents. He would never have hurt someone he loved, not for anything in the world. "I won't believe for a moment you did it intentionally. Therefore, it was an accident and not your fault."

CHAPTER TWENTY-EIGHT

RENARD STARED AT her. His greatest and ugliest secret he'd buried for ten years of his life aired and the woman didn't so much as gasp in scandalous outrage. Even Madam Clarice's careful mask had slipped when he'd confessed. Camille had believed he'd killed two grown men in cold blood—which had stung, bled like a fucking knife to the chest—but the suggestion of murdering his parents and the woman dismissed it with a wave of her hand.

He shook his head. "You can't know that."

"Then explain it," Camille said, her expression open, patient. "What possible reason would you have to trap the duke and duchess in a burning stable?"

"Of course I didn't trap them! But I started the fire, they went inside, and . . . didn't come out." Foolishness and naivety. When the flames had gotten out of control, he'd had this unmistakable moment of understanding, as if his childhood had been scorched from his body with the rest of the wood and straw.

"What were you doing?"

Renard came out of his thoughts at Camille's impatient tone. "Huh?"

"When the fire started, what were you doing?"

Shame turned the blood in his body hot. And there it was. His self-loathing, his and his sister's stolen innocence and strained relationship came down to one stupid act of rebellion.

His breath wasn't steady, and neither were his next two. "I was smoking my father's pipe. I'd stolen it from his desk and thought the stables would be deserted that time of day with the master and hands exercising four of the six horses in the pasture. And it was deserted, except for one other person."

Claws of guilt ripped at his gut from the inside. If he'd known Charlotte was in the hayloft, he'd never have gone inside. He'd have gone to the lake or the woods, or any other quiet place.

It wasn't until his parents had raced down at the first sign of smoke, rushing past the gawking servants and straight into the burning building that Renard had realized the extent of his folly, and what that folly may cost him.

"Does Charlotte know you've blamed yourself all these years?" she asked.

The thought of telling Charlotte made his stomach bottom out. "It won't come to that."

"She deserves to know, Renard. She believes you grew to view her as an obligation."

"By design." How could he ever allow himself to stay close to his innocent little sister? Not after what he'd taken from her.

He'd tell Charlotte one day soon. She deserved the truth. But right now, he needed the woman standing before him to know the truth. "Do you believe me, then? That I had nothing to do with those men's murders?" *Please believe me.*

Her nod was slow in coming, but when her gaze once again found his, he saw she'd accepted his words.

"You didn't hurt those men," she said, expression brightening. Only for that light to vanish into horror. "You didn't hurt those men," she repeated. A choking sound came out of her throat. "I ran for nothing. My God, Renard, I am sorry. I thought . . . It doesn't matter what I thought. I should have stayed and confronted you about my suspicions, but I *did* run and our son was lost because I—"

"Stop," Renard said, cutting her off with an uncompromising tone. "There was nothing either of us could've done for our son.

Don't you dare take on the burden of our son's death. You would've loved our child as I would've loved him. No." He stated his feelings as fact. "I *love* our son. Affection doesn't stop with death."

Her eyes turned glassy. She nodded once. For a moment, she looked truly lost. "Everything has gotten so muddled."

That it had. He could only imagine the hardships she'd had to go through the past year. Thinking he'd hurt people on her behalf, losing their child, living day to day not knowing where she belonged or how she'd live.

At least that worry he would correct here and now.

He wiped away a tear on her cheek. "After we marry and you are settled, I'll turn myself in for my parents' deaths." He'd had many months to think about the consequences. He explained them now. "I'm sorry, my current heir will no doubt make staying in Lux estate impossible. You'll most likely be banned from the premises, but I'm sure Hamish and Charlotte will look after you. And there are some funds I've set aside, with no ties to the title or properties. If you don't wish to stay with our relatives, you could find a small cottage somewhere to rent. It won't be the life of luxury you deserve, but you'll be looked after all the same—"

Camille's boot hit him square in the nose.

He looked down at the offending footwear. "Ow! Damn it." He dabbed at his nose. Why the hell was *she* angry? He was here to make everything right. "*Women!* Why must you always go for the face?"

"Because you are an idiot." Camille struggled to get her second off.

Renard picked up the nearest cushion and held it at the ready. "You're acting hysterical. I know this is a shoddy way to propose, but—"

The boot went wide when she threw it. His gaze followed where it landed beside the desk. He turned with a smug grin when a book came flying at his head instead.

He missed the immortal works of Shakespeare with a more lucky than agile duck-and-swerve.

The tome smacked into the desk and cracked the book's binding. Getting ready with *The Great Works of Byron* next, Renard tackled her to the chase before she could destroy another priceless piece of his friend's library.

She flailed beneath him, using her hands to strike at him when everything else lay out of arm's reach.

"Desist, at once!" He trapped her wrists together, underestimating her range, and rage, when she bit him in the hand. "For the love of God, Camille, stop! Don't marry me, then. Don't have anything to do with me or the title. I will tell my sister the truth. After that, I'm sure she'll still support you. I meant only to spare you from any unpleasant exposure—"

"You will tell no one, do you hear me?" She muttered something unflattering about men and their botched heroics. "Not only would your crazed shouts be more than exposing, worse, someone might actually believe your nonsense."

"Camille—"

"You *did not* kill your parents, Renard. You were fourteen. And it was an *accident*."

The conviction in her words clawed at the shame and regret that had taken up residence in his chest all those years ago. But those claws couldn't scratch deep enough to set him free.

"Release me," Camille said quietly.

Realizing he still held her trapped on the chase, Renard pulled away and sat at the foot of the furniture, putting his head in his hands. All this was his mess. Every bad thing that had happened to those around him could be traced back to that afternoon. He'd played with fate and ruined the plans of so many lives. Fate, in turn, had dangled love and contentment before him, and he'd nipped at the bait like a horse to the bit, even though he'd known better. Getting others involved had been a mistake. He'd gone after Camille with nothing but selfish need driving his actions, and nothing but tragedy had come of it all.

Even now he clung to the idea of saving her, when she clearly did not want a thing to do with him anymore. Perhaps she'd never cared for him, and it had all been a conceited illusion of his own making. God, he'd more than ruined Camille's life, he'd taken her innocence, her home. A part of him was devastated she'd ever thought him capable of cold-blooded murder. The other part knew, premeditated or not, he *had* killed.

A warm body pressed to his side. Renard looked up to see Camille sitting beside him, her face scrunched in concentration.

"I . . ." She started and stopped three times before she sighed and said, "I don't know how to comfort you. Kindness, warmth—they were things I was never taught. Emotions were unnecessary, nothing but liabilities. But you feel so much." She waved around the room, her gaze going to the books and shoes flung across the room. "You make *me* feel. Grand emotions and tiny ones, ones that make me want to scream and others that are so subtle, I need to whisper or they'll vanish." She rubbed at her forehead. "I can't understand what you're feeling right now. You in no way are responsible for your parents' deaths, but you disagree. Normally, I would call you an idiot and force you to admit I'm correct. It took my insufferable brother to point out the flaw in *my* logic." She smirked and offered a humbling shake of her head. "Your feelings matter, and it is possible they may not . . . be wrong."

Renard stared at her. If she'd serenaded him while wearing a man's trousers and vest, he couldn't have been more surprised. Her words stirred the dregs of kind feeling left in him, one particular feeling he dared not give name to. "Did you just admit to being wrong?"

She scowled. "Terrible listener as always, Your Grace."

"You said I was right." She'd said far more. *"You make me feel."*

"I said you may *not be wrong.*"

That feeling grew in him until its namesake became hope itself. "By extension, that makes you wrong."

She stood. "Never mind. You are an idiot. Everything must be a battle between us."

"No, wait!" He took her hand and guided her back to her seat. "Please," he said in earnest. "I must know. All this time I thought . . . Never mind what I thought. I need the truth, Camille. You ran to protect me?"

She bit her lip, but she did not look away. "Yes."

Renard's heart soared. She'd never admitted to sharing his affections. She still didn't now, but the words didn't matter. She'd never gone to the Yard, never wanted her connection with the dead men to lead back to him. She'd run *for* him.

The past year of anguish and worry disappeared. None of it mattered anymore now they were together again.

"Milly." He pressed a kiss to her hair, her temple, her cheek. He skimmed her mouth's edge when she pulled away and stood.

"It won't work, Renard," she said, though her flushed cheeks disagreed. "We are poison together. Now you tell me you have an heir who could take everything away. Can't you see that? You are titled and arrogant. I am prideful and cold. We'd make each other miserable!"

He watched her pace and was grateful to be alive. "You're right."

"You're not listening again—what?"

He stood. "You're right. We don't agree on anything. You refuse to be reasoned with, and I am the worst sober gentleman, *and* vain, *and* arrogant. Miserable, you say. Misery never meant a thing to me until you were gone where I couldn't follow. We are a futile combination. I won't deny it. You are common, I am an aristocrat. Society may damn us, may run us out of every town in England. And I will welcome it all." He took a step forward for each declaration until he'd backed her against the window. "You admitted you were wrong. You've changed over these months in ways I'm only beginning to understand. And, if you can change, so can I.

"I want to change for you, for me, for Charlotte. You make me want that. Being a better man never occurred to me before I met you. I thought I'd be forever a hollow vessel waiting for judgement day, but there's this voice that's been filling up that unending emptiness, a voice of reason and passion. *Your* voice." He placed his arms on either side of her head, trapping her with both his body and his gaze. "I thought I was being punished for my sins, but fate brought us together. I see now I was but a fool to not take you in my arms and hold you to me forever." He leaned down and spoke low in her ear. "For all your logic, you missed something important in your righteous speech of flaws and impossibilities. Something that puts paint to all of it."

Camille shook her head. "Affection isn't enough."

"Damn it, woman! I meant nothing of the sort." He grabbed her by the shoulders, his gaze intense. "We are perfect for each other because we're both too damn *stubborn* to lose."

HIS KISS WASN'T gentle. Rough and frenzied, it was a culmination of emotion over the past months: anger, regret, anguish, and love.

Camille folded into his embrace and pushed back everything he gave, a floodgate deep inside bursting open. Teeth clashing, tongues thrusting, fingernails digging in, their clothes torn from their bodies. They wrestled in a tangle of partial clothes and limbs to the floor, neither wishing to hand over control.

But after a moment, their manic embraces turned gentler, slower. The rest of their clothing was stripped off with care, the brush of fabric against naked skin heightening their passion instead of quelling it.

Renard pulled back suddenly and stared down at her. "I won't chase you anymore."

Camille stilled, her heart giving a painful *thud*.

"I'm going to follow you," he said.

Camille turned to him sharply, his words eliciting another, more frequent beating in her chest.

"Wherever you go, whatever you need, however long it takes. If you wish to patrol the streets and fight villains every night, I'll be there, offering support, flippant observations, and as many rocks as it takes for you to learn to trust me again."

He got down on one knee, handsome and statuesque in not a stitch of clothing, and took out a velvet box from his coat on the floor. "But there's only one rock I ask you take in the beginning, a symbol of my loyalty and faith in us."

Camille shook her head even as her heart was flying. "Marriage won't solve anything—"

He opened the box.

There, nestled in a silken pillow, was indeed a rock, the one she'd used to defend herself against Hawkins.

Her eyes filled with moisture as her voice filled with awe. "You kept it all this time?"

His eyes danced. "No matter the obstacle, I will overcome it for you. I will change to be a man you can rely on, show weakness to, and cherish you all the more for it. Whatever life I have left, I give to you, to do with as you wish. If I can spend the rest of my life arguing with you, I will consider myself a blessed man."

Remembering Lord Quickner's toast at the party, and the unfortunate near-death accident that had followed, Camille said with a tight gut, "You shouldn't tempt fate."

Renard's eyes blazed. "I'd tempt the very Devil for a chance at a life with you."

Camille's heart sang, somehow whole and pounding, as if the past year was nothing but a nightmare. Every conceivable reason to keep apart had burned to ash in his confession. He hadn't any involvement in the murders. Though she'd wished otherwise, there was no child between them to obligate his declaration. She'd done nothing in the past year but make the wrong decisions, brought on by wrong conclusions. But for once, the emotions in her heart felt right.

"I will not let you." She smoothed the sudden furrow on his

brow and did her best to explain. "You cannot overcome everything alone. I learned the power of family since I left. Without those around whom you can trust and rely on, we are weak, alone. If we are to do this, we will do it together or not at all." She smiled. "I will be there. As your wife."

Renard startled. "But you said—"

"I know what I said. I changed my mind."

He sighed, the tension leaving his shoulders. He laid her on her back and smoothed the hair from her face. "And I'm done being an idiot and asking questions when I should be kissing your feet in gratitude." Resting himself on his elbows on either side of her head, he kissed her forehead and promised, "Together, my Milly."

And their fates were sealed with a kiss.

CHAPTER TWENTY-NINE

T HEY'D LEFT FOR Gretna Green the instant they'd finished their reconciliation—two hours and several 'arguments' later. They'd lost so much time already, neither Camille's head nor her heart argued the need for expedited recompense.

Less than a week since their 'talk' and the vows were spoken, the documents signed, and the sight of Scotland's rolling hills were long in the carriage's posterior window. The carriage that lurched over a rut in the blasted road, informing Camille they were back on English soil.

"You wrote to Charlotte, yes?" Renard asked.

Camille nodded. "I told her only that we were figuring things out. Do you believe Charlotte and Hamish suspect?"

"That you are now the new Duchess of Lux?" Renard said.

"Duchess." She turned warm before cold reality sunk in. "What about the heir you mentioned? Will he really take you to court over objections to the line?"

Renard snorted. "I'd like to see him and his meddlesome mother try to take this away from us. I have you—nothing else matters. I'll crow our marriage from the top of Lux Manor's tower."

She smiled. "We have a tower?"

He kissed her knuckles, the warmth in his eyes doing more than the warming block at their feet to keep the chill away.

"You will have whatever you desire," he said. "Towers,

tarts . . ."

"Children?"

His other hand covered their intertwined fingers. "Yes, my dear. If you are willing?"

"You married me not knowing if I would sire an heir? Isn't that all you aristocrat males desire in life? Aren't you afraid your heir will inherit the title, if not win it by petition?"

He shrugged, the action so sweet, she wanted to fling off the wool blanket across his lap and replace it with her, astride him.

"None of that matters. I married you, Milly, *for you*. The manor and title can fall to that sniveling Mr. Norris or the devil himself."

Camille did take him for a ride after that, a ride that lasted the next several hours until they pulled up to their home in the country.

And, for once, Camille had not one complaint about the excessive rocking of the carriage.

➤➤➤◆◀◀◀

A RAPPING OF knuckles on the chamber door woke him.

Renard eased out of bed—careful not to wake his duchess—wrapped a dressing gown around himself, and accepted a letter from his valet through a crack in the door.

"Thank you, Fredricks. Would you ask Cook to bake some tarts for this afternoon? I wish to show the duchess the parks."

Fredricks bowed. "Yes, Your Grace. Would you care to shave and dress before I go?"

Renard rubbed the bristle on his jaw that had grown quite long in the week he'd been away. Camille had giggled last night when he'd kissed down her bare back, saying the tickle had been maddening. When his mouth had found its way to the apex between her thighs, she'd come after the first sweep of bristle to her delicate lips.

He grinned and shook his head. "Perhaps I'll let it go for now. I *am* a married man."

Fredricks's smile matched that of the rest of the staff since Renard had returned home, duchess in tow. "If I may, sir, it suits you."

Renard didn't need to ask to which statement the man approved.

"Will there be anything else, sir?" Fredrich asked. "Would you like me to wait in case you need reply urgently?"

Remembering the letter in his hand—the first of dozens of forthcoming invitations and callers, no doubt—Renard dismissed his valet's offer and told him to take the next few hours to enjoy a spot of breakfast. Glancing back at where the sheet had fallen to expose his wife's shoulder, Renard's body tightened. "The duchess and I will be indisposed for the rest of the morning."

Fredricks bowed again, amusement in his eyes. "Very good, sir."

Closing the door, Renard was prepared to throw the letter on the vanity and take full advantage of his wife's nakedness when the insignia on the seal stopped him cold.

He glanced Camille's way, determining she still slept.

Crossing to the window to read in the faint light seeping through an opening in the curtains, he broke the letter's seal with shaky hands.

Come to the club, or your secrets will reach your sister's ears before the authorities.

Madam

The older woman knew, somehow, of his reconciliation with Camille.

Renard stared at the note, the happiness of the past week leeching away into a spreading numbness that left him feeling nothing but the icy-cold floors underfoot. Fate had made its final decision.

He folded the letter and placed it back in its envelope with care, his actions slow, his thoughts a riot of chaos.

For years, every night since his parents' passing, he'd gone in search of his death, and every morning, he'd met the light, forced to suffer another day as a walking, empty vessel. Until he'd found that light in the dark, fierce and clever, holding a rock to hold off ruin and death as if they'd never touch her without consent, as if she'd deny the ugly truth of how some monsters took and never got what they deserved.

He wouldn't regret. Not one second. His actions and secrets had led to this moment. To the woman in his bed. His duchess who now bore his name.

He'd waited on a chair's edge every morning at breakfast since confessing his past to Madam Clarice, prepared for the bold headline on the front of *The Daily News* that would destroy his family's name and reputation.

Back in public view, his name and new wife would be on the lips of every gossip and worth a great penny to a Madam who coined in secrets; his reprieve was over. His cousin-heir would leap at the news and use the scandal to bolster his suit for the title.

"You're frowning," Camille said sleepily from the bed.

Renard tucked the letter into his waistband and smiled. "I was thinking." He went to her side of the bed and sat so he could place a kiss on her forehead. "I didn't mean to wake you. Go back to sleep, my love, and dream of our life together."

"Hmm." Her lashes were already fluttering closed. "Together . . ."

Renard's heart squeezed at the sight of her, perfect and lovely, sleeping peacefully after a long night of sex. She was his heart and his soul. He glanced down at her silhouette under the sheet, imagining she carried their child.

He prayed it was so. Prayed it with a piety and fear he hadn't felt since the day she'd left. *Let her be with child.*

If their vigorous coupling—the twenty or so since they'd

reconciled—wasn't enough to sprout the seed and he did lose his claim to his title, then his new brother-in-law would see to her care. He knew it as he knew Hamish would treasure his beloved sister, Charlotte, a sister who deserved to hear the truth from him and not the gossip rags.

Renard laid a hand over his heart and prayed some more, for Charlotte's happiness and understanding. He wouldn't pray for more time. Time was a measure of beginning and ending and had no hold on the bonds in his life. Love was unending and forever, and the goodbye he must face now would not be an end to anything. He swore it like an oath to God.

He kissed her lips this time, softly as to not wake her. Afterwards, he wrote a few words on a slip of paper and left it on the nightstand beside his wife before he went to the connecting chamber door to dress. He looked back once to etch the image of his duchess in his mind, his saving grace and partner.

To the angel in his bed or any who might be looking down upon him from on high, he whispered with sincere gratitude, "Thank you."

And he left.

CAMILLE LEFT HER dreams reluctantly. Stretching across silken sheets, she smiled at the light filtering through the curtains. She was warm and the day was bright.

And she was happy.

She knew it was more a particular person contributing to her happiness and not the comfort—though it was impressive—of her surroundings: the thick rugs covering the cold, wooden floors, the plush mattress beneath her body stuffed with the softest of down, the floral wallpaper done in a welcoming background of sky blue.

Camille rolled over to give her husband a show of gratitude, but the bed lay empty.

She sat up, bringing the sheets to her chest. "Renard?"

The dressing chamber door stood ajar.

She padded over to peek inside, the sheet doing nothing to ward off the chill. The room too was empty.

She checked behind the door and even glanced under the bed before she sat on its edge, at a loss. If the man had gone to break his fast, the least he could have done was wake her. Perhaps he was being gallant and hoped to surprise her with pastries in bed.

Camille smiled to herself and was prepared to dig back under the covers and feign sleep when a piece of parchment on her nightstand caught her eye. Opening it, Camille frowned.

The letters were so jumbled and the paper so ink-flecked, Camille gave herself a headache making out the words. When she did, her heart stopped.

Someone knows my secret. I must leave to make amends. Meet me at the Cock 'n Hen when you can.

Renard

Someone knew? How? The letter said 'make amends.' She flipped the paper over, searching for an explanation, but there was nothing.

Was someone blackmailing him? Were they threatening to go to the authorities and spin some nonsense about Renard being culpable for the previous duke's and duchess's deaths?

Dizzy from the flash of thoughts, she flung the sheet off and scrambled into the dress Renard had unbuttoned and discarded last night in their fervor for bed.

None of this made sense. Surely, a duke's word would give any constable pause? It *had* been an accident.

He'd told her to meet him at the tavern. Did that mean he meant to turn himself over to the authorities quietly to delay their names being dragged through the gossip pages?

Camille cursed at the unending row of buttons at her neck

and left the top half of her dress gaping as she dragged on her boots. Forgoing corset and stockings—but having a mind to wrap a modest shawl around her exposed back—she ran out the chamber door, flew down the stairs, and ran into the foyer.

What a fine time to claim heroics. Stupid man.

She loved him. More than scandal, more than big houses, and ridiculous gifts. That dumb cousin of his could have the title, could take the whole of England for all she cared. She'd leave this house. She'd leave the whole country if it meant they'd be together and he wouldn't be subjected to false accusations. But the idiot didn't think to ask her how she felt about all this.

She'd have to teach him what marriage was between a man and a woman. No, she'd teach him what *their* marriage would be, between him and her. Rules they could not only live with, but live by. Rules of love and trust, of acceptance and *common sense*, for heaven's sake!

Camille raced out the door, not giving a damn for a different set of rules that came to mind when she took two hands to raise her skirts and ran in search of a coach-and-four.

THE TAVERN'S MAIN floor was empty when Camille arrived.

Expecting Scarlet to shuffle out from the back any moment, Camille poured herself a drink and sat at the bar.

She ached from riding in the carriage. By the time she'd been free of the damned thing, she been ready to have it chopped for firewood. Mind in chaos, she'd dismissed the driver with directions to head to the Lux Townhouse.

The long miles had left her mind open to imagine the worst-case scenarios at her leisure, and her imagination was vast.

Renard could be in irons by now, having turned himself over to Scotland Yard. He could be dealing with underhanded blackmailers in a dark alley. The man could have been put upon by highwaymen on his way to the damned city!

Finding her glass empty, Camille poured herself another shot of whiskey and contemplated hiring the 'Merry Men' for a city-wide search for a fair-haired man in need of a swift boot to the head.

How could he run from her, without a word?

The internal question didn't sit well, knowing she had done the same less than a year ago.

She shook herself from her guilt. There'd be plenty of time to apologize to her husband, *after* she knocked sense into him.

If only his note had mentioned where *he* had gone. For all she could do now was sit and wait. Meeting at the tavern meant he must have been in London, but it was a big city, and any number of meeting places were barred to her, even with her new status as a duchess. Many admitted only men, for starters. Others would be unlikely to believe she *was* a duchess before the gossip rags started spreading the news.

Insufferable elite! What good was a title if it gained you nothing when in need?

Of course, there were the tried-and-true ways of gaining information, and spies were more reliable.

Camille called out Scarlet's name.

Leaving her drink, she wove through the back rooms, finding the place quiet. Circling back to the bar, Camille noted none of the chairs had been taken off the tables since last night's closing. No one was here. But the front had been open.

Had Scarlet forgotten to lock up last night?

Camille glanced at the clock. Manny and Scarlet would be in to open in less than an hour, if memory served, which it always did. Scarlet was lucky she'd been the one to stumble in and help herself to the bar instead of someone far more thirsty—or malicious.

Camille smiled with no small amount of smugness and relief at something to preoccupy her mind.

It would be nice to lecture her friend for a change. Camille went behind the bar and took up a rag and set herself to polish the glasses, eager for Scarlet to walk in and see her thus, waiting and full of advice.

Her mind quieted at the monotonous chore: rubbing circles into a glass from bottom to lip and setting it aside before grabbing another, and another, stacking the glasses three high before starting another.

She grabbed the last to be polished when the door opened. Catching a glimpse of fair hair, Camille whirled around to give Renard the tongue lashing he deserved.

But the man who entered was not Renard.

CHAPTER THIRTY

T HE MAN ENTERED the Cock 'n Hen with a swift but labored walk, a large, bulky bag dragging behind him. His hair was indeed a similar shade to Renard's, but his clothes and smile were a sad imitation.

Camille squinted at the man's face, partially obscured by a facial scar on one cheek. "Lord Slasbury?"

He tipped his bowler hat in greeting but said, "Try again."

Camille frowned. That was right. The real Marquess of Slasbury was older and overindulgent, to hear Charlotte describe the man.

This man was nothing but an imposter. Her stomach dropped.

Camille's gaze locked on the man before her. *This* was the man who'd nearly drowned Charlotte. The man who'd meant to skewer Hamish at the ball. The man who'd taken a chunk out of that artless bruiser Hamish called a friend, *Ralph*. A man she'd since come to know by the name, Percy.

What was he doing at the tavern? He was supposed to be locked in a cell. How had the man known she was *here*?

Camille's grasp on the rag slipped, and the cup in her hand fell to the floor in a shower of glass. "Did you follow me?" She reached for the shotgun under the bar. Was he after Hamish again? "The Duke of Camine isn't here," she said. Thank God she hadn't asked for her brother's assistance with Renard and the law.

A few inches more—

"Please don't. I'd hate to hurt you." His words were soft, but his gaze was hard as it flicked to where her hand had disappeared. Something in his expression said she'd never catch him by surprise. Her only chance was to run. And even a child on these streets knew a heavy weapon would make escape harder. When she placed her hand back where it was visible, he continued, that hard look replaced with a friendly smile. "Your confusion is understandable."

His rapid change in temper had her palms going clammy. She'd known another man whose mood would change on a whim, and how violent the previous Duke of Camine had become when angered. Camille kept her voice low, cordial. "Who are you?"

"My apologies. I know you so well, you see. I forget we haven't officially been introduced." The man smiled and tipped his hat in a fine display of genteel manners. "Nicholas Brandt, at your service."

Had they released him on a lack of evidence? Did he know of her connection with Renard? Was he angling for another way to strike at Charlotte? If she stalled long enough, Scarlet or Renard would show up and—

"No one is coming," he said, his smiling eyes knowing. "Your friend Scarlet and those obnoxious Merry Men will find their hands rather full in a few short minutes." He winked as if they were co-conspirators. "Lovely surprises I planted along the waterway." He grinned. "And I wouldn't concern yourself over the Duke of Lux coming anytime soon, either. He is quite busy with other matters." He held out a chain ending in a small, familiar key. "I may have borrowed your key. I hope you don't mind?"

Camille's hand shot to her neck, where the key to the Pony should've been. Had she dropped it after her reunion with Madam? "Where did you—"

"Not to worry," he said, checking the timepiece from an

inner pocket of the dark vest he wore. "The duke should arrive back in the country a few hours from now, long after our time here is over, when he'll be informed you left, quite suddenly, without a word to anyone where you were going."

Whatever the man meant by '*surprises*,' there was little doubt Syd and the Merrys could handle anything short of an incendiary device. The taunt about Renard, however... "He knows I'm here," she said. "He wrote me a letter and asked me to meet him—"

"*I* wrote that letter."

There was no deception on his face. Camille froze. "No." It wasn't possible.

"A neat trick." Nic shrugged. "Not all that impressive. Something I picked up in the Home Office." He pulled out a piece of paper from his coat, the exact shade and thickness of the parchment used by the Louis estate's steward. "His note was nothing special. Two words: I'm sorry." He tossed the note on the bar between them and snorted. "How dramatic."

Camille swallowed. "Home Office?" The man worked for the government? She glanced down at the note while panic set in.

It hadn't been Renard's handwriting. He wasn't here. But the letter had been on her nightstand. Icy fingers of disgust and violation left her trembling at what could have happened. "You were in my room." Then why the theatrics? "If you want revenge on my brother, why didn't you just kill me while I slept?"

"Kill you?" Nic made a face. "No, no. You don't understand. I had to get you *away* from the duke, don't you see? I've been so impatient. Made too many mistakes lately. I won't make the same one again. We needed time and privacy, away from all those nosy servants. Now we can finally get to know each other, no rush, no interruptions."

Nails gouging into her palms to keep her hysteria at bay, Camille backpedaled through his confession. "I don't understand. What do you want with *me*? I don't even know you."

"Don't say that!" The vehemence in his words made her step

back. He cleared his throat and seemed to collect himself. "You may think you don't know me, but I've been there for you. I've always been there." Anger settled over his features once again. "If only everyone would stop *getting in the way*. You'd see. You'd *know*. Morons, all of them!" Nic was too far in his rant to notice her flinch at his raised voice. "To think that idiot Quickner thought to keep you from me as well. He's lucky you were there when he drank the bullet."

Camille struggled to keep up with his illogical ramblings, but at the mention of Lord Quickner, everything inside her went cold. "*You* put the object in his drink?" That was impossible. She'd watched the servants pour. "The footmen, they filled the glasses."

"You'll find, my darling woman, that I am a man of many faces, many disguises. It is my specialty." He grinned. "*That*, and a few others."

He'd impersonated a footman and tried to kill Lord Quickner? Even if she believed something so unlikely, there was no reason. "Why?"

"He interrupted our walk."

Did he mean that time they'd met at the lake? The depth of her situation set in.

Her brain stalled for time to come up with a plan. "Why did you want me away from them?" she asked carefully.

His face brightened. "I have a gift for you."

The change in subject threw her. "A . . . gift?"

The spark in his eye was terrifying. "I saved the best for last."

With a flourish, he bent down and opened the drawstring of the bag at his feet, revealing a body stuffed unnaturally inside. A dead body.

Hawkins.

The cuts across his face and throat were vicious, but the angles and depth were a perfect match for two others Camille would never forget. Terror leeched the warmth from her body. "*You* killed Flank and Grey?"

Nic turned Hawkins's face towards him with the toe of his

boot. "They were in the way. This one kept spouting how he would get revenge for his men. He thought to lure you here and make you suffer. Hawkins never even considered it was someone else picking off his friends." He shook his head, his gaze sliding over her like snakes in the grass. "Mindless idiot. To think someone as perfect and righteous as you would need to lower yourself to wash your hands in their blood."

He'd been the one hurting people the entire time. The one stalking her. Her thoughts blurred with focused anger. "You went after Syd." Seeing how crazy the man in front of her was, she didn't believe for a second the man hadn't meant for Syd to fall. Near splattered her friend on the cobblestones for what? A relationship?

He continued his monologue, taking no notice of her inner struggles. "I've known you were special from the beginning." He laid his hand over hers on the bar, his skin cold. "Watching you run with that dislocated shoulder was marvelous. And when you turned to face them with nothing but a rock . . . sublime!"

Her skin crawled where his fingers squeezed hers, his manic delight like oily ice seeping into her body. "You were there in the alley? When Hawkins came after me?"

"Who do you think set those morons up to it?" He waved his other hand as if his inaction wasn't relevant. "It was just a spot of fun, and you were another helpless victim at that point. I thought you were another rabbit to watch die to pass the time. But you were more than I ever imagined. You attacked like a devil, going straight for the face. I fell for you then and there." His smile turned into a sneer. "And then that fool went and stole your victory from you."

Renard. Camille's body froze. Nic wanted Renard. There was no way this lunatic wouldn't go after him. Was that why Hamish and Charlotte had been targeted too? Their connections to her?

"Once your brother agrees on a sizable dowry, both he and his duchess are forgiven, of course," Nic said, as if they were discussing an outing to the theatre. "Neither will have need to fear my justice after things are settled."

Camille's brain stuttered. *"Settled."* Did he mean . . . "Marriage?"

"A strange sentiment for me as well. Never understood the practicality of binding oneself to such worthless whores. But we will get along famously," Nic said. "A woman of your intellect will require little condescension on my part."

Marriage. Then the snake didn't know everything; he must have escaped his cell recently.

Renard and she hadn't told Charlotte or Hamish about their vows. When word reached the populace, Nic would know there was only one way to break her ties with Renard.

Camille backed into the shelf of liquor bottles behind her, needing the room to breathe. His insanity had taken over all available air. He'd somehow formed a fictitious connection between them, one obsessive and dangerous enough the man couldn't see his desires had no hold in reality.

Not missing the distance she put between them, he frowned. "There's no reason to doubt me." He indicated Hawkins's body at his feet. "I brought proof of my affections."

Flank, Grey, now Hawkins—*gifts*, he'd called them. "Like flowers or confectionery."

"Of course." His expression changed with a tilt to his head and a subtle country accent. "No worries, miss. I made them suffer for what they did to ya."

Rapid-fire images bombarded her conscious mind. Camille clutched the bar, the sinking in her stomach doubling with the worst kind of obliviousness. Glass shards dug into her boots, but she felt nothing.

"You were my driver to the Quickners' estate," she whispered.

He nodded, seeming pleased at her connection. "I'd been preparing to assume that marquess's identity for months for another job. I knew the real Lord Slasbury had no wife, no attachment. He hadn't returned from his travels in ages. And it happened to be the perfect cover to get close to you."

She couldn't breathe.

He hadn't just watched her from afar. Every flash of fair hair in the streets, every blond curl under a grocer's hat; he could've been anywhere.

All her nightmares and fears, her doubts and ill luck, had been *him*.

She'd underestimated him as a threat. More like overestimated her own skills. A monster who flourished in the dark and was welcome in the light.

Growing up in the cesspool of London's finest gutter, she'd seen death and poverty from an unforgiving society. But the creature before her was a different monster altogether: Fangs, claws, and cleverness, shifting faces like the perfect half-hour gentleman, without any known weaknesses.

"You realize now the gap in our intelligence, don't you?" His pitying smile didn't match his triumphant tone. "Good. I don't like repeating myself, and your recognition will eliminate any rebellion you had planned. Not that I'd mind conditioning you to my liking." His smile turned reptilian. "No, I wouldn't mind the fight at all."

Camille blinked and a sudden urge to laugh brought her mind back into sharp focus. She took stock of the shotgun under the bar, the trigger mechanism too slow for their close proximity. She rubbed the rag in her waistband, too short for a makeshift garrote. The letter opener in her skirt—that she'd taken to carrying after leaving the club—would be a last resort against an opponent who'd use any weapon against her. And while she'd love nothing better than to remove her boot and smash in the man's nose, that too would not be enough.

Her gaze flicked to where the clean glasses she'd polished sat, waiting for use.

Camille turned her gaze back on Nic, a sense of direction bringing relief and hope. Intelligent or not, brutal or not, this monster was a man.

And all men had a weakness.

Madam had been right all along; there were skills one acquired working in a pleasure house that made all the difference in the battle between sexes. Time with the Ponies had given her more than one skill to use against the worst narcissistic vanity: ingenuity, acting, and flattery.

Swallowing her disgust, Camille adopted her best doe-eyed impression of Victoria. "You've been watching over me this whole time? But . . . but you never said a thing?"

He noted her light tone with a tugging of his lips before it turned into an ugly sneer. "That mangy *dog* got in the way." His tone turned accusing. "And you fell all over yourself to get him between your legs."

He'd watched her since the beginning. Camille pushed past her dread. She needed to keep his thoughts off Renard and back on himself or her plan wouldn't work.

"He saved me," she said innocently. "I thought he was the one killing those bad men, and I was grateful." Her Victoria impression changed into the hardened governess of Sensa's character. "He lied to me. He used me. I'll destroy him for tricking me!" She turned back into the sweet dove once again and gazed up at Nic's face, imagining Renard's kind eyes instead of the black pools before her. "You were my hero the entire time."

Nic smiled, that icy expression melting into one of merciful benevolence. "He *did* deceive you. Despite your brilliant mind, you are but a woman. I should have realized he'd snared you with his title and lies. But not to worry." He held out his hand. "I will take care of that fool soon enough and you will have your revenge."

Spoken in the same nauseating tone Mr. Richmund used to recite poetry. Camille rearranged her face into what she saw as Madam's bored mask. "He wouldn't be worth your sport." Camille took his hand and steeled herself against the wet feel of his lips on her knuckles. "There's no need to bother with him now. Now that you have found me at last."

She walked around the bar, her hand still in his.

He watched her with a sharp gaze, his eyes not straying from his prey.

When she was within reach, she lifted her free hand and palmed his scarred cheek. The smile she offered was sweet, submissive, infused with all the awe of religious worship, and the secret desire for blood.

With the force of her full weight, Camille knocked him off-balance towards the bar and slammed his face into the stack of glasses.

The glass shattered on impact, burying shards into Nic's cheek and forehead. He roared.

Camille tore herself free from his grip. She rushed for the door when her legs were kicked out from underneath her. Struggling, she avoided his grasping hands and staggered to her feet the same time he did.

Eyes wild, he yanked the largest piece of glass free from above his eye, spattering blood across the bar.

"Bitch!" Blood ran into his eye, but nothing would draw his murderous attention away. The monster had fully emerged. He charged.

Camille darted away, fleeing for the door.

But the monster was fast and his grip brutal as he ripped her back by the hair.

She screamed at the pain, but her body responded faster than her mind.

The time to flee was over. Now it was time to fight.

CHAPTER THIRTY-ONE

"**W**HAT ARE YOU doing here, lordy?" a feminine voice asked from above.

Renard glanced up at the Prodding Pony's roof, seeing a familiar shadowed figure perched precariously on the edge.

Finding himself capable of smiling despite the gallows' steps he stood upon, he said, "Hello, wise sage." He held up two silver coins from his pocket. "Two shillings if you come down. Three if you promise to keep off the edge from here on."

He saw a flash of teeth beyond the dark hood.

"Still arrogant, I see," she said. "You looking for Camille? 'Cause she ain't here."

"No," he said, his stomach roiling. "The Madam and I have business."

The door to the club opened, revealing the woman herself, the kohl around her eyes highlighting an amused expression. "Not sure I can afford any more of your business. Come to steal another of my girls away?"

Renard frowned. He was in no mood for games. "Your letter was most direct. You wish a bribe to keep my secrets quiet, right? Then name your price."

Madam cocked a brow and chuckled. "I have no need for your company, nor your secrets." She turned in the open doorway, her dismissal clear. "Consider our previous arrangement void. All information is stricken from memory. You are no longer welcome in my establishment."

Renard gripped the door before it closed. "Wait! I received your letter. You threatened to reveal my secret."

Madam's smirk was sardonic. "'*Secret*?' Is that what it said? No specifics?" At his hesitation, she rolled her eyes. "Any idiot could see you enter from the street and know my payment for membership is divulging a *secret*." She waved him away. "Someone is having a go at you."

The doubt rising in him felt akin to dread. He'd told no one else, aside from Camille. "You give me your word, Madam. You swear it was not you?"

The woman cocked her head, her expression turning serious. "I would not lie about such a thing, Your Grace. What would it gain me?"

Renard took the letter and envelope from his coat pocket, the club's insignia unmistakable on the seal. "If you didn't write it, then one of your Ponies must have."

Madam stared down at the letter, her face turning ashen. "When was this sent?"

"It was delivered to my estate this morning."

"That's impossible," she whispered.

This day kept getting worse; one of Madam's girls had found out his past and was attempting to blackmail him for some unknown reason and amount. At least it appeared the Madam truly had no knowledge of the scheme.

"If you compile a list of the girls with access to your seal, we can uncover the culprit."

Madam continued to stare at the letter, her skin ghostly pale. "No one," she whispered again. "No one has access."

Renard breathed out his impatience. "I understand. No one wishes to believe their coworkers capable of such treachery."

Her head snapped up at that. "*You* don't understand. When I say no one has access, I mean *no one*." She pointed at the seal, her hand steady, but her voice shaky. "That insignia is locked up at all times, in a secret room only one other person, besides myself, knew about."

Renard rolled his eyes. "Then that person is responsible. What is her name?"

Madam shook her head, her voice dropping to a mutter. "It can't be. It doesn't make sense. How would someone else know?"

His temper snapped. "Damn it, woman! Give me the name if you cannot deal with the person yourself."

Madam glanced up at him, and Renard was taken aback by the fear on the woman's normally indifferent face.

"Something is wrong," she said emphatically. "She must be in danger." She swayed.

Renard grabbed the woman by the shoulders to keep her on her feet. Clearly, this subterfuge had hit the woman harder than first perceived. He lowered his voice until it was soothing, persuasive. "Shh, now. Give me a name, Madam. We will see no harm comes to her. *Who* is in danger?"

Madam's gaze locked on his, and Renard felt the woman's terror slide across their bodies and grip the heart in his chest. He knew the answer before her mouth formed the name.

"Camille."

The woman from the roof dropped down without a sound, her hood pulled back.

Renard didn't have time to gawk at the dark hair and big eyes of Camille's companion from the Quickners' party; his mind was consumed with Camille.

"Explain yourself," he said to Madam. "How could my duchess be in danger?"

Both women turned to him in surprise, but it was the younger one who smirked and said cryptically, "Damn. Scarlet was right." She glanced Madam's way. "How bad is it?"

Madam ushered them inside the club and closed the door, dropping her voice despite the deserted hall. "The club's seal is missing, and so is Hawkins."

The girl swore. "Where would he go? The Underground?"

"Lucien revoked his membership."

"What about East End?"

"The place is too large to search."

"You think he's next?"

"I fear so."

Renard swallowed his impatience as the women talked in riddles. "One of you, tell me what the hell. Is. Going. On."

"Two options," the girl said, holding up her pointer and thumb. "Either that scumbag oaf Hawkins learned not to bellow when he walks and stole the seal without a soul knowing in hopes of luring Camille into a trap, or . . ."

"Or?"

The girl glanced at Madam and back. "Or a killer is back on the streets and looking for revenge for unknown reasons." Her young face changed to a hard mask. "A shadow I owe a slice and swift push off a roof."

Renard shot Madam a hard glare, remembering what Camille had confessed about Madam's secret ledger and what must have been the other woman's suspicions. "I had nothing to do with any of that."

Madam swallowed hard, an expression of guilt falling over her features. "Understood." She nodded. "If Angel agreed to marry you, she believes in your innocence."

Renard didn't ask of which crime he'd been accused. "Now . . ." He bit back a growl, his waning patience slipping away into dark anger. "How is the duchess mixed up with this missing seal? And why does the connection put her in danger?"

"As I said, the seal is kept hidden," Madam said. "No one knew about its location but the two of us. The fact that it was used to send that letter to you, today of all days—when I am expected to meet with the club's suppliers and would be unavailable until late this evening—means someone wanted you sufficiently out of the way."

"Any way the seal was forged?"

Madam shook her head. "It was made by the finest engineer in Europe. No one could forge with such precision."

Renard snorted. "I've a man living on the docks who could."

"Mr. Gregori Whitney?"

Renard turned to the older woman sharply.

Madam smiled smugly. "Then no, you don't."

Way to go, crackpot. "And Camille?"

Madam wrung her hands, an action that left Renard's insides likewise.

"The bodies, Hawkins's disappearance, the club, you, everything comes back to her." Madam's voice lowered. "The question is, Your Grace, do you know where your duchess is presently?"

"At our home in the country. Probably still abed."

"Are you sure?"

"Unexpected."

Renard took off like a shot, hearing his wife's word over and over.

He cursed himself for not bringing his horse from the stable on the other side of the city. Like a fool, he'd walked, wishing to enjoy his last moments of freedom on his own two feet. That extra time could mean the difference between saving Camille.

His soul screamed for its mate. To think of her harmed was like carving the muscle from his chest.

"Are you sure?"

He was sure Camille was the best thing in his life. He was sure he loved her more than the air in his lungs. He was sure he'd sacrifice anything to bring her home. And he was more than sure the woman wouldn't be where she should for one intrinsic reason; she lived by the identifier 'unexpected.'

The stolen seal, the bodies, Hawkins, Camille's fleeing to the country . . . Everything felt staged, a play with its actors on strings. But the hands directing this script were dirty, manipulating, a twisted version of fate's ever-present guiding hand.

Who would do this?

"Madam will send word to my crew. They'll keep a look out for Camille and any suspicious men on the streets," said a feminine voice.

Renard startled at the girl from the roof, keeping pace beside him like they were on a relaxed promenade through the Vauxhall pleasure gardens and not running full tilt.

"Who are you—"

"Name's Syd. Camille is like an older sister, and if you say some asinine thing about staying out of danger, I'll remove one of your fingers with my knife."

Renard swallowed down the exact words *"It's too dangerous"* and really looked at his running partner. "Could you do it?"

She didn't smile—the situation was too serious for that—but her mouth flicked with brief amusement. "I'll give you the option between a thumb or a forefinger."

"Sporting of you."

He turned left at a bisecting lane, Syd following.

"Do you have any idea where you're going?" she asked.

His steps faltered. He'd been heading in the direction of the Lux Townhouse. But this madman was too careful to take her to a place filled with eyes and ears of dozens of servants. He'd use subterfuge to lure Camille someplace she felt safe, a place she wouldn't hesitate to go by herself while bypassing the town-house.

"Where would Camille go to get away from the club and her flat?" he asked.

"Turn here." Syd pointed to the right and took the lead through the alleys towards the docks. "There's a tavern. The Cock 'n Hen."

"I know it." He put on a burst of speed, shocked at how easily the girl kept pace.

She glanced his way. "What's your plan, lordy?"

"Find my duchess. Keep her safe. Don't die."

She snorted. "Fine."

"You agree?"

"No. Your plan is trash," she said. "We'll do this my way."

He eyed her young face and wraith-like body. The girl was little more than shrouded bone and confidence. "Do *you* have a plan?"

"Yes." She flashed him a grin that was all teeth. "Hope you're better at stalling than you are negotiating people off roofs."

He ignored his lungs burning from the exertion, not when all his efforts went to keep his mind from devolving into panic. "I've been accused of charm by the very best. How much time do you need?"

"Long enough for me to get word to my men."

"Your men?"

Syd smiled. "The best."

Renard wouldn't question, wouldn't hope. Whatever this young woman's skills and connections, he'd accept any help to get Camille back.

The tavern came into view, and Renard's body flushed with cold sweat. He rushed for the front door just as the girl's arm cut in front of him. He stopped when she did against an adjacent building's wall.

"Why are we stopping?" he asked.

Syd glanced from alley to alley, her face hardening. "He's here."

Renard looked around. Seeing nothing amiss, he frowned and couldn't keep the impatience from his voice. "A woman of many talents. Fortunetelling as well as wisdom, oh, wise sage?" He stepped into the street. "I'll take my chances."

"There's no sound. Something is wrong." She waved towards the quiet docks at his disbelieving frown. "You peers have your princes and titles of note you bow your heads to in reverence."

All traces of humor were gone from Syd's face, making her next statement settle like lead in Renard's gut.

"When you grow up on the streets, Your Grace, the only man you bow before is Death, and even the wee ones go silent when He comes calling." She stuck out her chin in the direction of the tavern. "Do *you* hear anything, Your Grace? Sailors preparing for sendoff? Children begging for scraps?"

He heard nothing.

"No." He crouched back out of view and willed his brain to think. He knew nothing of the streets. Warning signs and caution had never been a priority. He'd always run headfirst into danger, and that foolishness had almost made him rush into the bar without a thought.

Now that it was pointed out, the silence was unnerving. Not even the constant water flow from the Thames could be heard, as if danger were a blanket muffling the nature around them.

Renard bowed his head to the strange girl beside him and offered up pride, vanity, and arrogance, knowing somehow she'd just saved him from ruining their best chance at a surprise attack.

"We'll do this your way," he said. "What's your plan?"

Seeing he was finally on board, Syd's hard expression cracked with a predatory smile. "Find your duchess, save her, and one more thing."

He huffed. "Don't die?"

"Not today, lordy." She took out a knife from the belt at her waist and held the blade up to the light. "You're not squeamish at the sight of blood, are you?"

Renard paused. "No?"

Syd slapped him on the back. "Good man. Now, when you see Camille, say these words exactly . . ."

CHAPTER THIRTY-TWO

C AMILLE TWISTED AS she fell and hooked an arm around Nic's knee, sending them both tumbling to the tavern floor.

Glass shards scraped the skin off her palm where she tried to catch herself. Her head slammed against the floor. Stars danced before her eyes. Lifting herself onto her hands, glass bit savagely into flesh, but she blocked out the pain.

An icy hand curled around her ankle.

Shaking off the dizziness, she kicked at his arm, his shoulder, his face. Her heart pounded. Her mind screamed. The door was so close. She pawed for it, her nails shredding against the hardwood floor.

Her foot connected with a part of his face that crunched, and those cold fingers around her ankle loosened. She bolted to her feet and staggered towards the door.

The room spun. She stuck out an arm to steady herself and ran into a table, sending one of the upturned chairs to the floor.

She blinked, focusing on the hazy outline of the door, and took stock of her injuries.

Sprained wrist. Abrasions on her hands and cheek. Nausea and blurred vision, most likely a concussion.

She wouldn't get far, but then, she didn't need to. If she could make it to the docks, someone would see her, someone would remember. And someone would tell Renard she'd fought until the end.

Her bloody fingers slipped on the door handle. She grabbed it frantically. The latch lifted. She gave a cry of relief and—

A knife buried into the wood beside her head.

The sting on her ear told her enough about how accurate her opponent's aim was. She turned, her vision clearing with a new wave of self-preservation.

Nic's face was twisted and bloody, his breathing labored from the pain and inconvenience of a broken nose. He extracted a second knife from his coat, and then a third, and pointed the tips at her chest. He'd found his own feet but made no move to close the distance and restrain her. With those knives, there was no need.

He toed the glass at his feet, blood flecked and shining in the afternoon glow through the front windows. His voice filled with manic glee. "A glass? Magnificent."

Camille's fingers itched to pull the letter opener from her pocket, but the action would draw his attention, attention she needed elsewhere. "So glad you enjoyed it. There are a few left unbroken; I can always break off the others in your head next time and save that mangled face."

His gaze sharpened. The step he took in her direction was slow, deliberate. He knew she blustered, and he'd take his time proving she had lost.

He reached out his hand, looking every bit a gentleman; the bloody gashes on his face revealed the monster underneath. "Come with me now, pet. I will break whatever hold that mutt has over you and you will see the truth. We are made for each other."

Camille's hand automatically went for the handle at her back. Once he caught her, he'd never let her go. Her accusation came out on a whisper. "You're delusional."

Instead of taking insult, Nic seemed pleased. "Willfulness and intellect. You are a rare creature, Camille. It is a shame you can't see how well we suit." He patted at the cut above his eye and smiled as he held out his blood-coated fingers. "You see how beautiful and clean the color is? How easy it is to wipe the filth of our enemies away in a pool of beauty? You have such a knack for brutality. A rock, glass. I couldn't engineer a more perfect partner."

The sight of the blood, and the knowledge she'd been the cause, twisted Camille's already upset stomach. She backed away, her hands raised as if she could block his words. "You're wrong. I don't want to hurt anyone."

"Don't you?" He stalked closer, his eyes lit with hunger. "Did you not wish to see those men slain for what they tried to do to you?" He pointed to Hawkins's body. "Is it not better that animals like him are shredded to bits? Food for the crows."

"No!" She may have hated Hawkins and men like him, like her father, for taking advantage, for believing superior strength and a sick desire entitled them to do as they wished with those unwilling. "They deserved to be thrown in prison. Locked away where true justice meant living with their actions every day in a tiny cell."

"Cells are easily avoided *and escaped from.* A well-acted stomachache, a naive guard, an easy snap of the neck, and a quick wardrobe change. I walked right out the front doors without a single objection." Nic shook his head. "Imprisonment. An honorable sentiment, but men like them never see the wrongs done, only the people responsible for keeping them from their fun."

Like you. She knew better than to say the words out loud.

Nic was a man beyond reason or self-awareness. In his mind, only his fun, his desires, mattered. Even now, after she'd half-blinded him with bar glasses, he moved as if he had every advantage, as if it were a lovers' quarrel and not a statement of her desire to be rid of him.

"No more games." He offered his hand to her again. "Your efforts were commendable, but shortsighted. Admit defeat and submit to me, and all is forgiven."

Camille stared at his hand, feeling a crack opening in her

chest. Not a crack; it was her spirit breaking.

For every second of doubt over the past year, for every moment she'd hidden from Renard, the man she loved, Nic had truly won. Now she was alone and the only person to stand between those she cared for and a gutter grave.

Camille closed the distance between them and made to take his hand, but his fingers slid into her hair instead, where his fingers twisted at the strands painfully.

"Now you are mine." He leaned down. His lips hovered over hers in silent threat before he ordered, "Say you belong to me."

Camille watched victory and malice light his eyes and saw what horrors lay in her future. Even knowing his strength and the danger he posed to her family, the last of her spirit rallied, not yet done fighting.

Her hand slipped into her skirt pocket and tightened around the handle of the letter opener. She stuck out her chin, bringing them nose to nose, and said, "I am my own."

The door to the tavern banged open. A tall creature staggered in, his skin and clothes red as blood.

Renard was bleeding!

Drenching his fair hair, running down his face, and staining his collar, the wound was a bad one and needed medical attention before he fainted from blood loss. He held his arm and walked with a limp, as if more than his head were injured. His gaze fell on Hawkins's body on the floor and his eyes went wide as he swayed dangerously on his feet.

Letter opener forgotten, Camille rushed towards him, only to be yanked back by the relentless grip in her hair.

Nic wound her hair around his wrist, dragging her closer. His gaze narrowed at their new addition. "Someone got the jump on you before I could, Lux. What a pity. How did you find us?"

Renard smiled through the blood, but it looked like even that small gesture hurt. "I followed the silence." His gaze went to her. "A friend of yours says 'hello.'"

She must have mistaken the flash of something unidentifiable in his eyes. Was he feverish? "My friend? Is that who did this to you?" Was there more than Nic she must contend with? One of the creditors?

Renard leaned against the door as it closed behind him. He winced in pain, though Camille noted the action looked forced.

His gaze was steady and direct. "Said you owed her a tray of tarts."

Camille's mind whirled violently. Her focus pinpointed the discrepancies in Renard's speech and body language. He didn't slur from exhaustion or slouch from any pain. And his words . . .

Syd was close by. She—

Camille didn't glance outside or show any indication she understood. Somehow, Renard and Syd had come together and surmised she was in trouble. How was a mystery and a miracle she wouldn't question. She wasn't alone.

This wasn't over.

Nic laughed, the sound raising the hairs on Camille's neck. *He* wasn't fooled, either.

"Is this the best you could do, Lux? A diversion and a bit of pig's blood?" Nic laughed harder. "Should I expect Scotland Yard to come bursting through the front door?" He glanced at the door. "Amusing. But those lazy toads would fall to my knife like chaff at the sickle."

Charade over, Renard stood tall and wiped blood from his eyes, but the expression on his face wasn't dismayed. He grinned and crossed his arms over his chest as if his trap had already sprung. "Not the front door, no."

Nic released Camille and dove out of the way, missing a knife to the back.

Camille skirted out of his reach and gasped at the figure who'd snuck in from the back door.

"Syd!"

Her friend shot her a grin but kept her gaze locked on Nic, who'd risen to his feet.

"Sorry for the delay. Seems like someone set off a string of smoke bombs at one of the mills. The whole city is cramming every street north of Cable. Know anything about that, friend?"

Nic smiled, his teeth stained red.

Camille's stomach lurched. "Syd, he's—"

"We'll talk later, Cam." Syd brushed the side of her head where Camille knew her shorn hair covered a nasty scar. "First, Bloody Face here owes me a dance that's long overdue."

Nic sneered at her. "Clumsy footwork and a weak frame. You fell so easily last time. Hardly worth the dance."

"You wound me, sir," Syd said, continuing her circling. "'Course a bad partner is just as culpable for any missteps." She took a knife from her ankle and pointed it at him in invitation. "You must allow me to change your mind when it comes to my skills."

He eyed the weapon in her hands with interest, his indifference shifting. He bowed. "As you wish, miss. It shall be your last."

Syd gave a mock curtsey to match her mocking tone. "I'll take the lead, if you don't mind?" She ran the flat of her blade across the side of her head. "Wouldn't want you falling before I have the chance to shave a bit off the sides."

Camille watched the two predators circle and circle, each rotation mirroring the twisting of her insides. Their dance had already begun, a deadly one.

Syd glanced out the front window, as if searching for a way out, knowing she couldn't take on her opponent.

Camille had to stop this. Her hand went for her skirts and the weapon hidden there.

"Whatever you're thinking . . . " Syd glanced at her out the corner of her eye. "I'm insulted."

"Syd, please. You don't have to do this. I'll be all right." Camille offered a fraction of a smile, the biggest she could muster. "Nicholas was only protecting me." She forced her smile bigger and entreated upon whatever warm feelings the cold bastard had. She stepped towards Nic, feeling Renard stiffen across the room.

She kept her focus on Nic. She'd resigned herself earlier to the fact that she had no choice but to go with him while she found a way to escape. Now she'd offer herself willingly, ready to sacrifice her freedom and life if it meant the other two people in this room would walk away unharmed.

She came to Nic's side and looked up into his scarred face, willing her features to soften. "Now that my friend knows how happy I am with you, we can be together and no one will stop us."

Nic's returning smile filled her with relief, until he leaned forward and said in clear, sharp words, "Not to worry. I'll make sure *your friend* doesn't interfere, ever again."

Camille's blood ran cold.

"Good try, Cam, but there's no way I'd walk away now." Syd's gaze once again went to the window, and whatever she saw there made her smile. She stopped circling and straightened, her entire demeanor changing in seeming triumph.

"Apologies, *friend*, in my innocent diversion." The light from behind cast her body in a long, intimidating shadow. "But there are a few others clamoring to sign your dance card."

With a courtly flourish, Syd curtsied again.

And the windows behind her shattered.

CHAPTER THIRTY-THREE

FIVE FIGURES BURST through the windows like wolves, gracefully landing to the floor and rising to their feet together as if they were one animal.

The men were huge, muscled, and most were young. The largest man startled when he looked at Nic.

"That's the bloke from the party," he said.

Syd's gaze sharpened. "You mean the killer after the Duke of Camine? You sure, Zans?"

Zans nodded and ran a thumb across his cheek, the imaginary line the same as the scar across Nic's face. "Gave 'im that parting gift me self."

"The one supposed to be in the pens?" Syd's eyes lit up. "This keeps getting better."

The oldest of the group—a man well into his middle age sporting a bowler hat and a military stance—gave Syd a nod that she returned with a smile.

The man looked to Camille next. "Good to see ye, lass."

Camille's smile was warm. "You too, Pops."

Pops's gaze latched on to Renard and then Nic, pleasantries over. "Zans, ye said the snake had light hair." His eyes darted between the two fair-haired men. "Which one is our rabbit?"

Renard shuddered, hearing a death sentence in the forthcoming answer.

Syd inclined her head in Nic's direction. "Handsome here."

She backed up to the line of men, falling in rank at the head. "Do leave a bit for me, would you? Seems my fall from the Pony wasn't so accidental after all."

Pops's entire attention went to Nic. He cracked his knuckles and advanced, not seeming to care the younger man held a knife when he was bare handed.

"You made a mistake, boy." He glanced down at Hawkins, taking in a dead body on the pub floor better than Renard had when he'd first walked in.

For a moment Renard hadn't needed to fake illness.

"The others' misfortunes, I could forgive ye killing for what they did to Miss Camille. Even going after me business partner I took for more business. But not me Syd." Pops shook his head as if he were truly sorry. "Ye should 'ave kept your attentions to the other predators, because now there ain't a hole ye could shit in that I won't find. That me men here won' sniff out."

The men at his back smirked, a collection of amused expressions that brought the images of broken bones and bloody gashes to mind.

Nic sneered, his gaze darting from one threat to the next and finally landing back on the older man in front of him. "You're no threat to me, *Captain*. Word is you've lost your touch and that girl"—he jammed a thumb in Syd's direction—"over there is now your Merry band of dishonored soldiers' leader." He cocked his head, confidence in the gesture. "And seeing as how your alpha can hardly keep on her feet, I doubt the rest of your 'wolves' will be much of a challenge. I'll take you on one by one and leave your carcasses for the birds."

Pops shook his head. "Not very bright, are ye? I don' disagree ye got skills, but there be few predators that can take on a pack. Ye'd be smart to see the tail that sprout from ye bum and the ears upon ye head."

The men—and Syd—stepped forward together on his last word, showing the unity and coordination of the pack, ready to take off after their prey.

Nic's confidence wavered. With a scowl and a curse, he turned as desperate as a hare and spat at Camille, "I'll slip away and regroup. I'll return stronger than before, and not even your dogs will keep you safe. You'll never see me coming. Never know when your carriage driver or a passing acquaintance on the street is not who you think they are. You've not won. You've merely postponed what's inevitable."

Renard's insides clenched, hearing fate's whisper in his ugly words.

His threats hung in the air like hovering storm clouds until . . .

Syd clapped, slow and overly dramatic. Everyone stopped and stared.

When she'd finished, she dropped her hands and gave Nic a feral smile. "As far as evil rants go, that was by far the best I've heard." She held up her arm to Zans, and the giant lowered his head obediently to look. "See? I have goose pimples."

Nic's glare was murderous. "I'll strip off your skin and hang your pelt on my wall, wolf."

She winked. "Not if I tear your head from your shoulders first, *rabbit*."

Her last word set everyone in motion. The men converged, knifes and fists drawn.

Nic backpedaled, the snake slipping through their reach as he'd boasted he would, blocking stabs and fists from all directions as he sprinted for the front door, the 'wolves' trailing after him.

Everyone piled out onto the narrow cobblestones, Renard and Camille bringing up the rear.

As the narrow street's edge bordering the dark water of the Thames came into view, Renard heard a knowing *splash*, and his stomach dropped.

They waited—the eight of them—in a line, all leaning over the unguarded walk. Silence reigned as everyone held their breath waiting for Nic's head to break the surface.

The water's surface remained placid; two heartbeats,

three . . . ten.

Renard counted, holding his own breath until he couldn't anymore. "Think he drowned?"

Syd gave a sharp whistle.

Zans and the three other young men took off down the banks in opposite directions, following the murky water and offering a series of silent hand signals, before two of the four split off down bisecting alleys to check the river from lower down.

Markus squeezed Camille's shoulder. "Head back inside." He nodded to Syd.

She nodded back. "I'll run the perimeter up to Caring Cross. If he thinks to sneak away up stream, I'll cut him off."

Markus nodded. "I'll scout out front in case he circles back. Meet back here in twenty."

The two of them took off, leaving Camille and Renard alone on the waterway.

Without a word, Camille went back into the tavern.

Renard closed the door behind him and took in the broken glass on the bar and floor, glanced over Hawkins's body and then at the destroyed window, and finally stared at the woman who stood in the middle of it all, somehow not a drop of blood on her, as if heaven had protected one of their own from harm. The nasty wounds on Nic's face, the mess . . . Camille had fought until the end.

"You hit him with a glass?" He smiled. His little fighter.

"My first reaction was to use my boot, if that makes you feel better?" She seemed to take in the scene herself for the first time, her eyes wide. "Scarlet is going to kill me when she sees all this."

Renard didn't know who Scarlet was—the owner of the bar, perhaps—but he loved the way she said the words with relief. His duchess had friends, people who would most definitely care more for their friend's well-being before griping about a broken glass or two. People he couldn't wait to meet and thank for offering kindness and compassion in her past when he couldn't.

"Milly." His boots crunched through the glass. Any space

between them became unbearable. He'd thought he'd lost her. When he'd stumbled into the tavern and seen Nic's hold on her and the knife in his hand, his heart had stopped.

He reached for her and froze at the blood covering his hands, fingers, arms, everything. Dropping his arms, he stood back to breathe her in and convince himself she was safe, one way or another.

Camille flung herself into his arms, smearing blood across her dress and face when she buried it in his shoulder. "You came for me."

He cupped the back of her head in his hands and turned her face to look up at him, his body shaking with relief. "Always."

CAMILLE STARED UP at her husband—the drying blood crusting his hair and face, the crumpled condition of his wool coat, the complete *lack* of deadly injuries on his person—a mixture of relief and irritation surfacing now that the immediate threat of death was gone. "You left."

"I got a letter from Madam. Though it seems it was a ruse, as was the means with which you found yourself here, I assume."

He'd gotten a letter as well? "There *was* a letter, barely legible. I thought it was from you."

"You couldn't tell the difference?" He sounded angry.

"Are you blaming me for coming here? I thought you were turning yourself over to the authorities in some ridiculous self-righteous display of maintaining your honor."

"Honor has been a grand relief to many when the guillotine falls, but you . . . Do you expect me to rejoice that the woman I love was being a right idiot and got caught by a sadistic killer?"

She reeled back, but not from the insult, not really.

"What?" he said.

"You." She licked her lips, her brain repeating his words over and over, unable to stop her heart from beating wildly. "You called me an idiot."

"You deserved it."

She gazed up into his face, seeing the softness in his expression as he gazed back. He'd come for her. "You love me."

"More than anything."

"But—" Why? How?

"After everything, you doubt me?"

"No." She doubted herself. He'd gone to the Pony, believing someone there knew about his past secrets. "You went to Madam's?" That was how Nic had lured him to the Pony. There hadn't been a peep of claims or interest since she'd shown her face back in St. Giles. Ren had told Madam about his past to buy off the creditors, she was sure of it. "You told her to pay off the remaining balance. You really do love me."

He lifted her chin with his knuckle, his eyes dancing with amusement and exasperation. "For a woman who remembers everything, you don't listen well. I've been confessing my feelings practically since I met you."

"That's not fair," she said. "Men say poetic nonsense all the time. How was I to know you meant a word of it?"

He huffed. "I baked you tarts, woman! What else do you want? A sign? A carriage? I'll buy you ten of everything." He held her close. "I see it's going to take a lifetime to get through that stubborn head of yours." He smiled. "Rely on me, trust me. You take care of everyone else. Let me take care of you for a change. And one day, you'll learn to love me back."

Her heart soared. Her husband, her friend and partner, loved her, wanted her, believed in her. Against all of fate's tests and the machinations of a sadistic killer, they were here, together.

She slipped her hands into his, the last traces of doubt and fear slipping away. "Renard, I do love you. I've loved you since the alley."

Renard's startled expression broke into a smile that took up his entire face. "You love me—"

The tavern door opened.

They whirled together.

Camille snatched the letter opener out of her skirts and held it at the ready.

Syd strolled in. Her whistling cut off abruptly upon seeing their intertwined fingers and the weapon in Camille's hand.

She could only imagine the image they posed, the intimacy as they stood side by side, covered in blood.

Syd grimaced. "Guess I should have knocked."

Camille put down the knife but kept Renard's hand firmly in her own. She asked, even though they all knew the answer. "Any sign of him?"

Syd shook her head. "We'll check the banks after the next storm to see if any bodies show up."

Camille wouldn't dare to hope. "You think he's dead?"

Syd shrugged. "If the current doesn't do him in, the sickness in the water will." She ran a finger down her cheek. "I imagine those cuts on his face will turn to sepsis being in all that filth. I'd say I'm proud, Cam, but I wanted to be the one to send the bastard to a painful grave."

Camille squeezed Renard's hand before releasing it—letting him know she'd heard what he'd said and would give him her answer when they were alone—and flung her arms around her friend.

"I know I owe you apology after apology and you're probably still irked with me for leaving, but I'm so glad you're all right."

Syd squealed. "Ew, you smell awful. Wash before you hug people." Her easy laughter after everything that had happened sounded like music from the heavens. "You could rival Scarlet with the dramatics."

Camille pulled back and took a moment to search her friend's face, seeing the changes and maturity.

"Got something on my face?" Syd teased.

Camille smiled. Knowing the words 'you've grown up' wouldn't go well, she settled for a safer, "You called for backup this time."

Syd gave her a look. "Your shocked tone hurts." That look turned on Renard, who stood back watching them. "And *you*, lordy. I thought you said you were charming?"

He winced. "Guess only beautiful young women are susceptible. I'll work on my too-irresistible-to-not-want-dead allure *after* I find a way to stomach the sight of blood. Did I have to put it in my hair?" He stuck his finger in his ear and wiggled. "I had blood dripping down my collar the whole time."

"Head wounds are gushers." Syd shrugged. "Couldn't be helped."

Camille whirled on them. "You planned this together? How?"

"Wise sage was waiting at the club," Renard said. "When Madam made it clear she hadn't written to me, your friend here put it all together."

Camille wouldn't lament about the hand of fate again. She'd learn to accept the help without question. If the events of the past year weren't enough to make her a believer, nothing would.

Camille cocked a brow at her friend, thinking maybe fate had some help along the way. "Wise sage?"

"Shh," Syd said. "I like it. Makes me sound distinguished and reputable."

Camille dropped an arm around her friend's shoulders, grateful everyone had walked away unscathed, wardrobes excluded. "And fictional." Her gaze went to the cropped hair on the side of Syd's head, and thirteen months of guilt had her wrapping her other arm around the younger woman and pulling her close despite Syd's pleas for release. "I never thanked you for what you did, watching over me. I don't deserve a friend like you."

"Oh, get off me." Syd pushed her away, though gentler this time. She made a face and eyed Camille like a dog who'd learned to talk. "You *have* gone soft. Didn't think I'd ever need to tell you 'Thanks' is useless."

Camille's heart plummeted. "Syd—"

"We're *family*, Cam. You want to make up for all the worrying you caused with a mountain of pastries, I won't say 'no,' but I thought you knew by now that family has your back. Take my ruined outfit as proof!" She shook her head. "Since your genius mind apparently can't work all that out, I'll tell you straight: Keep your gratitude. I'll take the pastries."

Camille felt the embarrassing sting of tears in her eyes. Sniffling, she knuckled Syd's head until the younger woman shot out of reach.

"A mountain of pastries going to be enough?" she asked.

Syd tapped her chin with a finger. "Two mountains? I guess you can afford it now you are a duchess and all."

Camille's gaze shot to Renard, who shrugged.

"Not great at keeping secrets, that one," Syd said. "Or acting." She sniffed at his clothes and recoiled. "Did I not tell you to get *fresh* blood from the butcher? No one would believe you were newly injured when the wounds already smell."

Renard threw back his shoulders, succeeding in looking as distinguished as a wet rat in a frock coat. "Did you expect me to wait for the next available swine to walk through the door? I thought we were in a hurry."

"Arrogant *and* lazy, lordy. Not a good combination."

He puffed up, hackles raised. "What about you? 'Dump a bucket of blood over your head from the butcher,' you say. 'Pretend you're injured and walk in the front door.' That's it! How on Earth is any person to surmise a partner's plan from such vague orders?"

"It's called improvising!"

"It was a trash plan!"

"Better than yours, lordy. 'Find her. Save her.' That's not a plan; that's a goal list."

Camille watched the two bicker like lifelong siblings, her stomach performing a strange flip. No real anger laced their words. It was good-natured arguing, a mutual need to release the frenzied energies after their encounter with Nic.

Family.

Camille thought about the word. For most of her life, the word had conjured grey images of her mother and father and the cold and calculating relationships involved. But now there was color, vibrant and inviting, drawing her closer to those who'd come to be permanent fixtures in her life.

Syd, Scarlet, Charlotte, Pops, Renard: She shared no blood between the lot of them and yet she'd describe them as no less. Family. Through the trauma and anguish of her life, she'd collected that which she'd always longed for, without ever realizing. She'd been alone all this time, since before she'd stormed into the Prodding Pony and before she'd learned she and Madam *did* share that blood.

How easily people made connections, emotional and otherwise. There'd be no question that Pops and Syd would take Renard in as one of their own. The way Renard teased Syd so easily, how he returned the clap on his back as Pops came back in through the door, the connection was mutual.

No one else understood.

Except one.

Camille took in the scene, the people she cherished, and knew someone important was missing. Someone she'd denied for selfish and fictional reasons.

She did share blood with someone besides Madam, a member of her family who deserved to know what was in her heart and to hear the gratitude and apology that didn't come second nature to either of them.

CHAPTER THIRTY-FOUR

"ARE YOU ALL right?" The Duke of Camine didn't move from his chair behind his desk, but, upon Camille's entrance into the library—evidence of her run-in with Nic clear in her tattered dress despite the thorough cleaning and bandaging of her injuries—Hamish's entire body stiffened, coming alert to a danger that had long since passed.

His tone was carefully even, telling Camille he resisted his 'mothering' for her sake.

Hamish leaned forward on his elbows, his tone teasing, though his gaze remained assessing. "Shall I call for the physician for Renard, or did you dispose of him permanently? I confess, when you left a week ago, I hoped it was to set your differences aside."

Better to rip the bandages off cleanly, she thought. "The other man may need a doctor, but since we'd all like Nic Brandt gone, I'd say leave the monster to swallow every potion in reach and hope he dies of dysentery."

Hamish's chair overturned as he bolted from his seat. "At Lux Manor? Did anyone see him leave?" Gaze shooting to the closed door, most likely aimed in the direction of where the Duchess of Camine was sitting in the upstairs sitting room, he made for the exit. "I'll alert the staff. We'll hunt him down like the wily fox—"

"He's not there," she said, stopping him. "We were in London. Your fox is most likely dead at the bottom of the Thames."

Or holed up in a dark crevice, dying a slow, agonizing death.

Immediate danger reconciled, Hamish came back to her side and lifted her bandaged hand. The anger rolled off him, but his touch remained gentle when his voice was anything but.

"Tell me you stuck a knife in that bastard's eye."

Camille retreated at the violence in his voice and words. "I jammed glass in his face," she said, nauseous at the thought. "Then he jumped into the river."

Hamish gave her space, going back to his chair, righting it, and sitting back down with a simple, "Good."

"Something must be done," she said. "If by some miracle he survives . . . We can't keep glancing over our shoulders and getting away at the last minute. Eventually, our luck will run out."

Chameleons like Nic Brandt didn't give up; take away one mask and they donned another. Close one area of attack and his tactics changed. Where Scarlet used those traits as a means of righting the wrongs of those enslaved and desperate in Dockside, Brandt used such skills to kill, and kill well.

She knew the chance of survival was slight, but Nic had proved a roach of a man, managing to scuttle free in more unlikely scenarios.

Feeling the hand of fate settle ominously on her shoulder, Camille shook her head and said with certainty, "Someone won't walk away next time."

Hamish didn't balk or ridicule. He steepled his fingers and didn't scoff at the unlikeliness of her grave words. "Let it be him, then," he said finally.

"He could strike anywhere, at any time. The odds aren't in our favor."

"You underestimate our family, dear sister. That snake may have a talent for bloodshed, but he is but one. We are many."

Camille warmed at the mention of 'family,' but she did not relent. "*We* are liabilities to one another."

Hamish smiled. "Together, a pack of wolves can take down

prey far superior in strength and size. Or am I mistaken in that Renard finally succeeded in charming you to the altar?"

She placed her anxieties and concerns away in a box in her mind. She'd come for a reason. "Fairly certain *I* charmed *him*."

"As I said, hidden talents." Hamish offered two slow claps of his hands. "Bravo! Be sure to tell Charlotte. She'd be distraught if the gossip rags find out before she does. And I'd hate to bloody my fists on some poor journalist's teeth. Especially when there is no need for me to go to the mats over your relationship now that I've officially adopted you as my ward."

Camille's eyes widened. Ward. That meant she'd be a recognized and respectable member of the Hurstfield family. There'd be no reason for Renard's heir to question her connections. "You didn't?"

"Afraid so." Hamish shrugged. "I took the liberty of continuing to abuse my rights as your older brother to overstep that day you found me at the townhouse. After witnessing your encounter with Renard in my foyer, I could see it was a matter of time before the question of birth over the new Duchess of Lux arose." He waved his hand in an expectant gesture. "Come now, let's see how many shoes to the head I can avoid before you land a direct hit."

He'd made her his ward. There'd be no meddling heirs, no banishment from society. "Thank you."

Hamish startled at the gratitude.

There were depths to her brother she'd never imagined.

His reference to a fist fight had Camille smirking. "Speaking of hidden talents, tell me: Why would a well-to-do gentleman fight in the Underground Ring?"

Hamish's next jolt of surprise came with a string of curses. "You were at Lucien's?" More curses, and a confusing flushing of his cheeks. "I was earning an audience with Markus."

Markus? "The old man told you to beat a man to death?" Sounded like the captain.

Hamish rubbed his temple. "The man said in no uncertain

terms, 'Show me you 'ave the grit to stand in the streets.' It wasn't as bad as it looked."

"The man was bleeding from his ear holes!"

Hamish shook his head. "Guess he's cleverer than you thought."

"Who?"

"Percy."

Camille went back through her memories of that night. The smell of the unwashed bodies and dampness of the earthen walls. The memory opened and the scene unfolded as if she were standing back in that dark, cold tunnel. The Ring and the lantern lights shone over two figures, one with her brother's unfashionably long brunette hair and the other with curls of darkest black.

"Percy was your opponent?" Her mind shot from connection to connection to connection, her admiration for the slippery character doubling as the memory receded back into the quiet of her mind. "You *staged* a fight to win over the 'Merry Men'?"

Hamish winced. "I may have put on a *show* for the man to grant me an audience without putting anyone in harm's way."

Camille couldn't believe it. "You tricky devil. Pops never suspected a thing, then?"

"'Pops'?" Hamish frowned. "You know Markus?"

She knew *the whole family.* "Perhaps we should sit and have a real talk. There are many things I've kept to myself." Perhaps Hamish was right about their 'family.' Kin was not all blood, and Camille knew three others who had the skills and need for revenge against Nic as strong as either duke.

Imagining Syd auditioning for their merry band of 'family' by throwing knives at a target while playing the pianoforte in the duke's drawing room did have its appeal.

Hamish ran a hand over his face and chuckled. "Good thing Charlotte has all but frightened the terror out of me. I'm not sure I could take any more unexpected surprises otherwise."

Camille heard the unconditional love in her brother's voice. Love for a woman she herself loved like a sister. How different that superior tone sounded when in context of taking on the world for those you cared for, herself included.

Camille took in a breath and held before releasing. She hadn't come here for a cordial chat nor to solidify the knowledge that her brother was on her side. She may have been shit at reading when a man's words were sincere, but Hamish's actions, both before and after he'd taken her in despite their sorted connection and possibility of scandal, spoke volumes of a man she could rely on—a brother she could trust—no matter how ugly her past scars had grown.

Renard had once claimed her pride would get her killed, and he'd been right. She'd let her pride kill her dreams and her ambitions. Kill a relationship with a person who looked and sounded like her father, but with none of the flaws.

It was time to let him in. "I have a proposition for you," she said.

Hamish leaned back in his chair, his grin wide. "I've had surprisingly good luck with women using a rendition of those words."

Camille chuckled, remembering.

Charlotte's list. The fine lady had come marching into this office, her reputation and safety—everything deemed necessary by society—left on the cold streets outside. She hadn't balked or hesitated to take hold of her future.

Camille let her friend's fearlessness bolster her own resolve.

"There's a project, a shelter, I want to start for women and their children. Girls and widows, and wives, and orphans—anyone in a bad situation who needs help getting back on their feet or starting over." She licked her lips and rushed on before her nerves, and pride, had her racing for the door. "But there'd be classes as well, volunteer lectures from people who have knowledge or a skill that the women could learn or teach each other. I have a space already and a promise from the land holder the rents would be kept reasonable."

She'd need to send Madam Clarice a basket of specially made

riding crops for all she'd done on her end. Not only would Camille have the space, but the protection of the club and its network of secrets to give the home leverage should entitled men come hunting for those whom they deemed 'property.'

"I've calculated starting costs and any potential additional expenses like physician visits and building repairs. I won't lie: Even with Pops's offer to use the free clinic"—and Lord and Lady Quickner's promise of funds—"the price is steep, but as the women are able to work during the day, a portion of their income would go back into the shelter until they are able to earn enough for their total independence. Without the need to pay for food, the turnover should be within acceptable numbers." The more women she was able to get back into society, the more word would spread, and the more women would come for help, thus enabling women with both free education and a safe place to test those skills before setting back out into the world.

She'd refused to allow Renard to contribute in any way, needing this for herself. But she knew of Hamish's efforts in Dockside with Markus, how the expansion of the clinic and offering of spectacles had sent a wave of change through the rookeries, instilling the people with pride in their work and lives.

Hamish understood about pride and effort, and about earning both through compassion and nerve.

She pressed a hand to her heart and offered her brother everything she had. "I do not expect charity. I will pay you back once the home's running offers a profit, and I will find other investors. It won't be a risk. I *will* make this succeed. So, if you could trust—"

Hamish held a note out to her, his expression blank.

Willing the hope rising in her to retreat sensibly, she took the banknote and gasped at the amount.

Miss Forthright's Home for Female Companions would be more than a reality. Gratitude overwhelming, she nodded to her brother and said, "I'll pay you back."

"It's not a loan. It's yours." He leaned back in his chair, looking smug. "You'll be quite the heiress, now."

"Mine? No, Hamish—"

"It's yours," he said again. "Yours by right."

Camille shook her head. "Not even a proper housekeeper or lady's companion earns this salary or allowance, not in ten years of service."

"Not for services rendered." There was a glint in his eyes. His smile turned feral. "It's every last pence our bastard father had in the bank." He sneered at the note in her hands as if their father's ghost were attached to it. "I've no need for such a modest amount. Do with it what you will before I toss it in the bin."

'Modest amount' was a lie. There was no doubt Hamish had money enough to support a small country, but his generosity was for more than revenge. He offered her back her pride, even when she'd come here to offer it up as penance.

Emotion clogged her throat. A brother, family. She'd gone her whole life without one, and now when one was offered up to her, open-handed and warm hearted, she found she had no grand speeches or articulate words to express herself with.

"Thank you," she said simply. "I'm proud to call you my brother."

He looked away and cleared his throat. "No need for that. I'm being entirely selfish." He grinned at her, his eyes shining. "I've always wanted a sibling to boss around."

"Haven't you heard siblings are nothing but trouble?"

"Ah, yes, well, Charlotte is an exceptional case as a duke's sister. I won't have near the trouble with you."

She laughed, the sound full of new life, a new *her*. "You sound suspiciously confident. Care to share how you'll make me toe the line?"

"Easy," he said.

The brotherly mischief and shared camaraderie on his face made Camille want to throw her arms around him in a display of affection that would leave them both embarrassed. "Yes?"

"I'll leave the line keeping to Renard."

They both laughed, knowing there was no hope of keeping her from anything at all.

CHAPTER THIRTY-FIVE

R ENARD ASCENDED THE stairs to the second-story sitting room, managing to knock on the door and enter at his sister's voice without flinching.

The room was warm with a roaring fire in the hearth, a fire Renard wouldn't look too long at, else he see his future in the burning flames.

Charlotte sat reading in the chair by the window, a new set of spectacles showing off the expressiveness of her eyes. Upon looking up and seeing him in the doorway, she smiled.

"Renard! What a pleasant surprise. I thought I heard a carriage." She glanced into the hall behind him. "Is Camille with you?"

"She's downstairs with Hamish."

Charlotte scrunched her face. "I hope he doesn't say anything too disagreeable. I'm rather fond of the busts in that room."

Renard wouldn't put it past his duchess to throw anything not bolted down when enraged. "What makes you think the disagreeable one would be him?"

"Because women are seldom wrong."

Despite the damning reason for his visit, Renard smirked. "Please don't tell her that. I never win any arguments as it is."

Her grin brightened her entire face. "I make no promises, brother."

It was that grin that tore at him—how it reached ear to ear

and how her eyes danced with the joy of an easy gesture when she'd had no reason to smile for years. She sat there and smiled at him, not knowing what he'd taken from her, not understanding he was the reason her smiles had been so few and far between.

"Come, sit down." Charlotte patted the seat next to hers. "Tell me about your adventure. Woman's intuition says I may have reason to congratulate you." She stood and crossed for the bell pull. "I'll ring for tea and—"

"I killed our parents."

The entire room stilled at his words. He swore the fire banked before coming back to life.

Charlotte stared at him. "What?"

Renard swallowed. His body flushed with heat and ice, but he wouldn't look away, wouldn't run. Not anymore.

"I started the fire in the stable when we were children." He wouldn't falter or spin a tale of foolishness. He stated what had happened as fact and gave Charlotte the truth she was owed.

"I took Papa's pipe and went to the barn to taste my first tobacco. When I was done, I didn't put it out properly. Before I knew what had happened, some of the stray straw caught fire."

He saw the wall of flames in his mind as if it were that day. The lack of rain had left the wood panels of the barn bone dry. Everything had gone up in a matter of seconds. It was all he could do to throw open the gates and pray the last two horses would run for safety.

He hadn't run for help, hadn't cried out. Unable to move, he'd stood there and watched, unknowingly leaving his sister to burn. His fingernails bit into his palms. He lowered his head, no longer able to meet his sister's shocked gaze.

"Our parents died because I didn't think to check if someone else was using the quiet of the barn." His apology wasn't enough; it would never be, but the words must be said regardless, no matter how insufficient. "I'm sorry, Lotte. I'm so damn sorry."

The silence stretched between them, damning and awful. Renard bared it, knowing the wrenching in his chest would be nothing compared to the tortures of hell.

"You don't smoke."

His head snapped up. Certain he'd heard her wrong, he asked, "What?"

Charlotte shook her head. "Hamish said he'd never seen you smoke. It's not that you can't; it's because you *won't*."

The statement threw him.

She must be shocked indeed if she hadn't begun cursing his existence.

While he waited for her to lose her composure, he offered, "Other way around." The lingering smell of burning wood and flesh was a permanent fixture in his mind and a compulsory memory for his body. Too long in any gaming hell with its stale air and throat clogging vapors and he'd go running to the privy to relieve his stomach of its contents. He'd learned to steer clear of the hells and find his oblivion the smokeless and cheaper way: pubs, one where both working men and women co-mingled and where there was no chance a man would light his pipe.

"The smell still makes me sick. Whenever my city cook would put pork on the menu, I'd leave the house entirely, afraid one whiff of overdone meat would leave me running for the nearest chamber-pot. I had every grocer strike pork off our ingredients list in the country, just in case."

"Ren." Charlotte reached for him. "It was an accident. You no more caused their deaths than I."

He evaded her outstretched arms by sitting on the divan. The sound of her nickname for him grated. She was too trusting still. His little sister, who'd hung on his every word as children as if he'd been some hero she'd admired, she couldn't see he was truly the villain.

"It doesn't matter if it was an accident," he spat. "I started the fire, and they are dead. Society won't take well to parricide, no matter the circumstances. Our parents, you, all I've ever done is hurt those I love." He'd spend every single day worshipping the ground his wife walked, thanking God Camille hadn't condemned him after learning the truth. But his sister, his sweet, little sister would grow to hate him as much as he hated himself. He dropped his head in his hands, unable to meet Charlotte's gaze. "I'm the worst sort of monster."

He waited for the sound of the library door to slam shut. She must have realized now; she was better off without him in her life. Those years in the country alone hadn't broken her; she'd taken that silence and forged a life of quiet resolve so strong, not even Hamish had stood a chance. She'd grown into a formidable woman, no thanks to him—

"Renard Leopold Louis, if you ever say that again, I will never forgive you!"

Renard looked up and startled at the tears in Charlotte's eyes. "Lotte—"

"No." She shook her head, the tears falling down her cheeks. "All this time. All these years, I reached for you, waited for your grief to lessen so we could face our lives together as a family. But . . ." The word cracked with emotion. "You've carried this guilt by yourself, thinking I wouldn't understand." She offered her open palms, her gesture and expression pleading. "Renard, don't you see? If I hadn't been in the hayloft, if I had listened to Mother and stayed in the garden like I was supposed to, they'd never have perished. Mother and Father were there because of me, because *I* wouldn't listen. If you are set on carrying the blame, then I must shoulder its weight alongside you."

Renard shot to his feet. "That's nonsense, Charlotte! Of course you aren't to blame."

"Neither. Are. You."

Renard paused. The fierceness with which she said those three words resonated to the darkest depths of his soul, where guilt and shame had set roots so deep, his hope of reconciling their relationship had all but choked out.

Now that hope sprang towards the light, the stock so thin and frail, a single gust of doubt would rend it to the ground. He couldn't believe she forgave him. *Wouldn't* believe, else he break beyond all reparations.

"You . . ." Renard cleared his own throat of emotion. "You don't hate me after all I've done? Even after learning the truth?"

Charlotte huffed—a bad habit she'd acquired as a girl when he'd said something she deemed too asinine to deserve a response—but then she took both his hands in hers and looked up at him with a sister's love, grown and matured over years of learning to accept her own flaws and that in others. Eyes that saw past what a person was and saw who they truly were. "The truth remains: You are my brother and you've carried this secret too long. I do not hate you, Ren. I love you, for always."

Renard didn't wipe the emotion blurring his vision; he refused to look away from the compassion and understanding in his sister's eyes. She had grown strong and loyal and he'd tear Hamish in two if he ever said one word that suggested otherwise in her presence. Amidst his bluster of despising heroes, he'd secretly longed for redemption for ten long years. And in one simple conversation, Charlotte had given it to him, as if forgiveness were the very essence of her nature.

He put his head to her hands, fighting back more insufferable tears. "I don't deserve you as my sister."

"Bullocks!" She lifted his face, her expression turning thoughtful. "You never meant to hand me off to some man for your own need, did you?"

He dropped her hands and fell to his knees before her, begging for her forgiveness or praying she would hear the truth in his words, he didn't know. "I meant only to see you cared for before someone found out about the fire, and my involvement, and scandal ruined your chances at happiness. Making you hate me, pushing you away, it was so you would stay innocent."

Her gaze darted around them, to the home of his closest friend, now *her* home. "Seems I can manage my own trouble without your help." Her expression softened further. "And White's betting book? I saw the wager."

His eyes widened. "You saw it?"

She smiled. "Hamish."

He ran a hand through his hair, refusing to imagine when and how Hamish had snuck her into the club. If it weren't glaringly apparent they loved each other completely, he'd take his friend out back and beat him for taking his sister's safety too lightly. "The marquess—Nic—convinced me more funds would keep you safer, in greater comfort. Now that I know he was aware of my secret, he knew the exact words to manipulate me. He knew I feared for your safety and reputation. With his obsession over Camille, I can only think he meant to flee after the wedding, his winnings in his pocket."

The more he thought about it, the more he realized he'd been an easier mark than a gilded peacock walking the streets of the rookeries. What a right fool he'd been.

"I vow, I'll make it up to you," he said. Whatever it took. "I'll spend the rest of our lives giving you unsolicited advice and digging for bugs in the garden, hiring tutors and housekeepers you can terrorize."

"That's a start."

She pulled him to his feet while her mouth curled into a grin Renard knew was trouble.

"However, if you are set on punishing yourself, I may have a way for you to spend your days repenting."

He chuckled. "Now I'm afraid." *And overjoyed.* "Don't tell me it involves living with insects in my tea?"

Her grin grew. "I have been told they tend to invest the house with raucousness." She placed his hand on her stomach. "But perhaps the newest Hurstfield will also share the Louis family's fascination with exploring the outdoors, if Uncle Ren shows them the joy of it."

Renard's weighted heart lifted to unbearable heights. "You are with child?"

"It isn't official yet," she said.

"Woman's intuition again?"

She smiled. "It's rarely wrong."

He felt the strangest stirring in his sister's stomach—or perhaps that fluttering was in his own chest—and closed his eyes in awe. "I am to be an uncle."

For so long, the world around him had lain in shadowed despair. The light flooding in with the presence of his wife and the reclaiming and growing family now was blinding.

He opened his eyes and put conviction in his vow. "I will be there for your children, and you, Lotte, for as long as you'll allow me."

Charlotte shook her head, but her eyes were shining. "What a handful you are, Ren."

EPILOGUE

Two Years Later: Lux Country Estate

"HELLO, HUSBAND," CAMILLE said from the doorway. Renard, in full suit, let his book fall to his lap and propped his head on his arm from the bed. His gaze raked over her, his voice low when he said, "You're late, wife."

Her thighs squeezed when that sizzling gaze flicked up to her face. She smiled, knowing how she'd make up for her tardiness. "My business in London couldn't be helped." She closed the door behind her and walked to the edge of the bed. "Now that Charlotte has taken an interest in the Home, I'll have more time for another project."

He grinned that grin she loved. "Please tell me *I'm* the project?"

She leaned down and brushed a kiss over his lips. "Yes."

She squealed when his arms wrapped around her and pulled her onto the bed, flipping their bodies so he lay atop her.

"Thank God." He buried his face into her neck. "You've been remiss in fixing me. I hate being left unfinished."

She ran her fingers through his hair and smiled. "I'd say you're rather perfect as you are."

He lifted himself on his elbows and stared down at her, his eyes wide. "'Perfect'? No, that won't do. I've so many flaws, remember? There must be something you can direct your

320

attention to?"

She shook her head. "Nope. Your penmanship is impeccable. Those lessons have paid off."

"I *did* work rather hard."

"And you're nothing of an idiot now that you are so agreeable."

"That was the easiest fix," he said. "Since you're always right, I have no need for idiocies."

She bit her lip. They still quarreled plenty, *both* making mistakes. But they always worked through their disagreements with a forgiving nature, and lots of sex. The day since Nic Brandt had disappeared, Camille had taken to reminding her husband of her love every day. With lips and tongue and words filled with insult and innuendo—to Renard's preference.

He sighed. "Is there nothing else? Will you tire of me now that I am so close to your angelic status? I was looking forward to your insults and undivided attention."

She laughed. "I'm sure we'll think of something."

He kissed her on the forehead and rolled onto his side to snuggle her from behind, a comforting position they found themselves in most nights when they talked until their lips found other uses.

"Is your mama settled?" he asked.

"She is." Camille had been shocked two years ago when her mother had declined the offer to live at Lux Estate with her and Renard. It seemed she and Aunt Clarice had formed an attachment, one that kept them regularly in bed.

Her mother's transformation had continued to surprise and elate her. Rosy cheeks, tolerable if not amiable company—in small doses—and smiles, the kind that reached her brown eyes. Clarice and Mama had become so happy, they'd decided to let a house farther from the club, where the two women could live a more respectable life as 'companions' while Sensa took over the daily workings of the Prodding Pony.

"They invited me to a small ceremony to celebrate, unofficial of course, but we are both invited."

"Ah, love," Renard lamented. "The parties, the champagne, the *small talk*."

Camille brightened. "That's it!"

Renard chuckled. "My public discomfort?"

"No." She smirked. "You're still charming."

His eyes lit mischievously. "One of my worst flaws."

She hid her grin. "And handsome."

Renard drew her close. "I'll wear a bag over my head whenever we're together. *That* should stop any guests from asking me about the weather."

"How imaginative, Your Grace. The neighbors will think you quite eccentric."

"For you, my dear, I'd freeze off my nose, fingers, *and* toes."

"You tried that already." Remembering him waiting outside the Prodding Pony sent a new wave of love through her chest. She trailed a finger down his nose. "I've grown to admire your handsomeness."

"Then I'm forgiven?" he asked, an echo of that night so many lifetimes ago.

She pulled his head down and whispered against his lips, "In this one instance."

He brushed his mouth against hers in an unspoken promise of what was to come. "I'll take it." He kissed her again, but instead of dragging her towards the bed, like she was hoping, he pulled back after a moment. "You deserve happiness. You know that now, don't you? No one can take what you've built, what you build every day for those women at your shelter. Your goodness, your compassion—all of it is there for the world to see. I hope you see it as well."

Heart overflowing, Camille smiled at his concern and need for her to know her worth. "I know."

He blinked. "You do? But I had an entire speech prepared to prove your magnanimity."

She laughed and knew in that one action she'd forgiven herself her mistakes and accepted the past for how it had shaped her future. "I was angry for so long at my father for being a selfish and indifferent monster. Furious at my mother for being weak and letting his absence turn her into an empty shell. Furious at the world for believing a woman's worth lay in her obedience and silence." She'd let the last of her anger drift away ages ago and her life had been nothing but bliss thereafter. Not even Nic had made an appearance, leaving Camille to suspect she'd been wrong to think he'd survived. And with the trust Hamish had set up for her, there was no question of her respectability should any would-be heirs take offense, even if Mrs. Norris still sent letters that bordered on sulking.

"And now?" Renard asked.

Coming back, Camille grinned. "Now, I'm only furious at myself for agreeing for one blasted second I wasn't deserving of better."

Thank God for Charlotte and Scarlet and Syd and Clarice—four women who wouldn't accept of the roles thrust upon them. They didn't ask for forgiveness or beg for what was deemed more than they deserved. They took up the weapons in their own minds and carved out places in the world that didn't fit them. And now she was one of them.

Now she inspired others to do the same.

And she thanked God for the man who stood by her side, offering her support and friendship through it all.

A gentle caress to her cheek had her returning to her chambers and her husband.

"You're frowning, my love," Renard said. "You know how I feel about that."

She wrapped her arms around his neck and lifted onto her toes to press a quick kiss on his lips. "No need for concern, husband. This time, the thoughts were happy ones."

"Happy, you say?" His fingers skimmed her side, igniting fire under her skin. "You were thinking about me, then?" He snuzzled a sensitive spot along her jaw that sent the burning lower.

She gasped when his teeth nipped at her earlobe.

"Care to share?" he asked.

Her mind trudged through desire to come to some understanding. "Huh?"

He leaned back from her, his gaze amused. "Your thoughts, darling. Anything I should know?" His voice and gaze lowered. "Things you wish to try?"

She smiled at him, remembering that smile from the night they'd met, the life they'd begun together through differences and teasing. And, indeed, an idea came to mind. "I wouldn't say 'no' to another homemade tart or two."

"Oh." He released her, willing to stall his own desire to fill her belly. He held out an arm, the picture of the perfect escort. "Then shall we head to the kitchens, duchess?"

She nodded. "We should have the staff take the rest of the day off as well."

He frowned, his arm dropping in his confusion. "If you wish it, but won't you need assistance dressing for dinner later?"

"I'll be much too busy for that." She walked to the door and opened it, looking back at her husband, loving the way he followed her schemes wherever she directed. "Besides . . ." She infused her tone with her forthcoming mischief. "After eating custard off our naked bodies, the only thing we'll need is a bath."

She watched her husband's body ripple with understanding and bit back her smile.

He cleared his throat and straightened his already perfectly placed cuffs. His serious expression was ruined by his own mischievous tone. "We wouldn't want to alarm the cook when we bypass the need for proper plate ware."

She nodded, ever agreeable. "And, thanks to Hamish, our water heats itself."

Mock seriousness dropping, he drew her into his arms once again and smiled. "Remind me to send my brother-in-law a basket of tarts in thanks for ensuring a perfect marriage."

"'Perfect'?" Camille laughed. "All it takes to win your affections is a bit of pipes and water? And you called tarts a silly favor."

"It has nothing to do with the water." He pressed a kiss to her lips. "The only thing I need for a happy life is my family . . . you."

When he pulled back to gaze down at her this time, Camille saw a long future of happiness—years of bedroom adventures involving baked goods—reflected in her husband's eyes. She placed a hand on her lower stomach and knew that happiness would grow after they'd polished off a tray of tarts, and when Renard learned of the life growing in her.

She offered a secret smile and asked, "Shall we go scandalize our household, then?"

Renard bowed to his wife and offered her the lead in that wonderful future.

"After you, my love."

About the Author

An educated artist, J. M. Diedrich previously worked as a freelance columnist for the Independent Observer. When she's not writing steamy kissing scenes or driving her characters into life-threatening situations, she's binge-watching anime. She lives in Minnesota with her husband and two boys.